D0058003

New American Library Titles
by Karen White

The Beach Trees
Falling Home
On Folly Beach
The Lost Hours
The Memory of Water
Pieces of the Heart
Learning to Breathe
The Color of Light

The Tradd Street Series
The Strangers on Montagu Street
The Girl on Legare Street
The House on Tradd Street

To my precious Meghan.
I'm so proud to be your mother.

ACKNOWLEDGMENTS

Despite all the hours spent alone in my chair with my laptop, writing is never a completely solitary experience. Every book I've written has depended so much on the generosity of others willing to share their knowledge with me, and *Sea Change* is no exception.

My undying gratitude to Diane Wise, RN, MSN, CNM, a good friend and excellent source of information on all things related to pregnancy and childbirth. This is the third book in which her expertise has proved invaluable to me—please never retire!

Thank you to the lovely residents of St. Simons Island for your always warm welcome, especially Mary Jane Reed of the excellent independent bookstore GJ Ford Bookshop, Tommye Baxter Cashin, and Susan Kinnamon-Brock, who graciously agreed to read the manuscript before publication.

As always, thank you to the usual suspects—Wendy Wax, Susan Crandall, Tim, Meghan, and Connor. Thank you for your patience and love, and for always knowing when I need a swift kick of reality.

Even the seasons form a great circle in their changing, and always come back again to where they were. The life of a man is a circle from childhood to childhood, and so it is in everything where power moves.

—BLACK ELK OGLALA SIOUX HOLY MAN

Sea Change

PROLOGUE

Pamela

St. Simons Island, Georgia
September 1804

Storms bring the detritus of other people's lives into our own, a reminder that we are not alone, and of how truly insignificant we are. The indiscriminating waves had brutalized the shore, tossing pieces of splintered timber, an intact china teacup, and a gentleman's watch—still with its cover and chain—onto my beloved beach, each coming to rest as if placed gently in the sand as a shopkeeper would display his wares. As I rubbed my thumb over the smooth lip of the china cup, I thought of how someone's loss had become my gain, of how the tide would roll in and out again as if nothing had changed, and how sometimes the separation between endings and beginnings is so small that they seem to run together like the ocean's waves.

A pile of timber, remains of either a house or a ship, huddled like a frightened child, cradling a glint of metal in its wooden arms. I hesitated only a moment before sticking my hand into the opening created by two boards, my fingers touching something hard, small, and cold. I held up my find to the murky sun to see a wide gold wedding band, its edges smoothed with wear, an inscription inside mostly worn away. I squinted my eyes to see better, twisting the band between the pads of my fingers, managing to discern only a single word. *Forever.*

I held the ring tightly in my palm, wondering to whom the ring had belonged, and what journey had brought it to me. It was an omen, I thought, my own wedding to be in three days, if Geoffrey could spare the time from salvaging what the storm had spared of his cotton crop. I wasn't his first choice, but he was mine now, and I felt linked to the unknown owner of the ring with the single word. *Forever.*

I stared up at the sun and its valiant attempts to break apart the clouds. I knew it would win; the brightest days always followed the worst storms. This one had been a bad one, bad enough to have overtaken Broughton Island, killing every soul including baby Margaret, whom I had helped bring into this world only one week ago. I wondered why she had been allowed into the world for such a brief time, whether the birthing pains her mother had suffered justified such a brief existence. Or whether any lessons had been learned in a brief span of seven days. I did not understand it. As a midwife, I accepted it, but I would never understand it.

Two black skimmers arced down from the milky sky, so close to the waves it seemed they might be swept under as they searched for their supper. The birds were back. They always came back after a storm, but for the first silent days one would always wonder. Like the tides they returned to the place from whence they came, a constant to those of us who remained.

I watched the pair for a little longer as they skimmed and swooped, their barking yips loud on the empty beach. Then I retreated over the ravaged and debris-strewn sand, and on to the house I shared with my father and younger sister. I held the ring tightly in my hand as I walked, the hard gold formed into a circle, the shape's infinite line recalling beginnings and endings, and how sometimes it was impossible to distinguish between the two.

CHAPTER ONE

Ava

ANTIOCH, GEORGIA
APRIL 2011

I stood outside my parents' house feeling the heat from the black asphalt through my leather flats. My mother's impatiens bloomed in the clay planters that flanked the front door of the ranch-style house I'd called home for most of my thirty-four years. Even the heat wouldn't dare defy my mother by making her flowers wilt; Gloria Whalen ruled her garden as she'd ruled her five children, and disobeying her was as much of a rarity as a January snow in Georgia.

A bead of sweat trickled between my shoulder blades as the heat beat down on me and my new husband as if it were the middle of July instead of just spring. I tried to explain to Matthew that summers were like that in west Georgia, so sudden that spring was like a cool evening sandwiched between winter and high summer. Matthew was from the coast, so I figured he already knew a thing or two about heat and humidity.

Matthew held my hand as I faced my father and four brothers, my siblings ranging in age from fifty-five down to forty-five, assembled as either a farewell party or as a show of force to the stranger I'd chosen to marry. Even now, standing in a suburban setting, they could still be identified as the funeral directors they were. Whalen and Sons had been in my father's family for three generations, and the serious, solicitous expressions on all five faces were more genetic now than learned.

Their assorted wives and my various nieces and nephews remained inside by unspoken assent, perhaps gathered in sympathy around my mother's bedroom door, a door she'd refused to open since I'd arrived that morning. I'd called the day before, the day of my wedding, to give her time to adjust. Even Phil Autry, my fiancé of four years, seemed to have taken the news better than she had.

I let go of Matthew's hand and hugged my father. He held on tightly for a moment, then released me to hold me at arm's distance. I was used to this. Despite my being the youngest and the only girl, and being reassured that I'd been what my parents had hoped and prayed for, they'd always seemed too wary of their good fortune to hold me tightly. It was as if by their holding me close, the vagaries of fortune that had given me to them would notice and take me away.

"Can I try to talk with Mama?" I didn't really want to. I hated to leave with things unspoken between us, but I didn't want her to think that I was desperate for her approval. I'd outgrown that need along with Clearasil and braces.

My father shook his head. "Give her time, Ava. She'll come around. It's just been a shock. To all of us." He paused and settled a stern look on me. "You know how Gloria doesn't like surprises. She'll come around."

I hoped my expression conveyed my doubt about the sincerity of his words. My mother had been vaguely upset when I told her I was married. Although she didn't admit it, I knew she'd always planned a large wedding in her garden with all the frills for her only daughter. It wasn't until I told her I was moving to St. Simons that she'd had her meltdown. She had four daughters-in-law who lived within spitting distance, all more than eager and willing to cater to my mother and treat her like the matriarch she was accustomed to being. I'd grown up looking out my bedroom window, able to see three of my brothers' houses, all the same except for different-colored doors, with neat grass and identical black sedans in the driveways. It had always made me wonder which house on this street would be mine one day. The thought gave me nightmares—even more nightmares than I'd had after my oldest brother, Stephen, had taken me to the embalming room. It wasn't the cold reality of death that had scared me; only the thought of not living the life I had.

I went down the row of my brothers, standing in birth order from youngest to oldest, as was their habit—David, Joshua, Mark, and Stephen—and hugged each. Matthew followed, shaking each hand before turning to my father.

"I'll take good care of her, sir."

"You'd better. She's very precious to us." My father cleared his throat, uncomfortable with any expectations of expressed affection.

My eyes stung as I looked down the row again at my brothers, each face mirroring the same sympathy. I'd never felt as separate from them as I did then, the lone dandelion in a garden of sunflowers. I was suddenly unsure of my reasons for leaving, whether what I felt for Matthew was only a temporary balm for the constant restlessness that had dogged me since I was old enough to reason with the world around me.

I turned back to my father. "Tell Mama that I love her and that I'll call when I'm settled." I began to babble, something I'd always done when my emotions threatened to spill over. "My roommate is packing up all of my stuff and sending it, and I told her to keep the furniture, and we're having somebody bring my car. And Matthew's positive I won't have a problem finding a job with my background and credentials. So there's no need to worry, okay?" I wasn't sure why I was rambling about things we'd already discussed. Maybe a part of me wanted him to break down and tell me why I had to be kept at arm's distance. Or maybe I was killing time waiting for my mother to run out of the house and hug me and explain to me why, after all the years of feeding me and clothing me and teaching me right from wrong, she could let me go without saying good-bye.

Matthew touched my arm. "It's a long drive. If we want to get there before dark, we should go now."

As we turned toward the car, I heard my name shouted. I turned to find my mother's mother, my Mimi, walking as quickly as she could, considering her ninety-one years and her insistence on still wearing heels—albeit low ones—and holding something in her hands. I'd said good-bye to her earlier as she'd stood guard at her daughter's closed bedroom door, and wondered with some lingering hope whether she'd brought a conciliatory message from my mother.

"Ava!" she called again, confirming that she had my attention. She stopped in front of us, her blond hair—courtesy of Clairol as if we wouldn't suspect she should have a head full of gray hair—streaming around her face. We waited as she caught her breath, and I eyed the treasure in her hands.

"You don't want to forget this," she said, stretching out her arms. Sitting in her open palms was a square wooden music box, the old-fashioned kind that when you opened the lid you could look inside to see the working mechanisms underneath a clear glass cover. The lid was dented and stained with watermarks, but even though I hadn't seen the box in a number of years, I was sure the mechanism inside still worked. It had been refurbished by my brother Stephen, after I'd found it nearly twenty-seven years before.

After a brief hesitation, I reached out to her, allowing her to gently place the music box in my hands. Of all the things I was leaving behind me, I wondered why this would be the one thing she wanted to make sure I wouldn't.

"Just to remind you," she said, patting my fingers as I closed them over the top of the box.

"Of what?"

She had the odd gleam in her eye that always reminded me that she was half Cherokee, raised in the mountains of Tennessee without much of a formal education, but she was still the smartest person I knew. "That some endings are really beginnings. If you don't remember anything I've ever tried to teach you, remember that."

She enveloped me in a tight hug as I smelled the reassuring scent of talcum powder and Aqua Net. "I will."

Mimi glanced up at Matthew, and I thought for a moment that her expression was one of accusation. But when I looked back at her face, it was gone.

We said our good-byes and, with one last glance toward the house, I climbed into the passenger seat of the silver sedan and allowed Matthew to shut the door. I didn't look back at my grandmother, or my father and brothers, standing like despondent scarecrows who'd failed to protect their crops, identical in their tall, narrow builds, their hair the same shade of dark brown that matched perfectly with the somberness of their black pants.

I didn't look back because once, long ago, Mimi had told me it was bad luck, that if you looked back it meant you'd never return. It's not that this place held so much meaning for me; I'd always known I'd leave, even though until now I'd never figured out where I'd go. I suppose it's one of the reasons why I'd never set a wedding date with Phil, having always felt beneath the surface of my life the constant current of restlessness. A sense that there was something more waiting for me somewhere else. The moment I'd met Matthew, I felt that I'd finally found what I'd been looking for.

I sat back with my fingers still cupped around the small music box until Matthew took my hand and held it in his while he drove us to the other side of the state, to the island nestled against the great Atlantic where my new husband and his family had lived since the American Revolution.

Matthew's thumb rubbed the slightly raised birthmark near the base of my thumb on my left hand that looked more like a scar. My mother told me I'd had it since birth, but I'd always preferred to think of it as a scar from some daring feat I'd sustained in childhood with no memory of how I'd obtained it. There were times when I wished that all of life's scars were like that, medals of survival for a pain no longer remembered.

His thumb found the new gold band that encircled the fourth finger of my left hand and stopped. "You're not wearing your engagement ring." It wasn't an accusation, but more a statement of fact.

I stared down at my hand. I hadn't meant to leave the beautiful diamond solitaire ring in my jewelry box. I had worn the ring for three days—as that was all the time we had between the time we decided to get married and the actual ceremony. I loved the ring, the antique setting and blue-white round stone. But when Matthew had placed the gold wedding band on my finger, it had felt somehow wrong to wear it with another ring. I couldn't explain it, couldn't think of a way to tell Matthew that wearing two rings gave me the feeling of walking into my house but finding all the furniture rearranged.

"Sorry," I said. "I keep forgetting it. I know I'll get used to wearing them both, though. Promise."

He nodded, focusing on passing an eighteen-wheeler. I sat back and looked out the window, imagining our car on the map headed east toward the ocean. I'd never been to the coast. My family, mostly grown by the time I joined them, had been too busy for family vacations to the beach. Despite friends returning with summer tans and shell collections, I'd been secretly glad. There was something unnerving about the ocean, with its endless horizon lapping at the earth's edge. Matthew spoke of taking me sailing, and of kayaking through the endless marshes of his island, but I could only nod noncommittally. I was in love and eager not to disappoint, and hopeful, too, that he would help me to love the water as much as he did.

Late-afternoon sun slanted into the car as we reached Savannah, the warmth lulling me into a quiet doze. I half awoke to a familiar scent, realizing in my groggy state that Matthew must have opened the windows, as the breeze I felt on my face was warm and carried with it the scent of something I found familiarly intoxicating yet alarming at the same time.

Still only partially awake, I tried to turn my head toward the smell, and to push my feet against the floor of the car to prop myself up. But I was paralyzed, being held down by an invisible force as I tried to extract myself from the dark space between sleep and wakefulness. I heard the radio and Matthew's soft humming, but I heard something else, too, a sound like water rushing over sand. The old nightmare hovered just out of reach, dodging the periphery of my consciousness, threatening to descend and pull me to a place I didn't want to go.

The music box fell from my lap and slipped to the floor, my hands too numb to catch it. I struggled to open my eyes, to see what I was smelling, what I sensed creeping up on me, but I couldn't. The lid of the music box opened and the familiar song began to play, its tinkling noise unexpectedly jarring against the rush of the wind. I focused on it, on the feel of the box pressed against my paralyzed foot, and listened to a small whine of sound that grew gradually louder, forcing my eyes open in time to realize the sound was a person screaming. And that the person screaming was me.

CHAPTER TWO

It began the summer I turned seven: the summer of tornadoes and the wail of weather sirens and sleeping in our basement. Or maybe it all began long before then, before I understood the concept of time and how it runs in perpetual loops, spinning its spiderweb of hours until the past, present, and future are no longer separate, distinct entities.

On the day after my birthday, I stood in front of my house and watched as other people's lives fell into our yard. Most of it was trash—paper, ruined photographs, scraps of wood that could have been furniture or a house, but rendered so small and splintered that it had been impossible to tell. But there'd been a few treasures, too. An Instamatic camera, with the film still inside, had fallen into my mother's rose garden. And into the boxwood in front of my bedroom window, as if it were a gift meant for me, the music box had landed wet and scratched, but otherwise intact.

Gripping the box, I'd run inside to show my mother, to play the tune that I knew but couldn't place. She'd begun to sing words, words she said she'd sung to me as a baby. The song was an old lullaby and she'd sung it to all of her children. But there was something wrong with her explanation. Maybe it had been her insistence that I was looking for a story where there wasn't one. Or maybe it was because the words she sang seemed wrong to me, as if I could recall different words to the song if I thought hard enough, words that eluded me even now.

That had been the beginning of the nightmares, of dreams of being pursued and out of breath, of being surrounded by water and sucked beneath it while the air from my lungs rose in bubbles like tiny fish, floating to the surface while I lay on the sandy bottom. They'd been infrequent during my childhood, and almost nonexistent since my twenties. Until now.

I pressed my head into Matthew's chest, trying to register his words. He'd pulled the car over into a drive that crunched under our tires, holding me close while we both tried to understand what was wrong with me. And why in the two short months since I'd known him I hadn't mentioned my dreams to him. Even after we'd decided to marry and live on St. Simons, I'd not told him about my fear of water. Maybe because there were too many other things we wanted to talk about in our brief courtship. Or maybe I was hoping that my dreams and fear had been something I'd left behind in my twenties along with my need to please my parents.

"I'm okay," I said, raising the bottle of water he'd placed in my shaking hands to my mouth. "It's just . . . I didn't know where I was. And I couldn't move, and the windows were open and . . ." I stopped, not yet able to explain what it was that had terrified me.

His chest rumbled under my ear as he spoke. "It's probably the lingering smell of the paper plant in Brunswick. It's much better now that the EPA changed some rules, but some people are sensitive to it. I'm sure it's just something you need to get used to."

I nodded, hoping he was right. "I'm sorry," I said. I looked into his worried eyes, needing to reassure him. "I just want to get home. To start our life together."

He leaned down and kissed me softly. There was so much we still didn't know about each other, but the connection I felt to him when he kissed me, or touched me, erased any lingering doubts. It had been that way since the moment we'd met. Before I'd known his name, I'd *known* him in the same way a newborn baby knows his own mother.

Matthew started the engine and pulled out onto the tree-canopied road. "We're on Demere," he said, "and when we reach the small airfield we'll go through the roundabout and take a left on Frederica. Those two roads and Sea Island Road are the main three arteries on St. Simons. Once you figure out where you are in relation to them, you'll never get lost."

I nodded and tried to smile, but my jaw was stiff. The windows were still down, bringing the scent of the island into the car, an odd mix of salt and vegetation. It was new, yet strangely familiar, like when I was younger and would smell the newly waxed floors on the first day of school. The scent of the island tugged on my memory, a stubborn piece that refused to be dislodged no matter how hard I nudged it.

I tried to focus on the few turns he made, to remember how I could find the house on my own, but I couldn't. The large, lovely trees with their shawls of Spanish moss, and even the broken oyster shells on the roads were all new to me, yet, like the scent in the air, it was as if I *expected* them, expected to see them, and to hear the crunching of the shells beneath the tires. I knew how the spongy green moss would feel between my fingers and how the sun would look on the branches of the trees at sunset.

"You did a good job," I said, reaching for his hand and lacing my fingers with his.

"Of what?"

"Of telling me about this place. I feel as if I already know it. Like I've lived here my whole life."

He squeezed my hand. "I love St. Simons, and I hope you'll come to love it, too. And to think of it as your home."

I smiled, then turned my head away to look out my window, hoping he couldn't see the unease, the lingering sensation of the terror I'd felt earlier. Or the persistent restlessness that I'd thought vanquished when I said "I do" that seemed to cling to me like a stubborn web.

A sea of gold and green grass filled the scenery to the right of the road, rippling softly, as if someone walked through it unseen. I shivered again and closed my eyes, knowing what it felt like to step on the marshy grass, to hear the rasp of the stems as they moved together as if dancing. To smell the peculiar scent of rotting vegetation that had wafted into the car—the same scent that now made me think only of coming *home*.

Matthew slowed as he took another turn between two cement pillars with stone pineapples on top. The drive made no pretense of having once been paved. It was an ocean of white dust and crushed shells under a sky of green limbs that leaned down close enough to whisper, their thick foliage blocking the late-afternoon sun.

We drove a short distance until the trees began to thin, tapering back to small shrubs as if paying homage to the house at the end of the driveway. I knew it was one of the few remaining nineteenth-century structures on the island, but still its antiquity startled me, along with the odd feeling of familiarity fueled, I was sure, by Matthew's vibrant descriptions and stories of growing up as an only child in the old house.

We climbed out of the car and stood together but not touching, the song of hundreds of cicadas whirring in the trees around us. The gritty earth beneath my shoes seemed to shift as if supported by water, and I reached for Matthew's arm, feeling the need to anchor myself.

It was a simple two-story farmhouse, with a raised foundation, a porch supported by four columns, and two brick chimneys affixed to each side of the house. Three dormer windows sat perched over the porch roof like protruding eyes. What made this house different from other houses I'd seen before from the same time period was its tabby construction, an indigenous building material consisting of equal parts lime, water, sand, oyster shells, and ash. Matthew's description of it had been so good that I almost knew exactly what it would feel like under my fingers without having actually ever touched it before.

What appeared to be flower beds lay abandoned at the front and sides of the house, while farther back, where the forest began its eager encroachment, I could see what looked like a miniature house. It was made completely of tabby and boasted a single chimney, and stood some distance from the house on the edge of the woods, its front door replaced with nailed two-by-fours with no handle for entry.

With plans to explore the grounds later, I turned back to the house. The grayish tint of the tabby helped camouflage the house against the sandy drive, making it appear as a shadow cast from the towering live oak trees. It seemed as if the house were hiding from time itself, content to let the years bypass it unchanged, in the same way the breezes stirred the marsh grasses, leaving them to return upright again.

I took a deep breath, trying to fill my empty lungs with air. "You described it so well that it's like I've seen a photograph of it. I just didn't realize it was so . . ."

"Old?" Matthew laughed and drew me to his side. "But it's very livable, I assure you. I added the kitchen and downstairs bath three years ago, and added a bathroom and closet to the master bedroom. It's not a palace, but I think you'll be happy here." He turned to face me, cupping my face in his hands. "I know you'll be happy here."

His voice changed slightly, as if in reassurance, but I wasn't clear which one of us he was trying to reassure.

I stood on my toes and kissed him. "I will be. *We* will be."

In response, he swooped me up in his arms and, as if I didn't weigh anything, carried me up the front steps. After fumbling with a key and opening the door, he brought me inside and set me carefully on my feet. Like a little boy, he watched my face as I took in my new home, his smile hesitant. I stood in a small, high-ceilinged foyer with wide heart-pine floors polished to a yellow gleam, a narrow staircase against the wall in front of us with a heavy dark wood banister, the newel post worn by hundreds of hands over more than two centuries. I took a step forward to place my hand on it, feeling the smooth, cool finish before my palm touched it. I forced air into my lungs again, wondering whether this was what it was like to see ghosts.

Ashes. Despite the hum of central air-conditioning, I smelled ashes from the working fireplaces that I knew remained in every room. I looked at Matthew in confusion, then forced a smile when I saw the worry had returned to his eyes.

"It's beautiful," I said, taking in a formal living room with Chippendale sofas and red flocked wallpaper before walking through to the adjoining dining room. The walls were a dark blue, the rug and draperies all period patterns, the furniture and accessories antique yet surprisingly approachable. A beautiful arrangement of gladiolas and blue hydrangeas in a cut-crystal vase sat in the middle of the table, the aroma not quite masking the permeating scent of fireplace ash.

Passing a door to the left that led to a butler's pantry and beyond to what looked to be a kitchen, I walked through a doorway at the back of the dining room to what appeared to be a later addition of a cozy den, a large flat-screen TV looking incongruous mounted inside a built-in bookcase. It was tastefully decorated, albeit in a masculine style, but I couldn't help but think its existence was superfluous, and imagined I'd spend much of my time in the original parlor.

"So this is your bachelor pad," I said, wondering why he'd chosen to live here alone instead of living full-time near his clinic in Savannah, where he worked as a child psychologist. He had an apartment nearby where he spent the nights for the three days a week he worked there, but he always returned home to St. Simons. To this house.

"It's home," he said, his answer almost too abrupt. He took a step toward me. "I'll show you the rest of the house in a bit, but right now I want to show you the bedroom."

I laughed at the gleam in his eyes, the threads of tension that had been tugging at me since I'd touched the newel post suddenly snapping loose.

I nuzzled my nose in his neck. "As long as you promise me that we're all alone." I'd said it in a teasing voice, but Matthew pulled away, his dark eyes serious.

"What do you mean?"

My smile faltered. "I was just wondering whether the house was haunted. Aren't all old houses supposed to be?"

A shadow shuttered his eyes, and for a moment I didn't recognize the man I'd married.

"Hello?"

We both started at the sound of the woman's voice and a hard rapping on the doorframe. A petite woman in her mid- to late fifties with short, wavy brown hair stood smiling at us. She wore sandals, capris, and a sleeveless blouse—what I'd been told was the standard island uniform—and was smiling broadly. She held a bouquet of sunflowers, their stems wrapped in pink iridescent paper. "The door was wide-open," she said in explanation, but I had a feeling that a closed door had never held her back. She held up the flowers. "And I brought more flowers from Eternal Carnation to welcome the newlyweds."

"Is that the name of the local flower shop?"

She beamed. "Yes—right downtown in the village."

"The flowers are lovely," I said. "Thank you." I took a step forward and stuck out my hand to shake hers. "I'm Ava Whalen. I mean Frazier." I flushed. "I'm not used to my new name yet."

Matthew took the flowers from the woman and bent to kiss her on the cheek. "Thanks, Tish." He turned to me. "This is Tish Ryan. Not only does she own and operate Eternal Carnation, but she's also responsible for keeping this house running and making sure I don't starve to death."

She smiled at me, her hazel eyes sparkling. "Although I'm sure we'll talk about any new arrangements now that you're here, Ava. I knew Matthew's parents and feel sort of responsible for him. And you know how men are—they're kind of lost unless somebody puts food in front of them or clean laundry in their drawers."

"Believe me, I understand. I have four brothers."

"I know," Tish said.

Both Matthew and I looked at her.

Seeing our confusion, she continued. "When Matthew e-mailed me yesterday to tell me he'd be coming home today and bringing a new wife, he told me your name and where you were from, and I sort of put two and two together." She crossed her arms. "Your brother Stephen and I were married for about two months when we were both eighteen. You weren't even born yet. We've sort of lost track of each other over the years. Must admit to being surprised to hear that the Whalens had another baby, but I guess they never stopped trying for a girl. But there must be, what, nineteen years between you?"

"Twenty-one," I said. "I never knew he'd been married before."

"It was pretty forgettable. We were horribly young and it didn't last long. But you know how impulsive teenagers are."

She smiled at us, but I wasn't sure what to say. I didn't know how teenagers were. I'd grown up surrounded by adults, and never had time to experience any type of teenage rebellion. Except for my choice of careers, I'd always done what was expected of me, always hoping somebody besides Mimi would notice.

Tish glanced at Matthew, then back at me. "I guess I should be leaving—I can wait to get all the details of your whirlwind romance and wedding—in fact, I'm thinking of throwing a party to introduce you, but we can discuss that later." She held up the flowers. "I just wanted to make sure the lights were on and the flowers in a vase, but I guess you beat me to it. Oh, and there's a casserole and salad in the fridge and a loaf of French bread on the counter. Didn't know if you'd have had time to stop at the grocery store."

"Thank you, Tish," Matthew said. "I don't know what I'd do without you."

"Yes, thank you," I added. "I wouldn't even know where to find a grocery store, much less know what to cook or how to cook it."

Again, Tish glanced from Matthew to me. "Yes, well, there will be plenty of time for you to learn both, but in the meantime I'm here to help. I wrote down my name and numbers on the pad by the phone in the kitchen—call me anytime." She put her hand on the doorknob, then turned around. "Matthew says you're a bit of a history buff. I'm the secretary for the St. Simons Historical Society, and I'm always on the lookout for new members. It'll be a great way to get to know your new home. And

Matthew's family history. It's very fascinating, and even has a few skeletons hanging from branches of the family tree that you might find interesting."

"I can't wait," I said, almost meaning it. There was so much I didn't know, but maybe I already knew everything I needed to.

Tish shot Matthew another glance before opening the door and stepping outside. "Oh, before I forget, what line of work are you in, Ava? I write a blog about happenings on and around the island that's followed by mostly locals. I like to include a list of newcomers, and I always list occupations. It's a great way to drum up business, especially if you're new to town."

"I'm a midwife. I worked with a group of obstetricians back home, and I hope to find another similar arrangement here."

"A midwife?" Her brows rose.

"Yes," I said, unable to read her reaction. "I'm a certified nurse-midwife. Using a CNM has become a very popular alternative to a doctor-assisted delivery."

She put her hand on my forearm. "Oh, I'm sorry; I didn't mean for you to take offense. I know what midwives are. I actually used one for my second child. I'm just . . . surprised, since Adrienne . . ." She lifted her hand and waved it dismissively. "Never mind, it's not important." She smiled brightly. "It was a pleasure meeting you, Ava. The next meeting of the historical society is held the last Thursday of the month at seven. I could pick you up at six thirty if you like."

"I, um, well . . ."

Matthew put his hand on the door. "She'll call you and let you know. She'll need time to get acclimated first before diving into the island's politics."

Tish headed down the tabby steps. "Call me then. But go ahead and put it on your calendar just in case." With a final wave, she headed across the drive to a vintage station wagon with wood paneling on the side, her sandaled feet crunching over oyster shells as she walked.

I closed the door and, when I turned around, found that I was trapped between Matthew's arms. His eyes darkened as he looked down at me. "So. Where were we?"

I placed the flat of my palms against the hard smoothness of his chest, tempted to give in to the rush that always accompanied Matthew's touch. But something Tish had said prodded at me like a finger. "Who is Adrienne?"

His retreat was almost imperceptible, and I sensed it more than saw it. It had been that way between us since the moment we'd met, both of us so attuned to each other that it was as if we moved within the same skin. Matthew dropped his arms and stood away from me, and my body felt suddenly chilled.

"She was a midwife, too." His words were mechanical, as if he'd practiced saying those five words over and over again to eliminate any emotion from them.

"But who was she?" I asked. "Why would Tish have been surprised to find we were both midwives?"

He touched my shoulder, his long lashes hiding his dark eyes as he looked at where his hand touched my blouse. "Can we talk about this in the morning? I don't want your first night here to be spoiled."

I rubbed my hands over my arms, feeling the gooseflesh under my palms. I wanted to lean into him, to forget about Tish's look of surprise and Matthew's reluctance to tell me more, but it was as if an unseen hand urged me to press on. I shook my head. "No. I'd like to know now. Who was Adrienne?" I tried to inject humor I didn't feel. "Was she an ex-girlfriend?"

The eyes are the mirror of the soul. Mimi's words came to me as I looked into Matthew's eyes. It was the first thing I'd noticed about him as I'd stood next to a plant at the Atlanta medical conference meet-and-greet trying to blend into the foliage. He'd approached with some now forgotten comment and I'd looked into his dark eyes and simply felt my heart say *yes*.

But now as he faced me his eyes were shuttered, and I felt for a moment as if I were looking into the face of a stranger. *He is*, my mind shouted, but as with all things where Matthew was concerned, I brushed away the doubt.

"No," he said, his voice soft. "She was my wife."

Pamela

St. Simons Island, Georgia
February 1805

The young woman on the dirty mattress moaned again, her cries weaker now and hoarser from the screaming that had started nearly fourteen hours before. The moss-stuffed mattress was soaked from her sweat, the odor stifling in the small room. The fire blazed to ward off the chill from the winter day, but there was not enough heat to warm the cold that gripped me as I looked down at the expectant mother.

I dipped a clean rag into a bowl of tepid water and wiped the woman's forehead again, trying to give the only comfort I could. She was barely nineteen, and so slender she could have been mistaken for a boy except for the mound of her stomach. Her eyes flickered open, settling on my face in silent supplication. I had no reassurance to offer her, and I turned away to dip my cloth back into the water, indicating for the house servant, Etta, to heat more on the fire. My own child stirred in the womb, a gentle reminder of life's fragility.

Leaving Etta with the laboring woman, I walked wearily to the door and stepped into the narrow hallway, the winter's dusk casting shadows along the walls. No candles had been lit but would need to be soon if we were to navigate the stairs. It must have been the wife's task, or her servant's, so the lamps remained without fire and no light to fight the darkness.

A man stirred from a chair by the door from which I had exited. He stood, swaying on his feet, and I could smell the rum on his breath. "Is the child born yet?"

I shook my head. "No. There are . . . complications."

The backs of his knees hit the edge of the chair, causing him to crumple into the seat. He did not bother to stand. He stared at me as if I should know the answers to the questions he did not know how to ask.

"The child is feet-first. I have waited as long as possible for the baby to turn, but he is large and Mary is quite small. I can try to move the baby. It is dangerous and painful, but it might be the only way."

He looked at me, his eyes bleary in the dusky light. "Will that save them both?"

The baby in my swollen abdomen stirred again, and I pressed my hand against him to still the movement. "I will try. Perhaps you can send for someone to be here so you would not be alone. Perhaps a mother or sister . . ."

"I have no one. The fever took them all last summer." He raised the bottle to his lips again, then returned to staring in stupefaction at the wall.

"Then I suggest you begin to pray."

His eyes shifted toward me briefly as he lifted the bottle one more time, and all I could see was the suffering of the young woman on the other side of the door. I grabbed the bottle from his loose grasp and slung it against the wall, glass shattering like broken hope. He looked startled, but I knew in his state he could not hurt me. "Honor your wife, sir. She is dying trying to bring your child into this world. Respect her last hours by being sober."

A sharp pain on my left hand brought my attention from his slowly blinking eyes. A shard of glass the size of a thimble had embedded itself into the skin at the base of my thumb, on the left side of the knuckle. Angrily, I plucked the glass out and watched with surprise as bright red blood seeped from the deep wound. I tore a strip of fabric from the bottom of my shift, then wrapped it tightly across my hand to stop the bleeding.

Wiping my hands on my apron, I returned to the birthing room with slow steps, my own child now still and quiet.

∞

I did not return home until sunset the following day, my back and heart weary, my limbs leaden with exhaustion. I left the wagon and horse out front for Zeus to tend to while I went in search of Geoffrey. He stood on the dock facing Dunbar Creek toward where it bled into the Frederica River, watching the sun in its glorious descent. It always seemed to me that the sunsets on St. Simons were God's assurance that he had not forgotten us in our brutal home, this place of fevers, heat, and storms, but also a place of indescribable beauty.

Geoffrey folded me in his arms, our child moving between us. My father once told me that the Mocama Indians had over one hundred words that meant love, but as I looked into my husband's face I could not imagine that there would be enough to describe my feelings for him.

His thumbs brushed my cheeks as he searched my eyes with his unspoken question.

"The mother is lost, but I saved the child." I bent my forehead to his chest, remembering how I had bathed the small boy and placed him in his cradle, his father too grieved to hold him. I prepared his mother for burial and cleaned the house as best I could, then left with a stew simmering on the fire. I did not question my motives, knowing I was attempting restitution for my failure, punishing myself for my inability to save both mother and child. And knowing, too, that there was nobody else who would. I left instructions with Etta for care of the child, then sent for the minister. I had done all I could, and that was the most disheartening part of it all.

"My brave girl," Geoffrey said, kissing me softly. His eyes became suddenly fierce. "Never leave me, Pamela. Never. I could not face a day on this earth without you here by my side."

I touched his face with my left hand, the gold band suddenly heavy on my finger. It was the ring I had found on the beach after the storm, and it had seemed right to both of us that I would wear it. I held my hand up to him. "Forever, remember?"

He took my hand in his and brought it to his lips. "Forever," he said, but beneath his conviction I sensed his uncertainty, too.

We stood side by side and watched as the ball of fire sank into the river like butter melting in a frying pan. My child stirred again, reminding me how close life is to death, and death to life.

CHAPTER THREE

Ava

St. Simons Island, Georgia
April 2011

I awoke in the bed alone, the crisp sheets beside me smooth and unwrinkled. For a moment, before I'd opened my eyes, I thought Matthew was there, feeling the familiar sense of a presence pressed against my back. Since I was small, I'd imagined an invisible sister, her constant presence the creation of a lonely little girl surrounded by giant brothers. Mimi called her my imaginary friend, and Mama called her something best forgotten. As I grew into womanhood, I had left her behind, my need for an imaginary friend eclipsed by my career and relationships. But she'd never been completely forgotten, recalled only briefly during moments of loneliness, an unidentifiable shadow with the power to comfort.

I sat up, the shadow dancing away. I didn't know where Matthew had slept, only that he had been apart from me on our first night together in the house. Tears stung the backs of my eyes as I recalled our argument, and how I'd refused to let him touch me until I could understand why he'd avoided telling me, even in the short time we'd known each other, that he'd been married before. I wanted no secrets in my marriage. I'd grown up in a world of adults who suddenly began whispering their adult words when my presence was noted. It was as if the house was full of secrets, secrets like ghosts that dissipated as soon as you looked at them but always seemed to hover in the corners. I did not want to live in such a house again.

The sounds of my new home settled around me like a warm blanket, welcoming yet strange at the same time. The old house creaked and popped under its burden of years as unfamiliar birds cawed and yipped outside. I pushed back the heavy duvet and for the first time wondered whether Adrienne had lived in this house, had picked out the toile curtains and plantation shutters on the windows and planted flowers in the garden below. As my hands clutched the soft bedclothes, I wondered, too, whether she had slept in this bed.

I slipped from the four-poster to the floor, my feet finding my slippers before heading to my suitcase for a suitable bathrobe. All of my functional clothing, including my terry-cloth bathrobe and sweats, was being shipped to me. I was left with my honeymoon clothes, impractical things like sheer silk nightgowns, short skirts, and high heels.

There were no closets in the room but a large wardrobe, almost as tall as the ceiling, sat between the two windows, a tassel—matching the draperies—hanging from a key in the front keyhole. I tugged the enormous door open, wondering too late whether Matthew had left any of Adrienne's clothes inside. I let out my breath as I saw only neatly hung dress shirts, golf shirts, various pants, and shoes—all decidedly masculine. His scent was there, the enticing aroma of his shower-fresh skin mixed with his cologne. I closed my eyes and breathed deeply, my heart tightening in my chest as I felt the same visceral pull that I'd felt the first time I'd seen him. Then I remembered the closet door at the far end of the bathroom addition that in my anger I hadn't bothered to open, and my doubts resurfaced.

Not yet willing to face the possibility of another woman's clothes in the unexplored closet, I slid one of Matthew's dress shirts off a hanger and buttoned it over the tiny silk nightgown I'd been relegated to wear the previous night. I nudged open the bedroom door and was met with the enticing aroma of brewed coffee and something sweet and oven-warmed. My stomach grumbled, propelling me downstairs and to the inevitable confrontation.

I stood in the bright kitchen, all stainless steel and granite, but with beadboard cabinetry with glass fronts and a large farmhouse sink to make the modern touches look less incongruous in a two-hundred-year-old house. Beadboard wainscoting, rising three-quarters of the way up the walls, was capped with a small shelf holding antique plates. Freshly finished heart-of-pine floors gleamed beneath the antique plank table and bench seats, while cast-iron chandeliers, obviously very old and most likely originally created for candles, hung above the eating area and the large island by the sink. The Viking stove with six burners along with the heavy-duty double ovens made me think the kitchen had been designed by a chef, somebody who knew how to roll out dough, or make soufflés and puff pastries. Somebody who wasn't me.

I looked at the stove where a nut-covered bread loaf sat in a pan, a single slice missing, but my appetite had suddenly disappeared. I spotted the coffeemaker, where somebody—presumably Matthew—had set out a mug, a container of sweetener packets, and creamer. An ornate silver teaspoon sat on a ceramic spoon rest in the shape of a cotton boll, and the flowers Tish had brought the previous evening sat behind the mug inside another crystal vase of unknown vintage, their aroma adding to the enticing smells of the kitchen. The sweetener and creamer were the brands I used, and my heart squeezed again as I thought of Matthew calling Tish before we arrived and instructing her to make sure I had what I needed.

I had to see him, to work this out between us. I fixed a cup of coffee and went in search of my husband. I stood in the doorway to the kitchen, hearing only the sound of a ticking clock. I'd always found the noise unnerving, reminders of the inevitable passage of time. I didn't call out, knowing he wasn't there.

I turned toward the door at the back of the kitchen that led outside and headed toward it. The backyard was similar to the front, with scrubby grass and sand eventually giving way to the thick trees and brush. The small tabby structure I'd seen the night before sat to my right, looking as alone and forlorn as before.

Mosquitoes buzzed around me, darting around my exposed skin but not landing. I wasn't worried. I was one of the lucky few whom mosquitoes didn't bother with. I took a sip of my coffee, seeing the outlines of another garden, large stones marking rectangular plots. The humidity sat in the air like a wet veil, and I could feel my carefully straightened hair crimping into tight curls.

A path led from the garden area toward the woods, and I followed it as if a string were pulling me into the right direction in the way I imagined migrating birds fly south. I saw the sun reflecting off of water between the trees before I saw the creek and the dock that stretched from wooden steps built into the bank, an extension of the path where I stood. Two long benches facing each other had been built into the railings at the end of the dock. I could picture Matthew as a small boy sitting there with a fishing rod and staring at the sun-rippled waves the way he was doing now. His dark hair, burnished red in places by the sun, gleamed, and my throat tightened as I watched him dip his head as if in heavy thought.

I didn't move but he turned, our eyes meeting across the distance. He stood as I walked quickly down the steps to the edge of the dock and stopped, feeling slightly queasy as it swayed. Then, moving very slowly down the center of the boards and keeping my eyes averted from the water on either side, I moved forward until I stopped in front of him. I held my mug between us, holding myself back from forgiving him before I had a reason to.

My coffee returned a distorted reflection of my face as I took another sip, the liquid now almost too cool to drink. Still holding the cup between us, I said, "I don't want to be a hypocrite, so I'm going to tell you something I've been afraid to."

He didn't say anything, but I imagined his eyes darkening as I'd learned they did when he was deep in thought.

I swallowed. "I'm afraid of water." I kept my eyes focused on the coffee in my mug, trying very hard to ignore the sound of water lapping against the dock's pilings or the small snaps of water as fish and birds disturbed the surface searching for food. "The ocean mostly, but I'm generally uneasy near any large body of water."

I heard his intake of breath but I continued. "It's the kind of fear that gives me nightmares. Like the one I had in the car yesterday." I looked up, afraid of what I might see.

Matthew's expression softened. "And I've brought you to an island to live. I didn't even give you a choice."

My eyes met his. "I made my choice. I wanted to be with *you*. That's all that mattered. I hope with time I can . . . get over it."

He took the mug from my hand and set it on the bench behind me, then pulled me against him, holding me loosely, as if he expected me to pull away. "With my job I deal with a lot of childhood fears, so I know something like what you feel about water isn't something you'll 'get over' on your own. And I don't expect you to. But I can help you, if you'll let me."

"You already have," I said, then stopped, not yet ready to tell him that I'd known that from the moment I'd met him. Or that the first time he'd kissed me, I'd tasted the salt of the ocean, as if he carried this place within him.

The hum of a motor, no louder than the buzzing of a bee, approached and gradually grew louder until I could see a small boat navigating its way from the creek to deeper water. I tried not to think of the Atlantic that lay beyond, or that the salt water that moved beneath my feet was the same water that swelled against the island's shores. The waves around us increased, causing the dock to rise and fall. I closed my eyes and buried my face in Matthew's chest, locking my arms around him.

"Let's get off the dock," he said, trying to move me forward.

I stayed where I was and shook my head, still feeling the movement of the waves but feeling anchored, too, by Matthew's arms. "I want to know about Adrienne."

The muscles in his back tensed but I didn't step away. I took his hands and led him to the bench, where I carefully sat on the edge, away from the water, and held his hands tightly in mine.

"What would you like to know?"

I cleared my throat, trying to look at this situation in the same way I would a breech birth or any circumstance where I couldn't let my emotions lead me. It's what made me a good midwife. "How long were you married?"

"Five years. Five years, three months, and six days."

I hadn't expected an answer so specific, as if each day had been treasured enough to be counted. But he'd married Adrienne and loved her. Having known what it was like to be loved by Matthew Frazier, I knew with my troubled heart that he had cherished her and their time together. Once.

I looked away, unable to meet his gaze. "What happened?"

"She died."

Whatever it was that I'd been expecting to hear, it hadn't been that. My gaze jerked back to his. "How?"

He looked down at our entwined hands, his thumb gently tracing the birthmark at the base of my thumb. "In a car accident four years ago. She was by herself, and I didn't even know she was dead until the next day."

"I'm sorry," I said, realizing too late how stupidly inadequate my words were. And how insincere. It was through Adrienne's dying that Matthew was mine now. I clung to that selfish thought, unable to stop myself from holding on to it like some hot burning ember that gave light in the darkness, but also threatened to consume everything with fire.

"We were very young when we married. I was just out of grad school and celebrating, and she was working in a bar in Savannah—she wasn't a midwife yet. But her older brother and I had been friends, so I recognized her and we started talking." He shrugged as if that single movement explained the rest of what happens after a couple meets in a bar.

"Was she from Savannah?"

He shook his head. "From here, actually, although Adrienne was sent to Atlanta for high school. Her parents are older. They adopted Adrienne and John—from different families—when they were in their forties. They still live on St. Simons, although her brother lives nearby on Jekyll Island. I don't see a lot of them." He set his mouth in a firm line.

Never one to resist picking a scab, I pressed on. "Why not?"

A large elegant bird with blue-white feathers and spindly legs landed in the marsh grass on the bank by the dock. It stood completely still, its gaze seeming to measure our proximity as well as that of its prey.

"Because they think I killed her."

I felt the water move beneath me in slow motion, my equilibrium unsettled like it had been stirred with a spoon. As if sensing a change of mood the great bird took flight, leaving behind only a memory of a splash as I faced my husband.

"It's not true, of course," I said before he could. If we were to salvage anything from this conversation, I *had* to say it first.

"Of course not," he said, but the first unwelcome tinge of unease had already found its way to the base of my neck, the way a pebble slides into a shoe. "It was an accident, but, as many people do when they're grieving, they tried to find a reason, or somebody to blame for something that couldn't have been avoided."

"Is that why you didn't tell me?"

His thumb found my lone wedding band. "Mostly," he answered slowly, before lifting his face to meet my eyes. "But also because it's a part of my past that I don't like to revisit."

In the bright sunlight I could see gold flecks in his dark eyes. They weren't the eyes I recognized. They were different somehow, like those of a stranger. "Do you still love her?"

My voice shook as I said it, and he must have heard. He held my head between his hands, his stranger's eyes searching mine. "I love you, Ava. It's almost as if I always have, even before I met you. Can you understand that?"

Forever. The word touched the back of my mind like a dapple of sunlight on the water, floating precariously until obliterated by a cloud across the sun. "Yes," I said instead. "I feel it, too."

He pressed his forehead against mine. "I'm sorry," he said. "I don't want any secrets between us."

I kissed him in response, unable to speak words that might reveal my unease at how carelessly we'd kept part of ourselves from each other, or how secrets could cast their shadows long after the truth was spoken.

⸎

I looked around the mess that was my new kitchen. Pans, pots, mixing bowls, utensils, and various powdery ingredients coated every flat surface. I was in the middle of wondering whether I could salvage the burned banana bread by scraping off the charred edges when I heard a knock on the front door.

Relieved to have an excuse to leave the kitchen, I quickly rinsed my hands in the sink, then eagerly answered the door. Tish stood there with her arms brimming with plastic grocery bags, a bright smile on her face. "I brought you groceries. I was at the store and realized that Matthew was working today and you didn't have a car. I hope you don't mind."

I took several of the bags from her before stepping back to let her inside. "Of course not, and I really appreciate it. We're not expecting my car until next week. That's when the friend I'm paying to drive it could do it without missing work, so I'm a bit housebound. Matthew did say he wouldn't be staying overnight in Savannah like he usually does so he can come home, but I feel kind of guilty. It's a long commute for just one day."

Tish followed me back to the kitchen. "I don't think Matthew will mind coming back to see his new bride. He'd probably walk back if he didn't have a car."

I blushed as I began emptying the bags of milk, lettuce, chicken legs, a couple of steaks, and an assortment of fruits and vegetables. I was a little dismayed to discover that none of the bags contained even a single frozen dinner.

Tish began balling up the plastic shopping bags. "As soon as you start your job, you can commute together and even stay at the Savannah apartment if you can work out the same hours."

I laughed. "I see you've got my next career move all figured out along with my dinners."

She frowned. "I'm sorry. I'm trying to be helpful without meddling, but it's a bit hard for me—especially since you're practically family. It's just that . . ." She bit her lower lip as if arguing with herself about how much she should say. "Well," she continued, "it's just that Adrienne worked in the same family health services clinic as Matthew, so I assumed . . ."

I leaned against the table, feeling suddenly tired. "They worked together?"

"Yes. He was the child psychologist on staff, and she was one of the midwives. The clinic has a pediatrician and two ob-gyns, too—for all stages in a child's life. It made sense for them to work together, so I figured since you're a midwife, too . . ."

She was too busy staring at me to finish her sentence. "What's wrong?" she asked.

My fingers felt sticky from the flour and butter I hadn't rinsed off completely. "Don't you think it's odd that . . . well, that Matthew would marry two midwives? It's not like it's the most common occupation."

"It is odd, if you think about it. He actually was the one who encouraged Adrienne to go to school to become a midwife. She was sort of at loose ends after she graduated from high school, and Matthew helped her focus. And she was a good and competent midwife."

She stopped, as if realizing she'd already said too much.

"Just good and competent?" I prompted.

Tish shook her head, as if excusing herself from a personal promise not to meddle. Quickly, she said, "I just don't think it was her passion."

Our eyes met, and I waited for her to say more, but she didn't. Straightening, I said, "I don't think I'll be applying there. I'm sure there are other opportunities elsewhere, in Savannah or not. We'll figure it out." I forced a smile. "Would you like some tea? I was about to get myself a cup to steel myself for the cleanup."

"I'd love one," she said as she moved to the refrigerator and began placing groceries inside. "Then you can tell me what other talents you have, since apparently it's not cooking."

I laughed as I swiped hair off of my sweaty forehead, remembering too late that my hand still had remnants of banana bread ingredients. "I might not know my way around the kitchen, but I do know something about gardening." Lightly, I added, "I figure Adrienne had to be a remarkable cook, judging from her kitchen. Please don't tell me she was a master gardener, too."

Tish's face softened as she regarded me. "She did love her flowers. The brighter, the better."

My smile dimmed. "I'm a different kind of gardener. I like growing useful things—fruits and vegetables. That sort of thing." I belatedly realized that what I'd said, considering she was a florist, could probably have been taken as an insult.

She smiled good-humoredly. "Good. We'll get along just fine then—I'll bring you flowers and you can bring me tomatoes."

"Deal," I said, moving the bread pan to the sink, where I hoped Tish wouldn't notice it.

Tish's voice was muffled as she rearranged a shelf in the refrigerator. "You should probably know that Adrienne was a very good artist—sketched the island a lot and had made quite a name for herself." She closed the refrigerator. "The charcoal sketch of the house hanging in the parlor is hers."

I turned off the taps, feeling suddenly deflated.

She must have seen something in my expression, because she took my arm and led me back to the table. "Why don't you sit down and let me fix us tea? I know where everything is, and you look like you need a break."

I watched her fill the kettle and put it on the stove while unwanted questions kept pecking at my brain like a persistent bird. I accepted the steaming mug and focused on adding sugar from a bowl on the table—a light blue ceramic bowl I didn't like and vowed to replace—then took a slow sip before finding the right words.

"Last night you mentioned something about the area's history and Matthew's family tree, and that it had a lot of skeletons hanging from it. Is that what you were referring to? Adrienne's death?"

Tish took a sip from her own mug and shook her head. "No. Of course not. Adrienne's death was an accident—a tragedy, sure, but not a skeleton.

I was referring to an old ancestor—somebody who lived here more than two hundred years ago. It's become almost an island legend."

My family, being in the business of death, rarely spoke of our own family tree, as if to punctuate the finality of each generation's passing. Both of my parents were only children, and besides my maternal grandmother I knew of no other relatives who came before. It seemed as if the Whalen family extinguished itself after each generation, leaving a blank slate for the next. To hear that my new husband had a family tree blooming with full limbs that went back generations sent a little stir of excitement through me.

I blew on my tea, then took another swallow. "So Matthew's family has been on St. Simons for two centuries?"

"Oh, yes. They weren't one of the large landowners, like the Coupers of Cannon's Point or the Butlers of Hampton, but they were respectable farmers. Even had a few acres of cotton for a time. At least until the early eighteen hundreds."

Curious, I leaned toward her. "So what's the legend?"

Tish's eyes widened, and I recognized a kindred spirit who found the comings and goings of those long since dead sometimes preferable to the present. "Matthew's great-great-something-grandmother was purported to be a traitor to her country during the British occupation of the island during the War of 1812. She supposedly fell in love with one of the Royal Marines. They say when the British evacuated, she went with them, leaving behind her husband and young son."

"That's terrible," I said, my tea suddenly bitter, the oddest compulsion to cry heavy in the back of my throat. "Are these just rumors, or is any of it based on fact?"

"A little of both." She smiled. "Maybe this can be your first project with the historical society. Although . . ." Tish shook her head dismissively before standing to rinse her cup in the sink.

"Although what?"

She kept her back to me while she placed her mug in the dishwasher. "Adrienne was obsessed with the story. They say the woman's husband died of a broken heart, and that his ghost can still be seen on the beach after storms calling for his unfaithful wife. Adrienne thought it romantic; Matthew just thought it was sad and didn't see the need to be reminded of such a tragic story." Tish faced me again and shrugged. "You seem to be an independent-minded woman, so you can decide. But, as I mentioned before, it might be an interesting way to start learning about your new home and the family you've married into."

I nodded, trying to keep a relaxed smile on my face and push away the heavy pall of sadness that seemed to have settled on me like a shawl.

Tish picked up her purse that she'd slung over a chair. "I've got to get back to the shop. We've got a wedding Saturday, and the bride keeps changing her mind about the bridesmaids' bouquets." She rolled her eyes. "I'll be here at six thirty next Thursday to pick you up for the meeting. I'm usually running late, so I'll just honk the horn outside."

I didn't remember telling her I'd be going, but I guessed Tish had already made up her mind. I thought briefly of my brother Stephen's current wife, the shy and reserved Mary Jane, and imagined I knew why Tish and Stephen's marriage had been so abbreviated.

"All right," I said. "I'll be ready."

I walked her to the door and said good-bye, distracted by the thought of a heartbroken man calling out for his wife long after she'd gone. The image of him standing in a stormy surf sent a tremor through me, as if I could feel the cool spray of the water, and I quickly looked around for a distraction before my gaze settled on my cell phone on the front hall table.

Before I could talk myself out of it, I picked it up and hit the memory button. It rang four times before my mother answered. If she had a cell phone or caller ID on the house phone, I might have accused her of screening my call. But my mother had always had an aversion to the phone, as if she expected it to bring only bad news.

"Hello?"

"Mama—it's Ava."

A brief pause. "I figured you might be calling."

When she didn't say anything else, I said, "We got here safely yesterday. Matthew's house is beautiful. It's very old, and made from tabby—"

"Yes, I know," she said, cutting me off. "We lived on St. Simons before you were born, remember?"

Before I could give her the chance to grill me again about why I'd chosen to move across the state, I began to ramble, searching for something to say, something that would keep her on the phone long enough for me to memorize the sound of her voice. "Did you ever hear the legend about the ghost of Matthew's ancestor calling for his wife on the beach?"

It took her a while to answer. "I don't recall."

My gaze strayed to the front parlor, where it latched onto the framed charcoal sketch of Matthew's house. "Do you believe in ghosts?" I asked quietly.

Her voice sounded strained. "Come home, Ava. I don't like thinking about you so near the water."

I turned my back on the sketch. "What do you mean?"

"You've been petrified of water since you were a baby. It was almost impossible to give you a bath in the tub. I had to get Mimi to help me just sponge-bathe you in the kitchen sink. I thought you had outgrown your fear, but I worry about it now. Now that you're living so near the ocean."

I thought for a moment about telling her of my experience as we'd crossed the causeway to the island, of the recurrence of my old nightmare, but I didn't.

"I think I'll be happy here, Mama."

Her reply was quick this time. "I don't see how. You don't like the water."

"Matthew is here. My home is with him."

"Well, then. That's your decision, and you'll have to live with it." Her voice shook, and I thought she might be crying, but the image didn't mesh well with the mother I knew.

"You lived here, Mama. Four of your children were born here. Don't you remember how beautiful it is?"

Her pause was so long that for a moment I thought she'd hung up. Finally, she said, "All I remember are the storms, and how the ocean moves up on the beach like it's going to swallow it up. That's why we left. Because we didn't want to live in a place that could take away everything we loved."

My old restlessness returned, mingled with impatience. "I need to go, Mama. I've still got a lot of unpacking to do." I paused, feeling an intense longing for a childhood I'd never had, for things that could have been but weren't meant for me. Gripping the phone tightly, I whispered, "I love you, Mama." I closed my eyes, waiting for her to speak.

After a short pause, she said, "I know, Ava." I listened to her breathe for a moment before she said, "I have to go now, too."

"All right. Tell Mimi and everybody I said hello."

"I will. Good-bye, Ava," came from the other end of the phone before I heard the small click.

I held the phone in my hand for a long time, feeling as if I were waiting for more than those three little words, and wondering why she hadn't answered my question about believing in ghosts.

CHAPTER FOUR

Gloria

ANTIOCH, GEORGIA
APRIL 2011

A good mother loves all of her children equally. As each baby was placed in my arms, I found it almost impossible to believe that my heart was big enough to make room for one more. But it was. After four boys, my heart was full nearly to bursting. Despite my love for my sons, there was still a void in my home, a feeling of missing something I'd never even had. It was as if I knew my daughter long before we met, in reverse order, like displaying a frame without a photograph.

The first time I held Ava in my arms, my heart sighed. Like it knew I was finally complete. I loved my boys, but there's something special about a daughter. It's as if that tiny bundle of pink blanket and ruffles is a mother's chance to start over with her own life. That's what my own mother told me, although from what I can see so far, neither attempt has turned out as we planned.

I clipped the columbine and added it to the basket under my arm, its riotous red soothed by the soft lavender of the crested iris. These would look perfect in Henry's consultation office, offering simultaneous beauty and condolence. There was some sort of absurdity about displaying dying flowers in a place that was all about remembering life.

"Who was that on the phone?"

Mimi—I can't remember how long it had been since I'd called her Mother—sat in the shade of a thick wax myrtle, her long blond hair rolled up in curlers and tucked under a red-and-white polka-dot head scarf. I kept my own hair clipped short and in its own natural color—white—so I wouldn't look as foolish as a woman just past ninety who wanted to be thirty again. It was useless trying to tell her that that horse had left the barn long ago.

I stopped clipping and straightened, my hand on my lower back, knowing already that I'd be popping my pain pills and taking a long nap in the near future. How much longer could I go on maintaining this garden? Mimi's arthritis had relegated her to the sidelines years before, but that hadn't stopped her from barking orders to me as if it were *her* garden. And in my own house, too! But a promise to someone made long ago propelled me to nurture this garden, and I wasn't about to go back on my word this late in the game.

Maybe soon I'd be the one in the chair in the shade, but I was afraid I'd have nobody to boss. My daughters-in-law were good sorts, but not one of them understood a garden. They liked flowers and the pretty smells, but none of them felt the *need* to coax seeds from the rich earth, or comprehended how the changing foliage was a better indicator of the weather than that stupid channel they had on cable these days. And they certainly didn't appreciate the heirloom roses, descendants of those that had once been in Mimi's grandmother's yard more than one hundred years before and now claimed their spot along the trellises that surrounded the garden. They were the arms of the garden, like a mother holding in her children as if it were possible to fence time.

"It was Ava," I answered. "I guess she felt the need to let me know she arrived safely."

I felt her accusing stare on my back. "You should have said good-bye. And then you should have called her first so you could say you're sorry. You did apologize, right?"

I tugged on a weed so hard that I ended up raining clumps of dirt over my Oconee bells. As I bent to brush it off the leaves and delicate white flowers, I said, "I can't apologize when I know I'm right. She married a stranger and she's moving practically across the world."

I cringed even before Mimi snorted in outrage. "St. Simons is hardly across the world, Gloria. It's barely across the state, and you can make the drive in under seven hours. And Matthew Frazier isn't a complete stranger, as you well know."

I stiffened. "We were acquaintances of his parents; that's all. I know nothing about Matthew. He was a little boy when we left, and I don't think I laid eyes on him until yesterday."

Straggly weeds rose from the dark earth like hair on a balding man, and the forget-me-nots badly needed pruning. Ava would have known to do these things, and would sometimes head to the garden first when she visited. But my daughters-in-law knew only what they were told. They wore spotless gardening gloves, afraid to have their hands in the dirt. Ava and I had always known that sticking our fingers in the dirt was a lot like holding the past and the present in your hands, understanding that decaying plants nourished the soil for new seedlings. It was hard for me to fathom that all four of my sons had married women so different from me. Ava and I were different, too, but our love of fertile soil smothered a lot of our other differences in the same way new topsoil covers the weeds. I'd always believed that Ava's preference for useful plants over showy blooms was her way of separating herself from me. Not that it mattered; Ava could grow grass from a rock.

"You should go visit. Help Ava settle into her new house," my mother persisted.

Mimi was like a dog with a bone, refusing to let go of a subject until she got what she wanted. "You know I can't do that. Henry needs me here, and

I've got the house and David's children to watch, and all of my committees. If she wanted me to help her get settled, she should have stayed in Antioch."

"You should tell her, you know."

She'd gone too far this time. I dropped my basket and stalked toward her. "You know I can't do that. It's been too long." There were so many other reasons, but how can a person put into words a blinding fear and the tenuous hold of a mother's arms?

The polka-dotted head scarf flapped in the wind, looking ridiculous next to the serious expression on Mimi's face. "I meant you should tell her that you love her."

I stared into my own mother's eyes, unable to count the number of times she'd told me she loved me. "She knows," I said, before walking back to my overturned basket and the flowers that had fallen onto the green grass like spilled paint.

Ava

St. Simons Island, Georgia
April 2011

I stood in the parlor staring at the framed drawing hung between the two front windows. Despite the overhang of the front porch, the late-afternoon sun slanted through the plantation shutters and illuminated the dust motes that floated in the shafts of light like spirits.

The scent of a three-cheese lasagna cooking in the oven permeated the house. Tish had given me the recipe, after ensuring that I already had all the necessary ingredients, telling me it was foolproof and one of Matthew's favorites. Despite my misgivings, I'd managed to assemble all the ingredients and place them into the baking dish, following Tish's instructions exactly. I'd taken the liberty of adding more cheese than the recipe called for, wanting to make the recipe my own. I hadn't been exactly sure what that meant, but it was one of the pieces of advice my sisters-in-law had imparted to me as they'd handed me a recipe box with their favorites inside.

The air conditioner flicked on, sending cool air from the parlor floor vent. Living in Georgia all of my life, I'd grown up with central air, yet somehow, in this old house with the same floors Matthew's ancestors had walked on for more than two centuries, it seemed wrong.

Peering closely at the artwork, I could make out the three initials in the bottom right corner. *AMF*. I didn't know what the "M" stood for, but I was fairly certain the "A" and "F" were for Adrienne Frazier. I examined the sketch of the house, studying the fine lines and delicate shading. The bark of the trees was as detailed as a photograph, each curl of the Spanish moss replicated in exact shades of light and shadow. Even I had to admit that Adrienne had been an extraordinary artist. I stepped back, my unsettled feeling having nothing to do with the talents of the first Mrs. Frazier. It was something about the house in the sketch, something that seemed odd, but I had no idea what it was. It was like looking into a mirror and finding that your hair wasn't the same color you remembered.

I lifted the frame off the wall, then hurried out to the front yard, determined to discover what it was that was different. I counted the porch supports and the steps leading up to the house. I even counted the windows and the panes in each, and studied the slope of the porch roof. But the sketch was an exact replica.

I returned inside and attempted to lift the heavy frame back onto the two small hooks. Pressing the side of my face against the wall, I peered at the back of the print and tried again and again to catch the wire hanger on the hooks but without success. In a moment of exasperation and impatience, I shoved the picture hard against the wall, freezing at the sound of paper tearing.

Feeling like I might be sick, I flipped the frame over and was nearly giddy with relief when I saw I'd ripped only the brown paper that covered the back of the frame and not the actual sketch. Despite the deep gash, nobody would notice, as the rip would be against the wall. Determined now to rehang the frame, I picked it up again, pausing as I caught sight of something loose sliding beneath the brown paper.

Placing the frame facedown on the floor, I gingerly lifted the torn paper to peer inside. From what I could tell from the small opening, there were three sheets of drawing paper, kept together with a paper clip. Curious, I stuck two fingers inside and plucked them out. They were clipped together on all four sides, and face-to-face, so I couldn't see what was on the fronts. I was about to slip off the first paper clip when I heard the sound of crunching tires outside. Matthew was home. My horrified gaze went directly to the now slightly larger gash in the back of Adrienne's artwork. I knew I was being irrational, but I didn't want my new husband to think I'd vindictively vandalized the drawing.

Standing quickly, I tried for one last time to hang the frame, the wire catching on both hooks the first time. I began walking to the front door when I spotted the drawing papers on the floor. Without thinking, I yanked open a drawer on an antique mahogany chest and closed it just as the front door opened.

I stayed where I was, unsure why I was feeling like a child with her fingers in the cookie jar. Matthew set down his briefcase and came toward me. As always when I saw him again after even a brief separation, my chest seemed to constrict, and my breathing grew more shallow. I wondered whether I'd ever stop feeling this way, but couldn't imagine there would be enough years left in the universe.

There were no words spoken as he embraced me in greeting, then kissed me slowly. I had to gently push him away as we both became hungry for more. "There will be room for dessert later," I said. "I don't want my first attempts at cooking to be spoiled."

He raised his eyebrows. "I thought you didn't know how to cook."

I tugged his tie loose. "There's a lot you don't know about me." I said it teasingly, but his eyes sobered as we both considered the truth of my words. "I figured it couldn't be too hard to read a recipe."

He leaned in to give me a chaste kiss on the tip of my nose, but didn't say anything as his gaze moved to the low, square table that sat between the sofa and two chairs opposite. "What's this?"

For a moment I thought I'd left the drawing papers in plain sight. Relieved, I remembered the clear storage bags I'd left on the table filled with old cameras and film canisters. I'd thrown them into my suitcase as an afterthought when I'd packed up my apartment, not completely sure why I'd thought them important enough to bring with me. I shrugged, a little embarrassed. "It's just a little hobby of mine that I've had since I was a kid." I sat down on the sofa while Matthew sat next to me.

I emptied one of the bags onto the table. "We had a lot of tornadoes the spring I turned seven, and one of those old Instamatic cameras landed in the bushes in our yard. I found it, and then my brother Stephen showed me how to open it, and we found that it still had film inside. He drove me to the drugstore and had the film developed. I wasn't sure what I was thinking I'd find. I'd just started reading Nancy Drew mysteries and was probably thinking the pictures were a clue to some big mystery."

I used my thumbnail to pry up the film compartment cover, then flipped over the camera and felt the hard plastic of the film canister land in my palm. I held it up like a prized treasure.

"And what did you find?" His voice was a mixture of interest and curiosity, and I wondered why I'd felt embarrassed.

"It was some kid's fourth birthday party. There were balloons and a birthday cake, and everybody was wearing those conelike hats with the fake blue fur fringe around the bottom. It was a family party, with just the mom, dad, the little boy, and two girls who were a bit older. They were identical, and were even dressed the same, so I assumed they were twins."

He sat back against the cushion and put his arm behind me. "Did you recognize them?"

I shook my head. "No. The tornadoes happened three hundred miles away. There was no telling who those people were. Maybe if we'd had Facebook or something like that back then, we could have posted them and hoped somebody recognized them, but I figured I was given the camera for a reason."

"Sounds like something your Mimi would say."

I looked at him sharply. "You've laid eyes on her once in your life. How would you know what she'd say?"

"Because," he said, his fingers brushing my bare shoulders, "you talk a lot about Mimi. It just sounds like something she'd say."

"For a moment there, I thought you were thinking I was one of your patients." I took out the other camera from the bag. "Anyway, there was something about the twins. I knew I didn't know them, but there was still something . . . I don't know. Compelling, maybe? Recognizable? I thought it was because I'd always felt as if I had an invisible friend with me, ever since I can remember. Something I dreamed up because I hated being like an only child, I guess. Or because I needed somebody to talk to because my mom . . ." I stopped, not wanting to continue, then flicked open the film compartment and watched as another film canister joined the first. "I started going to garage sales and rummage sales. All of my babysitting money went to developing the film. I didn't even keep the photos after they were developed—I threw them all away. It was like in each picture I was expecting to find something I needed to know."

Matthew sat up, his elbows propped on his knees, his fingers threaded together. "Did you ever find it?"

"Apparently not," I said, indicating my most recent garage sale acquisitions that lay scattered on his coffee table. I began to gather all the canisters in a pile. "I have a job interview tomorrow in Brunswick, and I was hoping to find a place to have these developed while I was there. You did say I could have the car, right?"

His lips tightened. "Yes, but I was hoping . . ." He stopped.

"Hoping what?"

He finished unknotting his tie and slid it from the collar of his shirt. "I was just hoping we could fit in our delayed honeymoon before you started working, when you won't have any vacation time."

We'd been talking about our honeymoon, but once we'd arrived on St. Simons together it seemed that neither of us had been that interested in leaving again so soon. But I could tell, too, that our unfinished plans weren't the only reason he hesitated.

I kept my voice cool, remembering what Tish had told me. "What else were you thinking?"

He sat back on the sofa. "Well, I was hoping that you would come speak with the people at my clinic first. One of our midwives will be going on maternity leave soon, and we'll need somebody to fill in. We could add another midwife to the staff if it works out for everyone once Joyce returns."

I swallowed hard. I was used to forging my own path, without consultation. Mimi said it was something I'd been born with, an inherited trait that she claimed was part of my survival instinct. I'd never been in a life-or-death situation, but I used her rationalization to excuse my penchant for stepping first without looking, and blurting out the first thing that came to mind. Forcing my voice to remain calm, I said, "I know that's what Adrienne did. But I'd rather find a position just on my own merits."

He looked at me, and for a moment it was as if he were seeing someone else. Seeing *her*. He shook his head as if mentally shaking away an image. "No, you're right. I'm sorry. It should be your choice." He paused, considering his words. "I guess I'm one of those people who cling to what's familiar and easy for me. I should have known better."

I moved to him, slipping my fingers into his thick, dark hair, and touched my lips to his. "Work will be a good distraction—for both of us—and will make our reunions that much sweeter."

He held me close, but I couldn't push back the feeling that he was disappointed, that he'd wanted to relive a part of his past. A past that had included Adrienne.

Matthew abruptly pulled away. "What's that smell?"

I sniffed the air, smelling the distinct aroma of burning cheese. "Oh, no!" I cried, before rushing to the kitchen and throwing open the oven to let out a billowing cloud of smoke. Matthew reached around me and turned off the oven.

Grabbing the oven mitts, I slid the burned and thoroughly unappetizing lasagna out of the oven and placed it on top of the stove. My first dinner for my husband was one charred, lumpy mess that looked as appetizing as dirt. "I guess I forgot to set the timer." I felt the embarrassing sting of tears behind my eyes.

"It happens," Matthew said, slipping the mitts off of my hands. "Luckily we've got some great little restaurants in the village where we can get a nice meal and a glass of wine—or two."

After making sure the oven was off, he gently led me out of Adrienne's kitchen, the aroma of my failure following us like a ghost.

CHAPTER FIVE

Pamela

ST. SIMONS ISLAND, GEORGIA
OCTOBER 1805

The marshes had settled into their autumn blankets of gold and amber, shaking out the birds and insects like an old woman preparing for winter. The island was a different place now than in the spring and summer, devoid of its sound and scent until the rains of March returned and made it blossom again. In this way it was different from the ocean that changed colors without really changing, its relentless ebb and flood tides reminders of its brutal imperviousness to life and death.

I stood in the chill wind with Geoffrey's arm around me, the only warmth in the icy depths of my body. Our child was gone from us so suddenly that we were both still stumbling through the house and opening doors into empty rooms.

There were few mourners at Christ Church cemetery. The minister had given the service in the open due to the lack of a church building, the oaks weeping moss onto the small gathering, moving the sunlight from grass blade to stone. The words were brief, as befitted the short life of baby Jamie, the scattered and recent headstones in the new cemetery bearing silent witness to our grief as the small box was lowered into the ground.

I held tightly to Geoffrey's hand but did not cry. I'd seen too many childless mothers never stop. Instead, I took comfort in the warmth of Geoffrey's hand in mine, the reassurance of life in his touch, and allowed the grief to come to me without inviting it to stay.

My father and sister, Georgina, approached, the latter looking like a blond porcelain doll despite her black cloak and dress. She kissed me on each cheek, her lips cold and stiff, before reaching for Geoffrey to do the same. I looked away, remembering how before my return from Savannah after having tended to my ailing grandmother, Georgina had been sweet on him and had even hinted of an upcoming betrothal.

But that was not to be. Shortly before my return, he'd stopped calling on Georgina. I was unaware of the reason why, believing it had something to do with my sister's sometimes fickle nature, and her ability to never be satisfied with what she had, and to always desire to have that which she could not.

Several months had passed when I saw Geoffrey at the gathering in the home of a neighbor, and our eyes had met across the room as if we shared the same thoughts. He crossed the room to speak with me and did not leave my side for the entire evening. He began escorting me home from church services, and not long after, we were married. I could not feel guilt over Georgina's loss. She was beautiful and would have many suitors. But Geoffrey was mine. I had even come to believe that our being together was as much a part of the world order as the changing of the seasons.

"I've made stew and crackling bread for supper," Georgina was saying. "I didn't expect you would be wanting to go home yet."

I looked at my sister, realizing she was right. The quietness of the house might be my undoing. I smiled at her generosity. "Yes, thank you. That was very kind of you."

"You are my sister and Geoffrey is my brother-in-law. It is the least I could do."

Impulsively, she grabbed my hands, ungloved because I had lost my kid leather ones while attending to a birth, and Geoffrey's funds were low after the disaster of the past year's storm and the loss of his crop.

Georgina stared down at the ugly red welt on my hand. "What have you done to your hand?"

I pulled away, aware of the angry scar. "I cut it when I was delivering the Tetleys' baby last February. It became fevered and I thought I might lose my hand. I suppose I should be grateful that it is only a scar."

Geoffrey appeared at my side and took my hand in his again, bringing the scar up to his lips. "Are you sure you do not want to return home?"

His dark blue eyes settled on mine and I wanted to weep again. The child we had just buried was his as well as mine, and they had shared the same eyes. I placed my head on his chest, hearing his heartbeat. "Yes. Just be with me."

Georgina stepped back, averting her face, allowing Geoffrey to lead me out of the churchyard. A horse whinnied, and I started as a man stepped from behind our wagon. I felt Geoffrey stiffen as we both recognized the young widower Nathaniel Smith. He had a large cotton farm on Jones Creek, and so we should have had a lot in common. Instead, Geoffrey had an avid dislike of the man and we did not seek out his company. His wife had died eight years before, and he did not attend church services at the planters' houses. Without the social inroads a wife usually made, it was not that unusual that our paths would not cross even on such a tiny island.

Nathaniel took off his hat and bowed his head toward me and then at Geoffrey. "Mistress Frazier. Mr. Frazier. I am sorry for your loss," he said, his eyes serious. When neither of us said anything, he continued. "I was not aware of your recent tragedy or I would not have come to see you today. But I was told at your house that you were here and would likely be receptive to seeing me after I stated my business."

"Which is?" Geoffrey bit out.

Georgina appeared behind Nathaniel and stopped suddenly when she recognized him, her face losing all color.

He reached behind him and pushed forward a thin slip of a girl no older than ten or eleven wearing a dirty yellow head rag. Her skin was light, almost white, the skin where her left eye had once been knotted and twisted where it had been sewn together over the empty socket. She stared at us with abject fear, her spirit cringing as her body stood upright.

"This here is Jemma. Her mama was the midwife at my place until she died of a fever last month. Jemma helped her some and learned some midwifery. I do not have any use for her myself, but thought your wife might."

I stepped forward but refrained from touching the girl, afraid she would start running and never stop. "What happened to her eye?"

Nathaniel's eyes narrowed. "She got a bad infection and it had to be taken out."

I struggled not to cringe at the image of what an operation like that must have been like. No morphine would have been given to a slave child. I stared at Jemma, imagining what sort of sturdy soul she must have to have survived it.

"How much do you want for her?" Geoffrey asked.

I nearly wept from relief at the sound of my husband's voice. I thought I would have to beg him for this poor, wounded child.

Nathaniel did not spare the child a glance. "I was hoping we could barter. I have two field slaves at the end of their terms, and without a midwife anymore I fear for their safe delivery. The father is one of my Ebos, so those babies are going to be big. I cannot afford to lose mother and child."

Without waiting for Geoffrey to answer, I nodded my head. "Of course. Just have someone send word when it is time."

Nathaniel noticed Georgina for the first time and an odd light refocused his eyes. "Miss MacGregor," he said, dipping his head. "I hope you are well."

I faced my sister and watched as her cheeks became infused with color. She responded by dipping her head and staring at her feet.

I knelt on the ground by Jemma and smiled at her, trying not to look at the ruined eye. "I am Miss Pamela," I said. "And you are coming to live with us."

The little girl seemed to melt inside herself. Hesitantly, she took a step toward me, and I placed a firm hand on her bony shoulder. She trembled beneath my palm, and I felt an odd kinship with her. My own mother had died in childbed when I was nine years old. Of all the losses in life, there is no equal to that of a girl losing her mother before she has learned how to be a woman.

I turned to Geoffrey. "Before we go to my father's house, let us take Jemma home. Leda can feed her and give her a pallet next to hers in the kitchen house. I think they will find some comfort in each other." I thought of the very short and very stout dark-skinned Leda, who had cared for Geoffrey since he was an infant. She was a childless widow of undetermined years, still mourning the loss of her husband, who had died more than three years before.

Geoffrey lifted Jemma into the back of the wagon before assisting me up onto the front seat and taking his place beside me. As we pulled away into the road, I turned my head to see Nathaniel take a step toward my sister. Georgina looked, then fled in the direction of our father, who was emerging from the churchyard.

Facing the road, I said, "I know you do not like Nathaniel, but he would make a good provider for Georgina. I wonder why she does not allow Nathaniel to court her."

Geoffrey did not answer at first. Eventually he said, "Leave her to make her own choices, although I am afraid she already has." He held the reins in one hand and gripped mine with his other. "You have a faithful heart, Pamela, which is why I love you so. I will not abide a feckless love; it wounds the soul." His gloved fingers entwined with mine, and I marveled at the large solidness of them, at how they were strong enough to work the fields yet gentle enough to cradle a baby.

He squeezed my fingers almost too tightly. "Do you understand?"

I rested my head on his shoulder, forgetting our sorrow for a single moment. "Yes, Geoffrey. You know I do. I could never be unfaithful to you."

Forever. My fingers touched the gold band on my left hand, and for the first time in a long while I wondered about the original owner of the ring, and whether its loss meant that forever had become a finite thing.

"Good," he said without looking at me.

He returned both hands to the reins as I continued to watch him, wanting to ask him how he knew these things about Georgina, and knowing, too, that I could not.

Ava

St. Simons Island, Georgia
April 2011

After glancing one more time at the map Matthew had drawn for me, I folded it and slid it into the back pocket of my shorts. It had been a while since I'd ridden a bike, but I'd always been told that once you learned how, you never forgot. During my first wobbly attempts to move forward on the uneven ground, I was about to disagree. It was Matthew's bike and too large for me, but he'd been happy to move the seat to its lowest position to make it easier, and assured me that we would go buy me my own bike soon. I pushed off with one foot and lifted the other to the pedal and found myself miraculously upright and somewhat balanced. I moved forward, a breeze of tangy saltiness kissing my face, and I smiled at no one at all.

My job interview the day before—obtained by a recommendation from my previous employer—had gone well, and I was in a good mood. Matthew had even offered to drive me across the causeway to Brunswick for the interview, but I'd wanted to do it by myself. So instead he'd taught me a few breathing exercises to calm down if I started to feel rising panic as I crossed the bridge, and after three practice runs with him in the passenger seat, I'd felt confident enough to do it myself.

I slowed the bike as I approached Frederica Road, remembering from the map to turn right to head toward the village. I'd been to the small downtown area filled with tiny shops and restaurants when Matthew and I had had dinner after my kitchen disaster, but I'd yet to really see my new home. Matthew had promised to show me around over the weekend, but I didn't want to wait. I felt compelled to see everything through my own eyes instead of his, to interpret the sights without his memories attached to them. And I wanted to see the ocean.

A cold bolt of fear iced through me at the thought, and the bike swerved onto the narrow two-lane road. A horn beeped from behind as I hugged the side of the road again, keeping focused on the pavement in front of me as the car passed.

It didn't take long for a sheen of perspiration to coat my face and make my T-shirt stick to my back. The smell of the marsh consumed me, making me less aware of the bike beneath me and the wet blanket of humidity that kept the warm air close to my skin. The familiarity of it came at me in a rush of memory even before my current consciousness recognized the source of the sulfur-scented air.

I slowed my pace as I began to notice again the canopies of live oak trees, with their curled arms holding up the moss like a woman displaying her jewelry. In places the street appeared to be inside a tunnel, the moss and trees giving the illusion of traveling through time in shadows and light.

I somehow managed to negotiate a traffic circle without colliding with a minivan from Ohio in the wrong lane. The driver waved an apology to me and I waved back, wanting to tell him that I was a tourist, too. I spotted a Dairy Queen nestled under a live oak tree and slowed my bike to a stop, belatedly realizing that I had forgotten my wallet—which made me crave something wet and cold even more.

My calf was cramping, so I dismounted from the bike and began stretching, noticing as I did so a couple emerging from a building with a yellow-and-green-striped awning next to the Dairy Queen. The name Murphy's Tavern was written on the windows and on a sign hanging over the door, in addition to being painted on the dark green bricks near the roof just in case you missed the first two. A small cluster of people stood with cameras focused on the bottom of the trunk of a large oak tree next to the tavern. Curious, I walked my bike closer to find out what had captured their attention.

Carved into the stump of a giant limb of the enormous tree was a man's face in repose, his eyes closed as if in sleep. It reminded me of the death masks of famous people I'd seen in history books. It was extraordinary in its detail, but what really astonished me was that for the first time since I'd arrived on the island, I didn't have the feeling of familiarity that had assailed me from the moment I'd crossed the Torres Causeway and remembered the scent of an ocean I'd never seen.

"What is it?" I asked the man next to me as he began to take his camera out of its case.

"It's one of the tree spirits," he said, as if that should be enough of an explanation.

The woman, presumably his wife, frowned at him before refocusing her attention on me. "There are about seventeen of them on the island—most on public property—carved by local artist Keith Jennings. They represent sailors lost at sea on ships made from St. Simons oak trees."

A soft rush of liquid air chilled me as if I'd suddenly been submerged in a pool. I stared at the face again, seeing it now as a drowned man, imagining his open eyes staring at the water's surface as he sank farther and farther away.

The woman was staring at me oddly, and I forced a smile. "Thank you," I said, my voice weak. "How interesting."

I nodded to both of them, then began to walk away, my palms sweaty against the handlebars. I mounted the bicycle again, unsure of which direction to head. My original plan had been to visit the village and the historic St. Simons lighthouse. The pier and the St. Simons Sound lay behind it, both beacons for the island's visitors and residents. I had thought to make a short visit to the water, to view it from a distance from the safety of my bike.

A cold sweat erupted on the back of my neck, almost forcing me to turn my bike around and head back home. But then I recalled Matthew's face when he talked about his time spent on the water since he was a boy, of his great love of the smell and feel of the waves beneath his boat, and my promise to myself to try to love it as much as he did.

Squaring my shoulders, I turned my bike in the direction I'd been traveling and began pedaling as fast as I could before I changed my mind.

When I reached the intersection of Mallery and Kings Way, I spotted the restaurant where Matthew and I had eaten, the 4th of May, and got off the bike so I could walk it on the sidewalk to look in all the shop windows.

The village was an area of eclectic tourist shops and galleries in addition to restaurants where even the locals liked to dine. I kept my eyes focused in the windows and not in the distance, where I knew the St. Simons Sound pulsed, and beyond that the Atlantic Ocean. I remounted my bike when I reached Beachview Drive, pedaling slowly past the Casino—an event hall and visitors' center—then took a right onto 12th Street, where the St. Simons lighthouse stood sentry over the town and the sound.

Again, I considered returning home, although I still had almost eight long hours until Matthew returned. I had a brief flash of my mother telling me to listen to my fears, that they were there to keep me safe. But if I'd always listened to her I'd still be in Antioch, Georgia, married to Phil Autry, and dogged by a restlessness I'd given up trying to understand. With renewed determination, I set my jaw in what my mother always called my "belligerent Belinda" look, and walked quickly toward the din of screaming birds.

A cement sidewalk wound from the lighthouse toward the fishing pier that jutted out into the sound. I'd seen it on the map and knew what lay beyond the bend in the walkway, but continued to push my bike forward, afraid to pause even for a moment, afraid that I'd stop and be unable to move.

The first tremors of panic began with the sound of waves breaking over the large rocks that edged the beach, curtailing the water's encroachment. I stopped for a moment to take a few deep, calming breaths like Matthew had taught me, realizing as I did so that I'd chosen this spot well, that the brute force of the ocean's waves would be softened here, protected by the St. Simons Sound. Still, the cool, dark water seemed to taunt me with each slap of a wave against the silent rocks.

It was early enough in the season that there weren't too many people around, but enough to ground me in the present, to force me to smile at passersby, to feel the hard plastic of the bike's handle grips and the gritty rub of sand against cement beneath my sneakers.

I paused on the walkway near a gazebo, staring past the grassy patch of dirt that sloped down to the rocks and then to the sandy beach. Past the shore, the water seemed almost placid and still. But I could feel the pull and suck of the wet sand, and knew how the strength of the ocean was a deceptive thing, revealed only to unlucky sailors and swimmers who discovered firsthand the power of a wave and the unrelenting weight of water.

A rhythmic pounding on the sidewalk forced my attention away. A man, his arms and bare chest glistening with sweat, was jogging, his pace slowing as he neared me. When he was about twenty feet away from me, he stopped and bent to put his hands on his knees as he breathed heavily. It was hard not to stare at him. He appeared to be in his early to mid-thirties, with hair that was nearly white from the sun. He was well built and had cheekbones a model would kill for.

When he straightened, his eyes met mine and he smiled. I looked away quickly, ashamed to have been staring. I was happily married, but I wasn't dead. Still, it was no excuse to have been openly ogling a stranger.

I began to turn my bike around when the man spoke.

"Are you lost?"

I blinked at him, the sun hitting me in the face. "No. Why?"

He shrugged. "I ran by you about ten minutes ago and you looked—I don't know—lost. You didn't seem to be aware of what was going on around you."

When I didn't respond, he said, "Sorry. I didn't mean to bother you."

"No. I'm sorry. I was just . . . thinking." I looked back at the water. "Do you know how deep it is here?"

He shook his head. "I probably should, but I haven't a clue." He stared closely at me, and I could see his eyes were a startling aqua—not quite green and not quite blue. "Why?"

"I don't know, really. Just wondering." I hesitated a moment, then smiled. "Are you a local?"

"Pretty much. I live on Jekyll Island now, but I grew up here and my parents still live here. I'm spending a couple of days with them, helping with a few house projects." He jutted his chin at me. "What about you?"

"I've just moved here. Thought I'd explore a little bit on my own."

He nodded in the direction of Matthew's bike. "And biking is a great way to explore—just watch out for the tourists." His smile was warm and inviting, and the fear that had gripped me in a stranglehold loosened enough for me to wiggle free.

"Yeah, I already discovered that. Whoever thought those roundabouts would be a good idea in a place that's a major tourist destination?"

He laughed, and I found myself relaxing even more. Grateful, I reached out my hand. "I'm Ava Frazier, by the way."

His smile dimmed slightly as he extended his hand before shaking mine. "John McMahon," he said. "Are you related to any of the Fraziers on the island?"

"I'm married to Matthew Frazier. Do you know him?"

Although he kept smiling, his eyes suddenly appeared almost frosty. "Yes, actually. I do. We went to high school together." He looked as if he wanted to say more, but he clenched his teeth together in a visible effort not to say anything else.

"Oh," I said, wanting him to continue, yet somehow knowing I shouldn't ask. His eyes had gone flat when I mentioned my last name, and I could tell he was eager to leave.

He stepped back, looking apologetic. "And here I am without a shirt and sweating all over you—my mother would be so ashamed." He grinned again and the warmth in his eyes was back, and I wondered whether what I thought I'd seen in them had been only a trick of the light.

"It was nice meeting you, John," I said. "I hope to see you around."

"Most likely. I'm here all the time, and I'm bound to run into you at the grocery store—there're only two big ones."

I smiled and waved. "Good. I'll look forward to it."

He started to walk away before he paused and turned back to me, an odd look in his eyes I couldn't place. "Tell Matthew I said hello."

"I will," I said, then stood and watched him for a moment as he jogged away. I felt a sudden coolness and looked up to find that heavy gray clouds had scrubbed away the blue sky and obliterated the sun. I stared at the water, mesmerized by its transformation from gray to black, and with a dry mouth I wondered whether the view from below would be different.

Gripping my handlebars, I began retracing my footsteps and avoided looking at the water at all, wanting to make sure it was out of my sight before the first raindrops began to fall.

CHAPTER SIX

Ava

St. Simons Island, Georgia
May 2011

I stood in front of the antique cheval mirror in the corner of our bedroom as Matthew stood behind me to zip up my little black dress. He lowered his lips to my neck and I sighed, wondering when it had happened that his scent had become as familiar as my own.

"Do we have to go?" he murmured close to my ear.

I turned in his arms, lifting mine around his neck. "Since we're the guests of honor, I would say yes. And Tish would be very disappointed if we don't show up. She might refuse to help me learn how to cook."

Matthew's eyebrows rose in mock horror. "By all means, then, we should go. But nothing says we have to be the last to leave."

My response stilled on my lips as Matthew lifted my left hand from his shoulder and regarded it closely.

"Sorry," I said, pulling away and walking toward my dressing table and jewelry box. "I'll wear it tonight." Before he could say anything, I lifted the diamond ring from the velvet and slipped it on. Wiggling my fingers, I

said, "You know I love it, Matthew. I'm just not . . . used to it." I didn't add
that it felt superfluous, that the solid gold band by itself was perfect, and
that the diamond ring felt like it belonged to someone else.

Matthew took my hand and kissed it. "It doesn't matter to me whether
or not you wear it. I just wanted to make sure that you didn't hate it, because then I'd go back to the jeweler and exchange it for something you'd
like better."

I touched his freshly shaven jaw and smiled. "I know."

Without releasing my hand, he began walking toward the bedroom
door, pulling me with him. "Come on. I have a surprise for you."

Belatedly, I remembered the papers I'd stashed in the chest in the living
room and had promptly forgotten. I wondered whether he'd found them,
and whether I should tell him the truth of how they'd gotten there or think
up a story that didn't involve my almost destroying Adrienne's artwork.

To my relief, he pulled me toward the front door. "Close your eyes," he
said.

I obeyed and then felt his hands on my bare shoulders as he led me gently down the steps. "You can open them now."

My eyes shot open, then blinked in surprise. A bright, shiny red woman's bicycle, complete with basket and bell, sat parked in the drive next to
my car. Like a little boy, Matthew picked up the bike and brought it closer,
turning it around so I could see the small Georgia license plate on the back
with AVA written on it.

"I had to have that special-ordered, since none of the stock ones have
your name."

I grimaced. Having an old-fashioned name had meant I'd never had
stickers or any of the childhood paraphernalia sold at fairs or drugstores,
like my friends did. I once asked my mother why she'd done that to me.
Her explanation had been that it derived from the Hebrew word meaning
"life," and then she'd returned to her gardening as if that had told me all I
needed to know.

"How . . . ?" I had a million questions for him, but couldn't sort them
in proper order to say anything.

"I knew you'd want a bike, so I ordered it the day we got married. The license plate, too. It was delivered while you were in the shower."

He smiled, my heart remembering the first time I'd seen that smile across a crowded room, the smile that fit his tall, athletic body and tanned face. The smile of a man who would walk on a beach during a hurricane or sail a ship into a storm. It had entranced me then, and I found it no less devastating now.

"Oh, Matthew," I said, throwing my arms around him and kissing him before I turned back to the bike. "It's perfect! How did you know red is my favorite color?"

He looked startled for a moment. "Didn't you tell me? You must have at some point." Grinning again, he added, "Glad I got it right. I'd hate to have to ship it back."

"Don't you dare," I said, grasping the handles. I looked down at my black dress and high heels. "If I take these off I can go for spin." I looked at him hopefully.

"If you take those off you won't be going for a bike ride," he said suggestively. "Why don't I stick it inside the garage for now and you can ride it tomorrow."

Reluctantly, I handed the bike over to Matthew, admiring the view as he walked it to the detached garage behind the house before I slid into the passenger seat of Matthew's car.

Still trying to learn the geography of the island, I paid close attention to the roads this time as Matthew drove. We took a left onto Demere from Frederica Road, passing a small airport with what looked like toy planes sitting on the field, but which Matthew assured me could actually take off and land without a battery or remote controls. After we passed the airport, I spotted a historical marker indicating we were at the Bloody Marsh battlefield.

"Sounds ominous," I commented.

"That's where Oglethorpe's troops finally defeated the Spanish in Georgia." He took my hand in his and rested our clasped hands in my lap. "We'll come back and explore on our bikes. And Fort Frederica, too—

that's the old British fort that was built as a lookout against Spanish attacks. It's nothing but ruins now, but it's pretty interesting."

I must have seen pictures of the fort before, because in my mind's eye I could picture it clearly: its tabby walls and crenellated towers. I could even see the old cannons facing the marsh, aimed at invisible enemies. Smiling, I turned to Matthew. "I'd like that."

My gaze focused outside my window again, watching the light fade. Dusk seemed to come earlier under the sweeping oak trees, their heavy arms embracing the approaching night. We crossed a causeway over more marsh, passing a sign that read EAST BEACH. "Does Tish live on the water?" I asked calmly, although I could hear my blood beginning to move faster in my veins.

"Just a block away, although the lot between them and the beach is empty, so it's almost as if they're beachfront. Her husband—second husband—is an architect, and he built their house about fifteen years ago. It's pretty amazing—if you like new construction."

Reassured, I smiled at my reflection in the window, understanding what he'd meant. My parents' house where I'd grown up was a midcentury modern, all pointed angles, short ceilings, and man-made materials. But now uneven floors, creaking joists, and ancient heart-of-pine planks meant home to me, as if the generations who'd spent their lives within the walls of Matthew's old house still lived in every creak and dent. It wasn't the same as living with ghosts. It was more like living with one foot in the past, and I found it agreed with me.

Facing him again, I said, "My mother doesn't think I should be here on St. Simons, so near the water. She said that's why they left, that she didn't want to live in a place that could take away everything she loved."

His face tightened in a way I'd learned to recognize as his psychologist's face, thinking hard while still trying to appear as if he readily knew all the answers. "Sometimes a parent's fear can be transferred to their children. That could be the source of your own fear of the ocean."

I looked at him hopefully. "Do you really think so? That would make me 'curable,' right?"

"Without further analysis, it's hard to say. But we'll work on it." He squeezed my hand before returning his to the steering wheel.

I thought of telling him then about my excursion to the pier, but I stopped, another thought pressing against my tongue.

"Was Adrienne afraid of anything?" I felt foolish for mentioning her name, and turned my head to stare out the window again so I couldn't read his expression.

For a moment he was silent, and I thought he wasn't going to answer. Finally, he said, "Ghosts."

My head jerked back to him. "Ghosts?"

He nodded, his face closed to me. "She told me once that sometimes when I looked at her it was like I was seeing a ghost instead."

A chill like a cold breath wrapped my spine with ice. "What did she mean?"

He shrugged, but it was stiff, and I could tell he was forcing himself to remain aloof. "I never knew. She couldn't explain it."

I stared ahead through the windshield, barely registering the watery marsh to our left in the last throes of twilight. "Tish told me about your ancestor—how his ghost haunts the beach searching for his unfaithful wife. Did Adrienne ever see him?"

His lips tightened for a moment. "Look, this night is about you and me. I don't want to talk about Adrienne, okay? That's all in the past. Let's focus on us right now and our future."

I undid my seat belt and sidled close enough that I could rest my head in the nook of his neck. Kissing him there, I said with more assurance than I felt, "You're right. I won't think about her anymore. It's all about us from now on."

I closed my eyes, breathing in his scent as if it were oxygen, and thought of the papers I'd taken from Adrienne's frame. I remained silent, unable to break a promise so recently made.

We passed through a residential neighborhood, albeit one with narrow streets and sandy shoulders. Several houses had bikes and Red Rider wagons filled with sand toys parked at the end of driveways, as if a day at the beach had proved too exhausting to find the energy to move everything closer to the house.

Driving into a cul-de-sac, Matthew slid his car behind a Jeep with its top and sides open. Although we weren't on the beach, I sensed it was near the way a deer knows the hunter's tread. Feeling my unease, Matthew put his arm around my shoulders and led me forward to a large house of sand-colored stucco and a tiled roof. Arches hovered over the windows like eyebrows, the massive front double doors wrapped in glass and wrought iron. "It's lovely," I said, because it was, but I refrained from saying how out of place it seemed amid the sand and cabbage palms.

Matthew pushed open the door without knocking, reminding me that he'd grown up with this family, Tish having stepsons near Matthew's age. Somebody put a glass of wine in my hand as clusters of people moved toward us in greeting, hugging Matthew and shaking hands with me as I tried to remember names that were thrown at me like confetti.

I found myself marshaled from the marble foyer into a large and airy kitchen at the back of the house. It had obviously been recently remodeled, with a tumbled marble backsplash, granite countertops, and cabinets that looked like furniture. The fixtures and cabinet pulls were all wrought iron, in keeping with the Tuscan theme, and beautiful hand-painted tiles were embedded in the wall behind the sink, highlighted by under-cabinet lights.

"I thought my kitchen was beautiful—but this is magnificent," I said to Tish.

"Thank you. I'd like to take all the credit for it, but I had lots of help." She stopped, an odd look passing across her face. I looked again at the painted tiles, and the light fixture hanging in the breakfast nook, the familiarity of it all rubbing me like a bug bite.

"Did Adrienne help you with the design?"

Reluctantly, Tish nodded. "Yes. She knew her way around a kitchen, and I welcomed her input. She painted the tiles, too."

I nodded, the beauty of the space somehow diminished.

A slim blonde with her hair in a short pixie cut stood by the farmhouse sink, sipping from a water glass with a large slice of lemon bobbing at the top. She appeared to be in her late twenties and wore a closely fitting black knit dress.

"There's somebody I want you to meet." Tish pulled me by the arm and brought me over to the young woman. "Ava, this is my daughter, Beth Hermes. Beth teaches high school history at Frederica Academy and is a member of the historical society, too. You missed her at the last meeting because she and her husband, Ken, were celebrating their anniversary and impending parenthood on Amelia Island."

Tish put her arm around her daughter, and I felt a stab of envy as Beth smiled her mother's smile.

"Mom's told me so much about you. I'm so jealous about how you and Matthew met. I mean, you go to a boring medical conference and meet for the first time and then get married so quickly! I don't think I'd have the guts to do that. I married my college sweetheart." She rubbed her hand over her still flat stomach. "So far, so good."

I eyed her belly, desperate to change the subject. I didn't want to talk about my meeting Matthew. I could never explain in mere words what it had been like to meet somebody for the first time yet feel as if he'd been a part of my life forever. Saying it out loud made it rash and irresponsible, two things my mother had never allowed me to be. "How far along are you?"

"Five weeks. I hardly feel pregnant. I wish I would start showing to make it legit!"

I laughed. "I'm a nurse-midwife, so I hear that a lot. Trust me, you'll be showing before you know it. Then your husband will start to complain when you start borrowing his sweaters since yours won't fit anymore."

"She's seeing Dr. Shaw at Brunswick Family Medicine. Isn't that where you had your interview?" Tish asked while taking the glass from Beth and refilling it to the top with water.

"Yes, it is. They called me today with a job offer and I think I'm going to accept. So I guess I'll be seeing more of you," I said to Beth.

"And me, too," Tish interjected. "Since Beth is my only daughter, Ken is allowing me to be a co–birth partner. We're hoping for an all-natural birth, but we've got a plan B, too, just in case."

"As long as mother and baby are healthy," Beth and I said in unison, making us both laugh.

Beth looked down at my hand. "Your ring is beautiful. Matthew has such good taste." Her smile faded slightly as she caught sight of the red mark at the base of my thumb. "What happened? Looks like that was one nasty cut."

I rubbed it self-consciously. "I know—but don't worry. It wasn't caused during a childbirth. I'm a lot gentler than that." We both laughed. "I should probably make up some heroic story, like how I saved a small child from a bear attack, but it's actually a birthmark. I've had it all my life." I tucked my hand behind my back, suddenly self-conscious.

"Congratulations on the job offer, Ava," Tish said. "I think you did the right thing."

Our eyes met and I remembered my promise to Matthew. "Yeah, me, too," was all I said.

Tish frowned, her gaze redirected behind me. I turned and looked through the hallway to the front door and spotted John McMahon standing just inside the foyer, wearing a confident grin.

"What's he doing here?" Beth asked her mother under her breath, a similar frown on her own face.

"That's exactly what I'm going to find out," Tish said, excusing herself as Beth followed.

I was about to tag along to greet my new friend when Matthew approached with another glass of wine. I was shy in crowds and was the first to admit that wine smoothed over any social awkwardness. "You looked ready for another," he said.

"I was just thinking the same thing." I brought the glass to my lips and sniffed deeply its bright and fruity bouquet, if only to eradicate the pervasive smell of salt that wafted in through the open French doors. Voices spilled from the outside patio, and I longed to step outside into the night air but knew I couldn't. Not with the swish and fall of water against sand unseen in the distance. But the pregnant moon sat swollen in her fullness, il-luminating the night sky and putting the stars to shame, and I felt a longing to share the beauty of it with Matthew, to be sheltered in the maternal light with him.

Tish's husband, Tom, approached. He was tall and slender, with silver hair and an easygoing attitude that made me think that he and Tish were well suited for each other. He held up two cigars to Matthew. "Just got these from my friend in St. Barts. Can't let a night of celebration pass with-out a smoke, can we?"

"I didn't know you smoked," I said to Matthew.

"I used to smoke a pipe—a stupid idea I got in grad school because I thought it suited my profession. But now I smoke just an occasional stogie with Tom. He's a bit of an aficionado and is trying to convert me."

I resisted the urge to wrinkle my nose. I could somehow picture Mat-thew with a pipe—I'd seen a tweed jacket with suede elbow patches in his closet, after all—but I couldn't quite see him with a cigar. "Y'all go ahead. I'll be fine."

Matthew kissed me quickly. "I'll miss you."

I laughed while Tom rolled his eyes before leading Matthew across the room to a door. When he opened it, I spotted a wood-paneled library with floor-to-ceiling shelves crammed with books. Then the door closed and I was left in a room full of people I didn't know.

Sipping my wine, I began to explore the beautiful rooms of the Italian-inspired house. It wasn't what I would have thought of as a beach house, with its terra-cotta tiles and mustard palette, but the arched doorways and painted masonry and tiles were soothing to the eye. It was also a family home, with beautiful, yet sturdy and well-lived-in furniture and rooms. Tish and Tom had five children between them, including stepchildren and the pregnant Beth, and it was clear from the banquet-size rough-hewn din-ing room table and benches that all had been designed for large family gatherings.

I leaned against the doorway and saw my own quiet childhood with my silent parents and inquisitive Mimi, telling her about my day in greater and greater exaggeration to somehow capture my parents' interest. My brothers and their wives came for special occasions, but the house always seemed cramped, as if it were reluctant to make room.

A charcoal sketch of an old fortress planted in the middle of a marsh hung on the wall over a long buffet server. I stepped closer, knowing before I could make out the initials of the artist who had drawn it. *AMF.*

I looked more closely at the sketch, at the intricate depiction of the tabby walls of the fort and the delicate detail of an egret in the foreground, its eye warily regarding the artist. I'd seen photographs of the fort, so I knew what it looked like now. But this was a picture of the fort before time and the elements had rendered it obsolete and desolate, a time capsule catapulting me back to the past for a brief moment.

I raised my glass to my lips, realizing I'd already finished my wine. Just two glasses had created a pleasant cottony barrier around my head where sounds and colors were happily muted.

"Do you like it?"

Nearly dropping my glass, I turned in surprise. "John! So happy to see a familiar face!" I recalled Tish's expression when she'd spotted him at the door. "I didn't know you'd be here."

"Me neither. I wasn't exactly on the guest list, but I've known the Ryans for years—their son Rick and I were best friends in high school. Didn't think they'd mind me popping in for the big congratulatory soiree for you and Matthew."

I wondered whether it was the alcohol that added the sharp edge to John's words. "Well, I'm glad you're here. I've met a few people, but I'm not too great with crowds."

John studied me, his unusual eyes understanding. "Do you like it?" he asked, turning his attention to the drawing.

"Yes," I said without hesitation. "I do. The artist was extraordinarily talented." My eyes met his. "It was done by Matthew's first wife."

He took a sip from a can of beer. "I know." It took him a moment to swallow, as if something were blocking the way.

"Did you know her?" I blurted out. I shook my head. "Never mind. I was just thinking that since you knew Matthew, you would have known . . . her." I couldn't bring her name to my lips.

He looked at me oddly. "You didn't tell Matthew about running into me at the pier, did you?"

I stared down at my empty glass, desperately wanting more wine. I wasn't sure why I hadn't told Matthew about meeting John. I hoped it had to do with my desire to conquer my fear by myself, to wait until I was ready to show him how I'd taught myself to walk boldly near the water. To even let the surf lap at my feet. I shivered, knowing I'd merely taken the first step.

"I must have forgotten," I said, wishing he'd answer my question about knowing Adrienne, but too embarrassed to ask again.

"Ava."

Matthew approached, clutching the stems of two full wineglasses so tightly I thought they might snap. I smiled only because I couldn't think of what else I should do.

"Is that for me?" I asked, putting my empty one down and taking one of the glasses before allowing myself a healthy gulp. "John and I were just talking about the drawing. It's beautiful, isn't it?"

The air between them thickened, making me think of the atmosphere right before a thunderstorm.

"Hello, Matthew," John said, his voice tight.

"John," Matthew replied with a short nod of his head. "I assume you've met my wife."

"Actually, we met the other day on the pier. She was going for a bike ride and I was out for a run. I'm surprised she didn't mention it to you."

A pulse had begun in Matthew's jaw, yet his expression didn't change. "No, she didn't." He twirled the wine in his glass but didn't drink from it. "How are your parents?"

John raised an eyebrow, but his eyes hardened. "Still grieving. The death of a daughter is hard to take."

Pinpricks of clarity began to poke holes in my wine-induced haze as I watched the two men talk without saying what they wanted to. *The death of a daughter* . . .

"Your sister . . ." I began, not sure how to end.

John lifted his beer can at the drawing in a sort of toast. "Adrienne Mc-Mahon Frazier. She got all the talent in the family, I'm afraid."

AMF. Adrienne McMahon Frazier. Of course. I remembered the frosty glint in John's eyes when I told him who I was. I faced Matthew and saw him regarding me silently, the words he'd spoken to me on the dock loud inside my head. *Because they think I killed her.*

"Oh," I muttered, unable to think of anything else to say. I raised my glass to my lips, but somehow missed, spilling some of the red liquid on the front of my dress.

Matthew gently pried the glass from my hand and put it on the server. "Maybe you've had enough."

John slammed down his beer can next to my glass. "It's so rewarding watching how much you care for your wife, Matthew. I remember how you used to be that way with Adrienne." John faced me, his eyes wide and sober. "Be careful, Ava. He's not who you think he is."

He turned away from us and made his way toward the front door as people stepped back and avoided looking at him or at us.

"You should have told me," Matthew said quietly.

I stared up at him, almost not comprehending. I shook my head, the room spinning. "No. *You* should have told me." I wasn't even sure what I meant, only that there were things I didn't know about him, and it shamed me to understand this about myself, to know that I had willingly walked into my marriage with an almost-stranger because I loved him, ignoring all the other reasons that I still refused to acknowledge.

I walked toward the great room, toward the sound of voices. The wash of air blew through the open doors, propelling me outside. The world had begun to tilt, just enough to take away my fear and my mother's voice. I felt Matthew behind me, solid and real and, I kept reminding myself, not a means of escape. "I want to see the dunes at night."

I was down the steps before I could stop myself, following a sandy path illuminated by tiki torches, as a memory—or maybe it had been a dream—of dunes bathed in silvery moonlight slipped through my mind as sand slid beneath my bare feet.

"Ava. Stop."

It had ceased to be a dream. The sand, grown cool in the night air, harbored no warmth, and the sound of footsteps behind me made my throat dry. "No," I gasped out, no longer aware of who was behind me, or what might be in front of me. All I knew was that I needed to run, to escape whatever was pursuing me.

"Ava," I heard again, but the name and the voice no longer seemed to register in my foggy brain. I ran, my breaths like those of a panting dog, until wooden planks and a set of stairs opened up onto the wide expanse of shadowed sand and silver pale water. I looked out toward the empty ocean as if I expected to see something there, a surprising disappointment stabbing my heart when I saw how empty it was.

Strong hands grasped my arms. "Ava. You don't know what you're doing. Please stop."

I struggled, as afraid of what lay behind me as I was of what lay before me. But the hands managed to turn me around, and I recognized Matthew's beautiful face illuminated by the soft light.

"Matthew," I said, relief making my knees weak. I collapsed into him, and he lifted me in his arms before sitting down on a wooden step.

"What's wrong? Tell me so I can make it right." He kissed my forehead.

I opened my mouth to tell him, then stopped. "I can't," I finally said. "Just tell me you love me," I murmured into his chest.

"I love you, Ava. You know I do."

I nodded, but felt no relief as I remembered the hand-painted tiles in the kitchen, as if they were footprints of his dead wife walking though our home and marriage. "Please take me home."

He brought me to my feet and steadied me. "Let me put you in the car while I go tell Tish that we're leaving because you're not feeling well." I nodded and allowed him to move me forward until we'd made it to his car.

He clasped the seat belt around me before regarding me steadily. "Will you be all right for just a minute?"

I nodded, the world spinning in dizzying whirls. I watched him walk away, afraid to close my eyes and feel the panic of pursuit again. I began to hum, recognizing the tune from the old music box, realizing, too, that I was trying to block out the words that wouldn't quiet inside my head. *Because they think I killed her.*

I began to sing the half-remembered words even louder while I waited for Matthew to come and take me home.

CHAPTER SEVEN

Gloria

ANTIOCH, GEORGIA
MAY 2011

The sliding closet door in Ava's old bedroom caught on something as I tried to push it open. For years I'd dusted the mementos of a girl's childhood—the trophies, bouquets of dead flowers, dolls with vacuous eyes, and batons from her four years as a majorette. They were the milestones of my daughter's growing-up years, milestones for events I hadn't seen. Milestones of a life I'd been privileged to share but too afraid to be a part of.

I bent down and pulled a film cartridge out of the door track, then straightened to examine it. In a way I'd understood her obsession with other people's photographs, with staring into strangers' lives like Alice at the rabbit hole. And because I'd understood it, I'd discouraged it. Yet, as with all things between Ava and me, the more I said no, the more adamant she was to pursue it.

I reached inside the closet and closed my fingers around the necks of a group of hangers clustered in the far corner. The maroon and gold sequins

of her majorette costumes still sparkled, the pleats in the skirts still perfectly pressed. I'd made these for Ava, sewn each sequin by hand despite
Mimi's insistence that she be allowed to help. But I had done it all, each pull
and tug of the thread and needle proof that I loved my daughter despite her
arguments to the contrary.

With quick movements I slid the hangers out of the shoulders, then
gently folded each costume and stacked them inside a packing box. I had no
intention of mailing them to St. Simons. If Ava wanted them she'd have to
come home and haul the boxes up from the basement. My intention today
was merely to empty out the room, although I'd yet to make plans for what
to replace it with. I simply needed to erase the daily reminder that I had run
out of time.

"Don't forget these."

I turned to face Mimi, who stood in the doorway with a short stack of
old photo albums in her arms.

I straightened, my hand automatically rubbing the small of my back.
Frowning, I stared at them. "What are those?"

Mimi moved to the bed with its pink eyelet bedspread and let the stack
gently slide onto it, the leg of a quilted pink elephant stopping their progress toward the edge of the bed. "These are the albums I made of Ava when
she was a little girl. I thought she might like to have them."

I felt something pinching behind my eyes, an old hurt with no remembered origin. "I'm not sending anything to Ava—just packing things up.
Besides, I'd never send her any photo albums. For the same reason I never
made one for her in the first place."

I glared at my mother, but she was ignoring me as she sat on the edge of
the bed and flipped open the album that had been on top. "She was such a
beautiful child."

Unable to stop myself, I moved to stand behind Mimi. She was right.
Ava had been a beautiful child, with pale blond hair and thick-lashed
brown eyes. She hadn't left her beauty behind as so many children do, and
even now sometimes took my breath away. What added to the whole effect
was Ava's complete unawareness of it.

Her hair had never darkened as we'd all expected it to, and by the time she was approaching middle school, we knew the color was here to stay. It was at about that time that Mimi started coloring her own hair blond, and although she never said it out loud, I knew the reason why. I was grateful in a way only a daughter can be in that moment when she realizes that her mother is an extension of herself, another limb, another heart to bear the pain and shore you up at the same time.

I stood silently behind Mimi as she slowly turned the album's pages, pointing out Ava's favorite Halloween costumes—all handmade by me—of Christmas mornings, and our rare vacations to places like Rock City, Tennessee, and Mammoth Cave in Kentucky. We didn't go to the beach on vacation ever, despite the boys' pleading. It was easy to use Ava's fear of the ocean as an excuse, but like all other excuses in life, it merely danced around the real reason why, a ballerina on a darkened stage where you couldn't see the edge.

"You should send this to Ava." A long red-lacquered nail pointed at a large photograph taking up an entire album page. It was Ava at around two years of age wearing a pink crocheted dress with a pale blue satin sash. It had been made by Mimi's grandmother and given to Mimi when she was born. In the back hallway were the framed photographs of Mimi wearing the dress at age two and me wearing the same dress nearly twenty years later. I hadn't hung Ava's portrait next to them, even though I'd kept the space vacant. Ava had finally stopped asking me why.

"The photograph?" I asked.

Mimi shook her head without looking at me. "No. The dress. For when she has a little girl of her own."

I stared at the color photograph of two-year-old Ava, with the chubby cheeks and the pink dress that made her skin glow, remembering the day the photo was taken as if it were only yesterday. I'd taken the dress from the old cedar chest, a wedding gift from Mimi's grandmother. The dress had been folded between layers of tissue paper, safely stored since it had last been worn by me. If it were possible to travel through time, this scrap of pink knit would be the conduit, recorded by each generation with a photograph.

"It's too early. I'm sure she and Matthew won't be planning a family anytime soon."

Mimi snorted, something I, fortunately, had never learned to do. "She's almost thirty-five. And I know she wants children."

"How would you know?" I asked, afraid I already knew the answer.

"When you were hiding in your room before she left, Ava and I had a really long chat. That was one of the things we talked about."

I pressed my lips together, hating myself for doing so. Stephen said I looked like a prune when I did it, but I couldn't seem to stop. "What else did you talk about?"

Mimi snapped the cover shut, then twisted around to look at me. "Nothing you wouldn't want us to be talking about."

My finger wound its way into the pink eyelet of the bedspread, the same bedspread I'd allowed Ava to select when she was twelve, even though I warned her she'd grow tired of it as soon as she hit fourteen. As she got older, I'd catch her looking through catalogs or pausing at store windows, and I kept waiting for her to admit I was right. But she never did. It was one of the things I admired most about my daughter: She always meant what she said and never went back on her word.

"You should send her the albums."

I shook my head. "You know I can't."

Ignoring me, Mimi pressed on. "You could bring them to her. It would give you an excuse to visit." She looked steadily at me. "Every woman needs her mother at some point." I wasn't sure whether she was still talking about Ava and me.

I turned back to the closet and took out another handful of clothes on hangers. "I can't." I kept my back toward Mimi so she couldn't see the tears that threatened to spill over. How could I explain to her what I couldn't explain to myself? That I was trying to let go of the one thing I'd always been afraid to lose before I even realized that you can't lose something you never really had. Or that after years of holding on too loosely, I'd finally lost my grip.

The phone rang and I tensed as I always did, letting it ring until the answering machine picked up. Then I went back to folding my daughter's clothes into the box, as if by doing so I could somehow erase the biggest mistake of my life.

Ava

St. Simons Island, Georgia
May 2011

I kept the phone to my ear, counting each ring until the answering machine picked up with my eight-year-old nephew's voice telling me that Grandma and Grandpa couldn't come to the phone but that they would call back as soon as they could. I heard the beep, then clicked the off button on my cell before sliding it into my purse. My mother had hated the phone ever since I could remember, although Mimi recalled times when my mother was a teenager and the telephone had seemed like another appendage. It was just one of the many inconsistencies of my childhood, like falling leaves that seemed so small until they covered the entire lawn.

I peered out the front door, looking for Tish's station wagon. My first meeting of the historical society had been uneventful, as most of the talk had been about the ugly new concrete barriers running the length of the causeway, a new traffic light (a big deal on the island, apparently), and the first chain restaurant midisland. I suppose living in a two-hundred-year-old house had made me jaded, but everything else on St. Simons seemed so new by comparison that I didn't understand what the problem was. I'd kept judiciously silent, remembering that part of the reason for my being there was to make new friends.

The most productive part of the meeting had been my assignment to a project to document old graves throughout St. Simons, in known cemeteries and in cemeteries that were only rumored to exist on the grounds of the old plantations. Maybe it was my family's connection to cemeteries, but I was excited enough to volunteer for the project, and Tish was assigned as the team leader.

I glanced at my watch, realizing I still had fifteen minutes, then left the door cracked open so I could hear Tish's car approaching and meet her outside. I was about to sit down in one of the front hall chairs, but paused halfway as my gaze caught sight of the low chest in the parlor. I hadn't had time to pull out the pages I'd removed from the back of the framed sketch and examine them, and I hadn't wanted to ask Matthew about them until I'd had the chance to see what they were.

With quick steps, I crossed to the chest and pulled the drawer open, panicking at first when I didn't see them before I realized they'd slid into the back of the drawer. There were three of them, all stuck together with four paper clips on each side, and measuring about ten inches by fourteen.

I gingerly slid off each paper clip, careful not to catch one of the straight ends on the paper. Slowly, I placed the first page faceup on top of the chest and smoothed my hand over it.

It was another sketch of the house, this one done from an angle different from the one hanging in a frame. I noticed the way the artist had drawn the light on the side of the house, making me think of the bright mornings I'd experienced in my new home, imagining I could hear the terns and the skimmers by the creek bank. Even if I hadn't known who the artist was, I knew that whoever had drawn the sketch knew the house intimately, knew the way the buttery light slanted in through the windows at sunset, and how the oaks in the front yard seemed to cling together like siblings, their branches intermingling and graciously granting shade to the house.

I picked it up and held it for a moment, wondering who'd stuck this one and the two others behind the framed sketch. And why.

I flipped over the second drawing and looked at it closely. Blinking, I gripped both edges and lifted it to get a better look. It wasn't a sketch at all, but what looked like lines of poetry. The words were drawn in black ink, in a calligraphy style or by somebody with beautiful penmanship. Like an artist's would be. The capital letters at the beginning of each line were larger than the rest of the text, each stanza centered perfectly on the page.

There were no musical notes on the page, or anything else that might indicate the words were lyrics to a song, but as I started to read it was as if music had begun to play in my head, the words on the page fitting perfectly with each note like puzzle pieces settling neatly into their slots.

Oh, hush thee, my baby,
Thy sire be a king's knave,
Thy mother his true love,
Separated by the deep ocean's waves. . . .

My eyes jerked up to the small curio cabinet where I'd stored the music box Mimi had placed in my hands when I'd left home—the music box I'd found during the season of tornadoes that had twisted and turned so many lives. As if from afar, I watched myself walk across the room and purposefully flip open the lid of the box, the mechanism inside whirring and twitching like an old cricket until the music stirred to life with a tiny click.

I listened to the tune three times, singing the lyrics on the paper each time until I'd memorized them, stopping in midnote as the mechanism wound down. I knew the song, of course. My mother had sung it to me as a child, and probably as a baby, too. When I'd had the chicken pox and couldn't sleep, she'd stayed in the room in the rocking chair by my bed and sung it. But not these words. The words she'd sung had to do with a beloved child falling asleep inside the protected walls of a castle, his father a knight, his mother a lady. The lyrics I read were the words of a father separated from his beloved wife and his child across the sea, offering reassurance rather than rest, hope and potential loss instead of comfort and warmth. But they were words I'd somehow known long before I'd slid this paper out from behind the frame.

With frozen fingers, I allowed the paper to drift from my fingers to the top of the chest, then hesitated just for a moment before I picked up the third paper. I was vaguely aware of the sound of a car approaching on the drive, but I couldn't stop.

This drawing was a full-length pen-and-ink sketch of a young woman. She wore a long dress, maybe from the eighteen hundreds, and she was hatless, the wind buffeting her skirts, and the long ties of a bonnet held in her hands. She stood barefoot in what appeared to be sand, the edge of an unknown body of water creeping up behind her. My breath came in shallow gasps as I brought the sketch closer, only half noticing what appeared to be a tall ship with full sails in the distance behind her. My gaze focused on the woman's face, the way her dark hair came to a widow's peak on her forehead, the large almond-shaped eyes and high cheekbones, the delicate nose that was too pert for beauty but worked with the rest of her features to create a face that drew attention. I brought the sketch even closer. There was something in her eyes, something mute but telling at the same time. Something that spoke of love and loss and surrender. But there was more, too, more even than the question she seemed to be about to ask. The scent of ashes burned the back of my throat, choking me. *I know you.* The words tumbled from some unnamed place in my brain with the same sort of certainty with which one feels hunger or pain.

"Ava?"

I turned to find Tish in the doorway, her face full of concern. The sketch drifted from my hand onto the floor, and I sat quickly on the sofa behind me.

She took a step forward, stopping in front of the sketch and picking it up. "You have absolutely no color in your face, and there are beads of sweat on your forehead. Are you all right? Do you want me to get Matthew?"

I shook my head. "He's at work. And I'm fine, really. Just . . ." I indicated the sketch she held, hoping she'd understand by looking at it so that I wouldn't have to explain something I wasn't even sure I could.

Tish sat next to me on the sofa and examined the sketch. She looked at it for a moment before sitting back against the cushions. "So you found them. I'd completely forgotten."

I looked at her in surprise. "You knew about them?"

"Only by accident. I was in Brunswick to get Beth's wedding veil and dried bouquet framed in a display box. There's a store down on Newcastle Street that does a great job, reasonably priced. I saw Adrienne there and overheard her instructions to the clerk before she realized I was there. I had no idea why she wanted them sealed behind the sketch she was having framed, and Adrienne made it clear that she wasn't interested in talking about it." Tish looked away for a moment, her fingers tapping gently on the paper, as if she didn't want to say any more. Eventually she faced me again. "She died a week later, and I forgot all about it."

I nodded, not understanding any of it at all. "I found them when I accidentally tore the backing from the frame."

She held the sketch of the woman in her lap and regarded it silently for a moment. "This is so different from Adrienne's usual work, but it's definitely her style. And her signature." Tish pointed at the three initials in the bottom right corner.

"She looks familiar to me, but I don't know why. Do you have any idea who she is?"

Tish shook her head. "No. But she looks familiar to me, too. Like I've seen another picture of her somewhere. Maybe in a book?"

I looked away, the tingling feeling of familiarity raising the hairs on the back of my neck. "There's a drawing of the house, too—done at a different angle from the one hanging—and lyrics to a song. I can't figure out why any of these needed to be hidden. The words of the song are familiar to me—I think I've heard them before, sung to the same tune as the old lullaby my mother used to sing to me, 'Oh, Hush Thee, My Baby.' "

Tish wrinkled her brow. "I didn't know there were different lyrics."

I retrieved the lyrics and handed the sheet to Tish, watching her face as she silently read them, her fingers tapping on her leg as if counting out the measures to the old tune. "They fit; that's for sure."

"I know." I picked up the sketch of the house and showed it to Tish, too. "And here's the third one."

She frowned. "Why would she hide these?" Her eyes met mine. "Have you shown them to Matthew?"

I shook my head, forcing myself to hold her gaze. "I didn't want him to think I'd torn the backing intentionally."

Very slowly, Tish handed me the papers.

"You really don't know Matthew at all, do you?"

My chest burned. "What do you mean? He's my husband. I know him enough to have married him."

She reached her hand out to me, and when I backed away, she dropped it. "I know—I didn't mean that. Sometimes people don't have to know each other very long before they know they've found the one. And I know it's that way with you and Matthew—I see it when you're together. But I've known Matthew since he was a little boy. Around here we call him an 'old soul.' It's like he was born knowing what he wanted, and once he has it he doesn't easily let go."

"Like Adrienne?" The words had found themselves on my lips before I could recall them.

Tish stood. "I'm not the person you should be having this conversation with, Ava."

Avoiding her eyes, I placed the papers back in the drawer, telling myself I'd speak with Matthew about them when he returned.

I dipped my head. "Thank you, Tish. And just in case I haven't said it enough, thanks for the party, too. I'm just sorry we had to leave early."

Slipping her purse over her shoulder, Tish headed toward the door. "The only person who should be apologizing is John. I'm sorry he upset you. He's a good man—just confused and still grieving. I hope you can understand."

I picked up my own purse and followed her out the door, locking it behind me. I paused, watching Tish's retreating back. "Why do John and his parents think Matthew had anything to do with Adrienne's death? It was a car accident."

She turned back to me, her eyebrows raised. "I thought you knew."

I wanted to duck back inside the house to hold back the question, but I remained where I was. "Knew what?"

"It was a car accident in the middle of the night. She'd been heading north on Highway Seventeen in South Carolina, and her family said the only reason any of that made sense was because she must have been running away from something. They were grieving and looking for reasons. Regardless of why, somehow her car swerved off the road over a bridge and into the marsh."

"How did she die?" My words were breathless, forced between my lips.

"She drowned."

I closed my eyes and focused on my breathing so I wouldn't forget to fill my lungs with air. Footsteps approached, and Tish's arm went around my shoulders. "Are you all right?"

I wasn't, but I nodded anyway. "I will be. Really. It's just . . . a shock." *She drowned.*

"You don't look all right. Look, we don't have to go to the cemetery today. The project will take weeks, so starting today or tomorrow won't matter. I've got plenty of help at the shop, and you don't start your new job for a week, so we can go another time."

I shook my head. "No. I'm fine. Let's go. Please." I was eager to refocus my thoughts, even if it meant studying old graves. Anything but the image of Matthew's first wife trapped inside a car underwater.

Tish released me with reluctance and I followed her to the car, my footsteps suddenly uncertain, as if the ground beneath my feet had turned to water, and I had no choice but to allow myself to be swallowed.

CHAPTER EIGHT

Pamela

St. Simons Island, Georgia
December 1806

The shrieks from the hog shed seemed to crowd out the light and all other senses from the kitchen house where I stood with Leda and Jemma, stirring great pots of pig fat to make lard. The heat from the blazing kitchen hearth nearly consumed us as sweat poured down our faces despite the frigid chill in the air outside. We squinted through the steam and tried to think beyond the slaughter to the bacon and ham we would have all winter.

Sweet potatoes roasted on the fire while Leda stirred the pigskin in oil for crackling. Nothing would be wasted. From the hogs' hairs to make brushes or the entrails for chitterlings, all the meat from the snout to the tail would be used in some fashion. I had learned that to be wasteful is to do without, and I thought back with some shame and longing to my grandmother's Savannah dining room, where I would push my plate away with food still upon it.

I turned to say something to Jemma and stabs of sharp pain gripped me, folding me over my distended belly. A small hand smoothed the fabric of my apron as if trying to brush away the pain, and I looked down at Jemma, whose face tilted up to mine. Still silent, still scarred, but healed in most other ways. Her months of silent sobbing had finally eased enough that Leda had finally welcomed the girl into her kitchen, where Jemma shone in the light from Leda's smile. I thought that in the two of them they would each find the mother and daughter they both longed for. And although they had formed a strong bond, when I was near it was to my skirts Jemma clung in her wordless affection.

"Thank you, Jemma. It is only the first pain. I think we will have plenty of time." I could only hope that my words were true. There was still so much to be done.

Jemma's brow puckered in concentration as she closed her good eye and began slowly moving her hands over my belly, tracing the outline of the child within. I did not know how much of her knowledge came from her mother's instruction and how much was intuition. Regardless, she had quickly become an invaluable assistant to me, always knowing when it was time to push and when it was time to stop. And which mothers needed sterner coaxing and which ones only comfort.

I peered toward the open door, wanting the fresh air deep in my lungs. I needed to find Geoffrey, to let him know it was time. We had lost a still-born boy in February, so tiny he had hardly appeared human. He had been born in the chamber pot, and it was Jemma who had taken him and prepared him for burial beside his brother, Jamie. I had bled a great deal, and Leda had told Geoffrey that he should prepare himself to let me go. He had not left my side, holding my hand as if to push his own life force into my veins. And he had.

Geoffrey had been barely able to look at my swelling body as soon as I had confirmed my condition. I prayed daily that my body would not betray me, that I would deliver a healthy baby so that I could still his fears. But for both of us the fear of separation was a touchable thing, a fist of ice that settled in the blanket with us at night, and joined us at the table in the morning.

Giving Jemma a reassuring pat on the shoulder, I stepped out into the cold December air, rubbing my hands on my arms to warm them. I searched for Geoffrey, his tall and broad-shouldered form usually easy to spot towering over most of the field hands and the neighbors who had shown up to help, just as we would reciprocate at their farms. Instead, my gaze caught that of Nathaniel Smith. I had not seen him since I had helped his two field hands deliver healthy boys not too long after Jemma had come to live with us the previous fall, but was not surprised to see him today. The skies hung low and gray, pregnant with moisture, and we all feared that it was cold enough for rain to turn into a rare snowfall. Geoffrey wanted to get the hogs slaughtered, their meat hanging in the smokehouse, before the first flake fell.

I dipped my head in greeting, then realized Nathaniel was no longer looking at me. I turned my head to see Georgina walking slowly from the farmhouse to the kitchen, dressed as if heading to church, and knew she'd be no help in the kitchen today. Since our father's death the past summer, she had moved in with Geoffrey and me, into the bedroom across the hall from us that had once been Jamie's. But she looked lovely, her cheeks pink with the cold, her dark green cape setting off her eyes. I looked with surprise at her red leather gloves, recognizing them as the ones Geoffrey had given me for my birthday the previous month. He had seen them on a trip to Savannah, and even though we could scarce afford them, he had purchased them because red was my favorite color.

The child stirred again just as another pain sliced through me, sharp as broken glass, its jagged edges tearing at my insides. My knees buckled, and I barely grasped the stair railing to keep myself from pitching forward down the steps. I heard Georgina cry out, and then strong arms lifted me into the air until I found my face pressed against the hard wool of a man's coat.

"Geoffrey?" I cried out in a haze of pain that glowed red around the edges.

It was not his voice that answered. "It is Nathaniel. Geoffrey went to the Sinclair farm to seek more help before the weather sets in. Tell me where to bring you, and then I will ride as fast as I can to go fetch him."

"Thank you," I whispered, unable to catch a breath between the waves of agony that had seized me in their heavy arms.

"We have a birthing room set up behind the parlor," I heard Georgina say, and then I closed my eyes and prayed for unconsciousness to release the pain.

I opened them again and found myself on the bed in the little room that Jemma and I had set up for when my time came. I tried not to think how I was three weeks early, or that my pain was constant now instead of in slow waves. I would not be able to bear it should it last as long as my labor with Jamie had. I needed Geoffrey, and I called out for him again.

"I will go fetch him." Georgina's hand touched my forehead, and I felt the leather of the red gloves slide across my skin.

"No." It was Nathaniel's voice, and even I could recognize the tone of his voice that brooked no resistance. "I will get Geoffrey."

I looked into his eyes for the first time and saw that they were the color of the ocean during a storm, gray with blue around the edges. They were also kind eyes, full of concern, and I remembered his young, delicate wife, whom he'd brought from Boston and who had lasted only two summers on St. Simons before dying in childbed. They said his friends had feared for him, that he had taken to walking the beach during storms as if waiting for fate to intervene and take him to see her again. He squeezed my hand, and I knew that I could trust this man, because he knew how to love deeply.

He turned to Georgina. "Stay here and comfort your sister. But first go send for Jemma." His heavy boots marked his departure from the room.

"Jemma," I called out, but the word was cut off by a scream coming up from inside my womb. I reached for my sister, who sat calmly in a chair at my side. "Get Jemma," I whispered.

She was slowly slipping off the gloves, one finger at a time. "I will. But I want to make sure you are comfortable first. Should I take off your skirts? Or get water?"

My head thrashed from side to side on the pillow, the pain nearly blinding me. "Jemma!" I croaked. And then I heard the door of the room bang open and felt her small, sure hands on me, and I knew that everything would be all right.

I slid from wakefulness to unconsciousness as easily as a pelican diving under the ocean's waves. But I forced my eyes open when I felt Jemma's warm breath on my face, her hands on my shoulders. This was how she always let me know when she had to say something to me, and I did my best now to listen.

Her one good eye flickered with concern, her face beaded with sweat. Georgina stood behind her with a pitcher of water, her skin white, her hair now fallen around her shoulders in beautiful curls.

"What is it?"

Jemma held her hands where I could see them, cupped and facing each other about a foot apart, as if holding a watermelon on the top and bottom. Slowly, she moved her arms so that her hands were sideways, and despair cut through my agony like hot oil in water. "Is it breech?" I gasped out. I remembered the pain when I'd stepped from the kitchen house, and wondered whether that was when the child had flipped itself, sealing both our fates in the span of a single breath.

I was about to tell Jemma not to worry, that as long as my water remained intact we still had a chance to hold the baby in, to keep it for another three weeks and hope and pray that it would move again. But before I could ease the words past my lips, Georgina pressed a wet rag against my mouth to moisten it, while at the same time I felt the trickle of water between my legs.

The despair darkened my vision, a black shadow that clouded out the day. As if seeing the same shadow, Jemma brushed Georgina away and held my face in her small, capable hands and pressed hard. My gaze met hers, and a strange calm infused my spirit. She could move the baby. I had shown her how to do it myself, how to ignore the screams of the mother and to reach up and feel for the baby's shoulders and head and to do what Mother Nature would not. And if I could withstand the pain, then I could survive it.

The door opened and Geoffrey ran into the room smelling of wet wool, snowflakes sticking to his greatcoat like stars. I reached for him and he kissed me, but not before I saw the abject terror in his eyes.

He nodded, his blue eyes nearly black with worry. Another pain roiled through me and I cried out, making Geoffrey wince. He placed his head down on the mattress beside me, his hand clutching mine. "Do not leave me, Pamela. There is no life without you."

I found the strength to place my hand on his cheek, the gold of my wedding band stark against the pallor of my skin. "Forever, remember?"

He looked up, his face stricken. "Come back to me. Whatever happens, come back to me. Promise."

A new wave of pain rose and crested, stealing my breath.

"Geoffrey, come." I had not seen Nathaniel until he spoke and placed a hand on Geoffrey's shoulder.

Geoffrey kissed me on my cheek, his lips against my ear. "Promise me."

"I promise," I whispered.

I felt him leave, then gave myself over to the pain and the surety of Jemma's guiding hands, and the hard pressure of the wet cloth as Georgina pressed it against my mouth as if trying to stifle the very breath I craved.

Ava

St. Simons Island, Georgia
May 2011

I'd biked or driven past Christ Church and its cemetery several times since I'd moved to St. Simons, but had never entered the gates. I would stop across the street from the main gate on a small dirt parking area and peer at the Queen Anne–styled church. It had been built in a cruciform design with a trussed Gothic roof, its grounds dressed in bright blooms and paternal oaks, accessorized with gray and white tombstones and mausoleums. But I had held back from going inside, not really sure why. I wasn't afraid of cemeteries; they'd been a part of my childhood. It wasn't fear at all that kept me from entering, but more of an expectation of a discovery—the discovery of something I wasn't sure I wanted to see.

Tish parked her car in the same spot where I usually stopped with my bike. After reaching into the backseat for two notebooks and a box of number two pencils, we exited the car and crossed the two-lane street. It was still fairly early, and the churchyard seemed deserted. But that didn't mean it was empty. The weight of years hung in the air like moss, a pervading sense of events happening just beyond my peripheral vision.

"The grounds are beautiful, aren't they?" Tish asked as she led the way through the gate and up the brick path toward the church.

"Yes. And huge. I didn't expect it to be so big. A person could get lost in here."

"It's been known to happen. Islanders have been buried in this churchyard for more than two hundred years. We've actually got quite a few famous people, too."

I nodded, listening with half an ear as I studied the massive trees around us. "These oaks must be a million years old," I said, tilting my face upward.

Tish laughed. "Not quite. There's an old saying that live oaks take a hundred years to grow, a hundred years to live, and a hundred years to die. From old photographs and drawings of the church, the experts say that these trees are well over two hundred years old. There's a lot these trees have seen."

She continued up the path, but I stopped, admiring the oaks and remembering the tree spirit of the dead sailor, and wondered whether the trunks of the oaks were darkened from absorbing the sadness of this place for over two centuries.

Tish waited for me under the triangular portico. "You have to take a peek at the inside of the church before we tour the cemetery. It's really lovely."

I followed eagerly, needing a sanctuary before facing the silent voices outside.

Tish opened one of the white double doors and we stepped inside, the atmosphere heavy with the fragrance of flowers and muted air. The interior was all dark wood and sweeping support beams. Despite the darkness, the small Gothic stained-glass windows in the chancel area and the large one in the rear of the chapel depicting a biblical scene allowed the sunlight to trickle in, transforming it into a kaleidoscope of color as it settled on the walls and benches of the small church.

Speaking in hushed tones, Tish said, "Although the families held services on this spot as early as the mid–eighteenth century, the parish wasn't officially established until 1807."

I looked around at the Victorian architecture, recalling the Gothic roof outside. "It doesn't seem that old," I said, wincing at Tish's admonishing look as I realized I'd forgotten to lower my voice.

Tish continued. "They didn't actually have a church building until 1820. Unfortunately, the Yankees destroyed it during the Civil War, and desecrated the cemetery while they were at it." She frowned and narrowed her eyes, making me think the event was a lot more recent, and that she'd been personally affronted by the soldiers' sacrilege.

I craned my neck to see the soaring ceiling and to admire the stained-glass windows. "When did they rebuild it?"

Tish smiled smugly, reminding me of the high school math teacher she had once been. "Anson Dodge paid to have it rebuilt in the early eighteen eighties in memory of his dead wife, Ellen. She's actually entombed under the altar." She nodded in the direction of the chancel. "Of course, the church is relatively new compared to the cemetery. The oldest grave we've found is from 1803."

I closed my eyes for a moment, feeling the peace of this holy place, the warmth of the sun brushing my face in a rainbow of colors. If I could choose to be buried anywhere, it would be in the cemetery watched over by the steeple of this serene church. Facing Tish again, I said, "That seems like a lot of graves for us to document."

"The cemetery is pretty well documented already. Mostly, I thought our task today would be jotting down the family names, so that if we find another grave on the island with the same name, it will make cross-checking easier. Lucky for us, some of the graves found on the old plantations were reinterred here. But I'm afraid there might be more out there."

"Hasn't anybody else looked before?"

"Sure, and a lot of marked and unmarked graves have been found. But I think there are more we still haven't found, and I put a proposal through that if I'm able to find proof of hidden cemeteries, the Georgia Archaeological Institute will let us use that new equipment that can see beneath the earth. Sort of like a portable X-ray machine, I guess." She shrugged. "I don't need to know how it works—just how to work it."

She motioned for me to follow, then headed back to the door. "A Civil War buff with a metal detector found the remains of those black Union soldiers on Folly Beach a year or so ago, which gave me the idea. I think the ground still holds secrets, and it just takes a determined woman—or two," she said, indicating me with a jut of her jaw, "to discover them."

We walked down the aisle past wooden pews with hymnals stored neatly into pockets on the backs, our footsteps muted by the red carpet. I walked slowly, listening for the hidden sounds I imagined I could sometimes hear tucked behind ordinary life, but all was silent in this church. My peace was short-lived when I realized that Tish was leading us back to the door we'd come in, back out to the cemetery where the bright sunlight chose sides, illuminating only what it wanted to.

Tish handed me one of the notepads and took a pencil from the box. "Here, take these. I figure if you get started on this side, and I get started on the opposite side, we'll meet in the middle just in time for lunch. And mark where you find any that are too faded to read. We'll come back for those with paper and flat crayons to see if we can lift off the words that way."

I looked around at the meandering paths, and the way they circled, then straightened, then seemed to disappear amid the canopies of trees and bushes.

As if reading my mind, Tish said, "You have my cell number if you get lost. Just call—or shout. I won't be far."

"Sure," I said, watching as an older man wearing sandals and socks, a large camera around his neck, walked through the main gate with a woman wearing lime green cropped pants and a pair of sparkling white Keds. I knew they were together by their matching wraparound sunglasses. They began walking slowly in my direction, and I felt an odd relief to know that I wouldn't be alone among the dead. I didn't believe in ghosts, but there was something hovering in the heavily scented air, something that made me feel that if I turned my head quickly enough, I'd see what it was.

With a brief wave, Tish walked away. Pulling out a pencil, I wrote, *Page 1*, at the top of the yellow pad and underlined it three times before I leaned over the first cluster of tombstones and began to read. My back grew stiff and my fingers grimy as I wiped at mold and lichens that gathered on the small stones close to the ground in shady areas. I knew my face matched my hands as I found myself wiping tears for the number of young children laid to rest in the sleeping ground, and the young men whose graves were decorated with small Confederate flags who'd been born on the island, yet died far away on the battlefields of Pennsylvania and Virginia. Some were barely older than sixteen.

I wrote the same family names over and over: Couper, King, Butler, Hamilton, Demere, Wylly—used as either a surname or middle name and sometimes as a first name. The island had once been dominated by these families, and it made sense that they would have intermarried. As I jotted down their names and dates, I was able to form a sketch of their family trees in my brain, imagining the trunks with long branches that entwined and threaded themselves with neighboring trees until it was hard to distinguish where one started and the other ended.

Sweat dripped in my eyes as I straightened to stretch my back, pinching my shoulder blades together with a reassuring pop. My sandals and feet were nearly brown. Despite the bright green grass in front of the church, most of the cemetery was covered in sandy dirt and dead oak leaves.

I straightened, realizing as I did so that I was completely alone. A family of four had wandered into the cemetery shortly after I'd started, but even they seemed to have disappeared. A cold sweat enveloped me, the skin on the back of my neck tightening. I moved down the path, trying to orient myself, but felt hopelessly lost. I remembered a story one of my brothers had told me, about two American tourists at Versailles who during a tour of the gardens had found themselves somehow transported back in time to the era of Marie Antoinette and her court.

A sense of urgency pressed against the spot between my shoulder blades, prodding me to walk quickly. I stepped off the path when I thought I recognized a tall, circular grave marker, hoping it would lead me back to the front of the church. Hurrying forward, I nearly tripped over a low iron fence, my feet managing to stop in time. I stopped, my breathing coming in small, short gasps, the air suddenly thin.

Pressing my hands against my chest like that would somehow help my lungs gather air, I studied the area inside the fence, where about fifteen graves sprouted from the sparse grass like a garden of stone. Most appeared very old, with cracked and faded markers, with a few whiter and newer ones near the front. My gaze seemed drawn to three graves at the very back, one larger on the end next to two tiny ones.

As if the others didn't exist, I stepped over the low fence and moved to the back of the plot. I pressed my eyelids closed and tried to catch my breath, wondering why the placement of the other graves in the front and the larger one set with the two small ones seemed so wrong, like they weren't supposed to be there.

Slowly, I knelt before the larger stone, forcing myself to look as my right hand lifted to touch the words carved into the marble nearly two hundred years before.

GEOFFREY GRANT FRAZIER
Beloved Father and Friend
B. 1781 D. 1815
Life is a span, a fleeting hour
How soon the vapor flies
Man is a tender transient flower
That in the Blooming dies

The taste of grief, of dry hollowness and bitter breaths, filled my mouth. I sat back on my heels, nearly reeling from the force of it, incomprehension flooding me as if I'd gone to sleep and awakened in a foreign place with no understanding of where the roads led or what language I was expected to speak.

Reluctantly, I lowered my hand, my fingertips brushing the letters and numbers on their descent before turning to the next two stones. They were tiny, only about one-third the size of the first one, and only a few short lines were scratched into the creamy white surface.

JAMIE HAMILTON FRAZIER
B. 1805 D. 1805

and

MICHAEL MACGREGOR FRAZIER
BORN AND DIED THE FIFTH OF FEBRUARY, 1806

I shot to a stand, then stumbled backward toward the front of the small plot, unable to move my gaze, yet also unable to stay too close. I didn't understand any of it, this sudden vertigo that left me feeling as if I were flying and falling all at the same time. I focused on the trees and the ground and the metal chain of the fence, all things recognizable and familiar, things whose purpose and presence I understood.

Pausing just inside the fence, I realized I'd dropped my notepad and pencil. Being careful not to allow my head to dip beneath my heart and make myself more light-headed, I slowly crouched to retrieve both items and found myself face-to-face with the newest grave in the plot.

It stood alone, set aside the way a child puts away a favorite toy to preserve it, the pink granite glowing in the muted sunshine allowed in by the oaks. Dead roses, wilted and brown, slumped against the headstone, a wreath with a faded yellow ribbon with the word "Daughter" leaned against the other side in defeat. Slowly, I read the words chiseled on its bright face.

ADRIENNE MCMAHON FRAZIER
Beloved wife of Matthew
Mother of unborn children
BORN MAY 29, 1981
DIED AUGUST 27, 2007

"She was a really nice lady."

The man's voice so close behind me shot me to my feet, my notepad and pencil flying. I turned around, hoping to find a living, breathing person.

"Did I scare you?" His words were thick and rounded, as if they came from a mouth filled with marbles.

The man standing just on the other side of the fence had the smooth, untroubled skin of a child, but his brown eyes seemed to carry the witness of years like a much older person. His face was round with ruddy cheeks, a soft blond stubble on a patch of his chin where he had apparently missed with his razor. His hair was thinning, but prematurely, I thought, as he didn't seem to be much older than mid-forties or so. His most arresting feature, however, was his nose. It zigged and zagged at odd angles instead of a straight line, as if it had been broken many times and never set. He was a big man, and I wondered whether he'd been a boxer or some sort of fighter to have earned a nose like that.

He wore a plaid long-sleeved shirt buttoned up to the neck, and jeans worn a little too high for current fashion. His knees were covered with pads tied behind his legs, just like my mother wore when we worked in her garden, and he carried a trowel.

"Just startled me, that's all," I said, wondering whether I should be scared after all. Despite his smile and expression of concern, there was something different about him, something that set him apart from most people, yet I couldn't name exactly what it was.

"You dropped your paper," he said, then leaned down to retrieve the yellow notepad.

"Thanks," I said, reaching out and trying not to wince as I saw the skin on his wrists and hands. Long and purple keloid scars climbed from his fingertips and beyond his wrists, twisting and thick like the roots of an old oak tree. They were old scars, but the skin still appeared pink and raw. I lifted my eyes and met his gaze, but he didn't seem to notice that I'd been staring.

"I'm Ava Frazier," I said, introducing myself but not offering my hand, then waited for him to do the same.

Instead, he looked back at the gravestone and repeated, "She was a really nice lady."

"There you are!" Tish came marching down the path, her feet stirring stones. She stopped in front of us and smiled at the man. "Hello, Jimmy. It's good to see you."

The man beamed as Tish embraced him, his hands dangling by his sides as if he were unsure what to do with them. Tish turned to me. "So, y'all met?"

"Sort of. I'm Ava Frazier," I said again, hoping to prompt him.

"I'm Jimmy," he said, smiling warmly. Despite his oddities, there was something engaging about his open face and dark eyes that made me smile back as if we were old friends.

"Jimmy Scott," Tish added. "The best landscape architect on the island, if not in the entire state; isn't that right, Jimmy?"

Jimmy's cheeks flushed a bright pink that mimicked the color of his hands. "No, ma'am. But I do like flowers."

"He's being modest," Tish said, and I noticed for the first time the red wagon filled with containers of greens and blooming flowers, the over-abundance spilling over the sides like children dressed for a party. "You going to tend to your family?"

"Yes, ma'am. It's time. Thought I'd plant roses on Adrienne's grave first. Not too much sun here, so they won't last, but her mama asked me to."

I felt relief at his words, not bothering to wonder why.

Tish patted his arm. "You're a good man, Jimmy. And I'll be calling you later this week to talk about my side yard. It's gone wild, and I need a good plan for it."

"Yes, ma'am." He dipped his head toward me. "Nice to meet you, Ava Frazier."

"You, too," I said, then turned to follow Tish out of the maze of paths and gravestones. When we were out of hearing, I asked, "Who is he, exactly?"

Tish looked over her shoulder to make sure we were out of earshot of the large man. "He really is the best landscaper; everybody uses him on the island. He's lived here his whole life and is sort of a fixture in the community."

"Is he . . . ?" I wasn't sure how to finish the question.

Tish brushed her hand through the air. "It's not what you're thinking. He's extremely intelligent in things that matter to him. I had him as a student and he's brilliant with numbers, but couldn't memorize a poem or write a coherent sentence if his life depended on it. He studied horticulture at the University of Georgia and did real well—although I will admit that I and some of his other teachers at the high school tutored him quite a bit for his English and writing classes, helped him with his papers, that kind of thing. Didn't need any help whatsoever in the math and science classes, though. He does have a few issues with his speech, which makes him socially awkward at times, which sets him apart, but other than that he's completely normal—if there's really such a thing."

I thought for a moment as we headed toward a main path, relieved to see the church in the near distance. "Was he born that way?"

"Yes." Tish trudged on, her footsteps suddenly heavier, and I saw sweat drip down her cheeks. Tish paused and faced me. "Although if he'd been given speech therapy when he was younger, it might not be as pronounced. That's just one of the forms of abuse that poor boy had to put up with."

"What do you mean?"

She stopped, her face troubled. "When Jimmy was only five years old his father tried to drown him in the bathtub. That's not what the police report said, but, well, people talk. Luckily his mother was able to intervene in time, not that she didn't pay for it." She shook her head. "Mary Anne—

his mother—was a nurse, so I'm sure she took care of a lot of things that never saw the light of day. God only knows what that woman and her children suffered. Floyd Scott was a brutal animal, and I know it's not right to speak ill of the dead, but it was a good day when he died."

"What about his hands? Did his father do that, too?"

We were in the middle of the path between the front door of the church and the main gate. Tish glanced toward the church as if to make sure God wasn't listening. "In a way, yes. Jimmy's dad was on one of his drunken binges and set the house on fire with everybody in it. Jimmy tried to save his mother and two little sisters—and him being only fifteen. That's how he got those awful burns on his hands and arms—but they all died. It was a tragedy, for sure, but good came of it, too. Jimmy survived and was taken in by another family on the island. And that mean son of a bitch was dead."

We started to walk toward the gate again when I recalled how I'd first seen Jimmy at Adrienne's grave. "It was the McMahons, wasn't it? Who took Jimmy in after the fire."

Tish nodded. "They didn't know the Scotts, but they'd been foster parents for years. That's actually how they came to adopt Adrienne and John—they were foster children first. Anyway, Jimmy needed a home, so they opened up theirs." She sighed. "I know the McMahons were real good to him, but Jimmy still grieves for his real mama like he does his two little sisters. He sometimes pretends that they're still alive and he's waiting for them to come home. I think it makes it easier for him to accept why they're not here."

We walked the rest of the way to the car in silence, the heat oppressive now, the atmosphere of the cemetery too crowded with stories of those who'd lived and died. I climbed into the car and closed my eyes for a moment, trying to block out the image of scarred hands and a crushed nose.

Forever. I heard the word as if it had been spoken inside my head. I glanced back once as we drove out of the parking lot, catching a glimpse of the three tombstones in the rear of the enclosure, and remembering the inscription, *Beloved Father and Friend.* It wasn't until we were driving away, the Gothic steeple of the church sliding by my window, that I realized what thought had been pecking at my brain, trying to get my attention. *Where was the wife and mother? And why was there no mention of her on Geoffrey Frazier's tombstone?*

I faced forward, staring ahead at the road but still seeing the three lone gravestones, the absence of the fourth as real as granite and as palpable as a heartbreak.

CHAPTER NINE

Ava

St. Simons Island, Georgia
May 2011

What is the taste of fear? Is it the acrid taste of adrenaline that coats the mouth? Or is it the salty tang of ocean water as it fills every cavity, pushing out the air needed to breathe? I lay in my bed inside the shadowed world between sleep and waking where foreign thoughts clouded my brain, and I felt the edges of the old nightmare rumble past me, stirring my subconscious with a stiff breeze.

But Matthew's naked body pressed against my own, anchoring me to this place, and the terror subsided, calming me as the salty taste dissipated like early-morning mist over water. Yet as sleep eluded me I realized that what I feared most was no longer the actual dream; it was not knowing where the words had come from.

I slipped quietly from the bed, knowing that sleep wouldn't find me despite it being only dawn, and threw on a T-shirt before padding barefoot downstairs to the kitchen. I made a pot of coffee and, while waiting for it to brew, pulled out a notepad I'd discovered previously in one of the drawers, and began to make a list. *Salt and pepper shakers. Dishes. Toaster.* This last was starred. The gourmet toaster oven that dominated a large portion of the countertop seemed to do everything but actually toast bread, and all I wanted was the basic model with four slits in the top. I might not cook, but I did know how to make toast if I had the proper equipment. *T-shirt for Mimi. Seeds for Mama.*

I tapped the pen against the last entry several times before finally striking through it. And then rewriting it. She'd lived on St. Simons but grew none of the plants so abundant here in her Antioch garden. Some plants might not do as well away from the coast, but I thought she would at least like to experiment. It was one of the things I loved best about my mother: her inability to accept no as an answer. I'd once asked her whether that was the reason she kept trying for a girl after having so many boys. She'd placed her hand on the crown of my head as if I were a delicate orchid and had been about to say something when she stopped suddenly, removed her hand, and told me to go do my homework. I'd thought many times about asking her again, but I never seemed to be able to find the courage.

I pulled two cups from the cabinet and poured coffee into one with my left hand while I added *coffee cups* to the bottom of my list. Adrienne was everywhere in this kitchen, and by replacing the small things first, I hoped to slowly exorcise her until I no longer felt her every time I stepped into the room.

Slipping on a pair of flip-flops that I'd started keeping by the back door—next to Matthew's much larger ones—I headed outside. Full summer was less than a month away, yet the air already seemed drenched with water, the marshes painted in shades of green. The birds were more abundant now, too, and their barks and calls had become so familiar to me that they no longer awakened me in the morning. I'd begun to wonder whether I could ever sleep anywhere else, as if their absence would awaken me instead.

I sipped my coffee as I stared at the old garden plot and remembered Tish telling me that Adrienne had loved her flowers. I recalled, too, how she'd said midwifery wasn't Adrienne's passion, but that she'd been competent. I wondered whether Tish had merely meant to make me feel better, or if her words meant something else entirely.

My gaze strayed to the small tabby outbuilding with the boarded windows. It appeared to be as old as the main house, and it had a chimney at one end of the structure. It was large for a potting shed, but its placement by the garden made it the perfect spot. Placing my empty cup on the back step, I walked through the overgrown grass and stopped in front of it, hearing crickets and the distant caw of an unseen bird. I tilted my head as if I expected to hear something else, as if this strange building came with its own sounds in the same way it was constructed of tabby and had a fireplace within. I closed my eyes, straining to hear . . . what?

Feeling foolish, I moved forward and up the crushed-shell steps and examined the two-by-four that bisected the opening. The nails connecting it to the wooden doorframe half protruded from the board, as if whoever had nailed them had done so quickly, like an afterthought.

Reaching up, I grabbed hold of the board and jiggled it, watching the nails shimmy. I thought briefly of just yanking hard, but recalled again how old the building must be, and how easy it would be for the wood frame to splinter or pull away entirely from the doorway.

I remembered a toolbox I'd seen in the detached garage and walked quickly to the other side of the yard to find it, my feet and lower legs wet from the dew of the tall grasses. Aiming the claw end of the hammer toward the nail heads, I pried the nails out of the wood with surprising ease, almost as if the tabby structure had been waiting for me to come and discover its secrets.

I decided to wait until later to unboard the windows and instead carefully leaned the board against the front of the little house and slowly turned the door handle, not at all surprised to find it locked. Somewhere in me, I must have hoped that it would be unlocked, as if the only reason it would have been boarded up was to keep the door closed.

I examined the handle in my hand. It was fairly new, and cheaply made, like the ones people put on garages or sheds to be a deterrent, if not a preventive. I knew I should wait for Matthew and ask him for a key, that even if the handle were inexpensive and easy to repair, what I might find on the other side might not be.

I ran back into the kitchen, listening for any signs that Matthew might be awake, and retrieved a butter knife from the drawer before walking quickly back to the deserted building.

Using a skill taught to me by my enterprising older brothers, whose popularity in high school was no doubt attributed to their access to the funeral home, where they were guaranteed quiet and privacy, I slid the knife into the jamb and wiggled it back and forth. When I heard the lock click, I dropped the knife, too eager to get inside to see where it landed or to even be grateful that it hadn't landed on my exposed toes. Thinking of Mimi and how she'd always told me that closed doors were only doors we hadn't yet opened, I pushed on the door.

The first thing that registered in my mind was the smell of ashes and the scent of cooked food from meals long since consumed. The second thing was that I'd been there before, stood beneath the low ceiling before the large stone fireplace dominating the far wall where the chimney stood on the outside. I blinked in the mote-filled light filtering in from the open doorway and from the slats of the boarded windows, and tried to understand how a place I'd never been could seem so familiar.

Easels stood scattered around the room on the scarred bare-wood floor, some open and some leaning against the tabby walls. Large partitioned folders with handles lay on an oversize thick-legged table in the middle of the room, several with curled and yellowed papers sticking out of the edges. A wooden caddy held stubby charcoal sticks and artist's pencils, and one of the easels held pads of drawing paper in various sizes, the covers of them, like everything else in the room, covered in dust.

I knew from looking at the space that this hadn't been where Adrienne worked, but merely a catchall room for her supplies and finished work. From the drawings and sketches I'd seen so far, I imagined she'd set up her easel on the beach or on a bluff overlooking the marsh or on the pier. I didn't know what she looked like, but I pictured her with white-blond hair and aquamarine eyes that were neither blue nor green, but not brown like mine.

I moved to the table and carefully lifted one of the smaller portfolios and slid a sketch out of its folder. It was a drawing of a baby, its sex undeterminable from the pose, its face invisible to the viewer as it stared away from the artist. All that was visible was the curve of a cheek, the soft roundness of a bare shoulder, the small nub of a nose.

Curious, I took out more sketches, discovering that all of them were of the same child from different vantage points. Some were of simply a baby's hand or foot. Although I went through every single sketch, I couldn't find a single one of the child's face.

I placed each sketch back where I'd found it, then replaced the portfolio, making sure I stacked it exactly where it had been. I didn't want to think about why I was trying to hide my presence here, only that I needed to.

A door at the back of the room caught my attention and I walked toward it, eager to leave the anonymous baby behind. The old wood door opened with little resistance, but angry hinges protested as I pushed it open until it hit the staircase wall behind it and I found myself at the bottom of a set of narrow stone steps. I hesitated, knowing that whatever room they led to had to be very small and dark, since from the outside the structure appeared to be only a single story, and there were no windows higher than the two on the bottom floor.

I had my foot on the bottom step when I heard a voice behind me. "What are you doing in here?"

I jerked back as if I'd been slapped, my foot sliding off the narrow step and throwing me into the door. "Matthew," I said, trying to regain my footing. "You scared me."

He moved from the door toward me. "What are you doing in here?" he repeated.

I looked up into his face, seeing a stranger. "I want to start a garden. I thought this would make a good potting shed."

His beautiful skin was a mottled red and tan, his eyes unrecognizable. "Did you not see the nailed board across the door? Or the locked door? How did you get in?"

At first I was embarrassed to admit how hard I'd worked at gaining access. But then I felt the slow-burning embers of anger. I stepped toward him. "Except for the path leading down to the creek and the dock, the rest of the backyard is overgrown and wild. It didn't occur to me that any part of your house—*our* house—would be off-limits to me."

"Not this place," he said as if I hadn't spoken at all, his gaze darting from easel to table to walls as if he were half expecting to see his dead wife. "Not this place," he said again.

"Is this her shrine?" I shouted, unable to see past my anger and only wanting to hurt him as much as he had hurt me. "Is it?" I shouted again as I used both hands to shove a stack of portfolios onto the dirty wooden floorboards. They landed with a thud that seemed to echo in the nearly bare space, a puff of dust rising into the air like a last breath.

The noise seemed to make him aware of my presence and he stared at me, blinking as if wondering how I had gotten there.

"I am your wife, Matthew. Me, Ava. Not Adrienne. I don't mind you hanging her pictures on the walls, or even talking about her if that's what you want to do. But I will not live in the same space with her, where she's allowed to lock doors to places where I'm not allowed. I will *not* live that way. I didn't marry both of you." I felt the hot, angry tears on my cheek and wiped them away, not wanting him to see how much this place and his protection of it hurt me.

He moved toward me, his face stricken. "I'm sorry, Ava. I didn't think . . ." He stopped.

"You didn't think what?" My voice shook, but I kept looking at him, willing him to say the right thing, whatever that would be.

He didn't answer but just kept staring at me.

"That I would mind sharing you and your house with her?"

Very quietly he said, "No. I thought that nothing else would matter once I met you."

I allowed his words to settle on me for a moment. "But it does," I said, my anger still like sharp rocks on a riverbed, hard and immovable even in a strong current. "It all does." I took a step back, wanting to clean up the mess I'd made but unable to start. I stared at the faceless baby sketches, spilled on the floor like milk and just as impossible to leave untouched. "What is in here that you don't want me to see?"

A shadow seemed to flicker behind his eyes like a walking ghost, transferring to the back of my neck like tiny, icy footsteps. *They think I killed her.*

He took a step toward me. "Why would you think that?" His voice was low, almost cajoling.

I raised my hands to indicate the room that had been off-limits to me until I'd forced it open with a hammer and a butter knife. Instead he reached for my hand, and as always when he touched me, my brain slowed to a subtle hum, blocking out reason and all conscious thought. I fought the numbness, trying to focus on the twinges of cold fear that had wound their way through what threads of consciousness he hadn't yet stripped away.

"I love you," he said, drawing me close. "Nothing else matters."

"But it does," I tried to say, but his lips had already descended on mine.

"Let's go back to bed," he said, attempting to pull me toward the door.

"Not yet." I turned around so he was pressing us both against the wall, the tabby hard and unyielding against my back. "Let me have this place for my gardening. Let it be mine and not hers."

His desire for me had darkened his eyes, but my anger was a needy thing, too. "Show me that it doesn't matter, Matthew. Show me that I'm your wife now."

I pulled him close to me as I felt his surrender, felt his need for me as if the two could not be separated. I pulled my shirt over my head and his eyes met mine. Silently, he lifted me so my legs straddled his hips, and he moved us so my back was against the smooth surface of the door.

My hands clutched at the muscles on his shoulders as we moved together in silent surrender, eradicating memories and exorcising ghosts, the easels against the walls witnesses to my first victory over Adrienne.

Gloria

Antioch, Georgia
May 2011

The old porch swing at the back of the house creaked its ancient rhythm in the late-afternoon haze. The temperature had been hovering in the high nineties all week, wilting my great-grandmother's roses. Their heady aroma clouded my thoughts, making me think of our time on St. Simons when Henry had worked in the coroner's office, and my garden was a barren yard of grass. Things had changed suddenly for us in our move to Antioch, and it had been a hard adjustment. In the end, it had all worked out, just not in the way we'd expected.

A yellow jacket landed stealthily on my forearm. Too weary from the heat to swipe it away, I sat staring at it, daring it to sting me. It seemed to slip on the dewy sweat of my skin before beating its wings and droning on to find a cooler spot.

"It is just too damned hot!" I said, not for the first time that week.

My exclamation brought down the corner of the newspaper next to me. "Gloria, you don't swear. Why are you swearing?" He didn't wait for an answer; the newspaper curtain went up again, blocking my husband from view.

I frowned down at my fingernails, spotting the broken nail I'd sustained while repotting my trilliums. Ava's hands were small and slender like reeds, whereas mine were as big as baseball mitts—something a mother of five had a great deal of use for. But our nails had been the same—short and without polish, with jagged breaks where a nail had dared to grow over the nail bed. Thinking about her made my chest hurt, and I fanned myself again with a rice-paper fan my daughter-in-law June had brought me from one of her mission trips to India. It was too small and too thin and mostly useless, but it had been a well-meant gift, so I used it. Frowning, I looked again at the back of the newspaper and murmured, "Because it's just too damned hot."

This didn't even bring a crinkle of notice from Henry. My gaze strayed from the old porch to the row of magnolia trees in the front yard. The milky white petals drooped in the heat. I had been married nearly fifty-six years ago under a similar row of magnolias in my hometown of Social Circle, Georgia, as had my mother, my grandmother, her mother before her, and so on up the family tree to way before the War Between the States. That's what Mimi called it, and she taught me everything I know. And some things I didn't want to.

I'd always imagined Ava marrying under these trees in the backyard of the house she'd grown up in, wearing the antique wedding dress that I had worn. I could picture her standing in the sunlight of the backyard, sheltered by the matronly magnolias, her veil glowing like an effervescent halo as she said her vows.

My sons had married in their wives' hometowns, in foreign churches or gardens that hadn't meant anything to me. But these trees were different. Mimi and I had planted them when Ava was a baby, marking each foot grown, each year, as an extravagant gift, too fragile to hold too tightly, yet too sturdy to keep.

I reached my arm around the back of the swing and rested my hand on Henry's shoulder. "What are we going to do?"

The newspaper didn't move. "About what?"

"About Ava."

Slowly and methodically, as he did all things, he folded the newspaper and set it on the floor of the porch. "I think it's out of our hands."

I leaned my head on his shoulder, knowing he was right but fighting it just the same. It wasn't in my nature—or Ava's—to let things take their natural course if that was at odds with our vision of the way things should be. We'd battled pest infestations, drought, and flood in our garden, tending the plants as a mother tends her babies to make sure they survived.

"I can't accept that."

His hand stroked my hair. "For the first time in your life, Gloria, you might have to. And she's happy. Happier than I've ever known her to be."

I brought my head up to look directly into his eyes. "How do you know?"

He looked sheepish. "Matthew's called several times. He wasn't sure if your brief conversations with Ava were enough to let us know that all was well with them."

I looked away and rested my head against Henry's shoulder again. "I wish she'd married Phil."

He was silent for a moment, the chains of the swing groaning as we moved back and forth. "We don't always get to choose who we love."

Closing my eyes, I allowed his words to seep down into me like a glass of cold iced tea, knowing the truth of them, but not wanting to hear them.

Henry continued. "Matthew's a good man, and he loves Ava and she loves him. Let's let them be happy."

"But how can they be? What if . . . ?" I couldn't say any more, my fear like a ball in the pit of my stomach.

He patted my shoulder. "No what-ifs, remember? We agreed to that."

His eyes met mine, calm and reassuring, and I was reminded of why I'd fallen in love with him all those years ago. And why he was a successful funeral director. He had a way of calming the spirit without having to say a single word.

"Aren't you afraid?" I asked quietly.

"I don't allow myself to be," he said, as if emotions could be willed. As if a mother could forget what it had been like to hold her baby's hands in her own.

I shook my head. "Mimi's having one of her headaches. That always means a storm's brewing." I looked up into the clear evening, at the stars pressing against the darkening sky and the crescent moon hanging above us like a knowing smile. "She's never wrong."

"We'll deal with it if we have to. It's what we've always done."

"But this is Ava," I said, as if that explained the past thirty-four years.

The sun sank low on the horizon, the last traces of it reaching through the magnolia petals and creeping up the steps of the porch. Cicadas began their last chorus of the day while the fireflies dimmed and glowed in unison. I kissed Henry gently on the cheek, then gave a big send-off with my legs, the porch swing swaying drunkenly in my wake.

Sighing, I stood, the swing bouncing against my legs. I walked into the house, the screen door snapping shut behind me, and Henry's newspaper pages fluttering like moths in the gathering gloom.

CHAPTER TEN

Ava

ST. SIMONS ISLAND, GEORGIA
MAY 2011

I pulled into the parking lot of the drugstore I'd passed on the way to work, hoping it would carry not only a few basic gardening tools, but also a film processing center. In the age of digital cameras, film processing had gone the way of vinyl records and Walkmans.

I was exhausted, yet exhilarated after my first day at my new job. It had mostly been a routine day of meeting my coworkers and a few patients, filling out paperwork, and learning where the restrooms were. Still, it felt good to be using another part of my brain again and, in time, to be helping babies into the world. My profession had always been more than a career for me; it defined who I was. And I tried not to think about how Matthew had married two midwives, even encouraging the first wife to become one. It was almost as if an unwritten script had dictated this small feat, and he'd accomplished it with relative ease.

I grabbed a small shopping cart at the front of the store, figuring I'd need it if I happened to find the pots I planned to scatter on the edges of the steps leading to both the front and back doors. Despite the abundance of rich green foliage surrounding the house, it looked abandoned and forlorn without potted flowers and shrubs close to the house.

Although I usually felt that fragrant blooms were extraneous in a yard, my mother's teachings refused to let go of me, and I found myself wanting the bright hues of perennials to bring color to the old tabby house. I tried to tell myself that it had nothing to do with Adrienne's sketch on the parlor wall that showed the house as it appeared now. As with the old kitchen house, I felt the need to make it my own, to make it different from how Adrienne had known it. It was almost as if I wanted her ghost to find everything unrecognizable and leave.

I was standing at the processing center at the front of the store and emptying my bag of film canisters on the counter when I heard somebody call my name. I turned to see John McMahon at the checkout near the entrance. He walked toward me, holding a can of shaving cream and two packages of photo paper.

I smiled tentatively, remembering the last time I'd seen him at Tish's party and his parting words to me: *Be careful, Ava. He's not who you think he is.*

"Hello, John. How are you?"

"I really should be asking *you* that, I think."

"Please don't," I said, turning my back to him. "He's my husband, and whatever differences you have are between the two of you."

He paused for a moment before speaking. "I'm sorry. You're right. I don't want my grievances with Matthew to get in between my friendship with you."

I turned around. "I hope we can be friends. But I also hope that you and Matthew will find a way to mend things between you."

He watched me closely, his eyes thoughtful. "Me, too," he said quietly. His gaze was redirected to the pile of film canisters on the counter. "Are you still using an Instamatic camera?" he asked, his eyes wide.

"Oh, no," I said, shaking my head. "Actually, these aren't even from my camera. I, um, collect these."

He raised an eyebrow.

"Just a hobby. I find them at garage sales and develop them. Stupid, I know, but it's fun."

"It's not stupid at all. It's actually pretty cool. Every human is a voyeur of some sort. You just have a unique way of exploring it."

Uncomfortable, I stepped back. "I'm not a voyeur. It's just . . ."

"Sure you are—like I said, we all are in some form or another. I'm just curious what it is you're hoping to see." I noticed how the dark pupils of his eyes appeared large against the blue-green irises, adding an intensity to his gaze.

My cheeks flushed, and I was relieved to see an employee approaching the counter. While I wrote down all of the information on the film envelopes and tore off my claim tickets, I was aware of John heading toward the checkout. I hoped he'd leave with just a wave so I wouldn't have to speak with him again. Regardless of what I said about our being friends, I didn't think Matthew would have seen it the same way.

I thanked the employee and wheeled my cart around, looking for the outdoor and gardening aisle. I was in the process of hoisting a large and heavy clay pot inside my cart when John reappeared.

"Let me help you with that," he said, taking the pot and placing it carefully inside the cart.

"Thanks," I said, brushing off my hands. I probably couldn't have lifted it inside without dropping it. Still, his presence made me uncomfortable.

"Are you mad at me?" he asked, his unusual eyes clear.

"No, of course not," I said, avoiding his eyes as I placed a trowel and two smaller clay pots in my cart.

"Good. Because I was going to ask you to show me the pictures once you get them developed. I think it might be kind of cool. Plus, I'm a photographer, too." He held up his shopping bag with the photo paper inside. "Although the project I'm working on right now is all about scanning old pictures and reprinting them in different sizes. No skill there, but it's fun."

I warmed to his open smile and easy manner, wondering, too, whether Adrienne had been like that. "You're a professional photographer?" I asked.

"Nah—just a hobby, really. But I enjoy it. I'm actually an insurance salesman." His grin revealed a deep dimple on his right cheek. "Needed something fun to talk about at parties."

I laughed. "Yeah, I guess so. Are you one of those purists who don't believe in digital?"

"Oh, no—although I do enjoy using my old thirty-five-millimeter. I like to experiment and resize certain photos. I'm actually working on an anniversary gift for my parents right now—" He stopped suddenly, like he'd just realized whom he was speaking to and shouldn't say more.

Being the youngest of five had taught me to speak up or I'd never be heard. Dissembling was for those who commanded attention through birth order or stature. My mother had always told me it was unladylike behavior; Mimi told me it was a surefire way to get what I wanted.

As if I hadn't noticed his hesitation, I said, "What kind of an anniversary present?"

His smile looked brittle enough to crack. "I have an old four-by-six photograph of my sister that I wanted to make into an eight-by-ten. My scanner at home isn't too great, so I thought they might do a better job of it here. Anyway, I need it to be bigger to fit into a really great frame I bought at an antique store in Savannah. It was a favorite photograph of theirs."

I continued to smile around the tightness in my chest. "That's a great idea. I'm sure it will mean a lot to them." I remembered a faded photograph Mimi kept on her bedside table of my grandfather wearing his army uniform before he was sent to Italy in World War II. In it, he was leaning against an old car with his arm around an impossibly young Mimi. They were laughing and looking at each other, and despite her having a shoe box full of old photographs, it was that one that she kept beside her bed.

"Yeah, well, I hope so." He glanced down at his bag. "Would you like to see it?"

I was struck dumb for a moment, wondering how I could refuse before realizing that I couldn't. "I'd like that." I really didn't want to know what Adrienne looked like; it was hard enough competing with her without knowing that she was beautiful.

John reached into the bag and pulled out a worn envelope with the flap tucked inside. With blunt, tanned fingers, he pulled out the photograph and handed it to me.

I didn't notice the water in the photo at first, and I was glad. The woman in the center of the photograph captured the viewer's gaze, obliterating everything else. I knew she and John weren't biological siblings, but they looked enough alike to have been related by blood. Her hair was white-blond, like John's, her eyes a bright green. She was beautiful, with perfect skin and features, but it was more than that. If charisma like that could be transferred onto paper, I couldn't imagine what its force must have been like in real life.

She stared out at the photographer with a Mona Lisa smile, but there was nothing timid in her gaze. I looked closely at her eyes. At first glance I'd thought they reminded me of John's, but I'd been wrong. His were easily read, his emotions quickly discerned. But Adrienne's seemed different, even in color, the bright green of them outlined with shadows. I held the edge of the photograph tightly, thinking that if I looked closely enough I could find the things she wanted to keep hidden.

"She's beautiful," I said, hating the word even as I said it, knowing it to be as inadequate as calling a tsunami a wave. I forced my gaze to take in the rest of the picture, seeing now that she was on a sailboat and standing on the teak deck, her hands grasping rope with a sureness that told me she knew what she was doing. She was looking over her shoulder, as if the photographer had just called her name. "Who took the picture?" I asked, reluctantly handing it back to him.

He kept his eyes focused on the envelope as he tucked the picture back inside. "Matthew," he said, his tone flat as he said the name. "They'd planned to enter some sailing race up in Charleston the following spring, so they were out a lot on the boat that summer."

"Did they do well?"

He stared at me for a moment before answering. "They never made it. She died at the end of August."

I wished I had the photograph again, to see whether it was the knowledge that she had only a few months to live that had placed clouds in her eyes. As if something like that were possible.

"I'm sorry," I said, as if it had anything to do with me. Like I would have stopped it if I could.

"Thank you," he said, his eyes clear again and his smile sincere.

I looked at my watch, surprised to see how late it was. Matthew was working at home and would be expecting me. "I should probably get going. It was great seeing you again."

"You, too," he said. He pulled out his wallet and handed me a card. "Call me when you get the pictures developed. We could go have lunch and we can look at them together."

"I will, thank you," I said as I pocketed the card, not entirely sure that I would.

"Great. I'll be seeing you then." With a little salute, he moved to the door, then paused, turning back to face me. "By the way, please tell Matthew that my parents are thankful for all of Adrienne's sketches he brought over today. I've been asking him for them for almost four years now. But tell him that it doesn't change anything."

Without waiting for me to respond, he turned around again and left through the automatic doors, their closing like a little whoosh of breath.

I felt the blood rush to my cheeks. Matthew and I had agreed to go through everything in the studio together over the weekend when we were both free and decide what to do with it all. We were supposed to have made the decisions together.

My fingers shook as I placed the items on the counter and paid with my credit card. *Why would he have done it all by himself?* I loaded everything into my car and drove out of the parking lot, realizing I'd forgotten the large clay pot in the cart, and not even caring, my mind racing with another, more troubling question: *What had he been hoping to find?*

Pamela

St. Simons Island, Georgia
July 1808

I knelt in the dirt with my basket, pulling the weeds from my herb garden, and gathering comfrey for Leda. Her rheumatism had gotten so bad that she could scarcely bend her fingers, and I had to take over many of the gardening duties. Jemma was a big help, but I could tell she preferred to mind little Robbie, and I allowed her. She loved my sweet baby as much as he loved her, and as soon as he could comprehend I would tell him that Jemma had saved his life and mine, and that more was owed to her than we could ever repay.

I sat on my heels, stretching my back and trying not to mind the emptiness in my womb. I had known after Robbie's birth that there could be no more children, and Robbie was the perfect child: sunny in disposition, bright and eager to learn. Still, I mourned the empty spaces in our house, the corners and rooms that should be filled with children's laughter and the padding of small feet.

Geoffrey had comforted me. Robbie was enough for us, and we would get used to the idea of having just one child. But when Geoffrey loved me at night, I knew in his soft murmurings that he was secretly glad. Because I had seen the terror on his face when I labored to give birth to our son, had seen the fear of learning that forever could mean the span of only a few years.

Robbie giggled, the sound like pollen to my heart, as Jemma held his small hand in hers under the shade of an oak tree while his plump and sturdy legs attempted to run. He was a cautious child and would stop at each tug from Jemma's hand. I suppose it was natural for him to be hesitant about a life that so easily could have been denied him. It was all Geoffrey and I could do not to jump up and save him every time he stumbled or ventured too far beyond our arms' grasp.

I turned back to my garden, my task made easier by the sound of Robbie's laughter. When Georgina and I had been small and our mother still alive, we had had a magnificent garden of scented blooms, descendants of clippings from our grandmother's Savannah garden. My father was a farmer, yet he had captured the heart of the daughter of a prominent Savannah family. He had allowed space in our vegetable garden for her frivolous flowers, hoping that it would somehow make up for bringing her to our desolate and sometimes hostile island. It had not. When I was eleven and Georgina nine, our mother had given birth to a stillborn boy, and soon after succumbed to a fever. One day she had simply fallen asleep and never awakened, as if neither her children, her husband, nor even her bright blooms were enough to make her want to cling to life. Even though I had been a few months short of my twelfth birthday, I had made a promise to myself to not allow myself to love anything with less than my whole heart.

I adjusted the brim of my bonnet to shield my face from the scorching sun as a rivulet of sweat slipped down between my shoulder blades. I longed for more help, for a new dress, for pretty flowers in my garden like Anna Matilda King over at Retreat Plantation. She refused to plant anything that didn't have a pleasing fragrance, and her gardens were legendary. But I had Geoffrey and Robbie, and my heart was full.

"Mistress Frazier."

I looked up to see Nathaniel Smith coming from the direction of the house, his hat in his hands. With effort, I straightened my cramped legs so I could stand, then waited for him to approach. He bowed his head in greeting.

Geoffrey's opinion of Nathaniel Smith had not altered since the horrible day of the pig slaughtering and Robbie's birth, but mine had. I slid off my gloves, the gold band on my finger glinting in the sun, and held my hands out to him. "You must call me Pamela. I am forever beholden and grateful for your assistance when Robert was born."

He grasped my hands in his gloved ones. "You owe me nothing. I was glad to be of service to you and your family. And you, of course, may call me Nathaniel." He dropped my hands and looked down at the ground for a brief moment. "I did, however, come in the hopes of asking a favor, but not as payment."

Robbie squealed and we both looked over to where Jemma was tossing him gently in the air and catching him. She saw us looking at her and shyly ducked so she could pull the side of her head rag over her face to cover the ruined eye.

"The girl is working out for you?" Nathaniel asked.

"Yes, thank you." I regarded him carefully, my forehead crinkling with worry. "I hope you are not reconsidering our barter."

"No, of course not. I am glad you have found her useful here."

"But that is not what you came to talk about."

He shook his head, and I could see he was uncomfortable with what he needed to say.

"Come," I said. "Let us go sit in the shade of the kitchen house and drink a cool glass of water and you can state your business."

He nodded his assent and followed me.

Jemma sat Robbie on her hip and was already heading to the icehouse to get ice chips for our water. We sat in the shade on a wooden bench Geoffrey had carved from the oak of a fallen giant and spoke pleasantries until Jemma arrived with our drinks.

Without further preamble, he said, "I've come to speak to you regarding Miss MacGregor."

"Georgina?" I asked with surprise.

"Yes. With your father gone, you will have assumed responsibility of your sister now that she is living under your roof."

"I have, but Geoffrey is the head of our household. If you would like to stay for supper, he should be in from the fields. . . ."

"No. I wanted to speak with you. Your husband and I . . ." His voice trailed away.

"Yes, my husband and you are not friends, although I have never been able to determine why. But I cannot make any decision regarding Georgina without consulting him—or her, for that matter. Georgina is visiting friends on Cumberland Island until the end of the month, but if you would like to call back then . . ."

He was shaking his head. "I have already asked her to marry me three times—three times in the last three years, and each time she has refused."

I was not entirely surprised to hear this, yet surprised to learn that Georgina had had contact with Nathaniel as I had not seen him or spoken with him since Robbie's birth. "Then why do you ask me? My sister has never been one to seek my counsel. She is able to make her own choices."

Nathaniel stared down into his hat. "Pamela, you are a kind and good woman. I knew you would not turn Jemma away, and would treat her kindly."

He looked away and I found that I, too, could not meet his eyes.

He continued. "It is partly the reason why I am offering for Georgina."

My glass froze halfway to my mouth. "I do not understand."

He finished his water in a large gulp, and I imagined that he wished there were something much stronger to drink. Staring down into his empty glass, he said, "I have been in love with Georgina from the first time I met her. You were living in Savannah at the time with your grandmother, but I received permission from your father to court her, and she agreed. I thought that we would be betrothed, but suddenly she stopped seeing me entirely, and it was then that I realized that Geoffrey was courting her."

I swallowed. "Yes. I know all this. And then I returned and Geoffrey met me. There is no bad blood between my sister and me because of it, I assure you. And I have often thought that you would be a good provider for her. Still, I cannot choose a husband for her. If you wish to court her, you would need her permission, not mine."

He took a deep breath. "Georgina needs her own husband and home, Pamela. I would be good for her."

His fingers tightened along his hat brim, his gaze dancing along the brick path that led from the kitchen house to the garden, and I knew there was more than he was telling me; it was there in the way he angled his body away from me and the way his eyes avoided mine.

I placed my hand on his arm. "Tell me," I said, so quietly that I barely heard the words myself.

He put his hand on top of mine. "Your husband holds you in high regard, Pamela."

I jerked away from him and stood. "I do not like what you are implying."

Nathaniel stood, too, his hat in his hands. "I do not mean to imply anything. Only that Georgina is young and beautiful, and that I would like to make her my wife."

"Do you love her still?"

He sighed deeply and I was reminded of how he'd mourned for his first wife. "Yes, I sometimes wish that it were not so, but I do."

I looked toward Jemma, where she'd sat in a grassy patch, allowing Robbie to run around her in circles, his short arms stuck out like little bird's wings. The fingers of my right hand clutched the gold ring on my left as I turned back to him. "I will ask her if you can court her, and if she is in agreement, then I will speak with Geoffrey. But if you love her, you will know that she is not easily persuaded."

His face relaxed into a smile. "Thank you, Pamela. I shall hope for word of your success." Bowing, and replacing his hat on his head, he said, "I should leave you to your garden."

I looked up into his handsome face, and asked the question I'd wanted to ask since the day of Jamie's funeral, when he had given Jemma to me. "Why do you and my husband dislike each other so much?"

He seemed startled by my candor, as most people were. Perhaps it was because I had lacked a mother's guidance, but I had learned that to get an answer, one needed to first ask.

His lips turned up in a half smile, but there was no humor there. "Your husband would be better able to answer that. I suggest you ask him." He tipped his hat, then left.

I stood where I was for a long time, listening to the laughter of my child and spinning my wedding ring around on my finger before returning to the garden, all the while wondering what Nathaniel had meant, and suddenly unsure that I wanted to know.

CHAPTER ELEVEN

Ava

St. Simons Island, Georgia
May 2011

I sat on the dock and watched the trees swallowing the light as the sun dipped lower in the sky, my empty glass of wine—my second—beside me. My heart fluttered like a dangling leaf as I forced myself to sit so near the water in a form of self-therapy or self-abuse—I wasn't sure which. Either way, my fear helped to divert my anger as I waited, twisting my wedding ring around and around my finger while I listened for the sound of Matthew's car. The low hum of a mosquito brushed by my ear, but I didn't swat at it, knowing it had no interest in me.

I closed my eyes, listening to the sounds of the marsh, of the thousands of invisible insects chirping, whirring, and buzzing, of the cries of birds I was still learning the names of, and of water whispering beneath me as it navigated through the tall reeds of cordgrass. My pulse skipped and jumped as I imagined what the currents carried below me, where they had come from, and where they were going. I opened my eyes and tried to focus on the solid sky, and recalled a John F. Kennedy quote I'd heard in a history

class once, something about how our bodies carry within us the same per-
centage of salt as the ocean—salt in our blood, sweat, and tears. He thought
it was the reason so many of us return to the sea, back to the place from
which we started. The thought only made me shiver.

I heard the sound of car tires on crushed shells, then waited for Matthew to find me, knowing it wouldn't take him long. I stayed where I was,
anticipating his gaze on my back and the sound of his footsteps, which was
now as familiar to me as my own. The back door opened and shut, but I
didn't turn around. I stared at my empty wineglass, forcing myself to remember that I was angry so that I wouldn't betray myself again as soon as
he touched me.

"Ava?" His heavy tread made the dock sway, and I wanted to clutch at
something to steady myself, until I realized the one thing I was looking for
was Matthew.

He stopped in front of me and I finally looked up. He wore an expression of concern and carried a large brown box taped shut at the top.

"This was waiting on the front steps. It's for you."

I barely glanced at the box, needing instead to get my words out before
his hands touched me and I would no longer be able to speak. "You went
through Adrienne's studio and cleared it out without me."

He placed the box behind him on the bench, then sat down next to me
on the dock, his long legs stretched out in front of him. He didn't move
toward me, but I felt his pull just the same, the way the ocean's tides felt the
moon. "I wanted to tell you before you had a chance to see it."

I watched his eyes, wondering whether I could hurt him, too. "I didn't.
John McMahon told me."

A shadow flickered behind his eyes as he regarded me steadily, but he
remained silent.

"He wanted me to let you know that his parents are glad to have Adrienne's sketches, but that it doesn't change anything." I swallowed, waiting
for him to explain to me why, or to ask for an apology, just so I wouldn't
have to continue. Eventually the word slipped past my lips. "Why?"

He took a deep breath, and for a fleeting moment I wondered whether he was using that brief respite to think of something to say that would explain his actions without telling me the truth.

"Because I didn't want you to have to go through all of that, all of those reminders of her." He filled his chest with air again, then slowly let it out. "And I wanted to say good-bye to her by myself. I'd let her go a long time ago, but I think I was holding on to the studio because I wasn't ready to let her go completely." He reached over and took my hand in his, my skin tingling where it met his. "I didn't do it to hurt you."

I didn't look at him, knowing that if I did, all would be forgiven. "But it still hurts that you'd make that decision after we talked about it."

"You're right. I didn't consider your feelings and I'm sorry. They were just preliminary sketches—nothing complete. And definitely nothing valuable, and I just wanted them out of there. It's done, Ava. I made Adrienne's parents happy, and you've got your potting shed. Can we put this behind us now?"

A strong breeze fanned the marsh grass, bringing with it the smell of the ocean, salty and wild. A tremor shuddered across my shoulders, but I closed my eyes against it and faced instead the darkest part of my mind where my fears lived, tucked away and hidden like a secret. "Did you find anything else? Any clue that might tell you why Adrienne left that night or where she was heading?" I thought of the faceless images of the baby and the words engraved on her tombstone. *Mother of unborn children.* Even in my anger, I couldn't bring that up now.

His hand slid from mine, the absence of his warmth more terrifying than the thick and heavy water that surrounded us. "Did John tell you to ask me that?"

"No. I'm asking because I want to know."

"Why, Ava? Why are you always looking backward when all I want to do is move forward?"

I stood, too drained to explain to him what he should have already known: that I must have been born looking behind me, searching for what pursued me, for what waited around the corner, for my elusive shadow sister. I'd learned very early on that if you only looked ahead, you might miss what was right there behind you, waiting to be revealed.

Matthew stood, too, and placed his hands gently on my face. "I'm sorry, Ava. You're right. And you have every right to ask that question. But don't you think that if I'd found something I would have told you? Wouldn't I want to erase any doubt in your mind that I had anything to do with her accident?"

Anger simmered inside me, charring the edges of my other emotions. "You can't erase the past, Matthew. If you think you need to just to protect me, then stop. I'm stronger than you seem to think I am."

An odd look came into his eyes, and I was reminded of something he'd said to me about Adrienne the night of Tish's party. *She told me once that sometimes when I looked at her it was like I was seeing a ghost instead.* Looking at him now, I thought I understood what she meant. Quietly I asked, "What were you hoping to find, Matthew?"

His hands dropped to his sides. "I love you, Ava. Isn't that enough?"

I thought of the time I'd fallen through the ice covering our backyard pool. I'd never gone near it in the summer, but I somehow thought I could conquer my fear if I could walk on top of it. My mother had jumped in wearing her silk dress and pearls to pull me out before I'd had a chance to gulp in a single mouthful of water. She didn't say a word to me as she dried me off and put me to bed in a warm, dry nightgown and let me eat chicken soup on a bed tray. I hadn't even understood why she'd bothered to jump in to save me until I'd heard her sobbing outside my door long after she thought I was asleep.

"No," I said, realizing how much truth a single word could carry.

He regarded me silently for a long moment, his thoughts unreadable. "I'm not going to ask why you were with John McMahon, but I hope you'll tell me. He's not somebody I would want you to cultivate a friendship with." I saw the anger in his eyes before he turned around and went back to the house, the door slamming shut behind him.

I swallowed the thick ball of tears that had formed in my throat, and wondered what I was supposed to do next. I'd never argued with my fiancé, Phil, and maybe that was why I hadn't ever felt like I should marry him, as if neither one of us possessed convictions worth arguing about.

My gaze settled on the box Matthew had brought out to me, and for the first time I saw the company name stamped on the outside of the box: NADENE COSMETICS. It had to have come from home, since I couldn't imagine anybody else I knew using a mortuary supply box to ship anything to me.

Grateful to escape the dock and the murmur of water, I scooped up my empty wineglass, then managed to pick up the box and carry them both inside to the kitchen before depositing them on the kitchen table. I was disappointed to find that the room was empty, remembering the advice imparted by my sisters-in-law about never going to bed angry. But what had transpired between Matthew and me was much deeper than anger. It was more of a rupture at our foundation, releasing questions and doubts that were easily transformed and disguised by love.

I moved through the silent house to the foyer, feeling the emptiness around me. I looked out the front windows and saw that Matthew's car was gone. I swallowed again and straightened my shoulders, imagining my mother watching and waiting for me to admit that she was right.

Walking resolutely back to the kitchen, I grabbed the large flashlight out of the walk-in pantry, then flipped on the back floodlights before heading toward Adrienne's studio. I'd been too angry to go there after Matthew had cleared it out, but now I felt a strong need to see it myself.

It was still bright enough outside to observe that the boards had been pulled from both windows, allowing the twilight to seep inside the dusty space as I stepped over the threshold. The canvases and easels were gone, as was the large table. Freestanding shelves holding an assortment of clay pots in all sizes now sat against one wall. Rows of hooks had been added to boards attached to the wall opposite the door, and from them hung spades and trowels, a shovel and a rake, and other gardening implements—some of which even I wasn't familiar with. Bags of fertilizer and potting soil were lined up like soldiers on a wooden pallet to keep away the moisture and bugs, and the windows had been cleaned of their grime.

I walked closer to the tools and flipped on the flashlight to see better, and noticed that most of the handles were red, and the trowel was all red except for the wooden part in the middle. It would have taken Matthew a long time to drive from place to place, since red handles were hard to find, and when I pictured him searching for gardening tools in my favorite color, my anger began its slip into guilt.

The door to the narrow stairs sat open, but I didn't venture up them. I remembered Matthew telling me how Adrienne was afraid of ghosts, and wondered whether it was this place that had made her think of the presence of the dead. It was all around me here, and I found myself expecting the fall of feet coming down the stairs, or the brush of a hand on my arm.

"Ava?"

I jumped, nearly dropping the flashlight. I turned to find Matthew silhouetted in the doorway, and for a brief moment I thought he was some-body else, somebody else whose presence I welcomed.

He walked slowly into the room, the dim light from the doorway behind him casting his face in darkness.

"You did all this. For me."

I felt him nod. "But I should have waited. It's just . . ."

I didn't speak, knowing he'd keep his thoughts inside as long as possi-ble, sifting them like flour, until the right ones came out. It was one of the few things I'd had to learn about him.

"I needed to do something. To keep my thoughts occupied." He sighed, and I felt the heaviness of his thoughts. "I had a patient suicide yesterday. A sixteen-year-old boy. I needed . . ."

I walked toward him and took his hands in mine. "Shhh. I'm so sorry. You have me now, all right? And I won't break; I promise. You can tell me these things. Maybe it will make it easier for you."

I walked into his arms like wind through water, and pressed my face into his chest, his scent again part of me.

"I'm not used to that. Needing help. I'm supposed to be the doctor with all the answers. The one who doesn't fail."

Pulling back, I pressed my finger against his lips. "You're human, Mat-thew. And I'm your wife—here to share the good with the bad. We said vows to that effect, remember? Don't try to protect me."

He nodded as my lips replaced my finger. He drew me toward him, and I allowed myself to be enveloped in his embrace. And in the moment before I closed my eyes, the flashlight caught on the corner of the wall by the stairs, where kudzu vines had begun to work themselves into a crack along the wall, climbing upward like a spider, relentless in its advance, like the doubt that crept around my skull and took root in my chest where my heart beat.

Gloria

Antioch, Georgia
May 2011

The morning birds chatted and argued in the branches of the pawpaw tree as I sat in the meager shade of my broad-brimmed hat, humming an old lullaby whose words I still remembered enough to be able to sing to my grandbabies. It made me think of the scarred music box Ava had found after the great tornado that had flattened towns across Alabama and Georgia, but had spared us so we could be a repository for lost things.

I'd never been one to collect antiques or dead people's belongings, not able to quite get over the fact that they were somehow tainted. It was like I thought that old age and death were contagious. I've since learned that there's some truth to that, but even back then I couldn't understand Ava's fascination with the tune from the old music box, or her ability to sing words to it she'd never heard before.

But it figures that Mimi would be the one to give the music box to Ava to take with her to St. Simons. The two of them had always been in cahoots, partners in crime. Secretly, I was glad of this, as if their bond—which couldn't have existed without me—somehow mitigated my inability to be the mother I wanted to be.

"Damn this heat," I said, fanning my blouse for the fiftieth time where beads of sweat had begun to trickle down my chest.

Mimi lay on the chaise longue, her blond hair pulled back by a large pink terry-cloth headband with an oversize bow, making her look like Cindy Lou Who. Her eyes were closed, her *People* magazine splayed open on her chest like a dead bird. My mother, who was only months shy of her ninety-second birthday, still felt compelled to sun herself for a short while each morning to "get some color." What she was really doing was getting more wrinkles, but I figured telling her would be a lot like watering a tree long after a fire has come along and burned it to the ground.

"If you're going to complain about the heat, you should garden at night." She hadn't even opened her eyes to speak.

I turned back to my plastic bags filled with paper towels soaking in water. The UPS store said they could ship anything, so I was about to find out. Carefully, I laid out my roses and forget-me-nots, hoping they'd make Ava homesick. But it was more than that, too. With each plant, clipping, and seedling I wrapped, I wanted my daughter to think of me and to remember that no matter what words went spoken or unspoken between us, we'd worked shoulder to shoulder in this garden. I needed her to remember that, regardless of how many times she told me that she wanted only a *useful* garden full of things to eat. Not that she knew how to cook them. I had failed her in that department entirely.

I knew Mimi sent Ava those albums, but I pretended that I didn't know. My mother had always liked playing with fire, believing that the heat would meld us into the real people we are inside, like melting gold to make jewelry. When I was old enough to understand this about her, I was a married woman with a baby about to be born, and I told her she was full of manure. I've long since learned that she was right, but I would never tell her so.

"Hello?"

I looked up to see Kathy, David's wife. She wore what Ava referred to as "mom jeans" with an elasticized waist that highlighted the backside of a woman past her prime. She always wore button-down blouses in various hues and sleeve lengths, but without variation despite her tucking them into skirts or pants or, in this case, mom-jean capris. I almost turned to my side to whisper a comment, as if Ava were still there, but stopped myself just in time.

"Hi, Kathy." I sat back on my knees, noting with dismay that she carried her gardening gloves.

Mimi raised a languorous hand in greeting.

"June mentioned you were sending clippings from your garden to Ava, and I thought I might be able to help."

"That's sweet of you, Kathy," Mimi said. "Gloria's getting too old to be working out in the sun."

I sent my mother a withering glance. "I'm fine—it's just been such a warm spring that it's like we skipped it entirely and went directly to summer." I patted the spot next to me. "I was working on the roses. Why don't you take over and I'll go get us some sweet tea."

I made my way to the kitchen, nearly gasping in the cool air-conditioning. Kathy was a good and dutiful daughter-in-law, but her hands were big like mine, her knowledge of the soil too limited and based on what she'd read instead of what she felt. Despite her good intentions, she was a poor substitute for Ava.

I washed my hands, then moved to the refrigerator and pulled out a pitcher of tea and a lemon to slice, pausing as I noticed the answering machine on the counter blinking. Closing the refrigerator with my hip, I placed the lemon and pitcher on the counter before retrieving a knife from the drawer.

Ignoring the incessant blinking, I slowly and methodically cut into the yellow skin, making perfectly equal slices before placing them in the bottoms of three glasses I'd filled with ice. Then, very carefully so as not to drip down the pitcher, I poured each glass near the top, then set them on a tray. I picked up the tray and was almost at the back door before I stopped.

With a heavy sigh, I placed the tray on the counter, then moved to the answering machine, my finger hesitating only briefly before pressing the "play" button.

"Mama? It's me. Ava. Can you pick up?"

Music from a radio played in the background, one of those new songs with the heavy beat that gave me headaches.

"I'd like to talk with you. I have some questions. If you're there, could you please pick up?"

The music continued, but faded slightly, and I imagined Ava walking with the phone as she always did. Since she was a toddler she'd been in perpetual motion, a restlessness dogging her as if she were making up for something lost. Then I heard the sound of a door opening and closing, and I knew she was standing outside. If I took a deep breath, I would probably smell the evening primrose of the summer marsh.

"I just wanted to know if you knew the McMahons." I felt her breathe in the small space before finding the next words. "Adrienne McMahon was Matthew's first wife. John is her brother. I haven't met the parents yet. But they took in a boy, Jimmy Scott, when his family was killed in a fire. I met him last week, at the cemetery at Christ Church. . . ."

There was a long pause and I thought she'd hung up. But then she spoke again. "Anyway, I was just wondering if you knew them, because . . . I don't know. I guess I just wanted to talk to you and I thought that would be a good place to start." There was only a brief silence this time and then just the simple words, "Call me."

When I hit the "delete" button my hand was shaking. I placed my hand on the phone and even lifted it and dialed the first number of the area code. But then reason took over and I slid it back into the cradle. What could I say to her that I hadn't already said? How could I make her understand that sometimes loving too much can be worse than not loving enough?

I opened the back door leading from the kitchen to the back patio, then lifted the tray, trying to still my hands so they wouldn't rattle the glasses too much. I set the tray on the table near Mimi, adjusting the umbrella so that it covered the iced tea but didn't cast a shadow on her upturned face, then returned to my garden, where the soil felt solid beneath my fingers, and the order of things was dictated by the sun and moon and not by the will of a human heart.

CHAPTER TWELVE

Ava

St. Simons Island
June 2011

I sat at the kitchen table in the milky white light from the large window. An early-morning mist hovered close to the earth, creating apparitions of the trees and brush, an optical illusion of branches growing in air and reaching toward the empty sky like a child's arms. I smoothed my shirt over my stomach, thinking of Adrienne and her unborn children, of the sketches of the faceless child, and turned my head from the window.

After nearly a month of little rain, we'd been saturated with almost two days straight of downpours and incessant drizzle. The absence of the sound of dripping water had awakened me, and I'd arisen to make coffee and wait to see whether the sun would come up and dry everything out enough for Matthew and me to take a leisurely bike ride around the island.

The steam from my coffee cup curled around my face as I took a long sip and eyed the stack of envelopes I'd retrieved from the drugstore with my developed photographs inside. I felt a little guilty, since I hadn't yet bothered to take the albums out of the box Mimi had sent me. I'd sliced open the top, but once I'd seen what lay inside I had immediately lost interest. I knew what was in those albums, knew that whatever it was I hoped to find wouldn't be found within the pastel-bound albums of my own childhood.

Moving aside the stainless-steel napkin holder and salt and pepper shakers—all new replacements—I moved the envelopes closer and selected the first one off of the stack. These photos were taken at what appeared to be a high school football game, with a poor-quality camera that left the images grainy and dark. I slid the garbage can closer to me and dumped the envelope inside before picking up the second one.

These were also easily thumbed through—random pictures of fields and fences, photographs a surveyor might have taken, perhaps, or maybe a person taking stock of a recent inheritance. I dumped those in the trash, too, without further thought. I didn't like to make up stories to attach to the pictures. Once I'd seen them, I lost interest. I was like a person sorting through a box after a move, searching for a half-remembered item, certain only that what she was looking for had not yet been found.

The anticipation I felt in opening every envelope slowly dissipated with each one, until I finally slid the remaining ones to the side before standing to get another cup of coffee. I heard Matthew coming down the steps, the creaks and groans of the wood as familiar to me now as the voice of a loved one.

I poured another cup and waited for him in the kitchen. He appeared, wearing bike shorts and a T-shirt, his tanned, muscular legs bare, his feet encased in socks and biking shoes. His mouth tasted of toothpaste as he bent to kiss me, accepting the coffee cup at the same time.

"Good morning," he said, his face still pressed against mine, our noses touching.

"Good morning," I replied, nibbling his lower lip gently between my teeth.

He leaned back to take a sip of coffee, his eyes dark and brooding, reminding me of our arguments about Adrienne's studio. And the making up that had lasted most of a night, but that hadn't completely eradicated the dark shadow of doubt.

"Ready for our bike ride? We should go now, before it decides to start raining again, and definitely before it gets too hot."

"Sure," I said, taking a sip of coffee and dumping the rest in the sink. "Give me a couple of minutes and I'll be right back." I ran upstairs to quickly change, then returned to find Matthew already outside, our bicycles side by side.

As Matthew and I settled on our bikes, he said, "I thought we'd go to Fort Frederica first, then head north on Lawrence Road until it ends. How does that sound?"

I nodded, eager to spend a relaxing day with my new husband, away from the house and the tabby structure in the back and all the secrets it wouldn't relinquish. I'd hung curtains inside, and brought in a large potting table that I'd painted a bright red. But I still couldn't seem to get Adrienne to leave, her presence like a midday shadow that stayed behind me no matter where I turned.

I'd finally gone upstairs to the windowless room, devoid of even a single stick of furniture. Matthew said that before the house was a studio, the upper portion had been used for storage. But whatever had been in there had long since been cleaned out, leaving only dust and cobwebs. The only light filtered up from the stairway, enough to illuminate the far wall, where the chimney from the fireplace below traveled up to the roof. It was made of large stones, creating an almost mosaic look to the tabby wall. A rustling noise had scurried around the perimeter of the room, and I quickly backed down the stairs and shut the door behind me, relieved to have an excuse to leave the oppressive silence and the feeling of unseen eyes on me.

Matthew and I headed down our drive, then through narrow streets as we made our way toward Frederica Road. The streets were deserted, allowing me to take in the scenery and the sides of the road covered with the coarse black needle rush. Matthew explained that the needle rush was an indicator plant for lower salt concentration, as if all water weren't just water; as if the level of the salt made it less dangerous.

I was so busy examining the foliage that I was surprised when I looked up to find ourselves on a tree-lined street with small shops on either side. Matthew stopped his bike and got off of it, and I did the same.

He reached for my hand, then pulled me to a live oak tree, and I understood why we'd made this detour. "It's a tree spirit," he said.

I nodded, unable to look away, the same sick feeling in my stomach that I'd felt the time I'd seen the first one at Murphy's Tavern. "Yes," I said. "It's beautiful."

It was, I had to admit. This one looked like an old sailor, with a long beard and mustache. But it was his eyes that arrested my attention. They were mere slits, as if in the midst of drowning he was closing his eyes for the last time. I shifted my gaze, studying the ridges and lines of the trunk instead, wondering how long the tree had stood there growing while the world changed above its widespread roots, and people lived and died while the tree remained.

Feeling unnerved, I turned my back. "Come on," I said, remounting my bike. "I want to see the fort."

We veered left at a Y in the road, staying on Frederica Road, passing Christ Church and the cemetery and eventually reaching the old fort about one-quarter mile past it.

We parked our bikes and, at Matthew's suggestion, skipped the visitors' center and followed our own walking tour of the old village and fort. He claimed that as a native he knew as much about the fort and the surrounding ruins of the village as any park service employee. After half an hour, I had to agree.

We followed a sandy path pocked with puddles and identified by markers as Broad Street that led from the interpretive center to the fort facing the Frederica River. We held hands, meandering over a boardwalk that crossed over a giant muscadine grapevine that Matthew said was thought to be more than two hundred years old. We stopped at the ruin of Captain James McKay's house, my attention captured by an enormous live oak tree behind it. A long line of lighter wood from a lightning strike bisected the trunk from top to bottom, calling to mind storms and frothy waves and a sky the color of slate. I shivered and Matthew put his arm around me.

"Somebody walking over your grave?" he asked, his tone light.

Mimi had once said the same thing to me, but I'd never before thought the words could be true. Needing to change the subject, I pointed up to the green ferns clinging to the trunk of the tree. "What's that? I haven't noticed them before."

"That's because when there's no rain, they turn brown and curl up and sort of hibernate until the next rain so you don't really see them. Then they green up and unfurl, drinking in the moisture they find on their host trunk. They can actually live for one hundred years without water. I'm sure there's a scientific name for them, but I've never heard them called anything else besides resurrection ferns."

"Resurrection ferns," I repeated slowly, liking the name and the way they cheated death, returning to start over.

Woodpeckers were everywhere, attracted by the thousands of insects that lived inside all of the ancient trees that now covered the old fort and village. The birds had probably always been there, nesting, feeding, mating, without noticing the gradual emptying of the village, the footprint of time pressing down on the town below them. And the resurrection ferns dying and being reborn, their beginnings and endings interchangeable.

We made our way past the abandoned ruins of the tabby barracks and out toward the edge of the water, where the cannons still stood lined up, ready to shoot at approaching enemy ships. I kept my distance from the water's edge, and Matthew stayed with me.

"It's beautiful here," I said, taking in the river and the encroaching marsh, the ancient trees with their shawls of moss, the ghosts of old buildings that sat unseeing under the blue sky, their roofs long since relegated to the wind. It *was* beautiful, but in an uncanny and familiar way that I couldn't explain.

"I thought you'd like it. I'm glad." He squeezed my hand, then kissed me lightly on the lips, lingering there for a moment before pulling back.

I faced the water, allowing a stiff breeze to lift the hair from my temples. Resting my head against his shoulder, I said, "I'm two weeks late."

Lifting my gaze to his, I studied his eyes. We hadn't been trying to get pregnant, but we hadn't been *not* trying, either. Still, I felt relief when his eyes smiled. "That's good news. Have you taken a pregnancy test yet?"

I shook my head. "Not yet, but we can pick up a test on our way home."

He let out an uncharacteristic whoop, then lifted me in his arms, twirling me in a circle. "I'm trying not to be too excited until we know for sure, but I'm thrilled."

"Me, too." I smiled up into his face, too caught off guard by my happiness to censor my words. For a few brief moments my restlessness had faded, my reasons for marrying somehow suddenly vindicated. But one looming specter refused to diminish, and I wanted it to go away with the rest of it and leave Matthew and me alone.

Pulling back slightly, I looked up into Matthew's eyes. His own smile started to fade before I'd even uttered a single word, as if we already knew each other well enough for him to be able to tell what I was about to say.

"I saw Adrienne's grave."

He didn't move or flinch.

"Were you the one who ordered the headstone?"

He nodded slowly, his eyes wary. "Yes, I did. Her parents didn't even want to discuss her funeral, much less her headstone."

Drawing in a deep breath, I asked, "What did you mean by 'mother of unborn children'?"

His hands tightened on my upper arms for a brief moment before he suddenly let me go. He shrugged, but there was nothing casual or unplanned about the gesture. "We'd always talked about having children. We both wanted them, but planned to wait until we'd been married for a while first. Actually, I was the one who decided that. She would have been happy to start a family right after we were married."

"And then she died."

There was a brief pause. "Yes. Then she died."

I heard what he didn't say, how he blamed himself for denying Adrienne that one thing she wanted, and how he'd attempted to record her wish for all eternity on her granite headstone. If it were possible, I think it made me love him even more.

I took his hand in mine and led him away from the river and to the path. We walked back hand in hand, but I felt his distance, as if Adrienne and her unborn children walked between us.

He stopped once to kiss me, his hand on the flat of my stomach, and I smiled up at him. Then the clouds returned to cover the sun, the rain emitting a soft and persistent drizzle that drenched without cooling, creating shadows where none had been before.

Pamela

St. Simons Island
October 1810

Our man Zeus rowed Jemma and me in the small dugout through the creeks and estuaries around St. Simons. We'd been to Sapelo Island for nearly two days helping deliver a set of twins for Amy St. Claire. It had been a difficult birth, the infant boy's shoulder blocking the birth canal and preventing his sister from being born. Jemma had massaged the woman's belly, rearranging the girl so that she wasn't pressing on her brother, then reached in to gently pop the boy's shoulder to allow him to slide out like a cork from a jug, resetting the shoulder as easily as plucking feathers from a chicken. I hoped the twins' relationship would not be as adversarial in the future as it had started out. I thought of my relationship with Georgina, and fate's finger that had chosen her to be my sister.

The change of season had come again to St. Simons, stealing the colors from the earth, replaced by shades of yellow and straw as the cordgrass went to seed, the wind dusting golden powder out over the marsh. The days were shorter, and as Zeus's oars slapped the water I looked up to see the night sky greeting the day sky, bright pinpoints of stars already spreading their canopy over us.

My father had read the night sky as a blind person would touch the face of a loved one, and I delighted in our time spent together poring over the stars as they appeared one by one. As a descendant of mariners, he knew about navigating by stars, about how the ancient Greeks and Romans had once steered their ships by the same constellations we could see today. It fascinated me to know the sky remained the same, gazing down at our changing world, at the endless ebb and flow of the oceans' tides, of lives beginning and ending. It made me feel insignificant yet at the same time part of the universe, feeling connected to one not yet born who might one day gaze up at these same stars.

A cool hand grasped my arm, and I straightened, realizing I had been half-asleep and liable to fall into the water. I sent Jemma a grateful smile, then looked past Zeus to see how close we were to our landing. I knew these waterways as if they were roads, knew the colors of each season as if they were dresses from my own wardrobe. There was something about this place that became part of you, and I sometimes wondered whether the salt water around me was what flowed inside me in my sweat and tears, marking me as a part of it. This comforted me when I thought of my own barren womb and the stillborn and buried children I had witnessed in my few short years on earth. Maybe there was no end, but merely a winding ribbon of water that brings us from this life to the next.

A hand waved in the murky distance and my heart leaped. "Geoffrey," I shouted, waving back, glad to have a physical movement to fully awaken me. The day had been warm, but the night was cool. My dress had clung to me with clammy sweat, but now I found myself shivering. I had been in such a rush to reach the laboring Mrs. St. Claire that I had brought only my summer shawl. "Please hurry, Zeus. It is so cold I am afraid I might catch my death."

He nodded, the whites of his eyes bright against the growing dark around us. The dugout rode lower in the water now than it had at the start of our journey as cedar absorbed water, making it harder to row. But all I could think about was my need to reunite with my husband.

As we neared the dock, I saw the slight cloaked figure standing behind Geoffrey, the brightness of her hair in stark contrast to her hood. My heart sank with disappointment; I hated having to curtail my joy in seeing Geoffrey, knowing I could not kiss him as I would like in Georgina's presence.

The scent of damp leaves and moist earth permeated the air like a newly dug grave. We had had a brief shower while crossing open water, but the dock here was stained a dark brown, and the tall grasses hung low with plump, glistening drops of rain. I knew the resurrection ferns would be almost near to bursting, verdant and full of moisture. I loved pointing them out to Jemma, who never tired of the tiny miracle taking place on the trunks of the trees around her.

Geoffrey held the dugout against the dock while Zeus lifted Jemma out, then helped me and my portmanteau onto the dock. My husband lifted my hand and kissed it, the thrill of his touch as startling as if we had been separated for two hundred days instead of only two.

"Everything went well, I trust?" he asked, tucking my hand into the crook of his arm as Jemma took my bag.

"Yes, blessedly so. Although the St. Claires already have six children; I cannot imagine how they will fit this seventh and eighth into their small house."

I had not meant to sound bitter, and only a squeeze from Geoffrey's hand told me that he had heard and was not condemning me for it.

"Georgina," I said. "How kind of you to come greet me. All is well with you, I hope?"

Nathaniel Smith had been courting her in earnest for nearly two years, ever since my conversation with him. Every day I hoped for some settlement between them, and not just for their sakes. I loved my sister, but I had grown to want my husband and son to myself without the hovering presence of another woman in the house.

Geoffrey had accepted the courtship, but only at my urging, and even tolerated Nathaniel's presence at our dining table on occasion. Still, no marriage plans had been announced, and I was afraid that Georgina would never marry if she didn't accept Nathaniel or move to Savannah—neither of which she seemed willing to do.

"I am well, thank you. I thought that Geoffrey might want the company, having no exact idea of the time you would be returning. He has been standing out here half the day, making himself sick with worry." Her voice was teasing, but there was another note there, too, something that reminded me of our childhood, when Georgina had complained to our father that I had won again at a game of scotch-hopper.

Geoffrey patted my hand that was curled into the crook of his elbow.

"In my defense, I was not out here all day, but only part of it. I brought Robbie once, as the boy is missing you sorely. He is asleep now in Leda's care, but I promised him that as soon as you returned you would go see him and at least kiss him on his cheek if he is sound asleep."

I rested my head against his cloak as we walked, feeling the scratch of wool against my cheek, my heart too full to count all of my blessings at once.

Geoffrey retired to his desk and his pipe in the small library with assurances that he would not linger too long, while I climbed the stairs to Robbie's room. I was surprised to find Georgina following me into my son's room instead of going to her own. It was full dark now, and I lifted my lamp high to see better, turning to Georgina with a finger to my lips when I saw Robbie's eyes were closed, his long, dark eyelashes fanning his soft cheeks.

Leda stirred from the straw pallet on the floor by the small child's bed Geoffrey had made. It had the faces of horses carved into the headboard and footboard, and although Robbie was fast outgrowing the bed, he was loath to part with it. I had long since warned Geoffrey that he would spend a lifetime carving bigger and bigger beds with horse faces for our son until we succumbed and got him a horse of his own.

"He be a good boy, Miz Pamela. Just an angel."

"Thank you, Leda." I looked behind her to the doorway where Jemma stood, silently watching, waiting to help Leda down the stairs. She was good that way, anticipating what needed to be done before I thought to ask her. She was the same in the birthing room, which was why I had come to rely on her more and more.

I leaned over my sleeping boy, shielding his face from the brightest light from the lamp. He was his father's child, all dark hair and blue eyes, the roundness of his face and limbs not quite hiding the sharpness of the bones beneath. He held our hearts in his chubby hands, and my breath caught in my throat every time I thought of him riding a horse, or growing too big for my arms to hold. I pressed my lips against his cheek, smelling his sweet little-boy scent, then straightened to find Georgina watching me, an odd glint in her eyes.

I moved the lamp, relieved to see that it had been only my imagination. But as I made to move past her, she touched my arm.

"I need to speak with you," she whispered. "In confidence."

Moving away from the sleeping child, I paused by the door. "Of course. You know you can speak to me about anything. We are sisters."

The sound of her swallowing seemed loud in the quiet room, punctuated only by Robbie's soft and rhythmic breathing. "I need you to make a tea. With pennyroyal."

The clock in the downstairs hall chimed softly, five minutes fast as always. No clockmaker had been able to repair it, and we had simply become accustomed to deducting five minutes each time it chimed. I stared at my sister.

"Pennyroyal? But that is . . ." I couldn't say it. "Do you need it for pain during your courses?" I dared not think of why else she might need it.

"No. It is not for discomfort."

My throat grew tight. "Then why do you need it?"

Her eyes were hard. "It is not for me. It is for a poor soul who has had to fend off the unwanted attentions of an overseer. She does not want to bear his child or the shame."

I glanced over at the sleeping form of my only son, the emptiness of my womb his sibling and my constant companion. I could not do what Georgina asked of me. I could not. I shook my head. "I cannot kill an unborn child. You cannot ask this of me."

"Is it not a sin that has put her in that condition? A sin that she was forced to commit? The pennyroyal would only right a wrong."

"No, Georgina." I shook my head again, as always at a loss in any argument with her. She was so forceful that until that moment I did not think I had ever not let her have her way. "Two sins will not make this right. I cannot and will not help you."

She lifted her head so that the light from the lamp hit the bottom of her chin, deflecting the light and casting each eye in shadow. "I know where you keep the pennyroyal in the root cellar, and where it is grown in your garden. You and Mother with your clever skills in the garden, ignoring me because I could not bear to get my hands dirty long enough to learn what the shapes of leaves meant. But I learned—enough, anyway, to make a useful tea." She took a deep, shuddering breath. "I thought you would want to help, but I see my faith in you was misguided."

She opened the door and stepped out into the hallway, but I grabbed her elbow, the movement making the light from the lamp cast apparitions on the wall behind her. "You need to know what you are doing. The amount of the pennyroyal leaves you infuse for a tea has to be exact. Any more can kill a person. Can you not understand that?"

Georgina turned to me, her voice a low hiss. "I understand, but do *you*? I only know that this woman will do whatever she needs to do, even if it kills her. She is that desperate. And if you will not help her, then I suppose I will have to do my best."

I listened as Geoffrey's footsteps crossed the hall downstairs, heading toward the stairs. Turning to Georgina, I felt my own despair, my own inability to say no to her reason. "I will help you. I cannot sit idly by and allow you to kill both the mother and child." Glancing in the direction of the stairwell, I whispered, "Meet me in the kitchen house tomorrow morning after Leda has cleaned the breakfast dishes. I will show you how to make a tea and the proper dosage. But that is all I will do."

She smiled brightly, as if I had just given her a present she'd been coveting. "Thank you, Pamela. I knew I could make you understand."

We both turned as Geoffrey came to the top of the stairs, bringing with him the scent of pipe tobacco, his candle flickering from his movement. He said good night to Georgina, then held out his hand to me. I gave my lamp to my sister, then slipped my hand into my husband's and allowed him to lead me into our bedroom. I felt Georgina's gaze on my back as I began to close the door, Geoffrey's free hand already on the hooks at the back of my gown. A cool breeze swept up the stairs behind us, bringing with it the smell of ashes and extinguishing the candle, throwing us into darkness as the door clicked shut.

CHAPTER THIRTEEN

Ava

St. Simons Island
June 2011

With bare hands I pressed the potting soil around the roots of the fragrant ginger lily, making sure I'd gone all the way around the plant squeezing out the air just like my mother had shown me. It was a showy bloom, tolerated only because it reminded me of my mother's garden and the time we had spent together there. This was the first day off from work I'd had since Matthew's gift of the potting shed, and I was determined to make up for lost time and show my appreciation.

I looked out of the cleaned window and saw the markers for my freshly dug garden, the white of the shaved wood even brighter against the black earth. Tiny tags stuck into the ground next to even tinier green shoots—my herb garden. I told myself that adding fresh herbs to my kitchen concoctions was bound to make them better.

After arranging the snowy white lily on the step below my petunias—another one of my mother's favorites—I straightened to admire the mix of colors of not only the blooms but of the pots as well. I checked my watch and saw that I had another hour before I had to meet Tish at an unmarked cemetery thought to be located in the vicinity of one of the old cotton plantations near the Hampton River. Figuring I could suffer through anything for just an hour, I resolutely opened the back door with the purpose of going through the cookbooks and recipes people had been throwing at me since my marriage and making a menu plan for the week.

I heard the sound of water from upstairs as I entered the kitchen. Matthew had two later appointments in Savannah and would be staying there overnight. I'd considered going with him, since I didn't have to be to work until ten o'clock the next morning, but I was looking forward to cemetery hunting with Tish, and I really needed to figure out what we were going to eat for the rest of the week and head to the grocery store.

My resolve lasted until I spotted the box of photo albums Mimi had sent. I'd placed the box on the floor next to the small desk in the kitchen, hoping it would prompt me to go through them and call Mimi to thank her. Carefully, I lifted the box and placed it on the kitchen table. I yanked a pair of pink-handled scissors—something else I needed to replace—out of a drawer and began to slice through the packing tape on the box.

Wadded newspapers from the *Atlanta Journal-Constitution* huddled on the top like dandelion heads, and I swiped them out of the way to peer underneath. I stared at the pale pink linen cover of the album on top, remembering sitting on Mimi's lap when I was a child while she turned the pages and told me stories of my childhood.

I took the pink album off the top and placed it on the table, knowing this was the first album because of the gold foil lettering Mimi had placed on the cover:

AVA JANE WHALEN

VOLUME 1

DECEMBER 1977 TO DECEMBER 1980

I opened the cover and turned to the first page, where I saw me as a toddler wearing a large red bow one of my brothers had most likely stuck onto

my nearly bald scalp, and sitting under the Christmas tree. I was holding a
rattle in one hand and reaching for a low-hanging branch of the tree with
the other. More photos showed me on my mother's lap or her holding me in
her arms. As I looked more closely, I realized that there were a few pictures
of me being held by my father or Mimi, but mostly by my mother. My
brothers and other relatives would be pictured next to me, with a hand on
me or around me, but I was always with my mother, her hands holding me
around the waist like a shield.

I didn't remember that Christmas, of course, but the pictures showed a
happy family, a normal family by most standards. But even when I was
perched on a lap or held upright, my face was tilted away from the person
holding me, my arms reaching toward something out of the camera's
viewfinder. Flipping back to the cover, I looked to see if I'd skipped a
page, wondering whether I'd missed earlier photographs, or even whether
I remembered ever seeing any. One in a crib, perhaps, or at my baptism. I
suppose being the fifth child made those sorts of pictures redundant. I suppose I should have been happy that I hadn't been dressed in my brothers'
hand-me-downs.

Standing, I took the rest of the albums from the box and placed them
on the table in numerical order. These were Mimi's albums, the same ones
she'd kept on the low shelves in her bedroom and allowed me to pore over
when I was a girl, the pages chronicling my life like a colorized memoir
without words. Mimi told me it was important to remember my happy
childhood, to be able to pluck out memories to smooth over rough patches
once I reached adulthood.

I wondered why she'd sent these, and why there'd been no note. From
the haphazard way they were placed inside the box, it almost seemed like
she'd been rushed. I imagined her, her blond hair half up with her pink
foam rollers, making her decision and acting on it all in the same moment.
I'd inherited that from her, I'd always thought, having been the student
who finished her homework five minutes before it was due, and who
planned to live the rest of her life with a man she'd known for only two
months before marrying him.

I made myself a cup of tea and sat down with the first album, then paged my way through each one, my face beginning to hurt when I realized how much I'd been smiling. I paused at the photographs of Lucy, my dachshund-terrier mix, who'd been rescued from a wet street when I was seven. My mother and I had almost hit her in the car as she huddled shivering in the middle of the road, her sweet brown eyes imploring.

"I think she needs to go home with us," I'd said, trying to keep my voice from rising in excitement, as if those words weren't the most important words I'd ever said to my mother.

"Ava, why on earth would you say such a thing?" Mama hated dogs and took every opportunity to tell us. They shed and they smelled, and—the worst sin—they might dig up the garden.

My mind skidded and raced, trying to come up with a compelling reason that would make my mother get out of the car instead of driving past the trembling ball of fur. Then I remembered something my third-grade teacher had taught us, and though I wasn't exactly sure what it meant, it had sounded profound at the time. "Because sometimes we have to be a hero and do the right thing, even if it's just for one person and even if nobody else notices." I paused. "Even if that person is a dog," I'd added, my fingers crossed tightly as I willed my mother to say yes.

She'd given me a peculiar look, her eyes bright and shining and her face speckled by the shadows of the raindrops on the windshield. Her hands had tightened on the steering wheel for a tiny moment, and then, looking at me one more time, she opened the door and stepped out into the rain without even opening an umbrella. Of all the things that happened that night, that was the oddest. Mama always got her hair done on Wednesdays, and that had been Wednesday night, and I couldn't believe she'd ruined her hairdo in the rain to go pick up a dog because I'd asked her to.

Luckily, Lucy hadn't been in the mood to run, because I don't think my mother would have chased after her. But afterward, even after Lucy had dug up Mama's tulip bulbs or peed on the carpet, it was at Mama's feet Lucy sat while we watched television at night, and it had been my mother who would sneak table scraps to the little dog—something forbidden to the rest of us—during meals. When Lucy died thirteen years later, I don't remember who'd cried harder—Mama or me.

I heard Matthew's footsteps on the stairs, then leaned into him as he stood behind my chair and put his hands on my shoulders. After kissing me good morning, he looked at the album spread open on the table.

"Nice haircut," he said, pointing to my junior-year school picture.

I slapped his hand. "Hey, perms were popular then."

"Where did these come from?" he asked as he made himself a cup of coffee from the new single-serve machine I'd bought. I'd made the decision to replace the coffeemaker after Tish mentioned that the old one had been her wedding gift to Matthew and Adrienne.

"Mimi sent them. They were in that box you brought in." I jerked my chin in the direction of the empty box.

He sat down with his coffee and slid his hand over mine. "I have to get to work, but leave the albums out. I want to look at them when I get back." He squeezed my hand. "I can't wait to see your baby pictures."

I couldn't help the silly grin that sprouted on my face, a regular occurrence since the two pregnancy tests I'd taken had shown two promising and very solid pink plus signs. "Why? So you can laugh at my hairstyles?"

"No. So I can picture what our baby will look like."

I frowned, remembering the missing baby photos. "The albums start when I was a toddler—I'll have to ask Mimi if there are any older ones. But I'm sure there's enough material for you to laugh at."

"Good," he said, before draining his cup and standing. "I'm going to be late if traffic's bad. If I decide to come home tonight, I'll call you."

I slid my chair back and stood. "Don't. I'll be fine, really. I'll be better than fine knowing you're not driving across the bridge at night after a long day of patients."

"What's this?" Matthew was peering into the bottom of the box, where I'd left a layer of wadded newspaper on the bottom. Leaning over, he reached inside and, after a brief rustling noise, brought up something small and pink.

"My dress," I said, feeling almost sick that I might have thrown it out with the box. I took the tiny crocheted garment in my hands, smelling the cedar chest Mimi had kept it in.

"I don't think it still fits," Matthew said, his laughing eyes making a mockery of his serious face.

I smirked. "This was made by Mimi's grandmother, and there's a picture of her wearing it, and my mom wearing it, and one of me—all when we were about two years old. Their pictures are framed in the hallway at my parents' house." I paused, feeling the old hurt again. "There's a space on the wall for mine, but for some reason Mama never hung my picture. I think Mimi stuck it in one of the albums."

"When you find it, we'll get it framed. And when we have our daughter, we'll get her picture taken wearing it, too." An odd look passed over his face. "How do you think she knew you were pregnant?"

"It could have just been a guess, but Mimi's pretty good at guessing."

He ran his finger over the pink knit. "Well, I sure hope it's a girl. Our son will feel foolish wearing a pink dress."

I laughed, and as we began walking to the door, my cell phone rang. I glanced down at it, recognizing the 912 St. Simons area code, but not the number. Thinking it might be Tish's number at Eternal Carnation, I picked up the phone from the table and answered it.

"Hello?" I said.

"Ava? It's John."

I glanced at Matthew, who was clipping his BlackBerry onto his belt.

"Yes. Hello."

"You're probably wondering where I got your phone number. I told Beth—Tish's daughter—that you'd already given it to me but I lost it. I hope you don't mind. I wanted to call you but didn't think it would be cool if I called your house phone."

I looked over at Matthew again, who now stood by the door with his jacket slung over his arm.

"No. Probably not," I said into the phone. "Look, this isn't a good time. . . ."

"I get it. I just was wondering if you'd picked up your pictures yet at the drugstore. I'd love to see them—and I've got some photographs of the island I took that I wanted to show you. I was hoping you'd meet me for lunch."

"Um, sure. Let me call you back."

There was a brief pause, and then, "Okay. You've got my number on your phone now. Call me when you have a minute. Bye." Without waiting for my response, he ended the call.

"Bye," I said into empty space, before putting my cell back onto the table and turning to Matthew.

"Was that Tish?" Matthew asked, putting his arm around me.

"Yes," I said, not even cringing at how quickly the lie came. "She's ready to get started, so I guess I'll be leaving right behind you."

"Take it easy in the heat, okay? Keep hydrated and wear a hat. I know we agreed to wait to tell people, but I think Tish should know you're pregnant so that if you're wilting in the heat, she'll know why and make you stop."

"I do know a few things about pregnancy," I said, smiling. "But I appreciate your concern. I'll tell Tish, if that will make you feel better."

"It will," he said. He gave me a lingering kiss with a promise to call me between patients, then left. I turned away before I could see his car disappear, wondering why I'd lied to him, and why I felt compelled to see John McMahon again. I slowly closed the door, feeling like the woman in a B horror film who walks into the darkened basement, knowing all along that whatever she is going to find won't be what she wants to see.

⤫

I sat at an outdoor table under a painted brick mural at Sandcastle Café in the village, sipping a glass of ice water. I was dying for an iced tea, but as I recommended to all of my patients, I had given up caffeine. I watched as a waiter brought a large pitcher of iced tea to a nearby table, and looked away.

"Sorry I'm late."

I looked up as John McMahon pulled out a chair and sat down across from me, placing a folder carefully on the table.

"Not a problem. I was just early." I took a sip of my water, trying to swallow the ball of guilt. Technically, I hadn't lied to Matthew. Tish had called right after Matthew had left, asking whether we could postpone our meeting until the following day. It had been an easy thing to slide my thumb down to the next "most recent" phone number and click on it. I liked John, but I would have been lying to myself to say that was the only reason I sought out his company. He added flesh to Adrienne's specter, gave her a voice. Matthew wanted to look only forward, but I could not as long as his first wife's death haunted our new marriage and continued to raise doubts in her family's mind. I wasn't naive to think I could prove his innocence and erase all doubts for them. But I had to try.

He looked at the small envelope I'd brought. "Surely that's not all of the pictures. You had about twenty canisters."

I smiled sheepishly. "I know. I threw most of them away—I always do. They weren't anything you'd want to see—trust me. But I kept a few that seemed interesting. I'll eventually throw them out, too."

Our waitress approached and took our orders, but only after I'd pored over the menu and discounted anything that might have mercury or too much salt and preservatives. I ended up with a plate of steamed vegetables that I knew would leave me hungry in a few hours.

When she'd gone, John indicated the envelope. "Can I see?"

"Sure. Although I'm not sure I understand your interest. It's not like I took them myself or it's anybody you know."

He held the envelope and regarded me. "No, but I think what you choose to keep says a lot about you. Maybe even things that you're not aware of." With a grin he opened the flap and slid out the photographs on the laminate tabletop.

Slowly, he studied them, placing each photograph on the table before examining the next. There was nothing remarkable about any of them—a family group wearing the same-colored shirts, gathered in front of a two-story brick Colonial; a bunch of children sitting on a diving board over an aquamarine pool and squinting at the photographer; an Easter-egg hunt with little girls in bonnets and pastel-colored dresses, their small feet in shiny black Mary Janes. I would end up throwing these out, too, but not until I received my next batch of film.

When John was finished he carefully stacked the photos and slid them toward me. "You didn't see why these photos stuck out to you? See any connection between all of these photos?"

"A connection?"

"Yeah, something they all have in common."

I fanned out the photos on the top of the table and studied the faces of strangers, wondering what I was supposed to see, wondering what I'd hoped to find when I'd first discovered the film in a discarded camera. I looked from face to face, then at the backgrounds, looking for something familiar, anything that would make this stupid hobby of mine make sense.

My gaze met John's. "No. Nothing."

John moved the photographs so that they formed an overlapping circle, exposing just enough of each picture to be able to compare them. "Sisters. All of these family groups have what looks to me to be sisters in them. They could actually be cousins or close friends, but in most it's obviously close family members—not that that would really matter if you're just looking for a photograph of an image in your mind you're trying to re-create."

I looked down at the photos again, recognizing immediately what he was seeing and what I must have seen, too. Leaning back in my chair, I smiled. Since my earliest memories, the only thing I've ever really wanted was a sister. Every birthday and Christmas I'd ask for a little sister. I didn't know why I'd been given brothers—all tall and loud boys who shed their hair and dirty laundry in the single bathroom I'd had to share with them when we lived in the same house. I'd studied with envy my friends who had sisters, annoying these same friends by inviting their little sisters on our playdates.

I chewed on the straw in my glass. "That actually makes sense, I guess, in a weird roundabout way." I stared into his cool blue-green eyes, wondering what it was about him that inspired confidences. I continued. "I'd always wanted a sister, which was unrealistic at best, seeing as how my mother was forty when she had me. But when I was eight years old my mother had a stillborn girl. I've never asked, but I'm pretty sure the pregnancy was an accident, and both of my parents had been thrilled. They even bought matching twin canopy beds for my room." I stared out at the passersby on the sidewalk, but saw only the empty bed I'd stared at for a year before the extra twin bed had been removed from my room.

"Mama carried the baby for five months before she lost her. I was there when she miscarried. Just me and Mama—there wasn't time to call for help. They named her Charlene, which is my grandmother's real name, and buried her next to my grandfather." I was thoughtful for a moment. "It's why I became a midwife, actually."

John regarded me silently, and I admitted to myself that I liked that about him. He would listen or allow me to change the subject without being judgmental.

I placed my glass back on the table. "And even though I was so young, I did everything Mama told me to do—got towels, and warm water, and called for an ambulance. Even later, when I thought about it, none of it grossed me out. Didn't even faze me. But Charlene died anyway. I think I grew up thinking that if I just knew more, I could have saved her."

He gave me a soft smile. "I'm a great believer in everything happening for a reason. Think of all the babies you've brought safely into the world because of Charlene."

I watched the waitress as she negotiated around the other tables with our orders in her upraised arms. "Yes," I said. "I think of her every time I help a mother give birth to a healthy baby."

We were silent as the waitress placed our plates on the table and refilled our drinks. Then I indicated the folder he'd brought with him. "Your turn," I said, placing a steamed zucchini in my mouth.

He slid the folder in front of me. "Just don't get food on them, okay?" He winked.

I opened the cover and found myself looking at a black-and-white photo of the St. Simons lighthouse. It was taken from the base looking up, exaggerating the height of the structure, somehow making it more formidable. I looked at the white brick building, trying to identify what looked off to me. Finally, I asked, "Has it always been brick? Seems to me I must have seen a picture somewhere that shows most of the bottom portion made of tabby."

"Must have been an old photograph. The original lighthouse was mostly tabby, but was destroyed by the Confederates when they abandoned the island in 1862. The existing lighthouse was built in 1872."

I stared back at the photo, wondering why it still looked wrong to me. I'd seen it in person on my trip to the pier, but I supposed I'd been too preoccupied at the time to notice that the lighthouse didn't look like it belonged.

"It's a beautiful photograph," I said. "I like your perspective."

"Thank you," he said, looking pleased as I flipped slowly through the photographs. They reminded me in a way of Adrienne's paintings that exhibited her love of the island and its people. John's photographs were of the marsh during different seasons, of shorebirds and driftwood, of sand dunes and sun-bleached houses. But there were people, too, shrimpers with grizzled faces, schoolchildren in a playground, and an elderly couple sitting on the beach holding hands. At Tish's party, John had said that Adrienne had all the talent in the family, but that wasn't true at all.

"You're a real artist, John. You should be trying to market these." My hands faltered as I flipped to the last two remaining photographs. I recognized the subject immediately. They were taken of a younger Adrienne, twelve or thirteen at the most, sitting in sand and staring at something outside of the picture. Her white-blond hair was still baby-fine, her face devoid of makeup but clearly showing the beauty she would grow into as an adult. But there was nothing childish in her expression, nothing that spoke of innocence or childlike dreams.

"You see it, too, don't you?" John asked quietly.

My eyes met his. "See what?"

The corners of his lips tucked into a frown. "Her expression is like an old woman's, isn't it? Like she's already seen too much." He paused. "She always believed that she'd die young. Even as a child, she would tell me that. Strange, isn't it?"

I nodded. "Tish called Matthew an 'old soul.' Maybe that's what Adrienne and Matthew saw in each other."

A shadow passed behind his eyes, and he opened his mouth as if to say something, then stopped. Instead he reached over and stacked his photographs, sliding them back into the folder and hiding them from sight. I waited for him to speak, and when he did I knew he'd changed his mind about what he'd wanted to tell me.

He smiled. "So, how's the project with Tish coming along? She told me something about it when I was in her shop last week picking up flowers for my mom."

"So far, so good—we've only done some preliminary work at Christ Church, but I'm meeting her tomorrow to do a remote site on the Hampton River."

His fingers drummed against the glass of his beer bottle. "Adrienne loved all that historical stuff. She was a member of the society, too." He paused. "Maybe it was because we were adopted, but Adrienne took a real interest in Matthew's family history. Did a lot of research, as a matter of fact. Had everything in a huge briefcase. She said there were lots of skeletons in the Frazier family closet and that it would make a good book. She planned to write it one day, but I guess she ran out of time."

I squirmed a little in my seat, wondering how close I could skate the line bordering morbid curiosity about my husband's late wife and obsession. "What kind of skeletons?"

"I wasn't all that interested at the time, so I pretty much listened with just half an ear, but I do remember a few things." He looked away, but not before I could see the regret that clouded his eyes.

"Like what?" I pressed, too far past the line to skate backward now.

He shrugged. "Well, we all grew up knowing about the Frazier ghost who supposedly roams the beach looking for his unfaithful wife. Adrienne claimed to have seen him once, and he was so real that she could see the lantern that he held. It was probably just some guy with a flashlight, but it was real to her. That was the thing about Adrienne—she had a great imagination. Her book would have been really great."

"Tish said something about Frazier's wife running away with another man. But it was a long time ago, right?" I took a sip of my water, shaking the ice cubes in the bottom.

"It was during the British occupation of the island during the War of 1812. Hard to believe people still care."

"Adrienne did." I thought for a moment. "What happened to her briefcase of notes?"

His eyes focused on his fingers peeling the label off the bottle. "Matthew has it. Or had it. I'm just surprised that he hasn't shown it to you, especially after you joined the historical society. He probably doesn't want you to think there's any stain on his family tree. Although treason is a pretty big stain. And infidelity." He raised his hand to the waitress to bring him another.

John's eyes were cool and unblinking, and I refused to look away. Lifting my chin, I said, "He's probably just forgotten about it. I'll ask him, though, because I'm curious. I can't imagine him wanting to hide something from his family's past. It's not like it has anything to do with him or me."

John leaned forward, his elbows on the table. "You don't think so? Adrienne was a big believer in karma: that we are punished for the sins of the past until we find a way to make penance. She was pretty sure that history was bound to repeat itself until we'd learned whatever lesson we were meant to."

I thought of the resurrection ferns, of their death and rebirth, and of how they could live for one hundred years without water. "You mean she believed in reincarnation of the soul?"

He was quiet for a moment. "Yeah. Something like that."

The waitress brought his beer over and then placed the check on the table. John reached for it and opened his wallet. "My treat," he said. "I appreciate the company of somebody who loves photographs of people and the island as much as I do." He slapped a credit card inside the black folder, then slid it to the edge of the table. "Besides, don't want Matthew suspicious if he sees the bill on your statement."

I leaned forward. "I'm sure he wouldn't be. I'm quite able to come and go as I please. I doubt he'd notice."

"Yes, he would." He made to push away from the table, but I placed my hand on his arm to hold him back.

"You and Matthew were once friends, right?"

He nodded. "Yes."

"Then why do you seek out my company if you think it will upset him?"

After a moment, he said, "Because I do like you. Because I like how you collect the forgotten photographs of strangers. And you like my photographs and think it should be more than a hobby."

I studied him for a moment, not doubting what he was telling me, but knowing, too, that his reasons weren't the main one. Quietly, I said, "I would like to be your friend, John. But a part of me believes that you're trying to either get information from me or you're trying to upset Matthew. And none of it is necessary." I took a deep breath, not yet ready for him to speak. "I know that you and your parents believe Matthew is somehow responsible for Adrienne's death. I don't want to trivialize your feelings, but from what I've heard it was clearly an accident. She was alone. Could it be possible that in your grief, you're just looking for somebody to blame?"

His aqua eyes appeared liquid, like a hot flame behind them was melting them into water. "Ask him where that briefcase is, Ava. Ask him why he didn't like her digging into his family history." He slid his chair out. "And then ask him where her appointment calendar is. She wrote everything in it—not just her appointments. She liked to draw things in it, too, in the margins. When Matthew gave her personal effects to my parents at their request, it wasn't there. He claims he doesn't know where that is, either."

My jaw hurt, and I realized I was clenching my teeth. "That doesn't mean anything, John." But even I could hear the doubt in my words.

We stared at each other for a long moment, our gazes not wavering. John broke contact first, his hand reaching into his back pocket, pulling out a small brown leather pouch secured with a yellow drawstring that he placed on the table between us. "But maybe this does."

I hesitated, then used my index finger to drag the pouch toward me before meeting John's eyes again.

"Go ahead. Open it."

Gingerly, I held the pouch in one hand. It weighed almost nothing, and for a moment I wondered whether it was empty, or held instead something immeasurable, like love or grief. My finger loosened the drawstring, widening the opening, until it hit something small and hard. Hooking my finger into it, I pulled it out into the light, the gold ring perched on my nail and gleaming dully, like a ship drowning in fog.

"It looks like a wedding ring," I said, my voice dry and raspy.

"It is. It's very old, over two hundred years old. It's been passed down in the Frazier family for generations."

I couldn't take my eyes off the ring, noticing the scars of years in minute detail, imagining the hands that had worn it, the things it had witnessed. "Who did it belong to?" I asked, although I didn't need to. I remembered Matthew telling me about a family heirloom wedding ring and how it had been lost. He just hadn't told me by whom.

"Adrienne. It was her wedding ring." He leaned closer. "Look inside," he said. "The inscription has had to be redone several times, but it's what was in it originally."

I squinted, trying to make out the elaborate font inscribed on the inside of the wide gold band, my hand shaking and making it harder to see. But I didn't need to see it; I knew what the word was before I said it out loud. "Forever."

I lowered my hand, placing it over my other hand to stop it from shaking. "Why do you have it?"

"She gave it to me. About a week before she died." He swallowed. "She told me it didn't belong to her."

The ring slid from my hand and landed on the table on its edge so that it began spinning and spinning in dying circles until John placed his hand over it, stilling it completely.

"What did she mean?" I could scarcely hear my own voice.

"I don't know. That's why I kept it. For evidence of something—I just don't know what. Yet. But I will."

I wanted to tell him that the ring and the missing briefcase and diary meant nothing, that they weren't evidence of a conspiracy to hide the truth, whatever it might be. That none of it had anything to do with Matthew. But I stayed silent as he read the unasked questions on my face.

He scooped the ring into his palm, then slipped it back inside the pouch. "And now you know why we think Matthew had something to do with Adrienne's death, either directly or indirectly. All we want is the truth. And I imagine that now you do, too."

Sliding his chair back, John stood. "There's a multineighborhood garage sale next weekend. You might be able to pick up a camera or two." He bent down and kissed my cheek, his lips cool on my hot skin. "I'll be in touch."

I said good-bye, then watched him leave, still feeling the cold, hard metal of the gold ring, recalling how there were no beginnings or endings in a circle, and how sometimes it was impossible to distinguish between the two.

CHAPTER FOURTEEN

Gloria

ANTIOCH, GEORGIA
JUNE 2011

I pushed the buggy past the coolers and red, white, and blue streamers, the triangular boxes of American flags alongside the supersize bags of chips and pork rinds. It was Wal-Mart's nod to the upcoming summer holidays, but it just made me depressed. My brother died in Vietnam, and it seemed almost disrespectful to remember his sacrifice with tortilla chips and salsa.

Mimi walked in front of me, moving much faster than any ninety-one-year-old had a right to. My knees and back ached from working in the garden, but I'd refused Mimi's suggestion that I use one of those motorized scooter buggies at the front of the store. I knew she was just being spiteful because of the stack of Depends coupons I'd pressed into her hand as we'd entered the store. It had taken both of us to haul the large bags of adult undergarments into the buggy, but we'd managed.

I followed my mother into the condiment aisle just as I began to hear Frank Sinatra belting out the song "New York, New York." Mimi stopped and began fishing around in her oversized purse as the song got louder and louder. After finding her cell phone, she squinted through the lower portion of her bifocals to see the screen. She looked up at me. "It's Ava."

I rolled my eyes. The boys had bought Mimi her first cell phone for Christmas. I didn't know what a ninety-one-year-old needed a cell phone for, but she'd been delighted. Most of her friends were already dead, so she used it mostly to annoy me with incoming calls from her grandchildren and great-grandchildren. It's not like she could read the numbers to make a call anyway, but the incoming calls were frequent enough to make me begin to dislike Old Blue Eyes.

I leaned as far to the side as I could so I wouldn't have to squat down or bend over, trying to check the prices on the various brands of ketchup. I'd taught Ava and all of my daughters-in-law that just because you had a coupon didn't mean it was going to save you money. Despite my instruction, I don't think Ava had clipped a coupon in her life, or actually noticed a price tag in the grocery store. She was like Mimi that way, always spur-of-the-moment, without giving too much forethought to any activity. Like marriage.

"She wants to know why I put the pink dress in the box, Gloria."

I busied myself straightening a shelf tag, focusing on the numbers without seeing them at all.

Mimi continued her conversation. "I didn't put it in there, Ava. I only put the albums in the box. I have no idea how the pink dress got in there."

I felt my mother's gaze like a hole being burned into the side of my head.

"Hold on, sweetheart. Let me get your mother on the phone."

I froze, my hands full of two jumbo containers of ketchup. I shook my head, but Mimi just stood there with her tiny phone held out to me. I had no use for cell phones, and certainly not in the middle of a Super Wal-Mart. I turned and stuck the bottles in the cart, then heard Ava's voice, small and tiny, as if it were coming from another world. In many ways, I suppose, it was.

"Mama? Can I just talk to you for a second?"

A flashback of the rainy night we'd rescued our dog, Lucy, swept through my mind. I recalled her small voice that carried thoughts too big for such a small girl, and how she'd crossed her fingers thinking I couldn't see. All these years later I still hadn't told her that luck had nothing to do with crossed fingers, but everything to do with opening your heart a little wider to see what would fall in. I suppose I was afraid to tell her that, not wanting her to learn the consequences: that the more you held inside your heart, the more you had to lose.

I took the phone, then pressed it against my ear. My clip-on earring dug into the side of my head, reminding me again of one of the reasons I hated the phone.

"Hello, Ava. Is everything all right?"

"Yes, Mama. Matthew and I are doing great."

She paused and I pictured her chewing on her nails or biting her lips, two nervous habits she'd had her entire life—I had no idea where they came from.

"I have some news and I wanted you to be the first to hear. We're not telling anybody else yet, but I wanted you to know."

I didn't say anything, not wanting to ruin it for her, although I already knew. "Yes?"

"I'm pregnant. Dr. Clemmens—that's my new boss and my obstetrician—says the baby's due date will be around February twelfth. Your birthday."

I squeezed my eyes shut and turned my head away from Mimi, who was pretending to study the sales flyer we'd picked up at the front of the store. "That's wonderful, Ava. I would love to share my birthday with your baby."

"With your grandchild," she corrected. "I think it's a girl, too. I know it's too early to tell, but I just have a feeling it's going to be a girl."

I blinked back tears and swallowed so she couldn't tell I was crying. "It's been a long time since I bought anything little and pink."

I felt her smile through the phone. "Thanks for the crocheted dress."

"Yes, well, I figured you'd need it eventually, and it's time I began cleaning out the house. I'm not going to live forever, and I don't want years of accumulated clutter to be my legacy for my children."

I had just made that part up, having no problem whatsoever with my children going through my attic and closets after I'd ceased to care. But the pink dress was hers, and it belonged with her. Stephen and Mary Jane were expecting their first granddaughter, and I'd seen Mary Jane eyeing the portraits of Mimi and me wearing the dress, so I figured it was only a matter of time before she asked for it. But it had never belonged to anybody but Ava.

"If it's a girl, I'll get her picture taken with her wearing it when she's two." Ava waited a moment, as if she wanted me to explain why I'd never hung her picture and why it had been put in one of Mimi's albums instead. But I didn't. There were no words to explain more than three decades of waiting for the right time.

"We were hoping that you and Mimi and Daddy would come for Christmas. I'd invite the whole clan, but I know they like to stay home for the holidays. Maybe after the baby's born we'll do a big reunion here at the beach."

The panic rose in me like a riptide at the thought of returning to St. Simons so many years after I'd left it forever. "I don't know, Ava. You know how I don't like the heat. . . ."

"Mama, Christmas is in December unless they've moved it and just haven't told me yet. The weather will be nice, and it's an easy drive. As long as you don't let Mimi behind the wheel."

I heard her smile, but it did nothing to quell the panic. I couldn't think of anything else to say.

"I didn't marry Matthew to spite you, you know."

I accepted the belligerence that had crept into her tone, knowing I deserved it now as much as I had when she was a teenager. It was a small price to pay for guarding my heart and preparing for disaster. "I know, Ava. I never said that you did. It's just, well, you know we're so busy here—"

She interrupted. "And you've got four sons and daughters-in-law who are more than ready, willing, and able to step in during your absence. I'd like . . ." She stopped, and I strained to hear her say that she wanted to see me, that she missed me, but I had taught her too well. "I'd like you to see my garden," she said. "The plants you sent are doing nicely. You know I don't like flowers in my own garden, but I put them there anyway, in a small section. For you."

I pushed back my disappointment. "I'm glad." I paused. "And I'd love to see your garden. It's just, well, you know how much I hate all the Spanish moss. I just want to take a big Hoover and vacuum it all up."

There was a long silence, then, "Say you'll come, Mama. Please."

I was surprised at how much I wanted to say yes. I missed my daughter, missed her in the same way I imagined I'd miss my sense of smell if it suddenly went away. My garden would lose so much of its joy and meaning.

"I'll think about it, Ava. After I speak with your father, of course."

"Thanks, Mama. I'll call Daddy, too, to get him on my side."

I couldn't stop the laugh that bubbled to my lips. "You always did have him wrapped around your finger. Don't expect things will ever change that much."

"Good." She paused. "I called and left a message on your machine—I guess you haven't had time to get back to me, but I was just curious if you knew Jimmy Scott and his family, and about what happened."

I stared down at the linoleum tile and at my feet in their practical low-heeled sandals, my chipped nail polish that screamed my need for a pedicure, forcing myself to remember. "Yes, I recall some sort of tragedy, but not how it happened or any of the details. We'd already moved, so I don't remember too much. It was a hectic time for us, with your granddaddy getting sick so sudden-like, and your daddy having to move up to take over the business. And your brothers begged to stay to watch the Fourth of July fireworks on the pier, which meant we ended up sleeping on mattresses, because the movers had already come. It's no wonder I don't remember much of anything else happening that summer." I swallowed. "Why do you want to know about something that happened so long ago?"

"Just curious, I guess. Do you remember Tish, Stephen's first wife? I met her when I first got here and she's become a good friend. We're working on a project to find unmarked graves in the area, and while I was at

Christ Church cemetery looking for graves, I met Jimmy. He seemed . . . I don't know, friendly. But Tish told me about his dad, so I was wondering if you knew them. . . ."

"Everybody at least knew *of* them. Jimmy was in Joshua's grade, so I heard a little bit about some of the troubles in that house, but that's it. And I never knew how much to believe, seeing as how it came from a ninth grader."

"Did you ever do anything for him? Because you were always so worried about us kids, about us having enough to eat, or if we were warm enough, or if our shoes still fit. You even made it your business to know about our friends and how they were doing, too."

I closed my eyes, and thought about everything she wasn't saying, about how there weren't any memories of me reading to her before she went to bed, or planning birthday parties, or talking over the kitchen table about crushes and best friends. Only memories of her being clothed and fed, and put to bed at night with a roof over her head. Things every ordinary mother did but without the frills.

Ava continued. "I just wondered if you knew about what was going on. It would be something you would have done, I thought. And Jimmy seems so nice, I'd like to think that there were people here who helped him."

"Like I said, Ava, I only knew them distantly and didn't really know what was going on until . . . until afterward."

There was another long pause, and I was getting ready to hand the phone back to Mimi so she could figure out how to turn the darned thing off when Ava spoke again. "Our house is on a creek, and I can go down to the dock by myself and it hardly bothers me anymore. And I've seen the ocean, Mama."

I slipped off my earring so I could press the phone closer. "Were you scared?"

"Yes. And I've only had a few more of those drowning dreams since I've been here. That's a good thing, don't you think?"

"It is." I was nodding into the phone, but stopped when I realized what I was doing. "Maybe Matthew can help you. Have you asked?"

"No, but he's suggested it. I will, though. Soon."

Mimi was now leaning heavily on the shopping cart and I knew we needed to go, but I was reluctant to say good-bye. "Are you drinking your milk? You need it now as much as the baby."

I heard the smile in her answer. "Of course, Mama. I'm a midwife, remember?"

"Of course."

"Say you'll come here for Christmas. Please?"

"I said I'd think about it. I'll let you know soon. Promise."

I looked up to see Mimi chatting with Holly Wright, one of Ava's high school friends. She'd once been a Pilates instructor but had contracted some kind of metabolic disorder that had caused her to balloon up to over three hundred pounds, forcing her to change jobs from fitness instructor to Wal-Mart greeter and get a motorized scooter. She enjoyed charging up and down the aisles of the store, accosting customers who'd managed to sneak past her at the entrance.

She stuck a smiley-face sticker on Mimi's blouse, but when I saw her approaching me I shook my head, indicating the phone as if my conversation didn't allow for smiley stickers. Fortunately, Holly retreated with a wave to show there were no hurt feelings.

"I've got to go now, Ava. Mimi's fading and I don't think I can carry her and the groceries out to the car."

Mimi scowled, but I turned my back and said good-bye into the phone.

I held the phone up to my ear after she'd hung up, wondering how long Ava could continue looking backward before she finally found what she was looking for.

Pamela

St. Simons Island, Georgia
June 1811

I woke up to the gentle sound of a woman singing and the pillow beside me cold and empty. In my half-awake state I imagined it was my mother singing, vaguely recognizing the lullaby she'd once sung to Georgina and me when we were small. But the voice was different, and I felt the sob in the back of my throat for the loss of my mother. My eyes snapped open before I could allow the grief to swallow me in its easy embrace.

I sat up, feeling the nausea that had assailed me for the better part of a month. I could find no discernible reason and had exhausted my own supply of tonics and powders. It left me dry-mouthed and heaving for most of the day, and as a result I'd lost a great deal of weight. So much so that I could no longer lift Robbie into my arms. I looked and felt like an old woman, with parchment skin and dark eyes that seemed to grow larger every day, eclipsing my face until I thought it might fade away completely.

I somehow managed to wash and dress without retching into the chamber pot, most likely because my stomach was empty, as I had not been able to eat the evening meal despite Leda's having made my favorite of bacon and collard greens. All I'd been able to tolerate had been a peppermint essence I'd instructed Georgina how to make.

The earth swayed as if I were on the deck of a ship, and I had to grab the doorframe to hold myself steady. Standing in the hallway I saw that Georgina's door was open, as was Robbie's. The clock chimed ten times in the hallway below, and I rushed down the stairs as fast as my aching body could carry me. I had not slept this late since my confinement with Robbie nearly five years before, the realization alarming me even more than my inability to diagnose what ailed me.

After ascertaining that I was alone in the house, I placed a shawl over my shoulders and stepped outside. It was the middle of summer, but the heat could not penetrate my frozen bones. It seemed, I thought, as if I walked in a perpetual shadow, either real or imagined, yet I couldn't find my way out from under it.

I followed the sound of singing to the kitchen house, expecting to find Leda and Jemma working while keeping an eye on Robbie as he played. He was a good and obedient son, never straying too far, and happily occupying himself until an adult was ready for play.

Turning the corner, I was surprised to find only Georgina and Robbie sitting in the shade of an oak tree. Robbie sat in front of Georgina with his back to her as she brushed his dark curls and sang to him.

Robbie saw me and broke away, stepping on Georgina's skirt and making her frown. "Mama, Mama!" he called as he propelled his body into mine, almost knocking me over in my weakened state.

"Darling," I said, as I squatted down to face him, his nearness somewhat restoring me. "You should have come to wake me up so that we could have breakfast together with Papa, as we always do."

He twirled a piece of my hair that had caught the sunlight. "Aunt Georgie said no. She said it was better to let you sleep. So we had breakfast with Papa instead."

I looked up as Georgina strolled toward me, the ties of her bonnet limp in the humidity. "I thought you could use your sleep. You work too hard, sister. Your body is telling you to rest."

I held my son in my arms and watched my sister approach. She had removed the pins from her hair so that it lay in thick waves around her shoulders. Stopping in front of me, she said, "I actually thought you would still be sleeping, so I asked Leda to prepare food for only Robbie, Geoffrey, and me. I'm sure I could ask her to make more."

The smell of fatback and beans wafted from the kitchen, but I did not hear the accompanying sounds of women talking or utensils banging against pots. "Where are Leda and Jemma?" I asked.

"I told them to take the laundry to the creek."

My eyebrows puckered. "But laundry day is Monday. There is no reason for them to do it again so soon. I had other chores scheduled for them today."

She flicked her hand in the air as if brushing aside a pesky fly. "Yes, but I thought their time would be better spent doing laundry twice a week instead of just once. I do not like to wear a dirty shift, and I would prefer not to wait an entire week before wearing a favorite again."

My head swam, and I wondered whether I should move from the sun regardless of how cold I felt. "Georgina, this is my household and I will run it as I see fit. I cannot have you interfering. It diminishes my authority and lessens the efficiency of everyone who lives and works here. Work should not and cannot be determined by your need to wear a favorite shift."

My stomach churned and I needed to retch, but I would not in front of Georgina. I had the distinct impression that she would enjoy seeing me in such a state.

She raised an eyebrow in the way I had seen her practice for years in the mirror to make her look haughtier. But all I could still see was a little girl who looked and acted too much like the mother whose death had seemed a personal affront to her.

"You were indisposed, and I did what I thought necessary."

I forced myself to stand, my hand clutching my son's small shoulder, grateful for any support. "I am not so indisposed that I cannot run my household. Please consult with me if you have any further ideas. I promise to listen, but everything does run well here, and I see little that needs changing."

Her lips curled, but I knew enough to know it was not a smile. "Yes, Pamela. I will remember."

The jangling of a horse harness reached us from the front drive, and we both turned with surprise to see Nathaniel Smith dismounting from the high seat of his carriage.

Georgina turned back to me. "Since you are feeling so much better, I will leave you to dine with your husband and son while I go take a drive with Nathaniel."

She patted Robbie on the head like a person would pet a dog, then walked quickly toward the house, where Nathaniel stood looking in our direction. He raised his hand in a wave, and I waved back, hardly aware of my own actions.

As soon as the carriage pulled away, I walked around the kitchen house, the smell of cooking food making the bile rise to the back of my throat. I swallowed and then, squeezing Robbie's hand, led him to the doors of the root cellar by the side of the kitchen house.

After struggling with the doors to open them, I told Robbie to wait outside for me, then walked down the steps into the cool, dark interior. It smelled of damp earth and growing things, much like I imagined a grave would smell, but the thought had never disturbed me. I had faced much worse things in life than I expected in death. I lit the lamp I kept hanging on the wall and went directly to the shelves where I stored my dried herbs and medicinals.

Holding the lamp high, I used my fingers more than my eyes to sort through the bottles I kept meticulously organized and labeled. My experience had taught me that ground powders were easily confused by sight. My fingers found the hole where the peppermint should have been, but as my gaze scanned the small jars and bottles, a dark space at the back of the bottom shelf caught my attention. Not needing the lamp this time, I reached in with my hand and felt the empty gap between two jars. The pennyroyal leaves were gone. The jar had been there the last time I looked, before I had become sick, but now it was no longer there. I pulled my head back to allow the lamp to reach the dark spaces. I opened my eyes wider, as if that might somehow allow me to see better, but the dim glint of the lamp found nothing to reflect, just as if I were staring into the eyes of the devil.

I sat back, dropping the lamp onto the hard-packed earth and bricks of the floor, the light extinguished as if a giant breath had suddenly snuffed it out. The damp green smell of the root cellar pressed against me and I turned to the side and retched, emptying what little remained in my stomach, and irrevocably shifting the tender bond between sisters.

CHAPTER FIFTEEN

Ava

St. Simons Island, Georgia
June 2011

I took a sip from the decaf iced coffee Tish had provided for our early-morning cemetery trek. I forced my eyes to remain open, concentrating on the sweet aroma of flowers that clung to the inside of Tish's car like a favorite memory. Two lavish floral arrangements from Eternal Carnation sat in the back of the wagon for delivery, their graceful stems and blooms waiting patiently under cellophane to be unveiled.

"So how far along are you?" she asked, peeking over the top of her large sunglasses—remnants from the eighties, I assumed.

"About six weeks. I'm due February twelfth." I felt the silly grin lift my lips again.

"So your baby and Beth's will be around the same age. We should start scheduling playdates now. With the way kids are raised nowadays, I under-stand everything is pretty much scheduled way ahead."

I absently rubbed my stomach, wondering whether the slight swelling I felt was real or just imagined. I hadn't had time to ask my mother what kind of pregnancies she'd had, whether she grew big with every child, and whether the size of her feet had changed. "I saw Beth last week when she came for her appointment, and I can't imagine either of us becoming that kind of parent."

Tish shook her head. "No, I don't think so either. Although it's sometimes hard to tell what kind of parent we'll be until we're holding that baby in our arms, or dealing with a screaming toddler in the grocery store." Her smile slowly faded. "Or dealing with any of life's surprises. I think sometimes the best mothers are simply those who make the decision to love their children every day, regardless of what happens. It sounds easy, really, but as an experienced mother, I know how very hard that can be."

I took a sip from my cup, trying to imagine the child growing inside me as a separate entity from myself, but couldn't. When each of my sisters-in-law were pregnant with their first children, my mother and Mimi made little pillows with cross-stitched tops that said something like having a child was like watching your heart exist outside of your body. It was too early for me to understand that, but a part of me already felt the surreality of a new life, the wonder of creating something where nothing had been before, the complete surprise of the unknown. And a small part of me was curious to know what genes would be dominant and easily attributed to a branch of the family tree, and which traits would appear from seemingly nowhere at all.

Tish slowed as we passed a small subdivision with garage sale signs announcing a neighborhood sale. She pressed her lips together, so I could tell she wanted to stop, but she didn't say anything.

"We can go check it out if you like," I suggested. "It's still really early, so if we just stay a little while we can still hunt for hidden graves before the sun really heats up."

She bit her lower lip as she strained over the steering wheel to see better. "I'm a notorious junker, and I promised Tom that I wouldn't buy anything else, but I'm like an addict. Besides, I happen to know that a couple who live in here have an antique store in Savannah. When they go to estate sales and have to buy an entire auction lot with good stuff and junk thrown in together, they can't sell the junk in their store. That's why they always have great finds when they do these garage sales."

"Come on," I said, feeling like a drug dealer, but wanting the chance to snooze in the car for a little while before I had to start combing through weeds. "I promise I won't tell Tom."

With a knowing look in my direction, Tish flipped on her signal and turned into the subdivision. She found a spot at the curb right in front of a driveway overflowing with boxes and furniture, and lots of primary-colored plastic children's toys.

Tish opened her door before turning to me. "I'm sure you'll be wanting to catch a nap, so I'll leave the car running and the A/C on. I've cracked your window a bit, too, so you'll have fresh air. But if you change your mind, just don't forget to take the key out of the ignition before you leave."

"Thanks," I said gratefully before resting my head against the back of the seat and closing my eyes. I must have fallen asleep immediately, because I didn't even remember Tish closing the door and walking away. Perhaps it was the sound of water trickling in a small fountain in the front yard, or the scent of the salt-drenched air that seeped into the car, but my old dream returned to me, a bruise lying right beneath my skin.

I knew I was sitting in the car asleep, yet another part of me could taste the salt water as it filled my mouth, feel it sucking me downward as I scrambled to stay afloat. My mind's eye could see light above me, and I saw my hands reaching upward. I knew they were my hands, because I recognized the raised birthmark on my left hand near the base of my thumb.

I awakened with a jerk, gasping for air. Forcing myself not to move, I made myself remember the dream, hoping to recall what had been so different this time. I turned my head toward the milling people in the yard, focusing on a little girl who was playing with a small kitchen set and talking on a plastic cell phone as she stirred something in a pot. I sat up straighter, remembering finally what I'd been fighting to grasp, a thought as thin and airy as smoke. In this dream I had been desperate to survive. My dream self did not want to drown, but struggled as if the life I was trying to save was worth living. In all the years I'd been having the same dream, this was the first time I'd understood this, a truth that no longer danced in the periphery of my consciousness but instead sat rooted in the middle of it.

I felt shaken, and completely unable to close my eyes and go back to sleep. I turned off the ignition, then left the car in search of Tish. I found her on her knees in front of three large boxes brimming over with very old-looking hardbound books. Next to her was a small stack of books, and in her arm she held three more while her other hand continued to rifle through one of the boxes.

She lowered her sunglasses when she spotted me. "Are you all right? You're looking really pale."

"I'm fine," I said, forcing a smile. "It was just a little too stuffy in the car." Turning my attention to the box, I asked, "Looking for anything in particular?" I was amused that Tish was a junker, but not all that surprised. Her car was ancient but classic in its quirky rattles and shakes, and certainly still worked. I should have recognized the signs the first time I'd seen the wood paneling on the sides of her wagon.

"I've read so many stories about people finding signed first editions of classic books in attics and yard sales. I keep thinking that could be me." She held up a tattered linen-bound book and frowned at it before tossing it back in the box.

"What are those?" I asked, indicating the stack on the ground next to her.

"Oh, those are just for decoration. You know, to prop up knickknacks to give something more height. I'm always looking for stuff for dressing my front window at the shop." She paused for a moment to study another book before handing it to me. "Here's a good one for you. It's not a first edition and probably not worth anything, but it's a history of St. Simons written in 1880. You might find some interesting tidbits about the area, not to mention Matthew's family. You did say you wanted to do more research, right?"

"Yeah, I do." I hesitated, then took the book and held it for a moment without looking at it. "John said that Adrienne had a whole briefcase full of notes about the Frazier family history, as well as a calendar she wrote everything in. It wasn't in her personal effects that were given to her parents after she died, and I can't find them at the house. I know you were friends, so I was hoping you might, well, have some idea of where they could be."

She contemplated me for a moment over the tops of glasses that rested on the middle of her nose. "Ava, I'm not the one you should be talking to about his. Have you asked Matthew?"

I looked back at the plastic kitchen set, where the mother was trying to pry the play cell phone from her daughter's small hand. "Not yet. He's very sensitive when it comes to Adrienne. And everything's so new between us that I don't want to rock the boat."

Tish stood and took off her sunglasses, her eyes serious. "Love isn't a buffet where you pick and choose the parts of your life you want to include in your relationship. You married all of Matthew—including his past—when you married him. Tiptoeing around sensitive issues and keeping secrets isn't good for any relationship." She looked up and smiled at a woman who paused for a moment at the book bin before moving on, then regarded me again with a somber expression. Lowering her voice, she said, "I hope you haven't been listening to rumors, Ava."

I thought of my lunch with John and the gold wedding band with the word *Forever* engraved inside. *Be careful, Ava. He's not who you think he is.* Instead of answering her question, I asked, "Do you know why Adrienne gave her wedding ring to her brother before she died?"

Tish looked at me sharply. "I didn't know that. All I know is that the ring had always been a little tight on her finger, and when she gained some weight, she'd stopped wearing it. I just assumed she was keeping it in her jewelry box or something."

"John has it. He said Adrienne gave it to him right before she died." I paused, wondering how much I should say. "She told him that it didn't belong to her."

Tish shook her head as if trying to jostle the words into an order she could interpret. "What did she mean by that?"

"I don't know, and neither does John. I was hoping you might be able to tell me more."

Sighing, she dropped the books she'd been holding and put both hands on my shoulders. "Do you love your husband, Ava?"

I stared at her, not knowing what to say. It wasn't because I didn't know the answer, but because I didn't know how to tell her how Matthew lived under my skin, and I in his, and that's where I felt like I had finally found where I belonged in this world. Instead, I said, "With all of my heart."

"Then prove it. Tell him about the ring and ask him what Adrienne meant."

When I hesitated, she prompted, "If you love him, you'll be able to listen to whatever he says, and then go from there." Her eyes narrowed. "You don't doubt his innocence, do you?"

"Of course not. It's just . . . I don't know. It's like we're both afraid we'll lose each other if we don't hold something back. He didn't even tell me about Adrienne until we were married. And I didn't tell him that I was deathly afraid of water."

I looked at her, hoping she knew all the answers. My mama did, but I'd learned over the course of my childhood that just because she knew everything didn't mean she would share those answers with me. Tish had become like a surrogate mother to me, but without all the filters.

She dropped her hands from my shoulders and her eyes softened. "You can't lose something you never had. You've got to learn to let go so you'll know how to hold on."

I jutted out my chin, unwilling to take her advice regardless of how right I knew she was. It was hard for me to discuss my feelings openly. I had been raised by a mother who spoke about everything except what really mattered. Except in her garden, where she cultivated the truth like a rare flower, allowing me rare glimpses into her heart.

"I don't think Matthew needs to know that I've been talking with John about these things right now. He's having a difficult time at work. One of his patients committed suicide and he's having to deal with the family's grief and his own doubts. He doesn't need this now."

Tish gave me a small smile before kneeling back down in front of the book bin, and began sorting through the ones she'd placed on the ground.

"I'm not going to tell you what to do, Ava. I think you can figure that out for yourself."

We paid for our purchases, then left, my anticipation of the morning dimmed somewhat by our conversation. I stared down at the cover of the book she had given me, the title printed in bold flaking gold print. *A Concise and Thorough History of St. Simons Island, Georgia,* by Richard Stanley Kobylt. I wondered whether the author had been as pompous as his title.

I flipped open the cover and began slowly turning the pages, hoping to indicate to Tish that I was ready for a change of subject. From the title page I could tell that the book had been edited and reprinted in the nineteen forties, which was why the binding was old but not as brittle as it might have been if the book were a first edition from 1880. I quickly skimmed a three-page acknowledgment section—which I found odd for a history book—before I paused at the sight of the word "Index" in block letters centered at the top of a page.

Ignoring my chipped and chewed fingernail, I used my finger to slide down the list of tiny print to see whether there might be anything of interest. About three-quarters of the way down the page, I stopped to read a chapter title: "The Ghosts of St. Simons Island." I wasn't really interested in ghosts, having never had a reason to have an interest, yet Adrienne's words about Matthew seeing ghosts when he looked at her stumbled across my memory. Running my thumb over the bottom corners of the pages, I flipped through quickly until I reached the indicated page, then slid the book open with my finger.

The chapter was filled with pen-and-ink sketches of the lighthouse and Fort Frederica, as well as a black-and-white photograph from the thirties of a portion of Dunbar Creek, known as Ebo Landing. From Tish and my reading I had already become familiar with these ghost stories, stories of the spectral British soldiers at the old fort, and of the proud Ebo slaves who'd drowned themselves, preferring loss of life over loss of liberty, and whose chants could still be heard in the marsh on quiet nights. There was also the more recent addition of the ghost of a slain lighthouse keeper from the late eighteen hundreds, whose footsteps could still be heard climbing the metal spiral staircase as if he were performing his nightly routine more than one hundred years after his death.

I skimmed the stories slowly, wondering whether the telling of these tales had altered with age, feeling slightly disappointed when I read nothing I hadn't heard before. But when I reached the last page of the chapter, I stopped. At the top half of the page was a sketch of a woman in early nineteenth-century dress standing on a nighttime beach, the moon an orb of light above her. The outline of a three-masted ship with full sails was visible in the far distance out on the water, yet nearby but behind her was the distinct shadow of a man facing another direction, as if he couldn't see her. The woman leaned forward toward the ocean as if she were searching for something. Or someone. I let out a gasp of air, realizing I'd been holding my breath.

"Are you all right?"

I held up the page to Tish. "Does she look like anybody you've seen before?"

She glanced at it for a moment, her gaze immediately returning to linger a little longer before she returned her attention to the road. "It's her—the woman in the portrait Adrienne had hidden behind the sketch of the house."

I nodded, unable to lift my gaze from the book. "I thought so, too, although I can't go home and check, because the prints are still at the frame shop. They've been ready for over a week and I just haven't had a chance to go pick them up."

Tish shot another glance in my direction but didn't comment on my reasons for the delay. Or my reasons for framing them. And I was glad, since I wasn't sure of the answers myself.

"What does the book say about her?" Tish asked.

Frowning, I quickly slid my gaze down the paragraphs I'd already read, feeling frustrated when I realized the only commentary on the sketch was the caption beneath it. Out loud, I read, " 'The spirit of a man thought to be St. Simons planter Geoffrey Frazier searches for his faithless wife after she fled with her British lover following the retreat of the Royal Marines from St. Simons on March first, 1815.' "

I looked up at Tish. "That's the same story you told me. Does anybody know any more to the story?"

She shrugged. "It's been so long, I guess it's just become a legend about people who lived here a long time ago. From what Adrienne told me, they never really knew what happened to her, only that she disappeared. It could be fact, or it could be rumor that she had a lover and left with him. There's no way to know for sure, although it would certainly explain her disappearance."

My finger traced the outline of the man's shadow, and I wished I could shine a light on his face, imagining I already knew what he looked like. "I saw Geoffrey's grave at Christ Church. That was the year he died, too— 1815. I remembered wondering why there was no grave for his wife, or any mention of her on his tombstone or on their children's."

"That could be because there's truth to the rumor, and she was not only unfaithful to her husband, but to her country, too. That would have made people want to forget her name as quickly as possible."

"I wonder if Adrienne discovered more."

Tish sent me a knowing glance as she slid into the parking lot of what looked to be a bait shop and put the car in park. "I'm going inside to get us some water bottles—I want you drinking a lot to stay hydrated. If you wanted to make a phone call, now would be a good time." She left the car, then pulled open the glass door of the shop, bells ringing to announce her presence before she disappeared inside.

I pulled out my phone and hit the memory button for Matthew's cell. He answered on the second ring.

"Hey," he said, the sound of his voice calling to mind warm nights and soft skin and the scent of moonflowers.

"Hey, yourself," I said. "Am I getting you at a bad time?"

"You can call me anytime, Ava. You know that."

"I know. I just don't want to interrupt you in the middle of a session."

"That's the only time I forward my calls to my secretary, Betsy, and if you need to speak with me right away, she knows to come get me."

I smiled into the phone. "That makes me feel important."

"Because you are." His mouth sounded very close to the phone, and I imagined I could feel his breath on my cheek.

I glanced at the darkened glass of the shop door and wondered whether Tish was waiting for me to hang up the phone before she came out. "Tish and I stopped at a garage sale this morning and I found an old history book that mentions your ancestor Geoffrey Frazier. His supposed ghost, actually. It doesn't really give any specific details about who he was or even his wife's name." I hurried on, not wanting Matthew to stop me. "And there's no mention of her on his tombstone or on his children's, like she'd been erased. Tish said that Adrienne kept all of her research in a briefcase, and I'd really like to see what she discovered." I closed my eyes, ashamed at how easily the lie had sprung to my lips. "I was hoping you knew where it was."

I knew Matthew was there, listening, because I could hear him breathing. But he didn't say anything for a moment. Finally, he said, "I'd forgotten about it, actually. I haven't thought about it—or seen it—in four years."

I was surprised at the disappointment I felt. "Oh, well. That's a shame." I glanced over at the door and watched as a man with a gray beard and a fishing cap stepped through it, the door jangling shut behind him. I thought about Adrienne's wedding ring, almost hearing the sound it had made as it rotated in circles on the table until John had stilled it. Just as quickly I made the decision that now wasn't the time or place to mention it to Matthew. Instead, I said, "I took your advice and invited my parents and Mimi for Christmas. I didn't get a firm commitment from Mama, but I think if we work on Daddy and Mimi we'll get them here."

I heard his smile, but his voice sounded tight. "I'm glad. Look, Betsy just gave me the signal to let me know my next appointment is here, so I have to say good-bye. I should be home by six. I love you."

"Great. I love you, too," I said. "I'm trying a new recipe tonight that Tish tells me you love . . ." I began before I realized he'd already hung up.

Tish didn't say anything when she got back in the car and handed me two large bottles of water. As she drove, I kept going over the phone conversation, wondering at what point Matthew's tone had changed, and why the old restlessness had taken hold of me again.

I looked down at the book splayed open in my lap and smoothed my palms against the sketch of the nameless woman. "He doesn't know anything about the briefcase," I said, deliberately not mentioning the ring.

"Not to worry," Tish said. "All the information is out there—we just need to find it." She pulled off the road onto a dirt drive that ended abruptly in a small clearing. She handed me an expensive-looking camera. "I've got it set on automatic, so all you have to do is point and shoot, just like I showed you. I have to make two deliveries and then I'll be right back—thirty minutes tops." She reached behind her again and grabbed the same yellow pad of paper and the box of pencils I had used before. "If you see anything out of the ordinary—anything that looks like it wasn't made by nature—take a picture of it and mark its location on the map you're going to draw, starting with this little clearing. I think this is where the old kitchen house of the Smith Plantation used to be, so any bones you find around here are probably just animal bones, but let's not assume anything yet. There are a lot of Smiths missing from the Christ Church cemetery, so they have to be somewhere."

I wanted to ask her about any Smith family records that might still exist, but wasn't in the mood to hear again about the Civil War occupation by the "damn Yankees" and their thieving, burning ways. "All right," I said, stepping out of the car with the camera and sketching materials.

"Don't forget these," she added, shoving both water bottles at me.

I saluted her with the bottles, then watched her drive away. I pulled out a pencil from the box, then placed everything else, except for the yellow pad, on the ground next to me before straightening to survey the area.

The inland forest was dense here, the trees less than one hundred years old. According to Tish, this middle section of the island had once been cotton fields and was one of the last large areas to be farmed. Now it was filled with live oaks and pines mixed with pignut hickory, laurel oaks, and sweet gum trees. I recognized many of them now, thanks to my long bike rides with Matthew. The sweet gums had become my favorites because of the spiky balls that fell from the tall branches and cluttered lawns and drives like childhood memories, each easily overlooked until they eclipsed the landscape.

The music of the inner island buzzed and hummed with unseen wild-life as I stepped forward out of the clearing and into the shade of a sweet gum. I picked up my pencil to begin drawing, but paused, sniffing the air. *Ashes.* The smell was strong, as if the fire had been a recent one, yet the trees were green and tall, with no sign of fire damage.

I tried to draw, but the smell of ashes proved to be too distracting; the more I ignored it, the more it seemed to hang in the air. Figuring I had time before Tish returned, I put down the pad and pencil, then headed in the opposite direction of the site of the old plantation house where Tish had indicated I begin my search. Instead I followed the smell of ashes, my feet compelled to move as if by some unseen force. Even if Tish had been there calling me back, I don't know whether I would have been able to stop.

There was a wide path between the trees, making me think it had once been well traveled, but not in recent years, judging from adolescent sap-lings that blocked the way in parts. I followed it for a short distance, the smell of ashes growing stronger, the trees thinning even more, until I reached another, larger clearing and stopped.

The ruins of a small house sat in the middle, its roof and front porch collapsed, the remains blackened by fire and charred bricks from the chim-ney still scattered in the yard. But surrounding the ruin—rising from the earth like a brilliant-plumed phoenix—grew the most beautiful flower garden of every color and variety, of every scent and height. Anemones huddled next to lady's mantle, while tall ginger lilies floated above Sun Flare roses. Weeds and grasses were kept back with a precise line delineat-ing garden from overgrown forest. The garden itself was part wild, yet part tamed, part cultivated, part accident. It was a dream of sight, a reality unrealized by most gardeners because of its sheer unwillingness to follow rules or expectations. It was the garden I'd always wanted to plant but had never allowed myself to.

I wondered whom the garden belonged to, and where the gardener lived, as the house was uninhabitable. Forcing my gaze away from the sea of color, I began to walk the perimeter of the property, looking not only for clues to who owned the property, but also for anything that might be of interest to Tish and our project, so she'd forgive me for not following the script.

Turning east, I walked slowly through thicker foliage, looking at the ground for bricks or stones or any indication that the garden was man-made and hadn't been spontaneously created. Leaves rustled and crunched as an animal smell permeated the air directly behind me. I spun as something low and dark darted through the foliage unseen. Startled, I stepped back, my terror intensified, because whatever it was that had scurried past me remained invisible yet nearby. A stronger scent of ashes and animal musk descended on me as a cold sweat erupted on my forehead. Panicking, I spun around, suddenly disoriented and forgetting what direction I'd come from or where I'd been heading. I began to run, my sneakers slipping on slick leaves and moist earth untouched by the sun under the canopy of trees.

I heard the sound of something running nearby, and I turned my head without stopping, looking forward just in time to avoid colliding with an oak tree. I quickly jumped to the side, my foot slipping on soil and leaves, my body twisting to try to regain my balance. I felt my foot twist before the pain in my ankle reached my brain, my fingers scrambling for purchase as I slid into some sort of gully. I skidded to a sudden stop, my mouth full of dirt and forest debris, my hand throbbing from hitting something hard and immovable.

The pain seemed to paint everything with a red tint, stealing even my voice as it swept up my body. I couldn't move, and I definitely couldn't stand, and through the haze of pain the fear grew like a fire fed by wind.

I lay on my side, my eyes clenched shut, trying to breathe through the pain so I wouldn't pass out from lack of oxygen. My hand continued to throb where it lay against the source of its injury, and when I looked down I saw a corner of a half-buried flat slab of stone protruding from the dark earth.

The rustle of leaves and the slow and steady sound of footsteps approaching turned my fear to terror. I tried to stay as still as possible, debating with myself whether I should shout for help, unsure how much time had passed, and whether Tish would even be back already to hear me.

I stared up through the trees at the small section of visible sky that seemed even bluer than I remembered, and I had a flash of memory of eyes of that same hue, and an inexplicably deep and penetrating sadness briefly replaced the pain in my ankle and centered instead in my chest, where my heart beat. Somebody began whistling, the melody seeming out of place yet oddly familiar. The whistling grew louder, the lyrics eluding me as the footsteps grew nearer. A long shadow fell on me as I continued to stare upward at the remarkable blue sky and wondered whether I was hallucinating.

The face that appeared above me was vaguely familiar, but none of the names that floated in my brain seemed to fit. Spots danced across my eyes as the man crouched down and reached for me. I stretched my arms toward him and whispered the name that seemed to form so easily on my lips: "Geoffrey."

CHAPTER SIXTEEN

Ava

When I opened my eyes again, I found myself lying on the rear bench seat of a pickup truck, my head elevated on something soft, and my leg propped up and stabilized between plastic bags of topsoil. An earthy smell permeated the inside of the cab, but it wasn't an unpleasant one. It reminded me of my mother and her large hands as she turned the soil with her bare fingers. In my half-awake state I saw her sifting through the dirt, showing me how the healthy soil lived beneath the dead and dried surface, and how sometimes you needed to dig to find it.

I came fully awake as the waves of pain throbbed up from my ankle, and I thought I was going to throw up. I clenched my eyes shut until the feeling went away.

"You just lie still, Miss Ava. I'm driving you to the hospital in Brunswick right now."

Despite the pain, I managed to prop myself up on my elbow, the memory of calling out a name I'd never spoken before and of being lifted off the ground toward a blue, blue sky crowding my thoughts. "Jimmy?" I pressed my head back against the rolled jacket pillow, trying to swallow down the nausea and pain. I remembered seeing flowers, and walking through the woods, and hearing something running toward me and then me falling. And I remembered hearing a familiar tune whistled by unseen lips. "How did you find me?" I managed through gritted teeth.

"That's my house."

I recalled the burned-out shell of a house and the heavy scent of ashes. "You live there?" I asked, surprised.

"No, Miss Ava. The house is all burned up—didn't you see? But I used to live there when I was little, and I still own it. Land prices aren't going anywhere but up around here." The way he jumbled his words and mispronounced others made me take a moment to translate what he was saying. And that was when I realized that I shouldn't underestimate Jimmy Scott.

I remembered what Tish had told me about the fire that had killed Jimmy's family when he was a teenager. I blinked in confusion. "But the garden . . ." I couldn't finish as a wave of pain consumed me, and I moaned to keep myself from screaming.

"It was my mama's garden, so I like to keep it up for her." He glanced at me over the back of the seat. "Does it hurt?"

I nodded, afraid to open my mouth, and resisted the urge to roll my eyes.

"Don't worry; we're almost there."

I propped myself up again in a sudden panic. "You need to call Tish and tell her where I am. She'll be worried when she doesn't find me."

"Don't you worry, Miss Ava. She's right behind me. She saw me as I was leaving, and I told her what happened, so she said for me to hurry and that she'd follow."

I gritted my teeth as he took a sharp turn and then the truck shuddered to a stop. The rear door behind my head flew open and I looked up at Tish.

"Oh, Ava. Matthew is going to kill me!" She turned her head toward the driver's seat. "Jimmy, run on inside and tell them we need a stretcher out here, stat. Make sure they know she's pregnant."

"Yes, ma'am," he said, then ran from the truck.

Tish placed her hand on my forehead. "What were you doing at the old Scott place? That wasn't anywhere near where I told you to start your search."

She looked close to crying, so I knew her scolding was to make herself feel better.

"I'm sorry, Tish. I smelled something burning, and I had to go see." I closed my eyes again, as if that might make the pain go away.

"Nothing's been burning in those woods for more than thirty years, Ava. You couldn't have smelled anything burning."

"It was the smell of ashes, mostly. It was . . . very strong," I said, unable or unwilling to explain the compulsion I'd had to follow the scent. I opened my eyes in time to see her giving me a doubtful look.

I realized my hand was throbbing, too, and when I lifted it to see better, I saw that the side of it was already a vivid blue under the skin. "I think I might have found something, though. When I fell, I hit my hand on something hard like a rock, but when I looked at it I could see that it wasn't a normal rock, but something that was curved on the edge and maybe manmade. It could be from a chimney or something like that, but it might be worth checking out."

A deep crease formed between her brows. "Let's worry about that later, okay?" She stepped back as the door by my foot opened and a woman wearing a white coat appeared. "I've called Matthew and he's on his way, and I'm not leaving until I know you're okay. I just want you to try to relax, and make sure anybody who touches you knows you're pregnant. Especially when they X-ray your leg."

I nodded as she disappeared from view; then I closed my eyes again and gave myself over to the pain and the healing hands of professionals, still seeing the vibrant colors of Jimmy's garden, and hearing my mother's lullaby whistled softly in the hushed stillness of an island forest.

❧

I took a sip of tepid tea from my mug, then replaced it on the coffee table. It had grown cold as I'd sat and stared at the same page of my *Midwifery*

Matters magazine for over half an hour. Since returning from the hospital the day before, I hadn't been allowed to move from the couch in the parlor except to hobble to the bathroom and back and then be carried upstairs to bed. Matthew and Tish had taken turns watching me with a constant vigil—Matthew because he was my husband and Tish because of a misplaced sense of guilt. Luckily, I hadn't broken any bones, but had still managed to twist or pull just about every muscle and ligament possible in my ankle. I had to wear a demobilizing boot for two to three weeks and stay off of it as much as possible, preferably keeping it elevated.

I chafed at the restrictions on my mobility, especially that I'd have to miss a week at work and then be confined to the office for another two. I was hoping to be able to at least work in my garden, and when Matthew left for Savannah and I was finally alone again, I was going to try to find out how one managed to plant tomatoes with an immobilized foot.

After giving me my tea and a kiss, Matthew had gone outside to work in the yard. I'd refused pain medication because of the baby, but I still felt groggy as a result of the entire ordeal. I lifted my head, listening to the quiet of the house and the faint sound of metal scraping against hardened earth. I closed my eyes to hear better—something Mimi had taught me— and heard again the rhythmic scrape and thud of digging. But the sound wasn't coming from the front yard; it was coming from the back, where I kept my garden and gardening shed with the newly painted red door and shutters.

Heaving my leg over the edge of the couch to the floor, I then pulled myself up before reaching for my crutches. My hand was still wrapped, mostly to protect it from my hitting it against objects, but at least it had stopped throbbing. It made it difficult to use the crutches, but I'd found a comfortable position so that the bruised part of my hand wasn't bearing my body weight.

I found my balance, then hobbled to the side window, where I'd have a partial view of my garden. I struggled to find a good vantage point between the slats of the plantation shutters, until I finally gave in and pulled the shutters back from the window, leaving me with an unobstructed view of the side yard and the entire gardening shed.

Matthew had discarded his golf shirt and was now wearing just an undershirt and shorts, and as I watched he shoved the tip of his shovel into the ground beside the shed. We hadn't talked about expanding my garden yet, or where, but it most likely would not have been where he was digging.

I pressed my cheek against the glass, my breathing fogging the window. Using the back of my wrapped hand, I wiped it clean and peered out again. I had never seen Matthew working in the yard, had never even seen him with a tool in his hand, although I knew he was handy and had built the small deck that led from the French doors off the dining room. He'd even rebuilt the dock on the creek. But he hadn't mentioned any projects to me involving my potting shed, and I stood where I was for a few minutes, listening to the scraping of the shovel, wondering what he was hoping to find digging so close to the foundation.

I lifted my hand to knock and get his attention, but before I could, he turned toward me. A sense of déjà vu descended on me, overwhelming me to the point that I was no longer sure of where I was standing or who I was. Our gazes met and, as I watched, he leaned the shovel against the shed and began walking toward the house.

I almost ducked out of sight, like I'd been caught doing something wrong. My head felt fuzzy, as if I'd been expecting to see something different, see somebody else walking toward me from the shed.

I'd made it back to the sofa by the time Matthew walked through the front door, but I remained sitting. I smiled up at him as he stood in the doorway, the smell of sweat and dirt only adding to the shock of desire that threaded through my every vein.

"You're supposed to be keeping your foot elevated," he said.

I looked up into his face, surprised at the sharpness of his words, and wondered briefly why I expected his eyes to have suddenly turned blue. "I was bored sitting on the sofa and I went to the window to see what the noise was."

He moved closer and took a seat on the antique wooden rocking chair next to the sofa. "You could have just waited and asked when I came inside."

My jaw stiffened. "I'm not a prisoner here, Matthew. It's okay for me to move around a bit before I resume my position on the sofa with my foot propped up." In case he needed proof, I lay back on the sofa and lifted my leg up on the pile of pillows Tish had arranged for me.

He rubbed his hands over his face, and when I saw his eyes again I saw they were filled with concern. "It's not just you I'm worrying about, you know."

I placed my hand on my stomach. "The baby's fine. He or she is much too small right now to care if I fall in a ravine and hurt my ankle. But I promise to be more careful." When I saw the look of doubt cross his face, I added, "Really. Besides, it's not like Tish is going to let me traipse through anything except a manicured lawn until this baby's born."

He smiled, and it was the old smile I had fallen in love with. "Good," he said. "Otherwise I'd be making you wear a bike helmet and knee and shoulder pads for the next eight months."

I relaxed against the pillow and smiled. I was about to ask him what Tish had put in the refrigerator for dinner when I noticed the dirt on his hands and under his fingernails. "What were you digging out there?"

He hesitated only briefly before answering. "I'd noticed kudzu growing through a crack in the wall of the shed, and I wanted to make sure I got it out at the root. Otherwise it'll have the inside and outside of your potting shed covered within the month."

I studied his hands, afraid to meet his eyes. "You dug a lot just to get to a root."

Again, he seemed to hesitate, as if his words needed measuring. "That's where the old root cellar used to be until my grandfather got locked inside while playing hide-and-seek with his brothers and cousins. Almost scared him to death—couldn't go into a dark room for the rest of his life. So my great-grandmother had it filled in and the doors removed. While I was digging I wanted to make sure that there hadn't been any settling, that the hole was still sealed. The old root cellar ceiling beams have long since rotted, and I didn't want the floor of the shed giving way while you're stand-ing on it."

"Then thank you," I said. His words made sense, but I couldn't shake the feeling that he was leaving something out.

He stood and sat on the edge of the couch. "I feel so protective of you. And not just now, because you're pregnant. I've felt this way since the first time I saw you." He smiled softly. "I guess you'll just have to bear with me." His thumb rubbed the ridge of the birthmark on my left hand while his eyes studied my fourth finger, where I wore only my gold wedding band. "Maybe we should sell your engagement ring and buy baby furniture with it."

Our eyes met, and I wasn't sure whether he was joking or not. "Mat-thew, you know I love my ring. It's just that when I'm working, or hanging out at home, it seems—I don't know—like too much. I do like it, but I like my wedding band, too."

I grasped his fingers and held tight, realizing that now was the oppor-tunity I needed to discuss the one thing I didn't want to. "When we first got engaged, you mentioned that your family had an heirloom wedding ring." I sucked in a breath. "Was that the ring Adrienne wore?"

His eyes darkened like the sky before a storm. "Yes. Why are you ask-ing?"

I held his fingers tighter, afraid he'd pull away. "Do you know where it is?"

He didn't hesitate before answering. "She lost it. While we were sailing. That last summer, when we were practicing for the Charleston regatta. She said it was too tight for her finger, so she stuck it in her back pocket and it must have fallen out."

I looked down at our entwined fingers that reminded me of the roots of the live oaks at Christ Church, long instead of deep, as if to reach through time itself. "Oh," I said, John's words spinning in my head like a ring on a laminate table. *She said it didn't belong to her.* I looked up at him again. "Who wore it before Adrienne?"

"My mother. I inherited it when she died, and I kept it until I had a bride to give it to." He was silent for a moment. "When I allow myself to think about it, I find myself wishing that I had waited to give it to you."

I bent my head and closed my eyes, remembering the word *Forever* engraved on the inside of the ring, and knew I couldn't tell him now about my meeting with John, or that the ring had not been lost. *She said it didn't belong to her.* I told myself that I knew now what Adrienne had meant by those words, that it had belonged to too many others to truly be hers. Later, cushioned by the space of time, I would tell Matthew what I knew and perhaps even get the ring back. But not now, when our marriage was still so new and fragile.

His phone rang and he answered it, turning away from me to carry on an abbreviated conversation with one-word answers. He hung up and went to the window and was silent for a long moment. Then he turned toward me, as if he wanted to ask me something, but stopped and instead said, "I'm going upstairs to take a shower. Do you need anything before I go?"

"What's wrong?" I asked, as if he could hide anything from me, as if I didn't know the dreams he left on his pillow when he awoke.

"I think you need to rest—"

"No," I said, cutting him off. "I need to know what's wrong."

He cast a reluctant gaze toward the stairs before walking back to where I lay on the sofa. Slowly, he sat again on the edge of the rocking chair facing me, his expression devoid of emotion, and I wondered whether this was what he looked like when he counseled patients. A tingle of alarm began at the base of my skull.

He took a deep breath. "That was an old friend of mine, Walt Mussell. We met in undergrad, but Walt went on to medical school and is now a radiologist. I asked him to read your X-rays."

I sat up. "But my doctors said there was no break, just a bad sprain. Why would you need a second opinion?"

He rested his elbows on his knees and folded his hands, much as I imagined he'd do during a counseling session. "My questions didn't have anything to do with your most recent injury."

"What do you mean, 'my most recent injury'?"

He paused, measuring his words. "Were you ever in a car accident as a child, or did you sustain a bad fall?"

I used my wrists to push myself higher on the sofa, and I winced as I put too much pressure on my injured hand. "No, never. Why?"

His face remained impassive. "Do you ever remember breaking your foot or your leg?"

"What are you getting at, Matthew? I'm not one of your patients. Just tell me what you're trying to say."

He steepled his fingers, and I wanted to grab his hands and shake them loose. I hardly recognized this man, this professional who listened to children who told him things most people didn't want to hear. "Your X-rays show healed multiple bone fractures in your foot and leg. They're old injuries, possibly sustained as a toddler or even as an infant, which is probably why your doctor didn't think to mention them. But I happened to see the X-rays, and because of my line of work am trained to question injuries sustained during early childhood. They're well healed, meaning they were set by a professional or at least by somebody who knew what he or she was doing." He paused, examining my face as if I were supposed to be giving him some sort of clue. "Usually those sorts of injuries for a person that young are caused by a catastrophic incident—like a car accident." He paused. "Or it could be a sign of physical abuse."

Images of my father's gentle face and of my mother's fingers brushing dirt from the gossamer petal of a lily filled my mind, completely at odds with what Matthew was implying.

"No. Absolutely not. My parents never laid a hand on me. Nobody did. They didn't need to. A look from my mother to show me she was disappointed was all it took to make me straighten up real quick." I shook my head vigorously, as if to add veracity to my words.

He leaned forward and placed a hand on my arm. "Sometimes children bury painful memories, Ava. It's a form of self-preservation that children develop to protect their young minds from things they're not ready to comprehend. I know you and your parents have your differences. . . ."

"No!" I shouted. "I'm thirty-four years old—don't you think at some point I would have recalled something? Because if that sort of abuse was sustained while I was a baby, surely it would have continued as I grew older, and *that* I would remember. And I don't." I glared at him, surprised to find myself close to tears. Quietly, I said, "Being emotionally distant is a far cry from physical abuse. You should know that." I shook his hand off and turned my face away, too angry and stunned to look at him.

I heard the rocking chair creak as he stood, and then felt his touch on my cheek, but I still couldn't look at him. "I know this is hard to hear, Ava. And that's why I had Walt double-check your films. But the X-rays don't lie. Something happened to you when you were a small child, something horrible. I've had too much experience in this to not know that whatever it was is still affecting you today. The difficulties with your mother, the way you feel alone even in crowds, your nightmares, and maybe even your fear of water." He paused for a moment and I waited, prepared for the final blow. "Even the way you rushed into a relationship with me."

I jerked my head toward him, aware that my shock and anger registered on my face. "I love you, Matthew. That's the only reason I rushed into a relationship with you. And it wasn't like I was the only one." I spat the words at him, but he didn't flinch.

"Would you allow me to speak with your parents?"

I swung my leg over the side of the couch, oblivious to the pain and discomfort. "And do what? Accuse them of unspeakable things? They have never laid a hand on me—I swear it. And I see no reason to disrupt their lives with baseless accusations. They're a bit too old for all of this trauma."

"Then let me hypnotize you. I use it a lot in therapy to bring back hidden memories. I think it might be helpful to you."

I fumbled for my crutches and stood. Matthew didn't help me, but I felt his eyes on me the whole time, knew he was ready to step in if needed. "There are no hidden memories to discover, okay? So I don't need to be hypnotized. I played a lot of sports as a girl. Maybe my injuries were more serious than I remembered. If it makes you happy, I'll call my parents and ask. But I don't want to hear any more about this, all right? You're always asking me to look forward, so let's do that. And I'd appreciate it if you wouldn't go behind my back and ask for second opinions on things concerning me ever again."

I hobbled out of the room and through the kitchen to the back door, struggled with it to get outside, and almost gasped for the fresh air of my garden when I finally made it down the steps.

Matthew didn't follow me, and I was glad. Because somewhere in the dark places of my memory, a seed of truth had become dislodged, bringing with it the images of flowers and the haunting melody of a song that was familiar and unfamiliar at the same time.

CHAPTER SEVENTEEN

Pamela

St. Simons Island
September 1811

We stood on the damp sand, our shoes sinking so that we periodically had to lift our feet and place them in another spot, only to begin the process all over again. I barely noticed as I focused on the words spoken by Reverend Matthews, carefully listening to ensure that Georgina said the correct words, and that she and Nathaniel would be properly wed.

Georgina had chosen the beach for the ceremony, and we had allowed it. It was the only decision regarding her marriage in which she had been allowed to voice her opinion, and Geoffrey and I considered it a harmless one. The wind whipped up white tips on the waves past the shoreline like little flags of surrender, and I wondered whether my sister thought that, too.

I watched their faces as they vowed to love, treasure, and obey until death parted them, the words flung from their mouths to the wind making them seem like wild and reckless promises. I could not help but wonder whether this had been Georgina's intention all along.

As soon as the reverend closed his Bible, the small gathering began its solemn retreat back toward the dunes, the guests' movements slow and awkward because of the sucking sand, but perhaps because of something else, too.

I had planned a small supper at our house to celebrate the nuptials before Georgina and Nathaniel left for their wedding trip to Savannah. But as I glanced up at the darkening skies, I wondered whether their trip would be postponed and hoped fervently that it would not. They needed to be away from this place; I needed them to be away. Even if it was only to be a few days, I needed to breathe freely again, to no longer feel the accusatory stare on my spine.

A hand touched my shoulder and I turned, expecting to see Geoffrey. Instead, I saw Georgina, her eyes wide like a child's and full of questions. I stopped and allowed the others to pass us by. I tried not to cringe from her touch, to meet her eyes as if I had nothing to hide.

"Speak quickly, Georgina. I must help Leda with the wedding supper, and the guests will be arriving directly."

Her eyes were restless, her fingers plucking at the pale yellow gown that showed perspiration under the arms already. She looked up at the sky. "I think it will rain."

"Most likely." I picked up my skirts. "Let us walk while we talk. Nathaniel will be waiting."

As if I had not said anything, she didn't move. "It bodes ill for a bride if it should rain on her wedding day." Her voice caught with the last words, and I looked closely at her, remembering the small sister who had stopped talking for a whole year when our mother died.

"We make our own good luck, Georgina. And Nathaniel loves you. That should mean something."

A sneer marred her perfect face. "What is love, Pamela? It is a fickle thing, a feckless plant that blows and sticks itself to a place with shallow roots until the next wind comes along." She looked at the water and frowned. "I hate it here. I always have. Mama used to tell me that she would take me away from this place, to Savannah or Philadelphia." Her eyes met mine. "She said she loved me, too, and see what has become of that."

My head snapped back as if I had been struck. "You are my sister. I will always love you."

Her eyes met mine, the clear blue reflecting the stormy skies above. "When Mama was ill and calling for me, Papa sent you in to nurse her. He would not allow me in, punishing me for something I did not understand. I did not see her again while she still lived. You went in, and she died. For years I believed that you had taken her from me on purpose."

I shook my head vigorously, trying to recall events that had occurred so long ago. "He was not punishing you. He did not feel you were old enough, or strong enough, to see Mama in her weakened state. I nursed her as best as I could, but she had given up long before. There was nothing I could do, except love you as a mother and a sister would. And I have."

"Then why do you not believe me? I did not mean to make you sick. If you had allowed me in to come see you, to explain, I would have told you that. I am not as expert on the herbs and leaves as you are. Can you not believe that it was an accident?"

I thought of the missing jar of pennyroyal leaves, and of the time I had painstakingly explained how to use the leaves to heal, and how much to use for baiting traps for the persistent crawling bugs that vexed us all on the island. Yet it was true that beyond that one instance, she had not worked with me in the garden, or in the kitchen house preparing my medicinals. Perhaps she hadn't remembered the proper dosages. Perhaps I had been wrong. But none of that mattered any longer.

"I want you to be happy, Georgina. That is all I have ever wanted for you."

She took my hand and squeezed my gold wedding band between her fingers. "My wedding ring does not say 'Forever.' What is between Nathaniel and me is not what is between you and Geoffrey. I think I have always hated you both a little because of it."

I watched the wind whip at my sister's hair, tangling and twisting the strands like little lies until it was unclear where they started and where they ended. "Tell me you do not mean that, Georgina. Tell me."

She stared past my shoulder, out toward the open sea. "I cannot have children; did you know that? And please do not ask me how I know—you will not want to hear it. But that is why little Robbie is so precious to me. He is part me, you know. We share the same blood."

I cannot have children. The memory of her asking for the pennyroyal tea flitted through my mind as a fissure of fear split open inside my heart. "Yes. You are his aunt." I wondered whether she could hear the way my words trembled, like dangling leaves in a stiff wind. "He loves you."

A broad smile brightened her face. "Yes, he does. I would hope that you would continue to allow me to see him. We do enjoy each other's company, I believe, and he would grieve as much as I should we be separated. I am his only living blood relative, after all. And if something should ever happen to you and Geoffrey, you would not want him to live with a stranger."

"Let us not speak of such somber matters on your wedding day. I wish you happy, Georgina. May we all have long lives, and may we find love eternal."

My sister raised a delicate eyebrow. "Do you really believe in such a thing?"

"I do," I answered without hesitation. "You will find it, too. You will see. That is why Geoffrey and I thought this marriage was best for you."

Her cool eyes settled on me once more. "Thank you, Pamela. You have made things so much clearer for me." She stepped forward and put her hands on my shoulders, then leaned in to kiss my cheek. Her lips were icy against my warm skin, and I felt as if I had been kissed by a corpse.

Without waiting to see what I might say, she dropped her hands, then marched forward through the sand toward her bridegroom, who was waiting for her, and looking at her in a way that made me blush and drop my gaze.

I turned toward the frenzied sea as the light changed in the sky, turning the water from green to gray, while in the depths below nothing changed at all.

Gloria

Antioch, Georgia
June 2011

I rearranged the snapdragons and passionflower vine clippings in the pale cream vase in the viewing room, comfortable with the other occupant in the room despite the fact that she lay horizontal in an open casket.

Helen Truitt had been Ava's fifth-grade math teacher, and a classmate of mine from elementary school through high school. It didn't unnerve me too much that my contemporaries seemed to be dropping like flies. I wasn't afraid of death, and not just because I was the wife of a funeral director and the daughter of a woman who still carried with her the Native American belief that the life of a man is a circle from childhood to childhood. I truly believed that my lack of fear had more to do with the fact that in my seventy-four years I'd learned that there were a lot more things worse than dying.

I stood before my old friend, eyeing her critically. Denise, the beautician Henry employed, had done a good job with Helen's hair and makeup, making her appear much as she had in life. Yet maybe that was the problem. I'd always longed to tell Helen that her hair was too dark and youthful for her complexion and age, and her makeup colors hadn't progressed much since the seventies. That was the main problem with death—that all the things you wished you'd said had to stay stuck in your throat. My throat was getting way too full with words.

I bent down to my basket of flowers to begin the next arrangement when I heard a sound behind me. I jerked up, knowing my back would punish me later for the sudden movement, and stared down at Helen, half expecting her to open her eyes.

"I don't think she's going anywhere, Gloria, so you can stop staring."

I swung around to the half-opened door and saw Mimi in her red sundress and matching red low-heeled pumps, the handle of her red patent-leather pocketbook draped over her arm. With her bunions I didn't know how she managed the heels, but I'd never known her to wear flat shoes since the day I was born.

I tried to appear calm despite the wild beating going on in my chest. Narrowing my eyes, I said, "How did you get here? Please tell me that June or Kathy drove you."

She scoffed as she walked inside and shut the door behind her, having to push on it twice to get it to close completely. "I didn't think you'd want either one of them to hear what I have to say to you." She put her hand on her hip. "You know, if you owned a cell phone we could avoid these kinds of situations."

My eyes widened. "You drove yourself?" I tried not to picture her behind the wheel of her 1982 Lincoln Town Car, mowing down stop signs and mailboxes. We'd long since hidden the car keys to avoid the long list of apologies and repair bills.

"Did you want me to walk? I'm not in my eighties anymore."

"But . . ."

"I've known you kept my car keys in Lucy's old dog dish under the sink ever since you took them from me. You know you can't keep secrets from me, so I sometimes wonder why you even try." Her eyes gleamed, and I knew she was talking about a lot more than just car keys.

I turned back to my flowers. "I can only hope that you didn't kill anybody."

I straightened again to look at her, aware that she hadn't snorted or tried to defend herself. Her eyes were soft, yet troubled, and my heart began its wild fluttering again. "What's wrong?"

"Ava called. She's been trying to reach you. She said it was urgent that she speak with you."

Relieved, I said, "If it's only about us visiting at Christmas, I told her I would think about it. . . ."

"No. She had an accident."

I dropped the flowers, petals scattering at my feet. "Is she all right? Is the baby . . . ?" I couldn't finish.

"She's fine, and so is the baby. She twisted her ankle real bad, but they say if she keeps off of it for a little while, she'll be just fine." Mimi moved slowly to a chair and lowered herself into it, using both armrests. I knew better than to ask whether she needed my help, but I kept a close eye on her, noticing how frail she'd become when I wasn't looking. I didn't want to see that, didn't want to recognize that one day Mimi would no longer be in my life.

"They had to take X-rays." Her eyes met mine and I found myself collapsing into the chair next to hers.

I stared at the open coffin across the room as Mimi continued. "She said that they found evidence of multiple breaks in her foot and legs from what appear to be childhood injuries."

I had to clear my throat twice before I could speak. "Ava played soccer and softball and hurt herself a lot. She was like a magnet for injuries." The old words sounded rehearsed, even to my own ears.

"That's what I told her. She was in a cast at least once, remember?"

I nodded. "But did she?"

Mimi was quiet for a moment, her chest rising and falling in shallow dips. "Yes. But she says that Matthew was concerned enough to have a radiologist friend of his read the films, and the doctor seems to think the breaks appear older than adolescence. That they seem to be from early childhood."

The silence grew until I could almost see it forming in the space between us. Finally I said, "What did you tell her?"

Mimi scowled at me as if I'd just asked whether she'd run down Main Street naked. "That the doctor is obviously wrong. Doctors make mistakes all the time. Ava seemed to agree."

"Oh," was all I could manage as I continued to stare at my old friend reclining in her coffin. I noticed a movement on the floor where I'd dropped my flowers, and saw a bright orange Gulf Fritillary butterfly on the stem of a passionflower vine, languorously flapping its delicate wings. As a child, I'd watched one emerge from a chrysalis I'd kept in a jar on my nightstand, amazed at how something so beautiful could have started out as a caterpillar. I stood and walked toward it.

"Don't pick it up," Mimi said from behind me, as if I didn't know this already, as if I didn't know that holding something too tightly could damage it irrevocably.

I walked toward the window with its heavy drapes and pulled them aside, then unlocked the window sash and slid it open, allowing in the sun and the heat of the day that pulsed up from the dark asphalt of the parking lot.

Moving slowly, I picked up the passionflower cutting and lifted it into the air, the butterfly's wings stilling from the sudden movement. I held my breath, then began to walk very carefully toward the open window. When I reached it, I held the stem outside and shook it gently. The butterfly stayed where it was for a moment, its wings straight up, then slowly lowering like a mother preparing for an embrace. Then it lifted into the air with rapid wing strokes and flew away.

I continued to stare after it long after it disappeared, remembering something June had told me after one of her mission trips to central Africa, to a country whose name I couldn't remember or pronounce, about how the women sang the same chant whether in great happiness or deep grief, and I wished I knew such a song, as my heart was filled with equal amounts of both.

CHAPTER EIGHTEEN

Ava

I placed my good foot on the bottom step and looked up. It had been a week since I'd been upstairs without being carried to either the bathtub or the bed, and I was more than ready to claim the house again. I wasn't scheduled to return to work for two more days, and I was already so bored out of my mind that I was afraid that if I didn't do something productive now, I'd go crazy.

I stepped up onto the first step, then lifted my booted foot to rest next to it before attempting the next stair tread. It took me several minutes, but I managed to make it to the upstairs hallway without hurting myself. Trying not to think about my conversations with Mimi and Matthew about old injuries, I hobbled forward into the master suite.

At the garage sale I'd attended with Tish on the day of my fall, I'd purchased a box of old photographs along with the history book. I'd almost forgotten about them until Matthew told me that Tish had brought the box and the book over and he'd stuck them in the closet.

The new closet add-on he'd built was something out of a design magazine, much like the kitchen. I tried not to think of what parts of it were Adrienne's ideas and which were his. Because, in the end, none of that mattered. It was my closet now, my house.

Still, I imagined I could smell her perfume when I opened the door, and wondered what Matthew had done with Adrienne's clothes. I'd found one of her dresses shortly after I'd moved in. It was tucked in a corner with Matthew's winter clothes—heavy jackets and thick sweaters that weren't worn too often on St. Simons. But I'd seen the bright colors and pattern that didn't look like something Matthew would wear, and when I'd pulled it out I'd smelled the perfume that assaulted me every time I walked into this closet. I'd taken the dress and given it to Goodwill. If Matthew ever asked about it, I'd tell him that it was my way of giving up the past.

The book and shoe box sat on top of my dresser, and I managed to tuck both under my arm and shuffle to the bed, where I dropped both. The floral bedspread had long since been donated, and now all we had was a cotton blanket pulled over the sheets. I'd been looking for a replacement, but nothing I'd seen in stores quite fit the mental image of what I thought it *should* be—a brightly colored quilt in a wedding-ring pattern. I'd never even liked quilts, and I struggled to understand my recent compulsion to acquire one.

I couldn't quite find a way to sit on top of the high bed, and the little steps were far too delicate for me and my boot, so I wedged myself against the side of the bed and opened up the shoe box before looking inside at the scattered photographs.

I sucked in a subtle air of expectation, the feeling quickly extinguished as soon as I spied the strangers' faces and their alien couches. I struggled to see what it was I continued to search for, disappointed with each foreign smile and nameless event displayed in fading Kodachrome.

With a heavy sigh, I picked up all of the loose photos from the blanket and shoved them back in the box, leaving it there while I pulled myself to a stand and picked up the book, wondering briefly how I was supposed to negotiate going down the stairs while holding on to something.

I hobbled to the top of the stairs and stood there, contemplating my next move as my gaze traveled around the hallway, coming to an abrupt halt at a single, dirty handprint on a door at the end of the hall.

Tish had arranged for a cleaning service while I was incapacitated, but their attention to detail wasn't up to my usual standards. I was one of those rare people who actually enjoyed housecleaning. It wasn't only that it soothed my mind after a hard week of work; it was more a compulsion to keep this house clean. I'd always been an adequate housekeeper, but there was something about this house, something that came close to a need for preservation for future generations and a reverence for those past.

The door led to the attic stairway, and as I stepped closer, I saw how large the handprint was, the fingers long, the palm broad, and I had a sudden picture of Matthew digging outside by my shed, and his dirty hands when he'd come inside. He'd gone upstairs following our argument and returned with damp hair and the clinging scent of soap. But I'd been outside in my garden, unaware of how long he'd been upstairs, or what else he might have done besides take a shower.

Slowly, I turned the door handle and pulled. It didn't move. I turned the old iron knob and tugged again, my brain sluggish as it took me a moment to accept reality. The door was locked. It hadn't been—I'd been up the stairs to give a cursory look at the attic right after I'd moved in. I'd seen the random stacks of old clothes and papers, antique furniture, and new suitcases. The air had been thick and musty, and it was definitely not a space I'd planned to spend any time in. I turned the knob in the opposite direction and jiggled the door, but the latch held firm. My gaze dropped down to the keyhole beneath the handle; I knew I'd find the key missing before my eyes even registered what they were seeing.

I sat down clumsily on one of the two Chippendale-style side chairs placed in the upstairs hallway for lack of a better space after I'd rearranged the furniture in the front parlor. I stared again at the handprint and locked door, almost hearing the scrape and thud of a shovel moving earth. Matthew had been looking for something in the old root cellar. I was sure of it, almost as sure that I knew what it was. And when he hadn't found it, he'd gone to the attic to look, but perhaps had run out of time and had locked it to take his shower, hoping to finish at a later time. He must have known that at some point I'd make my way upstairs again, and he'd wanted the attic off-limits when I did. Matthew knew me well, much better than I apparently knew him.

I looked at the book in my hand, the energy required to negotiate myself down the stairs gone. My cell phone rang downstairs from the hall table where I'd left it, and I recognized the ringtone I'd assigned to Matthew. I heard the beep alerting me to a voice mail message, and then the sound of the house phone ringing, and I finally understood my mother's aversion to the phone.

They think I killed her. A tremor of uncertainty crept up the back of my neck. I opened the book to a random page to calm down, to help rearrange my thoughts, promising myself that I would speak with Matthew when he returned home, clinging to the hope that I could believe whatever he told me.

I looked down at the book, to a chapter with the heading "St. Simons Island and James Madison's War." Unfamiliar with this war, I scanned the first page, looking for reference dates, then realized that the author was referring to the War of 1812. Seeing as how the actual war wasn't officially over until 1815, it made sense to call it something else. I grudgingly credited the stuffy-sounding author with the more appropriate name. I skimmed over a few more pages, reading about how the British, in their attempts to antagonize their former colony, had been plundering American ships and conscripting their sailors, conduct that had precipitated the declaration of war by President Madison.

I flipped a few pages, then stopped at another pen-and-ink drawing of a British officer tending to a child lying on a bed. I read the caption: *A surgeon of the Royal Marines tends to a young child with malaria. He is credited with saving at least one life during their short stay in February of 1815 before their evacuation on March first following the signing of the Treaty of Ghent.*

I stared at the uniform, imagining I could smell the musty scents of wet wool and leather. I looked, too, at the man's face, a nondescript depiction made by an artist who hadn't known what his subject really looked like.

The hair tied back with a black ribbon was dark, and I found myself shaking my head, as if I knew that the hair color was wrong, that it should have been a light shade of auburn.

I leaned my head back against the wall, feeling dizzy. After a few deep breaths, I flipped a chunk of pages over and looked down to see where I'd landed. The book lay open to the page I'd seen before of the woman on the beach with the figure of a man behind her. The name came unexpectedly and effortlessly to my lips. "Geoffrey," I said quietly, my fingers brushing the page, recalling the name I'd said as I'd reached for Jimmy Scott after my fall. I remembered, too, the blue sky and eyes of the same hue. But Jimmy's were brown. I knew this because I'd checked when he'd come to visit with Tish and brought a bouquet of flowers from his garden.

"Turn around," I whispered to the one-dimensional figure, with the unsettling feeling of knowing what he looked like, but unable to clearly see it in my head. My attention focused on the woman again, and I thought about calling the frame shop and having them ship the three framed prints to me. I immediately discarded the idea, as the prints were to be a surprise to Matthew, and if they were delivered, he might be the one to get to them first.

I studied the woman, the dark hair and the widow's peak, the almond-shaped eyes. *I know you,* I wanted to say. I tried to think whom she reminded me of or resembled. My finger traced the lines of her face, and I found myself desperately wishing that I knew her name.

I closed the book and struggled to a standing position with a renewed sense of purpose. I'd call Tish and ask her where I should begin my research. Maybe once I knew the woman's name, I would stop being rattled with the unsettled feeling I got every time I looked at her picture. Or thought of the graves of her husband and children and her own absent one. And maybe it would even overshadow my growing unease about Adrienne and her calendar, and the reason Matthew had locked the attic door and taken the key.

I put my hand on the newel post and paused, hearing the whispering of voices through the upstairs hall, a cadence of sound whose source seemed to come from inside my head. I closed my eyes, believing I could hear harsh words, but I couldn't distinguish what was being said.

I abruptly let go, as if the wood had become a conduit to the past I'd wanted to disconnect from, the voices now diminished but their echoes remaining like the glow on the screen of an old television set after it was switched off. The empty hallway greeted me as I stared around me, looking for a source of the sound, then began my long and precarious trip back downstairs.

I was on the bottom step when my cell phone rang again. I hobbled over to it and saw Tish's number flash up on the screen. I picked it up eagerly. "Hi, Tish. You must have been reading my mind. I was just about to call you—"

She barely let me finish my sentence before she interrupted. "Are you sitting down?"

I frowned into the phone. "Is everything all right?"

"It depends. It's not about Matthew, if that's what you're worried about. Are you sitting down?" she repeated.

"Sure," I lied. "What's up?"

Barely contained excitement danced in her voice. "You remember when you fell and you hit your hand on something hard?"

I rubbed the outer edge of my hand, no longer bandaged but still feeling sore. "Yeah, I remember. What about it?"

"Well, you told me that it seemed too smooth and shaped to be nature-made, so I went out there with my daughter, Beth, who, if you remember, teaches history at Frederica Academy and I thought might be able to give me some insight if we did find something."

She paused and I imagined her filling her cheeks with air as she waited for my response.

"And?"

"It's definitely a grave marker. What's so interesting is that we could tell it was probably a piece of scrap marble or taken from an older, broken tombstone because of its irregular shape. And it wasn't carved by anybody who knew what they were doing, either. A complete novice managed to chisel just the initials 'T.E.' and the date, 1815. At least, that's what we think it says, since it's apparent whoever did the carving had absolutely no skill whatsoever."

"Wow, that is a find." I paused. "Was there . . . anything else there?"

"Beth has a contact at the archaeological institute, so she called him and he sent out a few guys with tiny shovels and sifters to see if this was just a discarded stone or an actual grave site."

Again she paused, and I wished she were standing in front of me so I could shake her. "Did they find anything?" I prompted.

"Yes," she said, dragging out the "s" sound. "There are definitely remains, although they are terribly decomposed. It's too early to tell, but it looks like the body's been there for a very long time."

I swallowed, thinking how close I'd been to it. "About how long?"

"A very long time. There are mostly only bone fragments left, and what appears to be the back of a skull. But they also found a few metal pieces, including a small lead ball, and gold buttons."

"Are they thinking Civil War then?" I asked, remembering Tish's stories of the desecration of Christ Church cemetery during the Union occupation.

"Or earlier. One archaeologist said the button looked British."

I looked down at the history book I still held in my hand and imagined I heard voices again, smelled the thick odor of wet wool. "Oh," I breathed as a cool chill rippled through me. *Like somebody walking over your grave.* I shivered, remembering Matthew's words.

"The institute is very excited, and they promised they're going to make this a priority. They've already got the whole area taped off." I could almost imagine her cackling with glee. "Isn't this exciting?"

"Very," I agreed, still unable to completely eradicate the bone-deep chill that had settled in my veins like poured concrete.

"When do you go back to work?" she asked.

"Tuesday—after the long weekend. Why?"

"Because we need to visit the Georgia Historical Society's library and archives in Savannah. I have extra help at the shop on the weekends so that would be the best time for me to go if you could get the day off. They're open every first and third Saturday of the year, but I'm assuming they're closed this Saturday because of the Fourth of July weekend. Put it on your calendar for the sixteenth and we'll drive down together, all right?"

"Yes. That sounds great."

There was a short pause on the other end. "Are you all right? I thought you'd be more excited."

"I am. Really. It's just . . . I don't know. I think I'm tired of being cooped up here in the house." *And finding out things about my husband that I don't want to know.*

"Well, that will be over with soon, and Beth's on her way over now with a casserole. Y'all can talk about babies. I'm sure that will perk you up."

I smiled. "Yeah, probably." I thought for a moment. "Do you think the archives might have more information about Matthew's ancestors? I really want to find the name of Geoffrey's wife."

"Absolutely. The archives have everything—deeds, marriage records, newspapers—just about anything you want to know. If you can't find what you're looking for there, it doesn't exist."

My phone clicked, and I looked to see that Matthew was calling. "I've got to go, Tish. Matthew's on the other line. I'll talk to you later, okay? And keep me posted on what's going on at the grave site."

"Will do."

She hung up, and I hesitated only a moment before clicking over to Matthew's call. "Hey," I said as casually as I could.

"Hey, yourself. I was getting worried, because I'd called you before and you didn't answer. I kept picturing you sprawled in your garden among the tomato plants, unable to stand."

"There are worse places to fall," I said, a smile tugging at my reluctant mouth.

"Glad to know you're all right. It looks like I'm going to be late tonight. It's the birthday of one of the doctors in my practice, and I've been invited to join them for a little celebration. I'm afraid it's going to be way past midnight when I get home."

"Why don't you just stay in the apartment there?" I tried to tell myself that my reluctance to have him return home was about his safety and not about postponing asking him the questions I needed to ask.

"Because I don't want to be away from you any more than I have to. Besides, who would carry you upstairs to bed?"

"You don't need to. I've already managed to get upstairs on my own."

He waited for a moment before he responded. "I wish you wouldn't. It's not safe for you to attempt the stairs when you're by yourself."

I gripped the phone tighter, not wanting to wait any longer. "I tried to get into the attic, but the door was locked and the key was missing."

There was no pause this time. "Sorry about that. I had a feeling you'd try to go upstairs on your own, and might even attempt the attic stairs. But they're steeper and not very level, and it would have been too dangerous for you with your boot. Instead of telling you not to—which we both know would mean nothing to you—I locked it."

"But where's the key?"

He chuckled. "I was just thinking about that this morning. I have a reproduction American flag from 1812 in the attic and I wanted to hang it outside for July Fourth. But when I tried to remember where I'd put that key to open the door so I could get it, I drew a complete blank. Not to worry; I'm sure it will come to me. Hopefully in time for the holiday."

"Yeah, hopefully," I said, my relief at his plausible explanation tinged with something much heavier and darker. "So are you still coming home tonight?"

"Yes," he said. "I'd miss you too much if I didn't." He spoke the words close to the phone.

"I miss you, too," I said, closing my eyes, and felt him next to me.

"Don't wait up, and I promise not to wake you. But I'll see you in the morning."

We said good-bye, my eyes still closed as I imagined my husband's face, but behind my closed eyelids his eyes had turned blue.

❧

This time, the ocean sang with its own voice, the melody familiar, the lyrics garbled as if sung in a foreign language. I knew that I was dreaming, but I clung to that space between wakefulness and sleep, feeling something besides the persistent fear. I turned my head toward the music, hearing the old lullaby sung with the words that only I seemed to know.

My heart squeezed as if I were drowning, as if I couldn't draw air to breathe, but I was on land, my bare toes digging into damp sand, and the pain in my chest had nothing to do with sinking beneath the waves.

The sky was clear in my dream-night, the moon saturating all in a haze of blue. A form approached from over the dunes, the figure of a tall man, and my heart squeezed again, and I knew this pain as one of loss and a grief so tangible that my vision furled at the edges like a burning leaf. I opened my mouth to call out his name, but couldn't remember what it was.

The waves rolled up on the sand, their white crests like creeping ghosts along the surface of the water. I wanted to back away, but instead I felt myself stepping forward, toward the water, my clothes soaking up the water, making them heavy. A large wave engulfed me and I was in the water, unable to scream or shout or to see the shore where the figure of the man had stood. I opened my mouth, the salt water filling my lungs and stealing the words I wanted to say, snatching my breath. I awoke with a sob, my cheeks and pillow wet.

I sat up, startled to see the moonlight filter in through the slats of the blinds. I blinked, seeing a room that was familiar but not, the furniture and bed placed in the wrong spots, although I vaguely remembered helping to rearrange them myself. For a moment I imagined bare windows, the sashes open to allow in the air and scents of a summer night. And a quilt with a wedding-ring pattern on the bed. The vision was so clear I was sure I could smell the briny aroma of the marsh and the decay that meant death and life at the same time.

I lowered my hand to the mattress next to me, expecting to find the small body of a child pressed against mine, that shadow sister of my childhood dreams there to comfort me through the nightmare of my adult world. Instead, my hand fell on a broad and hard chest, and just then the name that I'd been searching for rose to my lips. "Geoffrey."

A firm hand touched my arm and the room settled back into familiarity, the furniture in its proper place and the plantation shutters back on the windows.

"Ava?"

I recognized Matthew's voice, and a breath of relief and uncertainty invaded the air between us.

"Ava? Are you awake?"

I collapsed against him, feeling the solidness of him against me as I gasped to suck enough air into me, as if I'd been without for too long. I nodded into his skin, unable to form words.

We lay silently for a long time, breathing in each other's breaths, his heartbeat strong beneath my head, the name spoken in my dream hovering like a specter above us.

"That was your third nightmare this week," Matthew said softly.

I nodded again, not wanting to speak, as if to do so would make the man I'd seen in my dream vanish and the grief return.

He pushed up on an elbow and looked down at me. "I can help you, Ava. Please let me."

I pressed my palm against his jaw, then up into his hairline, as if to reassure myself that he was real. "You mean by hypnosis?"

He turned his head and kissed the palm of my hand. "Yes. Your nightmares are trying to tell you something." I felt his eyes on me in the darkness. "A lot of adult nightmares are rooted in childhood."

I didn't say anything, afraid to acknowledge what we were both thinking: about how a child could have sustained multiple bone fractures with no memory of it. Or how an adult could have dreams of drowning when she'd never even been swimming.

"What if I don't like what I find out?"

"It's a possibility. But once a truth is discovered, a person then has something tangible to deal with."

I breathed in deeply, trying to catch the scent of the marsh mud again. "Will it make the nightmares go away?"

"Usually. And possibly your fear of water, too. It's been my experience that once the source of a fear is discovered, it disappears. It's almost like your subconscious uses your dreams to point something out, and once you notice it, it leaves you alone."

I thought about my imaginary childhood companion, and the shadow figure on the beach, and was no longer sure that I wanted them to go away.

As if Matthew could read my mind, he asked, "Who's Geoffrey?"

The moonlight behind him threw Matthew's face into darkness, but I knew he was watching me closely. "I don't know." I lifted my head and kissed him. I thought about telling him that I thought it was Geoffrey Frazier, and how his story seemed to haunt me. But I could not, as if in the telling I'd diminish something significant, relegating Geoffrey and his sad story to a familial anecdote and nothing more.

"Let me help you," Matthew said again, his voice whispered close to my ear.

I thought of Mimi's words as she'd handed me the music box. *Some endings are really beginnings.* I looked up through the darkness toward Matthew and wondered whether giving up the past could mean only looking forward, that this ending could be my new beginning, that trusting him would eradicate the doubt that clung to us like kudzu vines.

I reached for him, needing the solid feel of his bare skin beneath my fingers. "Yes," I whispered back. "I want you to help me."

He kissed me softly, then settled beside me and I sighed, tasting salt on my tongue and hearing the hum and roll of the ocean once more.

CHAPTER NINETEEN

Ava

St. Simons Island, Georgia
July 2011

Beth honked the horn when she spotted me sitting on the front steps, my crutches resting across my lap. I was hobbling toward her by the time she stopped the car.

"I could help you, you know," she said, sounding so much like her mother that I smiled.

"I know. But I feel bad enough dragging you out to come drive me around when I'm more than capable of doing it myself."

Beth moved to my side of the car and opened the door for me. "Are you kidding? It gives me something to do besides obsess over the baby and shop for baby clothes. I've got about a month to go before school starts back, so I jumped at the chance to be your chauffeur when my mom called."

"Well, in that case, I do appreciate your company, and I'm glad to know you weren't coerced. Your mom's not really one to take no for an answer."

"No, she's not." Beth caught me studying her spiky blond hair. Quickly running her fingers through it, she said, "Don't worry—it's just lemon juice to lighten it. I read all the mommy-to-be instructions you gave me at my last appointment, and I promise that no chemicals will touch my hair until after I've weaned Cletus." She patted her belly.

"Cletus?" I asked.

She giggled. "Yeah. Since Ken and I don't want to know the sex of the baby, we chose a generic name to call him or her before he or she is born. It was the only name we could think of that rhymed with 'fetus.'"

Laughing, I said, "Nice. Matthew will be disappointed that you called dibs on the name first." I glanced at her Prius. "Are you sure both of us and my crutches are going to fit in there?"

Taking my crutches from me, she said, "Oh, ye of little faith," and then deftly placed them between the two front seats. "Now sit down and make yourself comfortable before I change my mind."

I maneuvered myself inside and buckled my seat belt, preparing to brace myself if she drove anything like Tish. I was pleasantly surprised to find out that she drove like an old woman—assuming the old woman wasn't Mimi—and I wondered whether it was her pregnant state that made her err on the side of caution. I looked in my side-view mirror and saw the line of cars trailing behind us on Frederica Road, but said nothing. We were in the height of the tourist season on the island, and I figured most of them needed a lesson in patience anyway.

She pulled into the parking lot across from Christ Church, then helped me out of the car. "Got everything?"

I patted the camera around my neck. "Yep. I shouldn't be too long. I'm just going to snap pictures of the Frazier tombstones so we have all the dates and names for when we visit the archives."

"Great. Mom wanted me to check on the flowers in the church, clean them up a bit, and report back to her. That will probably take me no more than thirty minutes. Unless you want me to come with you and help navigate?"

I waved my hand. "I'll be fine, and I've got my cell phone in my pocket if I fall and can't get up." I studied her worried face for a moment. "Really, I'll be fine."

Her face relaxed. "You want to meet back here in about half an hour? Or if you're done sooner, just pop your head inside the church to let me know."

"Sounds like a plan," I said. She helped me across the street and down the main path, then continued straight into the church while I veered right toward the cemetery. I tried to remember which path I'd taken the time I'd been here with Tish, but found myself walking in the same circle twice. Eventually, I attempted a worn path in a direction that initially felt wrong, but after winding my way beneath the shade of the tall oaks and crape myrtles, I realized that I was finally headed in the right direction.

I headed toward the Frazier plot, then abruptly halted. Somebody was whistling. I turned my head and began walking in the direction of the sound, my crutches thumping on the packed dirt and fallen leaves. The leaves of the oak trees shimmied above me in the hot summer sun and I looked up, searching for the dormant resurrection ferns that were invisible now in their cycle of waiting.

I made my way out of the shade of trees and found myself in a semi-clearing with four small white granite tombstones set in a row like grinning teeth. I stopped, recognizing the red wagon and the back of the head of the man kneeling before one of the graves.

Jimmy Scott turned and smiled when he spotted me. "Hello, Miss Ava."

He wore a red University of Georgia baseball cap over his short-cropped blond hair, making his oddly shaped nose even more prominent. Even though he continued to smile, his brown eyes seemed darker, holding in a shadow he couldn't step out from under. I began to back up. "I'm sorry to disturb you. . . ."

He stood. Still smiling, he said, "You're not disturbing me. I was just whistling to my sisters while pulling up these old flowers and planning what to plant next." I remembered what Tish had said about how he still talked with the two little girls as if he expected them to come back. I suppose I would have, too, if I had lost all of my family and found myself alone.

I noticed his gardening gloves on his hands, and the uprooted purple cornflowers in his wagon, their roots like the arms of small children asking to be held. Jimmy indicated the stones with a sweeping gesture of his arms. "This is my family."

I took a step forward, like I would if I were about to be introduced to strangers, and paused in front of the first one. As if on cue, Jimmy said, "This is my daddy, Walter F. Scott. The 'F' is for Floyd, and that's what everybody called him. I didn't even know Walter was his first name until I saw it here."

The lettering was done in a simple raised block style and, except for one headstone, gave only the name and birth and death dates—the latter being the same for all four. I moved to the second grave, the only stone with an inscription: FROM THE WITHERED TREE, A FLOWER BLOOMS.

"And this is your mother?" I kept to the present tense, just like he'd done.

Jimmy nodded. "Uh-huh. Mary Anne Sinclair Scott. Everybody called her Mary Anne."

I lifted my camera from my neck. "Do you mind if I take a picture? Tish said to take as many as I can to go with our report."

"I don't mind. I take pictures here all the time. I keep wanting to see one of those orbs or something."

"Like in those ghost photos you see on TV?"

He nodded. "I've never seen any, but I keep hoping. I think it would be nice to know I'm not all alone, you know?"

I looked into his eager and hopeful face, remembering sitting at the dinner table with my whole family, yet still managing to feel as if I were sitting by myself, the people surrounding me like holograms projected from somebody else's life.

"Yeah. I know," I said as I snapped the photo, then followed him to the next two gravestones.

"These are my little sisters, Christina and Jennifer. Everybody called them Tina and Jenny, but I called them something else." He smiled shyly.

"What did you call them?" I asked softly.

He slapped at a mosquito that had landed on his arm. "Scooter and Skeeter." He smiled broadly, as if he weren't talking about two small children who had died in a fire before their third birthdays.

I squatted down in between the two stones, reading the names and dates: Christina Mary Scott and Jennifer Ann Scott, both born on September fifth, 1977, and dying together on the same day, June thirtieth, 1980. I looked up at Jimmy, trying to see what he was seeing. "Why those names?"

"Well, I called Tina 'Scooter' because that's how she crawled. Never wanted to crawl the regular way, but scooted on her diaper using both feet out in front of her to pull herself along. It was like she was too impatient to walk and didn't have time to crawl. Made my daddy real mad, because she learned to walk when she wasn't even a year old yet."

"And Skeeter?" I asked, beginning to understand why Jimmy smiled, my own face letting go of some of the sorrow.

"Because she refused to talk and instead would just let out this high-pitched screech. She fell and hurt herself real bad when she was real tiny, and Mama said that's why she wouldn't talk, that it would come later for her. It never really did." His smile dimmed, remembering something I didn't have the heart to ask him about.

I stood, noticing his scarred hands again and trying to picture the fifteen-year-old he'd been, trying to save his family from the fire. "I imagine that you still miss them a lot."

He nodded matter-of-factly, as if we were discussing the weather. "Yeah. I do." He was thoughtful for a moment as he leaned over to brush dirt off one of the headstones. When he spoke he looked back at me, his eyes warm and familiar. "But I got a new mama and daddy, and a brother and sister."

"You mean Adrienne and her family?"

He nodded. "But it wasn't like they were taking their place, you know? It's just that it was a family, and I needed one, and that's how it worked out." He lifted a pot from behind his mother's grave that I hadn't spotted before, the vibrant red blooms of a swamp hibiscus nodding at me in greeting. "I got this from my garden, transplanted the roots and all so I could bring it here and replant it. Something keeps eating on it, so I figure it might do better here. It's funny how that works out sometimes."

"How what works out?"

Jimmy shrugged. "How sometimes flowers need to figure out how to bloom wherever they're planted." He winked. "Miss Tish embroidered that on a pillow for me."

I felt a genuine smile lift my lips. "I like that, Jimmy. I'll have to remember it."

I glanced at my watch, knowing I'd have to hurry to get back to Beth in time. "That song you were whistling—it was the same song you were whistling when you picked me up from that ravine. Do you know what it is?"

"Yep. It was a song my mama used to sing to Skeeter and Scooter, but they always liked it better when I whistled it for them."

"Do you remember the words?"

He pursed his lips and looked up as if asking for divine inspiration. In a pleasant baritone, he began to sing:

> *Oh, hush thee, my baby,*
> *Thy sire was a knight,*
> *Thy mother a lady,*
> *Both lovely and bright;*
> *The woods and the glens,*
> *From the towers which we see,*
> *They all are belonging,*
> *Dear baby, to thee.*

Stopping, he opened his eyes wide and looked at me. "There's more, but I figure you got the idea."

"Bravo!" I said, clapping. "You have a lovely voice."

His cheeks pinkened and he looked down at his tennis shoes. "Thanks, Miss Ava. I sing in the church choir with Miss Tish. She's the one who told me I should join."

"They're very lucky to have you." I worried my lower lip. "I'm curious, though, about the words. Do you know a different version, maybe? Other words that talk about a wife and child living across the sea?"

Again, he looked up at the sky as if in consultation with a higher authority before shaking his head. "Nope. Those are the only ones I ever heard."

I adjusted the crutches under my arms. "Well, thanks for the concert. I'll let you get back to work."

He nodded somberly as he watched me work my way out of the small clearing. I paused and turned back to him. "Which way to the Frazier plot? I'm a little turned around."

Jimmy pointed to my left. "It's real close, but I think he wanted privacy."

I was too afraid to ask who, so I simply thanked him, then made my way as quickly as I could down the path to where I recognized the small fence and the large granite marker in the front. When I saw blond hair instead of dark, my heart beat easier in my chest.

John turned as I hobbled my way over the chain fence and into the small enclosure. He'd been sitting cross-legged on the ground in front of his sister's grave but stood as I approached.

"Ava," he said in greeting, staring at my crutches. "I heard about your accident. Glad to see you up and about."

"Thanks." I lifted my palm. "I'm sorry to intrude. I promise to be quick—I'm just here to take pictures of the older graves to add to our report and maybe help me with some of my research."

He shoved his hands into the front pockets of his jeans. "I take it then that you haven't found Adrienne's notes."

I shook my head, thinking of the locked attic. "And Matthew doesn't know where they are, either."

"Like the wedding ring."

I checked my anger, knowing this wasn't a place for it. "She told Matthew that she'd lost the ring while sailing. He had no reason not to believe her. I didn't tell him that you had it. I was actually hoping that we could come up with some arrangement."

He raised an eyebrow in response.

"An arrangement?"

I took a deep breath. "It's a family heirloom, John. It belongs to the Fraziers, and I'd like it back in the family. I'll be happy to pay you for it."

His face darkened as if a cloud had suddenly obscured the sun. "No." He shook his head. "It's all I have left of my sister."

I put my hand on his arm and squeezed. "I'm sorry. I didn't mean to upset you. I'm a nurse and a midwife, so it's just my nature to fix things. The ring brings you no pleasure, John. Why do you hold on to it?"

He grinned, but it didn't make me want to grin back. "For evidence." He turned his back to me and stared down at Adrienne's tomb. MOTHER OF UNBORN CHILDREN. I thought again of the sketches of the faceless baby.

Very quietly, almost as if he were speaking to himself, he said, "She told me that it didn't belong to her. If it wasn't hers, then whose was it?" He turned his head toward me, spearing me with an accusing glare.

His expression told me that he had already figured out an answer, and I knew my own explanation that it had belonged to Matthew's mother and other women in his family wouldn't satisfy his need for blame.

"You were friends with Matthew once, so surely you would know that he's not the sort of person who would be unfaithful, and I resent your implication. I can't be your friend, John. Not until you accept the fact that your sister died in a tragic accident and that it was nobody's fault." I dropped my crutches, then began fumbling with the camera, eager to take the pictures I'd come for and leave John and his anger behind in this place of grief and shadows.

My hand shook as I focused on the three graves in the back, using my zoom lens so I wouldn't have to walk on my booted foot to get to the back of the plot. I lowered the camera slowly, reading Geoffrey's tombstone again. BELOVED FATHER AND FRIEND. BORN 1771. DIED 1815.

Beloved Father and Friend. No mention of being a beloved husband. No mention of a wife. And no space between or around him and his two children for a fourth grave.

I started at a touch on my arm. John stood there with my crutches, handing them to me. "I'm sorry. At least let me help you with these."

I let the camera drop around my neck, then reluctantly took the crutches. As I turned to leave, his words stopped me. "If you have any doubts, Ava, any doubts at all, I wish you would share them with me. Wouldn't you want to clear his name if you could?"

I didn't bother to turn around. "I don't need to," I said with more certainty than I felt.

I moved my crutches forward.

"Wait a minute—I almost forgot."

Reluctantly I stopped and waited while he dug something out of his back jeans pocket. "I went to a flea market last weekend with my mother and I found an old Instamatic with the film still inside. Naturally, I thought of you, so I bought it and then had the film developed. There was only one photo inside that I thought you might like, so I saved it for you. I've been carrying it around hoping I'd bump into you." He held out a small white envelope.

After a brief hesitation, I took it. Tucking the crutches under my arm, I slid open the envelope and pulled out the single photograph. Judging by the hairstyles and bathing suits worn by the two teenage girls, the picture had probably been taken in the mid-eighties. Both girls had the same dark brown hair, either permed or naturally curly. One wore hers with a headband, the other in a ponytail with a large bow barrette holding it in place against the pulse of the wind.

They were standing on the beach, their lanky arms carelessly thrown over each other's shoulders, the vibrant blue-green of the ocean matching the shade of their eyes. One was slightly taller than the other, and one had on a bikini while the other had on a one-piece. Yet it was startlingly obvious that they were sisters.

The shadow of the picture taker fell on them, but their expressions were easily read. The taller and presumably older sister stared blithely into the camera, unaware of her blossoming beauty, focused only on the now. But her sister, with a smile that touched only her mouth, had turned from the camera and was looking up at the taller girl, in her eyes a mixture of love and something else I couldn't define but felt as if I knew. Like watching a movie where somebody was stroking a dog, and knowing how soft the fur is without feeling it yourself.

"What do you think?" John asked. "Did I get it right?"

"Pretty much," I grudgingly admitted. "Except I never keep pictures that show the ocean." I looked down at the photo, suddenly unsure of my reason why. The surf lapped behind them, yet didn't appear any more threatening than the clear sky above them or the unspoken words between them.

"Why is that?" he asked, his eyes innocent again.

"I don't know," I said softly, focusing on the photograph but thinking about agreeing to Matthew's suggestion that I try hypnosis. I looked up and met John's eyes. "Thank you."

"You're welcome." He paused, examining my crutches with a frown. "Do you need help getting out of here?"

I shook my head. "I'm fine." I studied his face. "Just remember what I said about being your friend. I mean it."

He tucked his chin into his chest for a moment before looking back at me. Indicating my camera, he said, "I hope you find what you're looking for."

Our gazes locked until I finally looked away. "Thank you," I said again as I turned and began to navigate down the paths toward the church, wondering whether John had been speaking about my historical research or something else entirely.

❧

I lay back on the sofa, my head cushioned by two pillows, both feet propped up on the sofa arm on the opposite side. I glanced up as Matthew placed a cassette tape recorder on the low table in front of me.

"You're really into cutting-edge technology, aren't you?" I grinned in an attempt to hide my nervousness.

Matthew smiled back and shrugged. "I've been using this for years. I guess I could replace it with something more modern, but nobody's ever complained about it before." He looked pointedly at me.

"Just trying to help," I said, crossing my arms to stop myself from shivering.

"Ava," Matthew said, disengaging my hands from their death grip on my upper arms and taking them into his warm ones. "I know you're nervous, and that's okay and certainly normal. I've done this hundreds of times in the course of my career, and it's really helped a lot of people."

"Did you ever have somebody it didn't help?"

He avoided my eyes. "I've had a few patients who couldn't be hypnotized for various reasons."

I felt a twinge of unease. "But have you had anybody that you *did* hypnotize whose results weren't what you wanted or expected?"

He hesitated for only a moment. "Just once—when I'd just started using hypnosis therapy and I didn't have a lot of experience yet." He paused. "The hypnosis took an unexpected turn and we ended up deeper into the patient's past than we intended. But now I'm aware of how that happened, so I know how to avoid it." He squeezed my hands. "I firmly believe that any benefit that you will receive from hypnosis will far outweigh any unexpected discoveries."

I stared into his dark eyes and felt as if I were staring down a well-worn path that led to a familiar yet unnamed place. "Will you let me listen to the tape when we're done?"

"Of course. I won't censor anything. But you shouldn't need it. A lot of my patients say it's like watching a movie, where you remember pretty much all that happens."

I closed my eyes briefly, trying to imagine what images might be projected on the wall of my subconscious, and could see only a black screen. "What if I don't like what I'm seeing?"

He squeezed my hands. "I'll be here with you, and if you seem to be distressed in any way, I'll bring you out of it. Okay?"

I nodded. "What if . . ." I stopped, not capable of forming words to the thoughts that had grabbed hold of me ever since Matthew told me about my X-rays.

"No what-ifs, all right? We'll take this one step at a time, and deal with it together—whatever happens."

"Okay," I said, closing my eyes again as he placed an afghan over me and a warm kiss on my forehead.

Matthew stood and removed a CD from his briefcase, then placed it in the stereo. Soothing New Agey music filled the room, masking the ticking of the old clock and the sound of the refrigerator motor sporadically whirring to life in the kitchen.

"I probably won't ask you to load that CD onto my iTunes, okay?"

Matthew closed the blinds, then flipped off the lamps before seating himself in the armchair beside me. "Deal," he said as he leaned forward and picked up a notepad and pencil from the table. He had easily slid into the role of psychologist, and I barely recognized my husband beneath the professional persona.

"I've chosen a technique today that will open a crack into your subconscious. In the next few days or weeks, your mind will be allowing more and more memories to come to the surface. I don't want you to be afraid of anything that's revealed. I will either be here with you, or only a phone call away. I just want you to remember that whatever it is you recall can only help you along the path of healing."

I wanted to get off the sofa and leave the room, but I stayed, wanting to prove to him that he was wrong as much as I wanted to prove it to myself. "So what do I do?" I asked.

"I want you to close your eyes and relax. Concentrate only on breathing in and out, and when I speak, I want you to listen only to my voice." He paused. "Are you ready?"

I nodded and closed my eyes, allowing my head and body to sink further into the sofa; then Matthew began to speak, his deep voice low and comforting.

"In a moment I'm going to relax you more completely."

Breathe in, breathe out.

"In a moment I'm going to begin counting backward from ten to one. When I say the number ten you will allow your eyelids to remain closed. The minute I say the number ten, you will, in your mind's eye, see yourself at the top of a small set of stairs."

There was a brief silence in which I concentrated on the ins and outs of my breathing and pictured a staircase—alone, in a darkened space—with me at the top, illuminated in a bright white light.

He continued. "The moment I say the number nine, and each additional number, you will just move down those stairs, relaxing more completely. At the base of the stairs is a large feather bed, with a comfortable feather pillow. The moment I say the number one you will simply sink into that bed, resting your head on that feather pillow."

I could see the bed and the feather pillow at the bottom of the staircase, and I felt an urgency to reach it, an unexplainable exhaustion that overcame me as I regarded the pillow, eager to rest my head on it.

Matthew's voice continued slowly and steadily, bringing me down each step of the staircase, my level of relaxation increasing with each step until I stood on the bottom one.

"One," he said. "Now you're sinking into that feather bed; let every muscle go limp and loose as you sink into a calmer, more peaceful state of relaxation. I want you to imagine that you're just an observer of your own mind, drifting slowly down through your levels of consciousness."

His voice became the only sound in the room as it brought me slowly through my levels of consciousness, like being on an elevator where the upper level was where I was aware of everything, and the lower levels my subconscious mind. I could see myself on this elevator, could even imagine peeking through the crack in the doors as it descended through each level. I could almost feel the subtle jolt of the elevator stopping when I reached the bottom floor. I waited, staring at the closed doors.

"This is the part of your mind where secret memories from a long time ago are stored, memories that are sometimes so secret that even you have no conscious knowledge of them." He paused, and I saw the doors of the elevator slide open.

"Now I want you to imagine that you're at the end of a long corridor, a corridor so long that you can't see the end of it, but it's completely empty except for you. You begin walking down it and you notice that there are closed doors set in the walls on either side of the corridor. You stop in front of a door with a sign on it that reads 'Secrets.' It's locked, and there's a big brass key in the keyhole, and you know that this is the room where your secret memories are kept."

I stared at the key, my hand hovering over it as I continued to listen to Matthew's words.

"Your subconscious mind has locked things up in here to protect you from things that once hurt you or upset you or frightened you in some way. They're all memories from a very long time ago, and they can no longer hurt you. Your subconscious doesn't know this, and will continue to try to protect you until you face them with your conscious mind and let them go."

He paused again, and I watched as my hand hovered over the key.

"Just turn the key in the lock and open the door a little bit. In the next few days you'll start to recall these old memories, sometimes when you're awake and sometimes during your dreams, and each memory recalled will make you feel a little lighter, a little happier."

I felt the cold brass beneath my fingers, the latch giving way easily as I turned the key, the door opening without my having to pull on the doorknob. A triangle of brilliant white light spilled from the opening, and although I was listening to Matthew's voice, I found myself mesmerized by the light, moving toward it, resisting Matthew's directions to return down the corridor to the elevator.

I felt a presence beside me, urging me forward, and I reached out my arm and pushed the door open wider, so that I was completely swallowed by the bright light. I stepped through the door, feeling led by someone I couldn't see. I closed my eyes, and when I opened them I was outside, under a startling blue sky and smelling salt air. Sand sank between my toes as I stared out at the ocean as if in expectation.

"Ava?" Matthew's voice called from very far away. "Ava? Where are you?"

"*I'm on the beach,*" I said, hearing the surprise in my voice as I saw the black skimmers with their broad wings and jet-black caps, and heard the slap of the surf against the shore. Glancing down, I saw that my feet were bare, but I wore a long skirt that blew against my legs in the wind. Hair whipped across my face, and I noticed with the calmness of an uninterested bystander that my hair was no longer blond but a dark brown.

Matthew paused. Then: "Are you afraid of the water?"

"No," I said, feeling no other emotion except the surety of those words.

"What do you see?"

I told him about my feet and my hair as if I were describing somebody else.

Again, he paused. "What is your name?"

I didn't hesitate, knowing the answer in the same way I knew that my favorite color was red or that mosquitoes never bothered me. I lifted my chin to follow the flight of one of the skimmers, watching it spread its wings and soar above the crashing waves. I licked my lips, as they had suddenly become very dry, and said simply, "Pamela."

CHAPTER TWENTY

Pamela

ST. SIMONS ISLAND, GEORGIA
AUGUST 30, 1812

The three of us stretched out in the sand on the old quilt I had found in the bottom of a chest in the attic, the vintage of both items unknown. The attic was a treasure trove of family artifacts, a portal into the past, one into which I could not resist sticking my hand and pulling something into the present.

Geoffrey rested on his back with his eyes closed, his dark lashes curled at the tips, almost like a woman's. But there was nothing feminine in his face of tight angles and squared jaw. Even his blue eyes did nothing to diminish the strength and masculinity of his features. I knew this face, even in the darkness, like the image of a candle's flame that remains in the mind's eye long after it is extinguished.

A small smile drifted to my lips as I thought of the miniature portraits I had commissioned from a traveling artist. I had given the artist peppermint tea for a severe case of dyspepsia, and he was so relieved that he offered as payment the two miniatures of Geoffrey and myself. He had made a quick sketch of Geoffrey and me and promised he would have the paintings completed by the next time he came to St. Simons. It had been more than a year, but I had not yet given up hope that I would have my beloved's face preserved forever in oil paint.

Geoffrey's eyes opened and we watched each other for a long moment before he smiled that smile that made me think of the rising sun over the marsh. "What are you looking at?"

"You," I said. "I was thinking how lucky I am to have such a handsome husband."

"No." He reached up and twirled a long dark lock of my hair with his finger. "I am the lucky one."

I frowned. "Will you still say that when I am old and gray?"

"And even beyond." He used his hold on my hair to bend my head closer for a kiss. "Why such maudlin thoughts on a beautiful day?"

The wind had changed, fighting with the shorebirds, and the waves danced in response. "If I should die, who would you have raise Robbie?" The question had sat motionless in my mind since the day of Georgina's wedding, waiting for a day such as this, when none of life's pressures could interfere with calm thoughts.

"I would, of course. And Jemma. She loves him like a sister would."

"Not Georgina and Nathaniel? They are our only surviving relatives."

"No," he said, closing his eyes against me, knowing I could read them and see what he did not wish me to see.

I lifted my face to the wind, my hair whipping my cheeks, as if I could find the courage I sought in the salty air. "Why did you choose me over her?"

His eyes opened in surprise. "You do not know? She has never told you?"

I shook my head, feeling like a child, curious over the contents of a wrapped present.

"And you are sure you want to know."

I nodded, not sure at all, but like taking calomel to cure an illness, to hear the truth was important to my well-being.

His eyes were soft as they regarded me. "I found her with Nathaniel. They were both unclothed. I did not witness any more than that, but it was enough for me to know that I could not marry her."

"But Nathaniel . . . ?"

"He wanted to marry her, but she would not."

His eyes were shuttered, but I pressed forward, needing to know. "Why not?"

He did not look away as he answered. "She wanted only me, she claimed, although I believed her actions showed otherwise, and told her as much."

I felt faintly sick and turned away. "And that is the only reason you did not marry her?"

He pulled me down so that our faces were nearly touching. "I thank God every day that I found them. Because then I met you, and no doubts remained." He kissed me softly, then brought me down next to him, and I closed my eyes, trying to shut out the memory of the look on Georgina's face when I told her that I was marrying Geoffrey. I had not asked for her forgiveness, yet still, despite what I now knew, I wondered whether I should have, for her sake if not for my own. Yet I was with Geoffrey and Georgina was with Nathaniel, and all was as it was meant to be.

We rested for a long while, although I would not sleep and leave Robbie unattended if he should awaken. Instead, I nestled against Geoffrey and watched Robbie's back rise and fall as he slept. I placed my palm there, never tiring of the miracle of him.

"He is not going anywhere, Pamela."

I turned my face toward Geoffrey and nestled my head beneath his chin. "I would not put it past him, even in sleep. I did not know that a boy could be quite so fast and quite so full of energy all of the time."

Geoffrey's chest rumbled beneath my ear. "And to think you wanted a dozen."

"I still do," I said, thinking of all the babies I had helped bring into the world for other mothers, when all I wanted was just one more for myself.

I felt his lips on the top of my head. "But you are safe, and it comforts me to know that you will not die in childbed like Nathaniel's first wife. Although I am fairly sure that Nathaniel would like to fill his new house with many children."

I nodded, thinking of what Georgina had told me about her being barren, and the new house Nathaniel had built for them. It was enormous, with five bedrooms and an extraordinary flower garden that rivaled Anna Matilda King's at Retreat Plantation. Every time I saw it, I could not help but wonder whether the garden was a nod to our mother's memory, or a reminder to me of why I had an herb garden full of useful plants.

It was a warm day, but cooler on the beach with the ocean breeze and an overcast sky. We had finally received news of our country's declaration of war on Britain. Delivery of the *National Intelligencer* was slow here on the island, so our news was always delayed. Still, it was a surprise to know that our fledgling nation had been at war for nearly two months already, yet the view from our island remained the same.

The surf crept nearer, covering the tracks etched by the skimmers and temporarily sheltering the small creatures that burrowed in the sand. Foamy bubbles reflected the pewter sky, the image perfectly round and clear until the ocean pulled them back again. When we were children Georgina would tell me that the bubbles were like mirrors through which you could see through to another time, and if you followed them out to sea, they would take you to that place. I hadn't believed her, but there were times, like now, when I felt the ocean's magic, knew that the salt and foam that formed the ocean had nourished me in my mother's womb, marking me as a child of the sea to which I would always return.

"Do you think we will see any hostilities this far south?" I asked Geoffrey, my eyes still focused on the horizon, where the sea and sky met, the gray hues of both melding as if smudged by God's finger.

"They will want to blockade our busiest ports in Charleston and New Orleans, I am sure. Whether our navy will allow it is another matter."

"But what of us here, on St. Simons?"

"I think we are too small for them to notice. I am a farmer and not a soldier, but I cannot think why the British would want to come here." He held me tightly, and for a moment all I could hear was the symphony created by the soft sound of our son's breathing, Geoffrey's heartbeat, and the slow riffling of the surf. I clung to the peacefulness of it, memorizing all the notes, to be recalled if needed.

He continued. "Mr. Gould at the new lighthouse has promised to keep watch for British ships and to send an alert if they are spotted. We are in good hands, Pamela."

"I am glad." I thought of the stories of the atrocities of the British and their Indian allies in settlements up north, and I shuddered to think those same marauders would invade my home.

Robbie stirred and then opened his eyes, his face splitting into a wide smile when he saw me. His was a happy nature, and his smile each morning placed the sun in my sky even on cloudy days. He reached for the pickling jar that had become his constant companion, a gift from his aunt Georgina. Geoffrey had fashioned a strip of leather with holes punched into the top and held in place by twine to allow the imprisoned caterpillar air to breathe.

Georgina had found the caterpillar on her passionflower vine and had brought it to Robbie with a clipping, seeing as we had nothing to attract caterpillars or butterflies to our own garden.

At six years old, Robbie was smart and inquisitive, and studying his caterpillar had become a near obsession ever since Georgina told him it would change into a butterfly. The caterpillar had grown fat and shed its skin several times, and Georgina had been bringing fresh stems and leaves to Robbie on a nearly daily basis to satisfy its appetite. I did not question her presence, as Robbie's joy overcame any misgivings.

I stood and began gathering the contents of the picnic basket while Geoffrey pulled on his boots.

"Mama?"

I turned to Robbie. "Yes?"

"My caterpillar is sick."

Placing the dishes that had been rinsed by the ocean into the basket, I took the jar from Robbie and peered through the glass. The bright orange caterpillar with black spikes from top to bottom was perched upside down on a single leaf, preparing for its transformation.

I shook my head. "No, it is just getting ready to become a butterfly."

His eyes widened with excitement. "Right now?"

"No," Geoffrey said as he gently took the jar from me. "It will take some time, but soon."

A frown worried Robbie's brow. "Is it dead?"

"No," I said. "Just getting ready for its new life—that is all."

Still frowning, he looked between his father and me. "Is that what Leda is doing, too?"

Leda had died in the spring, her passing a terrible blow to us all, especially to Robbie. He had seen her wrapped in her brown blanket before burial, and I suspected that was where the source of his thoughts began.

"Leda is in heaven, sweetheart. With God."

He stared back into his jar, his forehead smoothing into the softness of childhood again. "I think she will be back. As a butterfly. Because she told me she would not leave me."

I swallowed a thick lump in my throat. I had not the heart to tell him otherwise. That was the hardest part about being a mother: the part when you realized that you did not know all the answers. I threaded my fingers through his dark curls. "You may be right, Robbie. But surely not a butterfly. I think Leda would be better suited as a queen if she came back. She always loved shiny things, did she not?"

He nodded vigorously, his smile returning. I watched as he stood, clutching his jar, wishing with all my heart that what I had told him was true, that we had the chance to become more than what we had been, to be given another opportunity to fix what had been broken, to forgive where forgiveness had once appeared unobtainable.

We walked down the beach as far as we could before heading up over the dunes, our footprints in the sand marking our progress, the ocean swallowing them after we passed as if we had never been there at all.

Gloria

ANTIOCH, GEORGIA
JULY 2011

I walked past Mimi's room, then did a double take and immediately retraced my steps. She stood next to her bed, which was covered in the same Indian quilt she'd had on it through nearly sixty years of marriage to my father. She'd once told me that I'd been conceived under that same quilt, which guaranteed that I'd never use it myself. That was something, as my teenage grandchildren liked to say, that was too much information.

"What are you doing?" I asked as I stared at the large hard-shell suitcase spread open on the bed like a butterfly under glass. She had disorganized heaps of clothing scattered over the pillows and the part of the bed that wasn't covered by the quilt. Inside the suitcase were similar heaps. I stepped close, stopping when I recognized what lay nestled between the clothes, the matching brass frames glinting under the overhead light fixture.

"I'm going to go see our girl, Gloria. Somebody has to, and it doesn't look like it's going to be you."

I stayed where I was, transfixed by my photographed childhood face staring up from the bottom of the suitcase. "Why are you doing this? Why now?"

Mimi's magnified eyes stared at me through her bifocals. "Did you not hear Ava on the phone? That's how I know."

"She's confused. She was carrying on about somebody named Pamela who had dark hair and wore long dresses. How can we help her if we don't even understand what she's upset about?"

Her gaze continued to hold my own, and I knew we were both remembering another time, when the moon sat full and bright in the sky and the scent of evening primrose hung heavy in the air like a cloak of possibilities.

She stepped between the suitcase and me and threw a stack of her multicolored velour sweats on top of the frames. "You have spent a lifetime living only half of your life, Gloria. You can only see how much you could lose. And Ava and I are asking you to look very hard now and see what you could gain."

Her hands gripped the side of the suitcase, and I noticed anew the blue veins that threaded the tops like road maps, and the small bones that seemed suddenly so delicate. Mimi was a diminutive woman whose personality had blinded me to seeing it all of my life. Until now.

Her voice was so soft I had to lean closer to hear her. "Have I taught you nothing? Why would God have made you my daughter if I couldn't teach you anything?"

My ninety-one-year-old mother was crying, and the shame cut at me. Very quietly, I said, "There is no death, only a change of worlds. You taught me that, remember? When Daddy died. It made me not afraid anymore." I choked on my own words. "It gave me the courage to do what I had to do."

She was silent for a moment before she spoke. "So are you coming with me?"

I took a deep, shuddering breath. I hated to be wrong, hated even more to be told I was wrong by my mother. "I suppose I'll have to. You're blind as a bat, and I'd be forced to call the Highway Patrol as a matter of public safety if you insist on heading out on your own. But I'll need at least a day or two to make sure Henry has meals in the freezer, and the ladies' bridge club has somebody to fill in for me. . . ."

Mimi slammed the lid of the suitcase closed. "I'm leaving in half an hour, with or without you. I'm sure your bridge club can make do, and Henry's a grown man, Gloria. Surely he won't starve without your supervision."

She was right, of course, but I wouldn't give her the satisfaction of telling her so. Instead, we both stared at the large suitcase on top of the bedspread as if it were a stain we weren't sure how to treat.

"I suppose I should call one of the boys to come get that and take it to the car," I said. "I hope Matthew won't mind bringing it into the house when we get there." I frowned at the circa-1968 mustard yellow American Tourister and wondered how somebody so old could still manage to pack so much stuff.

"Oh, we're not staying with Matthew and Ava. They're newlyweds, after all. June's sister has a vacation home on St. Simons, so we're renting it for a week with the option of continuing our stay if we need to. It's got two bedrooms, since I knew I couldn't sleep in the same room with you and your snoring."

I sighed, wondering how long she'd been waiting there in the open door by her suitcase for me to walk by and have this conversation. "Fine," I said, turning on my heel to go to my room and throw a few things into a much smaller bag. "But I'll need an hour to get ready. While I'm packing you can call Stephen on your cell phone and ask him to come load the car."

She grunted to let me know she'd heard me and wasn't happy, but as I left the room, she had the final word. "You might as well pack for a few weeks. We could be there for a while."

My steps slowed as I neared my own bedroom, my thoughts turning to the towering oaks of St. Simons and the resurrection ferns that hid in the trunks, and the road between here and there that no longer seemed so long. And as I pulled my suitcase from the back of my closet, I thought of Ava and whether my efforts to protect my daughter might mean losing her forever.

CHAPTER TWENTY-ONE

Ava

Beth Hermes lay on the table in the examining room wearing a blue cotton gown while I did my best not to spoil with the clomping of my boot the calming atmosphere that we tried to attain in the practice. I rubbed my hands together to warm them and then, making sure to protect her privacy by keeping the lower sheet strategically placed below the slightly swollen belly, lifted her gown to begin the external examination.

"So, how did your hypnosis session go?" she asked.

I hadn't yet come to terms with or even gotten any understanding of what had happened, and I wasn't prepared to discuss it with Beth. So I pretended I hadn't heard her and began her examination.

"Let me know if anything hurts or if my hands are too cold," I said as I gently palpated her abdomen, feeling for the uterus, and imagining the already perfectly formed, three-inch-long baby floating in its liquid world. I found what I was looking for exactly two fingerbreadths above the pubic bone.

"Good news," I said. "The baby's finally big enough that we might be able to hear the heartbeat today."

Her expression of disappointment surprised me until she spoke. "I thought this was just a routine appointment, so I didn't ask Ken or my mom to come. I know they'd like to hear it, too."

I smiled. "I understand, and we can schedule another appointment for you this week so Ken or your mother can be here. But they'll have plenty of opportunities later. Maybe you'll want this first time to be just between you and your baby."

I rubbed my own slightly protruding belly, still too early to hear the heartbeat, and waited for Beth to decide. Although rarely found on the "What Do You Want to Be When You Grow Up?" lists for little girls, I had never wanted to be anything other than a nurse-midwife. Maybe, as I'd told John, it had to do with my mother's miscarriage and the helplessness I'd felt. But deep down I'd always known it was a calling, something I'd been born to do. I was good at it, and whatever Beth decided I'd make it work.

Beth thought for a moment, then nodded. "Yeah, just me this time, but next time I'll bring both Ken and my mother."

I retrieved the handheld fetal Doppler ultrasound machine, then lubricated the transducer before sliding it where I expected the baby's heartbeat to be. Neither one of us breathed as we heard the muffled *thud-thud* of the tiny heart coming from the speaker on the Doppler, the sound so distant that it seemed to be coming from another time and place.

"Wow," said Beth, tears in her eyes. "It makes it so . . . real somehow."

I counted the small thuds, still not immune to the enormity of what we were hearing, or how strange it seemed that it was even a possibility.

When I was finished, I wiped off the skin, then pulled the cotton gown back down over Beth's slightly rounded belly. "Everything looks great, and you seem to be right on schedule for thirteen weeks," I said, writing my notes in her chart. "Your nausea's all gone now? And you're taking your prenatal vitamins?"

She sat up on the examining table. "Yes—to all of the above." She opened her mouth to ask another question, but, anticipating where she was trying to move the conversation, I interrupted her.

"Your blood pressure's a little high. Are you having any swelling in your ankles or feet?"

"A little, maybe. But it's summer and I just figured it was the heat."

"Could be," I said, looking at her chart although not really seeing it. I seemed to have a sixth sense when it came to other women's pregnancies, anticipating when a baby would automatically turn from a breech position without intervention and when it wouldn't. I could smell gestational diabetes before it was confirmed in a urine test, and predict preeclampsia before symptoms became severe. It was almost as if I'd had a lifetime of experience delivering babies instead of only a decade.

"I want you to keep an eye on your sodium intake. Continue to drink lots of water, and call me immediately if you develop any headaches that won't go away with Tylenol and rest, especially if you also have any blurring of vision. And before you leave, I'd like to draw some labs to get a baseline of your kidney function."

"I thought you said everything was fine," Beth said.

"It is. I'm just trying to make sure it stays that way." I jotted down a few more notes, then glanced up at the clock. I was running only ten minutes behind, a small miracle, considering how long it took me to clomp from one examining room to the next.

"So how did the hypnosis session go?"

I bit back a sigh as I recalled my hysterical phone call to Mimi and my inability to comprehend anything Matthew had tried to tell me. "We're not really sure," I said, glancing up at the clock so I'd have another reason to cut our conversation short. "Matthew says that what we gain from hypnosis is not necessarily what happens during the session, but what happens afterward—what our subconscious begins to reveal little by little, either in our dreams or in flashbacks while we're awake."

"And have you had any?" She swung her legs against the side of the table like a little girl. "Dreams or flashbacks?"

"I . . ." I started, then stopped, recalling the vivid images that had dogged me every single night since. *I've had dreams about the ocean my entire life,* I'd wanted to say, but couldn't. Because they were no longer like dreams to me, but a part of me, and I couldn't explain that to Matthew any more than I could explain it to Beth. "Not yet," I said. "Matthew says to give it time."

I smiled my official smile. "Well, I guess I'll see you Saturday for our trip downtown to the historical archives. I'll pick you and your mom up at ten, then my treat for lunch afterward. We'll celebrate getting this boot off my ankle." I waited as she slid off the examining table. "I'll leave your refill prescription for your vitamins at the checkout desk."

My hand was on the doorknob when she spoke again.

"I went to the archives once with Adrienne, too. She was also looking for information about Matthew's family. It's a shame you can't find all of her notes—it could save you a lot of time and trouble."

"Yeah, I know. But neither Matthew nor her family knows where all of her research went. Or her date book. I'll keep looking. And are you sure you want to go back and look for the same information?"

Beth laughed. "Are you kidding? I love that stuff—and I always find something new. Maybe I'll find something that's field-trip-worthy for my ninth graders. The last time I was there, I discovered an old letter from around the time of the Civil War that referenced a slave cemetery that's since been swallowed by the ocean. We used the documentation from what we knew with that in the letter to figure out where it had been. Nothing like having history under your fingertips to get kids interested."

She turned around to the chair where she'd left her clothes and then stopped. "Speaking of uncovering stuff, Adrienne told me that she'd found a hiding place in a wall while she was looking for something else. It was probably put into the wall when the house was built, since at the time you could be raided by the Indians or the Spanish. She said she hadn't found anything valuable in it, but I figure if she wanted to hide something small, that would be the place for it."

My mouth tasted of paper. "Did she mention where it was?"

Beth shook her head. "Not really—just that the space wasn't that big. Sorry I can't remember more."

"Thanks, Beth. I'll ask Matthew—he should know, seeing as how he's lived in the house his entire life."

We said good-bye and I shut the door behind me before shuffling to my next appointment, thinking of date books and hiding spaces, of the ocean and an attic door with a missing key. And of a husband whom I didn't seem to know at all.

⁂

I returned home before Matthew. After changing clothes and chopping salad fixings, I filled a large pot of water for my standby of spaghetti and sauce in a jar and turned on the fire beneath it to heat. Then I returned to the parlor, my hands on my hips, and spun around looking for any sign that would indicate a hidden panel in any of the walls.

I walked slowly through the parlor and the dining room, knocking on walls and finding nothing. I moved across the foyer and paused in the threshold of Matthew's study. I knew this was my home, and with the exception of the potting shed, he'd never made me feel as if any part of the house was off-limits to me. Still, this was his masculine domain, with the large antique partners desk and the rich mahogany paneling on the walls. I supposed that if I wanted to keep valuables somewhere in the house, this would be the most logical place. Which was also one of the reasons it would be the last place in the house I imagined Matthew's ancestors would keep a hidden panel.

I stood by the desk, examining the walls. All of Matthew's diplomas were hung in his office in Savannah, but I would have expected *something* to hang on these walls. I stepped closer, the empty walls at odds with what I knew of my husband, and saw small nail holes at eye level going across the wall opposite the door. They were at the perfect height for framed artwork, and it made me wonder when Matthew had removed them. I could see in my mind's eye the delicate strokes of pen and paper, the depictions of the view from the dock at sunset, or even of Matthew sitting here in this study. They had been Adrienne's artwork, removed because Matthew had decided it was time to move on. Or maybe because it was too hard to hide from the past with reminders of Adrienne staring down from the walls like knowing eyes.

Restless, I moved farther into the room, close enough to the wall that I could spread my hands flat against the smooth wood, could see the tiny whitened hole from where a nail had once protruded. I lifted my hand to knock, but stopped as the sudden aroma of pipe smoke seemed to drift through the air. I turned around, surprised to find the room empty.

Something heavy and deep sprang its roots like fingers up from my stomach to my throat, carrying with it the taste of bile and grief. I saw him—the man from the sketch in the book—standing by the window, a pipe in his hand. His skin seemed gray, his face thin, his hair lank and long. He was looking at me with an intensity I felt in the marrow of my bones, and I had the sensation that he was waiting for me as if I had just left the room. I knew this was a memory of something, a recollection dislodged like a rock from a high precipice, but if this was meant to recall a childhood event, it hadn't come from mine.

But the feeling in the back of my throat was real, the sadness and help-lessness, and I needed it to go away. "Stop!" I shouted to the empty room, and I was by myself again, the image gone from my mind, yet the memory lingering like the smell of pipe smoke that had filtered in from a past I hadn't known existed.

I wanted to lie down, to go to sleep and erase all of what I'd just seen. But I knew the images would pursue me into my dreams, as they had each night since my hypnosis session. They came at me like an old black-and-white silent film, flickering through my subconscious without words. Yet when I awoke, I remembered them, remembered words I hadn't spoken or heard.

And in those dreams I recognized this house, and the dock, and the beach—a beach that did not inspire terror, but instead drew me toward it as a place of sanctuary. None of it had anything to do with old bone breaks or my fear of water, and I would awaken angry and frustrated, and too con-fused to tell Matthew. How could I explain something to him that I couldn't understand myself? Mostly, I didn't want to give him a reason to put me under again, afraid of what else I might see.

I lifted my hand again to knock on the wall panel, noticing the raised birthmark at the base of my thumb as if seeing it for the first time. Something jogged at my memory, like the buzzing whir of an insect, then just as quickly vanished. I brought my hand down on the paneling and began rapping up and down, even below the chair railing and baseboard, listening for a hollow sound that might indicate a hiding place.

I'd gone halfway around the room before I remembered the boiling water in the kitchen. I checked my watch, saw that it was still early for Matthew to be home, then turned off the burner, placing the top onto the pot to keep it warm so that it would reach a quicker boil when I turned it on again.

I was in the foyer walking back to the study when my gaze settled on Adrienne's sketch of the house between the windows in the front parlor. I remembered the other sketch of the house I'd found inside the frame, and of the woman on the beach and the printed lyrics, wondering again why Adrienne had placed them there, and wanting desperately to see the picture of the woman again. I stopped, trying to remember where I'd placed the call ticket to pick up the framed sketches.

I stepped into the parlor, glancing around the room and hoping something would jog my memory. I slid open the drawers on the low chest and rifled through the magazines on the coffee table in front of the couch. I turned to leave, on the hunt for my purse as another spot where I might have shoved the ticket, when I spotted the battered music box on top of the corner curio cabinet. I was fairly sure I hadn't placed the box there, and assumed the cleaning people had moved it.

I hobbled over to it and picked it up to move it back to the chest of drawers and felt something hard and solid knock against the inside of the hinged lid. Carefully holding the box flat, I lifted the top and looked inside. Nestled in the small cavity over the glass covering the moving parts lay an old-fashioned door key, a dark-colored iron one that matched the rest of the keys in the house.

I stared at it for a long moment before taking it out of the box, the metal cold against my palm. With a shaking hand, I replaced the music box on the curio and returned to the hallway. Standing at the bottom of the steps, I looked upward, wondering whether I should bother going upstairs to see if the key fit in the attic door. Because I already knew that it did.

The sound of tires on gravel made me turn around, and I forced my hand to stop shaking as I made my way to the door and wondered how I was going to mention the key that hadn't been lost, but had been deliberately placed in a spot where I most likely wouldn't look.

As footsteps approached, I threw open the door, then stood there, surprised, as I watched my mother and Mimi walk toward me, my mother in front, because now that Mimi was older and slower it was Gloria's chance to not always be behind. Both moved slowly, as if they'd been sitting down for a long time. Maybe it was the relief of not having to confront Matthew yet, but I flew into my mother's arms, surprising us both. She hadn't hugged me good-bye when I'd left Antioch, and although she'd never been one for excessive physical displays of affection, it had been enough for me to miss it in the same way the sky would miss the stars.

She smelled like her garden, of sun-warmed earth and green growing things. She smelled of home and refuge, of the comforting aroma of the laundry detergent she'd been using all of my life. Her arms, almost reluctant at first, wrapped around my shoulders and hugged me tightly, then abruptly let go as if I might break. Or as if I might just slip away. It had always been that way between us.

I turned to Mimi, who'd caught up to us, and her arms, thinner than I remembered, hugged me to her bony chest, but all I smelled of her was love. She held me away from her, studying my face. "Pregnancy suits you, Ava. I've never seen you so beautiful. Isn't that right, Gloria?"

My mother's lips tightened as she nodded, but I knew she wasn't being stingy with words. Her eyes swam with moisture, and she'd rather be caught with the back of her skirt tucked into the waistband of her panty hose than to be seen crying in public.

I turned back to Mimi. "What are y'all doing here? I didn't expect you until Christmas."

Mimi was already walking to the front steps, my mother close behind. "You were crying pretty hard, child, when you called us. We figured you needed us now." She emphasized the word *we,* which meant it had been her idea. Not that I hadn't known that the minute I saw them walking up my driveway.

"Where's Daddy?"

My mother waved her hand in the air. "He's working. Says somebody has to be there to hold the fort down. Mimi and I came prepared to stay awhile. We're too old to make that trip without space in between to rest up before we go home again."

The three of us stopped at the bottom of the steps, each of us trying to figure out how to navigate the stairs with our various physical ailments. Eventually, my mother took over, helping Mimi up the steps one at a time— although it looked like they leaned against each other in equal amounts— and then I clambered up by myself, as I'd already had plenty of practice.

I showed them into the parlor and had them sit down on the sofa, and then I sat in one of the chairs across from them, not sure whose turn it was to speak. Finally, I ventured, "If you haven't already eaten, I was making spaghetti and salad for Matthew and me. I can throw in extra. And we've got two guest bedrooms upstairs; I'll just need to put sheets on the beds—"

"We've rented a house," my mother said, cutting me off.

"You're newlyweds," Mimi added, as if that explained everything.

"How long are you expecting to stay?" The words jumped out of me before I could pull them back. Mimi smiled, but Mama's lips tightened.

I tried to backpedal. "I mean, I'm glad you're here, but it's just a bit of a surprise."

Mama started to speak, but Mimi placed her hand on her arm to stop her. "Well, with the baby, and your ankle, and now this hypnosis thing, we figured you might need some backup."

I raised my eyebrows, still not sure whether I was happy to see them. At least with my mother here I'd have the chance to ask her questions about my pregnancy and babies. But I wasn't prepared to share with either of them anything about the clouds of doubt that hovered above Matthew. Not because I was afraid to prove my mother right, but because I was afraid to prove *myself* right.

"What are you holding?" Mimi asked.

I looked at my fist and realized I still held the key. Slowly, I turned my hand palm up and unfurled my fingers, the metal dark against the paleness of my skin. "It's the key to the attic. Matthew lost it, and I just found it." My voice sounded unnatural even to my own ears.

I met their eyes, but in each I saw the seeds of doubt.

I stood abruptly. "Matthew will be home any minute now, so I'm going to go put the water on to boil again and throw some garlic bread in the oven. Maybe he can show you the house—it's still a bit tricky going up and down the stairs. . . ."

The front door opened, and Matthew walked in, his smile hiding his surprise at finding my mother and grandmother sitting with me in the front parlor. I hadn't heard his car, and I felt at a disadvantage.

"What a nice surprise," he said as he placed his briefcase against the wall and walked toward me. He stopped midway and I realized that he was staring at the key in my hand. Our eyes met and his smile faltered slightly.

"You found it," he said.

"Yes, I did."

"Where?" He sounded genuinely curious.

"Inside the music box."

"Good," he said. "I imagine the cleaning people must have found it and stuck it in there. They're always moving things." He turned abruptly to hug Mimi and my mother. "It's great seeing you both. I hope you plan to stay for a while."

My mother stood to her full height, which was slightly less than the five feet, eight inches she'd once been. She pulled back her shoulders to look up into his face and stared Matthew directly in the eyes. "As long as it takes," she said.

I was taken back to the moment when I was small after I'd slipped through the ice of our swimming pool and she'd pulled me to the surface. I felt cold and warmth rushing over me as I had before, but this time I wasn't sure from what she'd come to save me.

CHAPTER TWENTY-TWO

Ava

ST. SIMONS ISLAND, GEORGIA
JULY 2011

I flipped on the switch to the attic light, then began to climb the stairs one step at a time, with Matthew directly behind me to make sure that I didn't fall. After a stilted conversation over my dinner of jarred spaghetti, garden salad, and burned garlic toast, Mimi and Mama had finally left. Matthew and I had each driven a car so Mama wouldn't have to drive at night, then helped them settle into their rented house.

In the car ride back I'd tried my best to accept Matthew's explanation that the cleaning people must have found the attic key and placed it in the music box. I'd rested my head on his shoulder and rubbed my hand over the growing swell of our child and pushed my doubts behind a curtain that seemed to become more and more transparent with each passing day.

"There it is," he said after reaching the top of the stairs. He pointed to an old leather trunk, on top of which sat a varnished wooden box. "My replica flag," he said in explanation as he crossed the attic floor to retrieve it. "Too late for the holiday, but I guess I don't really need an excuse to fly it."

I looked around the space, at the exposed beams and pink insulation and the accumulation of a family's debris seemingly lumped together by decade, and wondered whether a hiding place had ever existed up here.

"I saw Beth Hermes today," I said. "She told me that while she was helping Adrienne with her research, Adrienne mentioned an old hidey-hole somewhere in the house. That's actually what I was looking for when I found the attic key."

His face registered genuine surprise. "I'm not shocked that we have one, but I've never heard of it. I don't think my parents or grandparents were aware of it either, as it was never mentioned to me. Did Beth say where it was?"

I shook my head. "No, and Adrienne didn't tell her. It was small, so it wouldn't have held an entire briefcase, but I'm wondering if maybe that's where Adrienne put her date book."

Matthew was focused on unlatching the box and retrieving his flag. "Well, we'll definitely have to be on the lookout for it." He took the flag and replaced the box on top of the trunk.

Feeling disappointed, I looked around, noting that nothing seemed different since I'd last been there—the stacks of old furniture, the suitcases, the yellowed newspapers. I looked down at the floor, wondering whether the footprints in the dust had been there before. Glancing up, I met Matthew's eyes.

"Before I lost the key, I was up here looking for baby things," he said, as if reading my mind.

I nodded and averted my gaze. "Did you find anything?"

"Like Adrienne's briefcase?"

I didn't bother to deny that that was what I'd been thinking.

"No, I didn't. I have looked, up here and everywhere else, because I knew her parents wanted everything that belonged to her."

I thought of the empty closet, and the blank walls in his study, and asked the question I wasn't sure I really wanted answered. "How long did it take you to take down her artwork in your office? Or her clothes in your closet?"

He looked surprised, as if I'd asked him where babies came from or why a candle couldn't burn in a vacuum. "Within a month of her funeral. They seemed out of place somehow, even though we'd been married for five years." He stopped, measuring his words. "Because they didn't belong to me," he said, and I heard the words behind them, the words that said their marriage had been only a temporary thing, a passage of time in which nothing permanent remained. And I remembered what John had said about Adrienne's wedding ring. *She said it didn't belong to her.*

I forced myself to keep my voice steady. "So did you find any baby things?"

"I did," he said, moving through a narrow passageway between boxes and furniture. "Don't worry—it's not a crib or high chair. We'll buy new for that kind of stuff."

Carefully, I followed him, making sure my clublike boot didn't catch on anything and either trip me or start an avalanche. When he moved aside so I could see, I heard the air leave my lungs in a high-pitched wheeze.

It was a very old wooden rocking horse, the mane, nose, and eyes carved by the hand of an artist. Only odd patches of paint remained in random places, leaving pale, bleached wood with carved lines and curves, and eyes large and full of fire. It was remarkable for its beauty and testimony to good workmanship. But it was mostly remarkable for its familiarity.

"What's wrong?" Matthew asked, his voice full of concern.

I realized I'd raised my hand to my mouth. "I think I've seen it before."

"I don't think so, Ava. It was made generations ago by an ancestor and has never been anywhere outside of this house. Maybe you saw something similar?"

I reached out and touched the mane, and imagined I could hear a little boy's laughter and the sound of the runners rolling against the wooden planks of a floor. "I don't think so," I said, my voice so soft that Matthew had to lean his head down closer to hear me.

"Do you need to sit down?"

Before I could answer, he'd pulled an orange vinyl chair, circa 1970, over to me, wiping the dust off with his hand, then steadied my arm as I lowered myself into the seat.

A cold sweat clung to my skin, and I concentrated on drawing deep breaths, then letting them out. My head stopped spinning and I met Matthew's eyes. "I know I've seen it before. But not . . . here." I waved my hand to indicate more than the attic, to include not just the house but the world beyond it. "It was new. And the saddle was painted red." My throat closed on the last word. I clutched at Matthew's hand. "How did I know that?"

He kept his gaze focused on me and held my hand until my breathing had returned to normal.

Matthew pushed the hair off my forehead, the strands sticking to skin. "What's wrong? Are you all right?"

I shook my head, unsure even how to begin, but relieved to have finally found an opening. "I'm not sure." I met his gaze, measuring his emotions as I spoke. "I haven't told anyone, but since my hypnosis, I keep having these intense dreams and flashbacks of . . ." I paused, almost saying "me." I continued. "Of Pamela. She's definitely . . . not from this century. The clothes are wrong, and, well, so is everything else." My smile faltered before it began. "She has a husband and a son, and she loves them both very much. I feel that strongly, just as I feel everything else that she's doing and feeling." I bit my lip, trying to think of how to say it and knowing my inability to admit to it was why I hadn't told him before. "It's like I'm seeing her life through my eyes. Like I *am* her." I spoke very quickly, as if I were afraid that if I slowed down, I'd stop.

"She has a sister, Georgina, and Pamela loves her, but I don't think she likes her very much. She feels an obligation toward her. And I see snippets of other people, too, and places that are familiar to me now but that I can't name. It's like being on a roller coaster, with flashes of scenes and emotions thrown at me all at once." My head dipped. "Am I losing my mind?"

He squatted in front of my chair and looked up into my eyes. "No. It's totally normal after regression therapy for dreams—while you're awake or asleep—to become very vivid and real. And some of them are actual memories from your earliest moments in life, and some are just your imagination, a way your subconscious is trying to help you see a painful part of your past."

"Yes, but this is a whole *life*. In another century. How can that have anything to do with me growing up in Antioch?" I stared at him, unable to read his eyes, and it unnerved me. "Please, Matthew. Take me under again. Bring me back to that place. There's more I need to know." I didn't know that I had been going to say that, and the words frightened me. I *didn't* want to go back, but at the same time I knew I had no choice if I wanted answers.

Something flickered in his eyes, like a distant cloud sliding over the moon. "It wasn't a past-life regression, Ava. There's no firm evidence to prove that such a thing even exists. Usually what people are calling a past-life regression is just a matter of the subject having been unknowingly exposed to certain things that make them believe it actually happened to them in a previous life." He squeezed my hands, his eyes still foreign to me. "You've been talking a lot with Tish and Beth about the history of St. Simons. That could certainly be feeding your subconscious." Quietly, he added, "And remember. Those bone breaks occurred in *this* life."

I heard the clinical reasoning in his words, but I couldn't so easily dismiss what I'd been feeling and seeing. Mimi believed in the cycle of life and death, something my mother had taught me meant going to heaven when we died. But even as a young child, I'd known that wasn't the same thing. "Mimi's always saying that she tries not to be too good in this life, because she wants another chance to come back as a movie star." I tried to smile, but my lips got stuck halfway. "Pamela is too real for me to have made it all up."

"Our subconscious is a lot stronger than we can even imagine. It's our great protector, guarding our minds from seeing something we're not yet ready to face."

I shook my head, trying to erase his doubt. "Whatever it is, I can face it now. You make me strong. Don't you see that? I want to try the hypnosis again. I need to go back to that place." I tried to stand, but he held on to my hands so that I remained seated.

"No, Ava. No. You were supposed to go to your childhood, but I couldn't control what happened. I don't feel safe doing that again."

His hands tightened on mine, and I looked at him with a growing understanding. "You did that with Adrienne, didn't you? You did a past-life regression with her."

He lowered his head, but not before I'd seen his eyes and knew I'd spoken the truth. "Adrienne is dead. Can't we leave her buried?"

"We can't, Matthew. Not as long as you keep her alive with your secrets." I leaned forward, my head suddenly clear. "What did she tell you?"

I waited until he spoke. "We only did it twice. The first time was because she wanted help with a bad habit. And then the second time, she wanted to know more about her birth parents. She was adopted as a toddler, and she wanted to know more. Her birth parents were deceased, and she figured this would be the only way to really know. So I did. I probably shouldn't have. I didn't have a lot of experience, and I had no idea what I was doing. But she swore she was happy to play guinea pig for me."

"What did she see?"

He shook his head. "I don't know. She wouldn't tell me. She saw something that frightened her, but she kept it from me. She described what her parents looked like, and their house, but she deliberately looked away from the thing that scared her and would not tell me."

"Did she go back farther? Before that childhood?"

Our eyes met and I saw him struggle with telling me the truth or burying the past. "Into another life? She claims she did, but again, with all of her research I assumed she was playing the part of somebody she'd read about. That makes a whole lot more sense than believing your soul has been reincarnated."

I thought back to the conversations I'd had with Mimi about the subject, having no idea that one day I'd have reason to recall them. Holding Matthew's gaze steadily, I said, "Even General Patton said that he'd lived a past life as a Roman general, and Benjamin Franklin and Thomas Edison believed in reincarnation. I'm not saying that makes it real or not. It's like believing in ghosts—whether or not you experience them, there are too many people out there who have said that they have. Too much evidence to say that the universe doesn't always work the way we think it should or the way that we're taught that it should."

His face closed like a solid door, his hands pulling away, and the old fear of being alone swallowed me like a fog. "Don't," I said, hearing the desperation in my own voice, seeing in his face his own doubt. I clung to it, searching for its source. "What did Adrienne see?" I asked again. "Are you afraid that I'll see the same thing?"

Matthew looked down at his hands, his elbows resting on his knees, his fingers steepled in front of him. "I don't know. I really don't. She wouldn't tell me." His eyes were cold when they lifted to meet mine. "But it changed her. She wasn't the same after that. It ruined her in some way, made her separate herself from the life we'd lived together." I watched him swallow, the sound audible in the stillness of the attic. "She died six months later."

We sat in silence for several moments, listening to the creaks and moans of an old house at night, and I recalled something Matthew had said to me once about Adrienne. *She told me once that sometimes when I looked at her it was like I was seeing a ghost instead.* I thought I finally understood what she'd meant. I spoke, my voice a knife to the quiet. "I'm not Adrienne. I wish you'd look at me just once and see me instead of a ghost."

He stood and turned so he faced the rocking horse, his long fingers touching the mane that was so precise I imagined I could feel the breeze that blew it back over the horse's face.

"I feel it, too," he said. "The past. It seems to live here, in this house, parallel to the present." His hands smoothed the wooden flanks of the horse, then traced the edges of the saddle where the seat had been well-worn by nameless Frazier children. I felt a strong sense of déjà vu, as if I'd seen him there before, touching the horse, speaking to me.

Matthew continued. "I think that's why we all feel this connection to the past—because it's here in the furniture, the floors, the walls. They must carry inside them a sort of memory of those who've lived here before. That makes a lot more scientific sense than believing we've lived previous lives."

"Then prove me wrong," I said as I stood, gripping the back of the chair for balance. "Hypnotize me again and take me back. Let me tell you what I see." I took a step closer to him. "It was your idea to do it the first time, even though I had fears of discovering things I might not want to know. Now it's your turn to take that leap of faith."

He didn't answer, but kept his face focused on the rocking horse, his thoughts elsewhere. I walked up to him and placed my cheek against his back, my arms embracing him from behind, our child between us. "I would not pull away from you, regardless of what happens. And you're more experienced now; you'll be a better guide for me." I paused for a moment. "I'm not Adrienne."

"I know," he said, his hands covering mine. "Will you let me think about it?"

I nodded, knowing that was all he could give me for now, but knowing, too, that he had no choice. He had been the one who pushed me to face my past, and now we were both too far down that path to turn back.

He turned to face me, taking my hands in his. I stared down at our entwined hands and at the birthmark on the base of my thumb. "All right," I said. I stepped into his arms, part sanctuary and part drug, then allowed him to lead me down the stairs. I concentrated on each step I took while I tried to erase the memory of the look on his face when he'd seen the attic key in my hand, and the sound of a child's laughter that seemed to echo in the attic behind us.

Gloria

St. Simons Island, Georgia
July 2011

I parked the car in the dirt lot across the street from Christ Church, then sat where I was for a long time after I'd turned off the engine. Finally, Mimi nudged me with her bony elbow.

"I don't think that waiting much longer will bring the cemetery to us. I'm guessing we're going to have to get out of the car and walk."

With a sidelong glare, I hauled myself out of the car, then helped Mimi out on her side before scooping up the bright yellow gladiolus I'd bought at

Tish's Eternal Carnation. Leaning heavily on each other and praying that a fast car wasn't headed our way on Frederica Road, we crossed the street.

Since both Henry and I were transplants to St. Simons, we had no family members buried in the cemetery. Still, we'd attended our fair share of funerals here of friends and acquaintances, so I was familiar with the serene setting and the small church that sat in the middle of the grounds like a mother keeping watch over her children. It had been years since I'd last come down these paths, but like learning how to walk, finding my way through the meandering maze was a skill I hadn't forgotten.

I recognized the Frazier enclosure from Ava's description, and we paused at Adrienne's gravestone in the front, our arms linked. " 'Mother of unborn children,' " I read out loud, an icy grip seizing my heart. "She was only twenty-six when she died."

Mimi was very still beside me, her gaze focused on the older tombstones in the back. "Did Ava tell you that Adrienne was a midwife, too?"

I shook my head. "No, I don't recall."

"I think that's odd. And not just because Matthew married two women with the same profession, but that he encouraged the first to become one."

"What do you mean?"

Mimi shrugged, but her gaze remained focused on the three stones lined up in the rear. "Ava told me that he was the one who encouraged Adrienne to go to school and train to become one. Like he felt preordained to marry a midwife."

The chill that had surrounded my heart now spread throughout my body, making me shiver in the heat of the July morning. "That's not possible," I said, in the same tone of voice I'd used with my children when they were growing up and they told me they'd forgotten their homework or had run over the newspaper at the end of the driveway instead of bringing it into the house. This had always prompted them to fix the error, to go back in time to make things right. But in real life, there was no such thing as do-overs.

"Isn't it?" my mother asked, and I was a child again, asking where souls go when the body dies.

I took Mimi's arm and led her away. I felt her falter and held tight. "Don't worry; it's close by. If we pass a bench you can sit and rest a bit."

Mimi snorted. "You mean *you* need a bench. I could run a marathon." She shuffled forward as if to prove her theory.

"Sure. If the other competitors are snails and turtles, you might even have a chance of winning." Taking her arm again, I led her to the place where I'd been only once, but remembered as if it were yesterday. One doesn't forget the graves of four family members, whether you knew them well or not.

We followed the weaving path for a short distance until we found ourselves at another clearing with four simple white headstones. A man wearing a UGA baseball cap stood between two of the stones holding a large green plastic watering can, a red wagon behind him carrying two more cans identical to the one in his hand.

He looked up at us and smiled. I was struck dumb for a moment, his face immediately familiar to me but his identity evading me like a moth around a candle.

"Good morning, ma'am. Ma'am." He tipped his hat at both Mimi and me while I just stood there gaping.

"Good morning to you, young man," Mimi offered. "Are you . . ."

"You're Jimmy. Jimmy Scott. Aren't you?" I asked, wishing I had some of the water in the can to pour down my suddenly parched throat.

"Yes, ma'am. That's me." He continued to smile at us, but his eyes were wide as he waited for an introduction.

"I'm Gloria Whalen." I waited for a moment to see any recognition, but his eyes continued to regard me steadily. "And this is my mother, Charlene Zinn. You went to school with my son Joshua. A long time ago. We moved the summer after ninth grade. And you've met my daughter, Ava Frazier."

He took his hat off and swiped his sleeve over his forehead. "I remember Joshua. He was real nice to me. And Ava's real nice, too. She wants me to help her make an herb garden with little brick paths. She can't do any real lifting with the baby, so she's hiring me."

I smiled back. "She says you're the best landscaper around. I bet you get that from your mother."

His smile dimmed somewhat. "You knew my mama?"

I lifted the gladiolus I held in my hand. "Not well. We met when Joshua broke his arm and she was the nurse on duty. She was really good with him, said she had lots of experience with kids and broken bones, so it was a good thing we came in when she was there. That's how we learned that our boys were both in Mr. Morton's ninth-grade homeroom." I glanced down at the headstones and the proliferation of flowers on all four of them. "She showed me her garden once. I'd never seen anything like it."

"I remember that," Jimmy said. "But I didn't remember it was you."

I smiled as I recalled the petite woman with the quiet voice and warm brown eyes. "I bumped into her one day when I was picking up the boys at school and mentioned to her that I was having trouble getting my wisteria to creep, and she invited me to come have a look at hers."

"Daddy didn't like Mama to have visitors." He spoke without accusation or enmity, as if the words had tumbled about in his head for a long time until they'd settled into a place that seemed to fit.

I only nodded in response, not wanting to talk about the screaming tirade I'd received for the mere infraction of admiring his wife's garden. I held up the gladiolus. "I brought this for her." *For strength,* I thought. I swallowed, trying to collect my thoughts. "I always felt bad that I didn't do more. That I didn't pursue a friendship with her, even though I thought she could probably have used a friend."

I smiled, feeling close to tears, and felt Mimi's hand on my arm. "She told me something that has stuck with me all these years." I closed my eyes, felt wetness on my cheeks. "She told me that being a mother is like being a gardener of souls. You tend your children, make sure the light always touches them; you nourish them. You sow your seeds, and reap what you sow. She called her children her flowers." I clutched the gladiolus stems tighter and walked closer to Mary Anne's grave. "I wanted to thank her for that, because those words have helped me get through the times when being a mother was a lot harder than I'd anticipated."

I placed the clipping on the grave, then removed two stems from the bundle and laid them on the graves of the two little girls, leaving the father's grave unadorned. I looked up at Jimmy, almost expecting to see recrimination, but saw only thanks.

"Mama liked gladiolus," he said. "And I know my sisters would, too." He grinned broadly, looking just like his mother, and my heart broke a little.

Mimi pulled on my arm and spoke to Jimmy, as if knowing that my words had crowded my throat, making it impossible to speak. "We'll let you get back to work. I guess we'll be seeing you at Ava's house. We promise to keep you well fed and watered with lemonade and sweet tea."

"Thank you, ladies. It was a pleasure seeing you." He settled his hat back on his head and returned to his watering, taking care not to splash the gladiolus.

We turned our backs to him and began our slow progress out from under the shadows of the oaks and into the bright sunlight. I wasn't sure we had accomplished anything, but at least it was a place to start.

CHAPTER TWENTY-THREE

Ava

St. Simons Island, Georgia
July 2011

Tish and Beth were already walking down the front path of Tish's house when I pulled into the drive. Beth lived only a block away and had coffee with her mother just about every morning, so I had to make only the one stop. I unlocked the doors and waited for them to approach, rotating my ankle. My boot had come off the day before and I was still reveling in the lightness and freedom of being bare-legged again.

Beth opened the passenger door for her mother and stepped back. "Age before beauty," she said with a sweeping hand gesture.

Tish frowned. "But your legs are longer and it's harder for you to get in and out of the backseat because of your belly. Really, you should sit up front."

When it looked like Beth would argue, I intervened. "Look, why don't you take turns? Tish can sit up front on the drive to Savannah and Beth can sit up front on the way back."

They both looked at me with surprise before sliding into their respective seats. Tish patted my leg. "See? I knew you'd be a good mother. Already playing fair." She looked in the backseat as if noticing for the first time that the other half was empty. "Where're your mother and Mimi?"

"I invited them to come—Forsyth Park is adjacent to the archives, and it's a beautiful morning for strolling through it. But they insisted on getting started on setting up the baby's room. I'm not due until February, but they said it's never too early. Matthew and I have painted the nursery a pale green, and he brought down a rocking horse from the attic, but other than that we've just stacked a few purchases into a corner of the room. That's not good enough for either of them." I rolled my eyes despite being pleasantly surprised. "I mean, my mother already has so many grandchildren it's hard to believe that another one would be noticed, much less celebrated."

Tish glanced into the backseat before patting my arm. "It's because you're the only girl. There's something special about your daughter having a baby. It's like you have a chance to do it all over again."

"And fix the mistakes you made the first time," Beth added, leaning into the front seat.

"Right. Because look how horrible you turned out." Tish shook her head, but she was smiling.

I focused on backing out of the driveway, disconcerted by the easy banter between mother and daughter and trying to imagine doing that with my own mother. Gloria and Mimi were like that, I supposed, but I'd always felt as if I'd been left out of the loop.

"What's this?" Beth asked.

I glanced in the rearview mirror and spotted the *Concise History* book I'd thrown in the car before I'd left. "It's the book your mom and I found at a garage sale. I've only had time to skim through it, but it looks like there's some pretty good information in it. I thought if either one of you could read without getting carsick, we might be able to pick out a few names to guide our research. I already made a list of names from the photographs I took at the cemetery to add to the one we compiled when we were there. Unfortunately, the ones I took at the Frazier plot are too blurry to read."

"I volunteer my mom," Beth said, handing the book up front to her mother. "I'm finally over my morning sickness, and I'm not excited at the prospect of feeling nauseous again."

Tish took the book with an exaggerated sigh. "I guess I'll do it. Hang on while I find my readers."

I concentrated on driving while she dug into her enormous purse that looked more like a duffel bag. "Have you heard anything more from the archaeological institute about the remains I found?"

She clapped her hands down on her purse. "I *knew* I was forgetting something! I swear I'm having sympathy pregnancy symptoms with Beth, because I barely seem to be able to remember my own name most days." She closed her eyes briefly as if to compose herself. "Yes, Dr. Hirsch called yesterday afternoon. I would have called you immediately, but a bride came into the store and I spent two hours with her and her fiancé discussing their wedding. I'd completely forgotten until now."

"What did he say?"

"The groom?"

"Mom!" came the groan from the backseat, and I had to smile.

"Oh, right. Sorry. You mean Dr. Hirsch. Well, they've been excavating the grave, and it's pretty clear it's not part of the Smith Plantation cemetery, because it's too far away. They're thinking the body was placed in a relatively isolated spot on purpose. They're going to try to bring in some imaging equipment to see if they can find anything else, maybe even other remains, but that could take a while."

Her cheeks puffed out slightly, as if she were holding on to a secret, and I wanted to squash them with the flats of my hands like my brothers had always done to me. Instead, I kept my hands firmly on the steering wheel and asked, "So why do they think it was put there instead of the cemetery?"

"Because," she said, drawing the word out slowly. "Remember I told you that they found skull fragments? Well, they also found a bullet among the fragments and what looks to be the edge of a small hole in one of the bone pieces. The British occupation was completely peaceful—if you don't count looting and the release of slaves—and there were no documented casualties. So it looks like this was an isolated incident, and maybe even one that was covered up or overlooked."

"Really?" I asked. "But how could a war casualty—especially one in a peaceful occupation—be overlooked?"

Her eyes gleamed, and I wondered whether she'd missed her true calling as an archaeologist or historian. "The metal ball found with the skull fragment was too small to have come from a musket—so it probably came from a pistol. Both were standard-issue to both armies at the time, but the pistol was used for closer combat. But as there was no combat on the island, it begs the question, doesn't it?"

"Are you saying they think it could have been foul play?"

"They're thinking it's a possibility. But the lead ball isn't the most interesting thing they found in the grave."

Again she paused, but it was Beth this time who interjected. "Mom—just tell us already!"

"Well, it looks like the remains of a medical bag were also buried near the body. Of course, it would be too hard to tell if it belonged to the person or was just thrown in there, but they do seem to be from the same era. The leather of the bag is completely disintegrated, but the metal tools inside are mostly intact."

I frowned, remembering something I'd seen in the book. "Beth—flip to the index pages and find the section on James Madison's War—which is just another name for the War of 1812. There's a sketch of a British doctor tending to a child. I'm wondering if there's any mention of a name or regiment or something we can use for reference when we're in the archives."

She flipped through the pages and then began to read when she found it. "'A surgeon of the Royal Marines tends to a young child suffering from malaria. He is credited with saving at least one life during their short stay in February of 1815 before their evacuation on March first following the signing of the Treaty of Ghent.'"

I remembered reading the same passage, and smelling the strong scent of wet wool. "How could there have been a malaria outbreak in February? Doesn't that come from mosquitoes?"

Tish nodded. "Yes, but some forms of the disease, if not completely cured, will remain dormant and will then crop up later. I think the longest dormancy is something like thirty years, but I think a single year is more likely."

I nodded, thinking I'd had this conversation before. "What would they have treated it with in 1815?"

Tish pursed her lips as she thought. "You're trying my feeble memory here, but I don't think quinine was developed until afterward. I'm thinking they were still using Peruvian bark—not very easy to come by, unless you're a British surgeon with a stock of medicines you've brought back from the homeland, where there's an active trade going on with the suppliers on another continent." She tapped her fingers on the steering wheel. "I know Pierce Butler, the husband of the actress Fanny Kemble, who owned Hampton Point Plantation, died here of malaria after the Civil War. Definitely a disease that crosses social lines."

I shivered, thinking how lucky I was that mosquitoes had never liked me, and how such a simple thing as blood that mosquitoes found unappealing could have been a lifesaver in another time.

Beth's eyes met mine in the rearview mirror. "It doesn't give a name."

I nodded. "But it does say he was a surgeon in the Royal Marines. Maybe we can find a list of the surgeons or other medical personnel that were with the British regiments stationed on St. Simons."

"Under Admiral Cockburn's command," said Tish, squaring her shoulders. "I do know my St. Simons history. And don't forget we do have the two initials that were carved on the tombstone—T and E. Dr. Hirsch has better access to that kind of information than we do. If we don't find more information today, I can at least ask him to check to see if there are any names that match those initials."

"Aren't Dr. Hirsch's people doing their own search?" Beth asked.

Tish raised her eyebrows. "His 'people'? They're so underfunded right now that he practically wept with gratitude when I told him what we were doing today. He did have an intern call ahead for us—something I would probably have forgotten to do—to have files pulled before we get there, which will save us a lot of time."

She stuck her readers on her nose, then pulled out an iPad from her purse. "They don't allow pens or purses or backpacks in the archives, but they will allow laptops and tablets to take notes on." She reached into her large tote bag and took out two of her yellow notepads and two pencils. "These are for you."

I glanced down at her iPad screen and watched as she typed in list format, "T.E., Royal Marines, 1815." Then "ague," "malaria," and "War of 1812."

"What's ague?" Beth asked, reading over her mother's shoulder.

"It's what they called malaria back then," Tish said.

"Don't forget Geoffrey Frazier," I said. "Or any mention of the last name Frazier."

I kept my gaze focused on the road, listening to Tish type the eight letters, feeling sick and exhilarated at the same time.

❧

I found a parking spot on the street a block away from Hodgson Hall on Whitaker, where the Georgia Historical Society housed its archives. As we climbed the steep steps of the Italianate building, Beth said, "They have the Demere family Bible here, but mostly just random collections of papers from the various St. Simons founding families." She held one of the large wooden doors open, and Tish and I stepped into the air-conditioned space before her.

In a lower voice, Beth continued. "I'm afraid that most if not all of the stuff we've requested is noncirculating and not on microfiche, which means we'll be here for a long time. I'd suggest we each grab a box and jot down any names we come across, then cross-reference against the names on the list we compiled on Tish's iPad."

As soon as we entered the great hall, my gaze went upward to the soaring three-story-high ceilings, before settling on the inscription on the wall above the main entrance: NO FEASTING, DRINKING, AND SMOKING OR AMUSEMENTS OF ANY KIND WILL BE PERMITTED WITHIN ITS WALLS.

"They really make history fun," Beth said with a smirk as Tish walked past us to the main desk to show her photo ID and register.

We checked our bags, then made our way to the green-floored reading room. It was a long, rectangular room with tall ceilings and large, arched windows encircling the mezzanine area at the top, while bookshelves stood sentry along the walls in the lower portion of the room. Long wooden tables with lamps marched down the center. The room was empty except for an elderly gentleman poring over a thick book with a magnifying glass, a notepad and pencil nearby, and a librarian sitting at the large desk nestled between the tables. A nameplate identified her as Cathy Blanco. She gave us a stern look as we passed, just in case we were even thinking about talking too loudly. As if on cue, the three of us checked our cell phones to make sure the ringers were off.

We settled ourselves at the last table just as our research materials were delivered—four large boxes of bound and cataloged papers. Tish settled her iPad on its stand in front of us so we could refer to her notes while each of us claimed a box.

"Whoever gets done first gets the fourth box," Beth said.

"Oh, boy," I said, then put a finger to my lips to indicate to Beth that Cathy Blanco was watching us. I turned to my box and lifted out the first folder and settled it in front of me. With a breath of anticipation, I waited for my two table companions to do the same; then I opened the first folder and began to read.

Three hours later, with a crick in my neck and stiff shoulders, I looked up at Tish and Beth. From their expressions and empty notepads I had a strong suspicion that their frustration matched my own. The name Frazier was mentioned several times, but never Geoffrey's name, or any other name that seemed familiar to me or that appeared on Tish's list. There was also nothing referencing a malaria outbreak or the British occupation. I knew the odds were against our finding a mention in what remained of letters from two hundred years ago, but nevertheless I'd been optimistic. I was beginning to agree with Matthew: that somehow my very vivid imagination had conjured a different world and peopled it with characters whose names I'd seen somewhere but didn't recall.

I dropped my pencil on my pad and pushed the hair off of my face. "All we have here is correspondence between the plantation families on St. Simons, and all of their household papers. If our T.E. was murdered, I doubt somebody would have put it in a letter or kept a receipt for his headstone." I rubbed my eyes, which made them feel even grittier. I slid my chair back. "I just refuse to leave here empty-handed."

I walked over to the reference desk and the librarian looked up. She appeared to be older than me, yet I noticed that she had an earbud stuck into her left ear and what sounded like a tinny version of Pearl Jam leaking out the other bud.

With a single, efficient movement, she removed the earbuds, then slipped them into her desk drawer. "May I help you?" she whispered.

I nodded, trying to look more confident than I felt. "Do you have any old books, like nineteenth century, about legends or ghost stories of St. Simons?" I scanned my brain for any other source of literature that might have a nonfictional event at its core. "Or even poetry," I added.

"One moment," she said, and her fingers began to tap quickly on her computer keyboard. "We have quite a few books on those subjects that have been published in the last fifty years," she offered.

"No, unless those are reprints of books originally printed in the nineteenth century. I'm looking for firsthand accounts or writings."

Her pink-tipped fingers again dashed across the keyboard. "We have *A Concise and Thorough History of St. Simons Island* by Richard Stanley Kobylt," she said, her eyes reflecting the blue screen.

"I actually already have that one. Anything else?"

Her fingers tap-tapped again on the keyboard. "We also have a volume of verses penned by Royal Marines while stationed along the coast during the War of 1812." She squinted at the screen. "It was published in London in 1820, and we have a single copy. Looks like it was a donation from the Smith collection." She looked up at me. "Would you like to see that?"

I was only half listening, my mind trying to come up with new avenues of research. When I realized she'd asked me a question, I said, "Oh, yes. Sure. Thank you."

She tapped a few keys. "It will take a few minutes, but somebody will bring it out to you shortly." She opened a large drawer and drew something out and handed it to me. I looked down and saw that it was a bifold brochure. "If you're interested in St. Simons history, you might want to take a look at the Smith collection at the Savannah History Museum. It's not far from here, although you'll need to take your car. You might find it helpful."

I looked down at the brochure, where the portrait of an older man in profile dominated the front. His white sideburns were worn long, his high cravat touching his jawline. It was clear that in his younger years, Mr. Smith would have been a very handsome man, even by today's standards.

Cathy Blanco stood to see the brochure better. "Sort of like an older George Clooney, huh? Pretty successful gentleman, too. He owned a medium-size but very profitable cotton plantation on St. Simons at the beginning of the nineteenth century. He ended up selling everything, then moving to Boston with his son and a freed slave. I believe his son came back to St. Simons, and it must have been his descendants who made the donation to the museum. You'll have to visit the exhibition to learn all the details." Her teeth parted in what I assumed was a librarian's grin, as if she were afraid that if she smiled too much it would be like speaking too loudly. "Unfortunately, this job means I know very little about quite a bit."

I held up the brochure. "Well, you've been very helpful. Thank you."

I returned to the table and the last batch of letters from the fourth box, getting up again to retrieve the book that had been delivered to the front desk. The cover, gently worn but definitely old, was in a mauve-brown cloth with gilt titles on the front and spine: *A Collection of Verse*. I thought of Mr. Kobylt's book and realized that book marketing in the nineteenth century didn't include catchy book titles.

Carefully, I opened the cover, the scent of dust and years wafting out from between the covers. I gently flipped through the pages, skimming amateurish and melodramatic prose about battles, longing, and passion—sometimes all three—and was about to close the book and return it to whatever crypt it had been sleeping in when the title "Lullaby" caught my attention. Holding the book open, I read:

Oh, hush thee, my baby,
Thy sire be a king's knave,
Thy mother his true love,
Separated by the deep ocean's waves;

The text seemed to swim before my eyes, and I began to hum the familiar tune—the same melody of the lullaby my mother had sung to me, the same one that Jimmy whistled. But these were the words I remembered, the words Adrienne had written in beautiful calligraphy and hidden in the back of the frame.

I blinked to see more clearly, and quietly began to sing the next verse.

Oh, hush thee, my baby,
I am coming home to thee,
To love, serve, and honor,
My true love, thy mother, for eternity.

A throat clearing from the frowning librarian brought my head up, and I stopped singing. I looked at my table companions to see them both staring at me expectantly.

"What is it?" Tish whispered.

"I'm not sure." My gaze skipped to the bottom of the page. *Submitted by Mrs. Catherine Enlow.*

I turned the book around so that Tish and Beth could see. "These are the lyrics I remember, Tish. The same ones that Adrienne had stuck behind the sketch in my parlor."

"Enlow starts with an 'E.' That's something, right?" Beth asked.

My breath felt icy in my lungs as I closed my eyes and heard the lyrics again in my head as if I'd always known them. "It might be," I said, surprised at how normal my voice sounded. "The words were written about a 'true love.' Maybe that true love was his wife." I rubbed my hands over my face. "It's a long shot, but we can give the last name to Dr. Hirsch and see what he can turn up. Maybe Catherine Enlow's husband was stationed on

St. Simons. And once we find his name, we can hopefully find out what happened to him."

Tish held up her hand and I gave her a high five, trying to stop the trembling of my limbs.

I was excited by my find, but disappointed that we hadn't learned more about Geoffrey, or Pamela, or Georgina, or any of the other characters who plagued my dreams.

I was about to suggest we pack everything up and head out for a late lunch when Tish began tapping her pencil against her page. "That's interesting."

"What?" Beth and I said in unison.

I hoped Tish would be more forthcoming with her information than in the past, as I didn't think I had the patience to pry it from her piece by piece.

"Well, I guess this caught my eye since you're a midwife, Ava, but in several pieces of correspondence that I've read through, when they're talking about the birth of a child, they've mentioned the same midwife. The first name didn't stand out to me—probably because they don't mention a last name—but now I'm recognizing it. They do say that she came from a small farm on Dunbar Creek and was responsible for delivering many of the babies all the way from Sapelo to Cumberland from around 1800 to 1815. I haven't seen any mention of her past 1815."

"So what was her first name?" I asked, resisting the impulse to grab her notes and look at them myself. Instead, I kept my gaze on Tish's notepad, wondering why the air around me seemed to suddenly lack oxygen.

Her pencil eraser bobbed up and down on the pad, almost in slow motion, the sound like small explosions. Her eyes met mine. "Her name was Pamela."

CHAPTER TWENTY-FOUR

Pamela

St. Simons Island, Georgia
February 1815

I sat up in my bed, blinking in the milky winter predawn light, listening again for the sound that had awakened me. My expelled breath rose in silent puffs, disappearing over the bed quilt like a dream upon waking.

Geoffrey's fever of the previous summer had returned two days earlier, starting with a numbing headache, then chills and fever. In the summer, I'd administered Peruvian bark to Geoffrey and Robbie, and I thought I had cured them. I had heard of recurrences of ague, but had not expected it nevertheless. I knew enough to know that the symptoms would repeat in two- to four-day cycles unless I could find the rare bark. And each cycle would be harder and harder to bear until the patient got better on his own, or didn't.

I quietly slipped from the bed, even though I knew it would be near impossible to wake Geoffrey. The fever exhausted him, and his body needed its rest before the fever returned. After sliding my feet into my slippers and taking my wrapper from the foot of the bed, I stepped out into the hallway, letting the door shut behind me with a quiet click.

I paused, listening to the reassuring sound of the clock downstairs, then waited to see if I heard anything out of place.

A soft cry came from Robbie's room, and I stood frozen where I was, praying I had imagined it. If the ague had returned to Robbie, he was far less prepared for it than Geoffrey. But then the noise came again and I marched quickly to his room, pausing on the threshold, the sickly smell of camphor mixed with lavender permeating the air.

By the light of a single lamp, Jemma stood over Robbie's bed, rubbing the ointment on his chest. The old rocking horse with the red saddle that Geoffrey had made for Robbie when he was still a little boy stood outlined by the dim light of the window. He was too big for it now, but would not hear of our removing it to the attic.

"No," I half said, half sobbed as I stepped forward into the candlelight and for the first time noticed the presence of another person in the room. I started as I recognized one of the Coupers' house servants from Cannon's Point, Young Martha.

"What are you doing here?" I asked, alarmed.

Instead of answering, she said, "Jemma sent Zeus for more wood to keep Master Robbie warm for when his chills start. I helped her with the poultice. T'always works for Master Couper when he gets croupy in his chest."

I was disoriented, wondering why Young Martha was in my house, but my concern for my son refocused my attention. I sat at the head of the bed and saw the glassiness of Robbie's eyes, the way his sweat-soaked hair stuck to his forehead. I bent to kiss his cheek, my lips burning with his heat. I looked up at Jemma with alarm, but she soothed me with the calming gaze she used with expectant mothers.

"It be all right, Miss Pamela. Jemma taking good care of Master Robbie," Young Martha said.

"Why are you here?" I asked again, my uneasiness growing.

She stood a little straighter, pushing her shoulders back. "We got British soldiers at Cannon's Point. I come to tell Jemma and Zeus."

I was glad for my empty stomach, knowing food would not have sat easy with that news. We had known the British had invaded Cumberland

Island, and Mr. Gould at the lighthouse had been true to his word and kept watch for any sign that they had set their sights on our St. Simons. Since we were only a small farm, we would not have been the first to know that we had visitors. I also knew that our Zeus was sweet on Young Martha, and my uneasiness settled into worry.

"Is it peaceful?" I asked carefully, recalling stories Geoffrey had told me and that I had read regarding the British burning the White House in Washington and the massacres up north at the hands of their Indian allies.

"Yes'm. The British officers are gentlemen and speak kindly to Master 'n' Mistress Couper. But they using Cannon's Point for they headquarters, and they soldiers say that if we go with them we be free."

Jemma's eyes met mine and she slowly shook her head. I looked back at my son, the relief making me weak.

"Mama?" Robbie said.

"Yes, sweetheart?"

"I don't feel good."

I placed the back of my hand against his forehead, my skin feeling scalded. I looked up at Jemma. "We have no more medicine. His father has the ague as well."

There had been so much sickness since last summer that I had nearly run through my stores of medicines. The Peruvian bark, which I mixed as a powder with wine, was procured only through barter, and the war with Britain had made it almost impossible to obtain. Jemma and I both knew the camphor rubs or bleeding would not bring about a cure.

"They be a doctor soldier at Cannon's Point, Miss Pamela. I know because I fetch him for Miss Rebecca, who be in a delicate way. They call him Dr. Enlow."

I heard a movement in the hallway and then Zeus came in with an armload of firewood. After depositing it on the hearth, he stood nearby, avoiding eye contact with me.

Young Martha stood, sparing a single glance toward the sick boy in the bed before turning back to Jemma. "We is goin' now. Come with us and be free."

Jemma didn't look up but shook her head. Young Martha headed toward the door and I stood. "Zeus?"

He didn't look at me.

I had no idea how Geoffrey would do the spring planting without Zeus, but I was not in control here, and the sound of Robbie's crying refocused my priorities. I nodded my head once, not in dismissal or understanding, but perhaps in a mixture of both, then watched them leave.

Jemma squeezed out a rag in the washbasin and placed it on Robbie's forehead. I put my hand on hers, stilling it. "Thank you," I said.

She nodded once, just as I had, then continued to bathe Robbie's face. A spasm shook him, his pallor almost yellow. Quelling my rising panic, I kept my voice calm. "I will get dressed now, then see what we still have in the root cellar and bring you what I can find. And then we will see if they will keep down tea and broth."

It felt good to be organizing my thoughts with plans of action; I knew I needed to keep moving forward so I would not become mired in more dangerous thoughts. Geoffrey continued his deep sleep as I washed and dressed, his long body a still lump under our quilt. The image haunted me as I left the room.

The cold morning air stung my cheeks as I approached the kitchen house, the grass beneath my feet heavy with frost, the hum of insects banned by the turn of seasons. Even my morning birdsongs were different, the warble of the wrens and sparrows taken over by the cackling of the newly swollen population of the clapper rails. But my birds and their songs would return, along with the colors of the marsh in spring, the inevitable cycle of life that seemed so far away during this dead season of winter. There would be no spring for me, I knew, if Robbie's laughter and Geoffrey's touch were not a part of it.

I lit the fire in the cold hearth and brought in water for the kettle, then lit a lamp before descending into the root cellar. I wore the house keys on a chain around my waist, and took out the long key to the new lock I'd had Zeus install on the door. I felt safer knowing that only myself and Jemma had access to my medicines and herbs.

The metal felt icy against my skin as I pulled on the handle and let myself down the steps. I walked past the potatoes and other food stores, my candle held high, stopping in front of the narrow shelves where I kept my jars of herbs. I stared at the near-empty shelves, having known already what I would find. Camphor, lavender, and peppermint—none of which could help Geoffrey or Robbie.

The candlelight on the wall trembled, and I realized it was from my own shaking hand. I walked quickly up into the meager sunlight, trying to warm the chill that had settled in my bones. I was at a loss as to what I should do. Georgina would be of no help, with her dormant garden of useless blooms. She relied on me for whatever ailments she or Nathaniel might have, as did many of our neighbors.

I allowed my anger at the loss of Zeus and what it would mean to Geoffrey to invade my sense of despair, almost welcoming it as a woman welcomes an impending birth as a means to end nine long months of confinement. I was angry at these faceless British soldiers who did not know me or my family, yet chose to take away our livelihood without recompense, remorse, or the courage to meet us face-to-face.

With a newly restored sense of purpose that at least managed to keep the despair temporarily at bay, I gathered eggs, then brewed tea for both Geoffrey and Robbie and delivered them to Jemma, feeling confident to be leaving them in her care. I was a poor rider, mounting a saddle only if I had to, so I hitched up one of our two horses to the wagon and headed toward Cannon's Point on the banks of the Hampton River.

The elegant mansion with its tabby foundation and wooden upper story and a half boasted a broad stairway that led to a wide piazza, providing views of the Hampton River and surrounding marshes. But today it was hardly recognizable for the tents and campfires spread on the grounds surrounding it, groups of blue- and red-coated soldiers clustered around fires like roosters to a hen.

I did not go up to the mansion, as my business did not involve the Coupers. If the British could take what belonged to my family, then I knew from whom to extract payment. I expected to be stopped and questioned as

I made my slow progress up the main drive, and I did receive odd looks, but I suppose I did not appear threatening, as nobody stepped forward to intervene.

Aware of how suddenly my good luck could end, with shaking fingers I tied the horse and wagon near the kitchen house, then made my way around the big house, examining the faces of soldiers I passed, looking for a pleasant countenance of someone who would not give me trouble.

A solitary man sat on the mounting block at the front of the great house, shaking out a rock from his boot. He appeared young, not more than seventeen, and when I spoke he stood immediately, placing his stocking in the dirt and no doubt gathering more stones.

"I am looking for Dr. Enlow," I said with authority, so as not to brook any questions. "Could you please direct me as to where I might find him?"

"Yes, ma'am," he said with a thick Cockney accent. "'E's in the medical tent—that's the big 'un at the end of this 'ere line of tents."

"Thank you," I said, then walked quickly away before he could ask my purpose.

The tent was easy to find. It had the biggest fire in front of it, with a large cauldron of boiling water hanging over it, and a makeshift line of rope was strung from two limbs of an oak tree, where strips of drying linen hung limply. A long, narrow table sat in front with medical instruments on top, as if they'd been cleaned and were in the process of drying. Many of them I did not recognize, but others, like the amputation saw and forceps, I did. A broken boat oar stood by the cauldron, while a man sat near the heat of the fire, his forehead and cheeks red from the alternating cold and heat. His light auburn hair was pulled back in a queue, and he wore a white linen shirt and a wool vest. He sat at a makeshift desk made from a barrel, a portable letterbox sitting on top opened to what appeared to be a blank piece of paper. I watched as he dipped his pen into the inkwell, then paused too long before writing the first letter, so that a blot of ink smeared the page.

"Dr. Enlow?" I asked, my voice giving away none of the fear I felt. I was not afraid of this man, nor of the British invaders. I was afraid of what healing I could not do, of medicines I did not have nor knew how to use.

Mostly I was afraid that this man could not give me what I needed, and that I would be left without hope.

His eyes were a fine gray, steady and intelligent. He seemed surprised to see me, yet recovered enough to stand and give me a quick bow. "At your service, ma'am."

"My husband and son are quite ill with ague, and I am in need of Peruvian bark to treat them. I am presuming that you have enough for an entire ship."

I half expected him to mock me. I was a mere woman making demands of the all-powerful British navy. Even I would have had trouble keeping a smile from my face if our roles had been reversed. Instead, I was surprised by his response.

"How old is your son, Mistress . . . ?"

"Frazier. I am Mistress Frazier. My son, Robbie, has just turned eight years this past December." My voice caught on the last word, and his eyes softened.

"I have a son the same age. I believe I can understand the concern of a mother who would march through an enemy encampment—without reproach, it would seem—to demand medicine."

I nudged aside my relief at his understanding, clinging to my anger until I had what I needed. "Do you have it?"

His brows furrowed. "I do. Not in great quantities, but I am fairly certain I can procure more. But how do you know that is all you require?"

"I am a midwife, and have some knowledge of the healing properties of various herbs. What I cannot grow here, I trade for with my own herbs. Geoffrey—my husband—and Robbie had an episode with the ague last summer, and I used up what I had left of the Peruvian bark. It worked well, but the ague has come back. I have heard of that happening, and know they need more of the medicine to make them better." I swallowed, not wanting him to see weakness in my tears. "My son barely survived the last bout. He is still not strong."

"And you are sure it is the ague? Peruvian bark is an expensive medicine."

I stiffened. "We have already paid the price for this medicine. You have told our people that if they get on your ships, they will be free. I had hopes this would make it a fair barter. I . . ."

He held his hand up to stop me. "No, Mistress Frazier, that was not my question. I was inquiring as to whether I should see the patients, to ensure they are being treated with the correct medication. If you will allow me, I would like to see them for myself."

My knees buckled, and it was only then that I realized how stiffly I had been holding myself, as if I held the burden of the world on my shoulders. His hand, strong and reassuring, held on to my elbow until I was steady.

"Thank you," I said. "That would be kind, but unnecessary. I am quite capable. . . ."

He lifted his uniform jacket from the back of his chair and put it on. "It is not a question of your capabilities, Mistress Frazier, but of a simple consultation to ensure the best treatment."

He began fastening the large gold buttons on his jacket. "You have undoubtedly paid a high price for my services already. But can I hope that I might ask you for one thing more?"

I stilled, the disappointment making my knees weak again. "I assure you, sir, that I have no money to give to you."

"It is not money I require, just your woman's mind. As a mother, you are best qualified to help me." He picked up his leather medical kit and gently placed a few instruments from the table inside it.

"I am not sure what you mean, sir."

He indicated the small writing box. "I have left behind in Northumberland my beloved wife, Catherine, and my seven-year-old son, William. I have not seen them for more than three years, but I have tried to bridge my absence by writing verses for them. You see, when I was at home I would create my own words to lullabies—since I do not know how to write music—for William. This way, my wife can sing to our son with my words. It is almost like the three of us are together again. My hope is that he will not have forgotten me when I finally return home."

We had begun walking toward the place where I had left my horse and wagon. Despite his enemy uniform, I found myself liking him. His love for his wife and son made us kindred spirits, and I prayed that he was inclined to feel the same.

"And what is it that you require me to do?" I asked. He helped me up into the wagon seat and I took the reins as he climbed in beside me.

"I have been unable to move beyond the first stanza. It is quite baffling to me, as you have probably noticed that I am rarely at a loss for words."

Despite my gnawing worry over Geoffrey and Robbie, I could not help but smile. "I had noticed," I said dryly. "What do you have so far?"

He cleared his throat and in a strong tenor voice sang,

> *Oh, hush thee, my baby,*
> *Thy sire be a king's knave,*
> *Thy mother his true love,*
> *Separated by the deep ocean's waves;*

"You have a lovely voice, and I recognize the tune. It is an old Scottish lullaby, is it not? My own mother used to sing it to my sister and me when we were small. There are many families here whose original homes were in Scotland, so it is not so strange that it would be familiar to us here."

"Good! Then you can help me with the rest of the lullaby, as you will know where words need to be inserted to keep the melody going."

I looked down at my worn red leather gloves and took a deep breath, the cold air biting as I drew it into my lungs. "It is not too long a drive, but I can see what I can do," I said, thankful for something else to shift the worry from my mind.

We had begun only the second line of the second stanza by the time we approached the house, my newly regained spirits plummeting when I recognized Georgina's carriage out front. As I pulled the wagon up next to it, my sister appeared at the front door, her eyebrows raised in surprise as she noticed my companion.

Without waiting for assistance, I flung myself from the wagon seat and ran up the steps to greet her. "Is everything . . . ?" I couldn't finish my sentence.

"They are fine, Pamela. Both husband and son are resting, their fevers and rigor gone for now. Jemma sent word that Geoffrey and Robbie were ill again, so I brought over food and my Mary. She is young, but she has been helping her mother in my kitchen since she was seven, so she should be a good help to you, and that will allow Jemma to assist you in your nursing. I must confess that I was not a little put out that the request did not come from you." She appeared troubled for a moment. "Most of our field hands and house people have gone with the British. I would have thought that Jemma would be gone, too, but I see she is as loyal as ever."

I looked into my sister's clear blue eyes, but saw no guile. But I could not help but consider her gift suspect. She had never given me anything that did not come with a high price.

I sensed a presence beside me, and introduced my sister to the doctor, watching carefully as her gaze passed between the two of us as if she could read something that was not there.

Feeling wary, I thanked my sister, then led the doctor upstairs, saying a prayer under my breath that my beloved husband and son would be cured, and that I had imagined the dark shadows that crossed Georgina's eyes when she had seen me approaching with Dr. Enlow.

CHAPTER TWENTY-FIVE

Ava

St. Simons Island, Georgia
July 2011

I opened my eyes and blinked, my finger rubbing the birthmark on my
left hand, a faint memory of the woman, Pamela, doing the same thing.
I sat up on the couch and saw Matthew, his elbows resting on his knees and
his fingers steepled, a deep frown on his face.

I sat up and pushed the afghan off my lap and retrieved the music box
from the curio cabinet. I opened it, allowing the delicate notes to drift
through space and time. "Now do you believe me?" I asked.

"Believe what? That you absorbed a lot of information today at the archives? That you have a brilliant imagination that has created intricate details of the lives of people who lived here two hundred years ago? Yes, I can
believe that. But can I believe that these are your memories from a life you
lived before? No. It's simply not logical."

I snapped shut the lid of the music box. "Then how do you explain this?
How could I have known those lyrics if my own mother didn't even know
them to sing to me? And how would I know Pamela's name?"

He sat back in his chair and allowed his shoulders to relax. I knew he practiced this for patients, so they wouldn't be aware that he wasn't as calm as they needed him to be. "You saw the proof today, in the old book of verses. The words were written two hundred years ago, so they've been around for that long. The tune itself is from medieval times, so it's been around for a long time, too. That's all logical; don't you see? You heard the words once, maybe twice—maybe in school, or on television, or whatever—and your subconscious remembered them. And you told me yourself that Tish found mention of a midwife on St. Simons named Pamela—which means you most likely read it somewhere before. Doesn't that make a lot more sense than this other scenario of a past life?"

I placed the music box on the table between us, and focused on keeping my voice calm—something I'd learned from him. "I keep seeing Pamela in a boat, and on the beach, and she loves the water. And I feel that love; I feel it as if I've lived by the water my whole life instead of being petrified by it." I took a deep breath, wondering whether I really believed what I was about to say. "I want you to take me sailing. I can't say that I will ever love it as much as you do, but I don't think I'll be frightened of it anymore."

He had started to shake his head before I'd even finished speaking. I crossed the space between us and curled up in his lap, my head tucked between his jaw and shoulder. "Don't you see how much I love you? That I trust you to keep me safe? That I mean it when I say the hypnosis has changed me in some degree, that it may have lessened my fear of water enough that I would allow myself to go on a boat with you?"

My head lifted and fell as he breathed in and out so softly that I thought he'd gone to sleep. Finally, he said, "I can't imagine any part of this as being a good idea."

"Remember before my first job interview you taught me those breathing exercises to calm me so I could cross over the causeway to Brunswick? If I feel panicked I'll know what to do. But I won't need to; I know I won't. You'll be there." I lifted my head and met his gaze.

"Are you sure?"

I nodded, almost feeling the spray of water against my skin. "I need to do this."

Our lips met, and I saw the stars behind my closed eyelids, my blood thrumming through my veins like a fast-moving river toward the ocean. He held me, and I was no longer afraid.

We broke apart as the front door burst open and Mimi and Gloria appeared on the threshold, their arms burdened with shopping bags.

Matthew and I immediately went to them and took their bags, noticing as we did the pastel-colored toys and the very chubby teddy bear peeking out from the top of the largest bag.

"Don't look!" Mimi said, trying to close the top of a bag where what looked like a windup mobile sat perched on top.

"We've been working on the baby's room all day," my mother explained, "but we needed a few more things. I think we're going to have to extend our rental agreement on the condo for a few more weeks. I'm afraid this project is going to last a bit longer than we originally thought." She didn't look the least bit apologetic.

Mimi straightened, rubbing a hand on the small of her back. "I hope you don't mind, Ava, but a frame shop called today and I answered the phone. They said your order had been ready for over a month and they were calling to remind you to come pick it up. Since I brought a picture for the baby's room that needed framing, I figured we could kill two birds with one stone."

Before I could protest, she indicated one of the bags Matthew was holding. "They're in there."

From the bag he slid out four tissue-wrapped frames. Looking up at me, he asked, "What are they?"

I wasn't sure how to answer, no longer remembering why I'd had them framed. Maybe the very fact that Adrienne had hidden them made me want them displayed. Or maybe even then I'd wanted something tangible, some kind of proof that what I was experiencing existed outside of my own mind.

"I thought I'd make them a gift for you, but I'm not really sure now."

Our gazes met briefly as he tore open the tissue of the first frame and stared down at it for a long moment before looking back at me, a question in his eyes.

It was the picture of the woman standing on the beach, her dark hair tangled by the wind. "I found them behind the frame of Adrienne's sketch of the house. Tish said that the last time she saw Adrienne, she was at the frame shop, having her sketch framed and asking for these to be placed inside."

Mimi and my mother collapsed into chairs, and a part of me knew I should be getting them water or something to help them cool off. But I couldn't look away from Matthew's face and his expression, which looked like a person who'd just been punched so hard it had sucked the air from his lungs.

"The last time she saw her . . . ?"

He didn't look as if he could finish.

"Before Adrienne died." I touched the frame. "I think this is Geoffrey Frazier's wife."

"Why?" he asked, his voice rough.

"A similar sketch appears in the old history book I found at the garage sale, identifying her as his unfaithful and treasonous wife. The artist must have drawn it from the same portrait Adrienne did." I paused, seeing again dark hair whipped by the ocean's wind, feeling the strands stinging my lips. "I think this is Pamela."

"Because that's who you see when you're under hypnosis?"

I shook my head. "No." I searched for the words that might explain why I recognized her. "Because when I look at her picture, it's almost like I'm looking in a mirror."

His eyes widened as he took in my fine, wavy blond hair and slight build—so unlike the willowy and brunette Pamela.

Without saying anything else, he sliced open the next one, the lyrics of the lullaby written in calligraphy. I watched as his eyes scanned the page before meeting mine.

"Those are the lyrics I found in the book of verses at the archives. The ones I knew but didn't know how. Adrienne must have found them, too, in her research. And loved them enough to write them down." I paused. "Or because they had a special meaning for her, too."

He dropped his gaze and opened the third package, this one the sketch of the house that had seemed different to me. We both studied it in silence.

Finally, I said, "It's different from the one that hangs on the wall. I couldn't figure out what made it that way until just now." I tapped my finger on the glass. "Look—there're curtains on the windows instead of shutters, and there are no flowers anywhere. Not even in pots."

I moved my finger to where the kitchen house was visible in the background. "And there's a large double door leading into the cellar that doesn't exist anymore." I drummed my fingers, building courage. "This is the house I see when I'm dreaming or under hypnosis. It's the house Geoffrey and his wife lived in."

He didn't respond but began stacking the frames, holding on to them as he stood. "Why would you think I'd want these framed?"

The words stung, and I was embarrassed that he'd said them in front of Mimi and my mother. I hunted for a suitable answer as I thought of all the ways I'd tried to erase Adrienne from this house, yet still I'd felt the need to frame these prints. I considered everything I'd learned about the subconscious mind from Matthew, and little pieces in my brain began to shift and slide. I cleared my throat. "Maybe because I thought Adrienne was trying to say something and that I was meant to figure it out."

The look of alarm I read in his eyes frightened me more than anything he could have said.

Mimi, standing stiffly, shuffled over to us. "Don't forget the last one. I brought it in and they were able to frame it today at the store. It'll spoil the surprise, but I can't wait any longer for you to see it."

I sent her a grateful look as I pulled the fourth tissue-wrapped frame from the bag. I started to cry before I'd ripped off the second strip of tissue paper. The image of me posed in the pink crocheted dress with the pale satin sash blurred in front of me.

"We thought you could get a photo of Matthew as a baby and hang them together in the baby's bedroom."

I swallowed my disappointment, wishing they'd brought the portraits of Mimi and my mother wearing the same dress, wanting to finally hang them all together. Instead, I smiled, then kissed Mimi on soft cheeks that smelled faintly of face powder.

"It was your mama's idea," Mimi said.

Gloria pulled herself to a stand. "Well, since you'd already sent her the dress, I figured it was fitting to start her own photo collection. Make sure you leave room next to yours for your daughter's portrait."

"Or I could hang all four in the hallway," I blurted out, knowing it was my sense of hurt that had made me confrontational.

"Maybe," my mother said as she picked up one of the shopping bags, her tone an easy dismissal. Changing the subject, she said, "Matthew and Ava, could you bring up the rest, please? Mimi's just about give out from this heat. Just leave them outside the baby's room, because you're still not allowed inside."

"I can hear you, you know," Mimi muttered as she took the framed print from me and began her slow ascent up the stairs.

I turned to Matthew, hoping to apologize for breaking my promise to allow Adrienne to remain buried. But he'd already left the room, the door to his study closing softly behind him.

⸎

Two weeks after Adrienne's framed prints had been returned to the house, I stepped out into the back garden and handed Jimmy a sweet tea. He took his gloves off as he accepted the glass, and I watched his hands as he drank, wondering whose they reminded me of. His fingers, even under the pink welts of his scars, appeared delicate and fine-boned, not at all what I would have thought a landscaper's hands would be. But then I remembered the beautiful flowers of his own garden, and the patience required to grow them, and it seemed fitting that his hands would be small enough to cradle delicate blooms.

"That's real good," he said. "Thank you." He finished it with a last huge gulp, then placed the empty glass on the step behind me.

"My mama made it—she's got a way with sweet tea, doesn't she?"

"She sure does." He jutted out his chin in the direction of my potting shed. "I know you said you didn't want any flowers, but I think we could have a real pretty garden right there in front of the shed. Maybe some bougainvillea or azaleas against the wall, and a few rows of red shrimp plants or staghorn ferns in front? That way all that color will be the first thing everybody sees when they walk from the front yard to the back. And we could connect it with a brick path leading from the herb and vegetable garden."

He lowered his voice, as one does in deference when entering a church. "Adrienne loved flowers. I helped her design her garden. There were even pictures of it in lots of magazines; did you know that? I could help you with yours, too. It would be different, though—Ava's garden." He frowned. "Or maybe we need to wait until you've lived here for a little while."

I used my hand to shade my eyes from the sun so I could see his eyes better. "Why, Jimmy?"

He shrugged. "Then you'll know what you want to take root, and what you want pulled out."

My skin tingled, like I had stepped out of a sunny spot and into the shade. I turned away from him, focusing on the brick paths and the stakes he'd already marked in the ground. I could see what he was envisioning, the spots of color against the grays and beiges of the tabby, like vivid memories against a canvas of time. But I could see, too, the sketch Adrienne had made of the house as it had once existed, a house devoid of any color or anything that wasn't practical or useful. I stood, it seemed, with a foot in two worlds, unable to determine which was the right one.

"I'm not sure . . ." I began, but stopped as Jimmy placed both fists on his hips, something I always did when I felt frustrated. He was still smiling, but I could tell that he was pretty much set on planting flowers in my garden.

"Why don't you like flowers, Miss Ava?"

"It's not that I don't like them; it's just . . ." I paused, trying to think of words that would explain all the years at my mother's side tending to her plants, but never feeling as if they were mine. Her varieties hadn't been colorful enough, or big enough, or wild enough. They were beautiful, as a serene lake against purple mountains would be, unless you were looking for the wide expanse of frothy ocean against a cerulean sky.

What was less explainable was my aversion to colorful blooms in *this* house, something I'd felt even before I'd known that Adrienne was a gardener.

"I do like them," I said firmly, having given up on offering an explanation that would make any sense. "I'm just wanting to focus on one thing at a time right now, and that would be my herb and vegetable garden. Maybe next spring . . ."

My words trailed off as Jimmy walked toward his ever-present red wagon and wrested something out from under the bottom of a pile of plastic flatbeds. He clutched a slim leather briefcase that looked like it had seen better days, the light brown leather almost tie-dyed with water stains, the handle on top too warped to carry comfortably.

As he neared, he unhooked the clasp in front and flipped the briefcase open. "Just in case you change your mind, I went ahead and drew up a plan." He slid out a few pieces of paper and then tucked the case under his arm. Holding up the pages for me, he said, "I know you liked my mama's garden, so I thought maybe we could go back there and you could tell me what parts you like the most. Not that we'll want to copy it, but just to give me an idea of what . . ."

His voice seemed to disappear into the humid air, all sound ceasing for what could have been minutes or hours. I was staring at the latch plate of his briefcase. Although it was scratched and pitted, I could see that three initials had once been engraved on the brass, although only the first two were still legible: *AM*.

My voice sounded hollow. "Jimmy, where did you get your briefcase?"

He looked up from his garden plans, surprised. "I found it."

His brown eyes were clear as he regarded me, and I knew he was telling the truth.

"Where did you find it?"

"In the water."

He was beginning to sound defensive, so I forced my numb lips into a smile. "What a lucky find. Was it in the ocean?"

Jimmy shook his head, his red baseball cap shaking in unison. "No. I was fishing in Dunbar Creek and there it was, sticking in some tall grass right on the bank. I barely had to get my sneakers wet to get it." He twisted so that he held the briefcase away from me, like he expected me to snatch it from him. "It took about a week to dry it in the sun, but it's almost good as new."

"Was there anything inside?"

"Yep. A bunch of papers. But they were too wet, and the ink had smeared all over the place, so I threw them out."

"Just papers? No book—like a daily planner or anything?"

He shook his head. "Nope. Just papers."

The numbness had spread from my lips to include my entire body. "How long ago was this?"

He closed one eye and looked up with the other, as if he were thinking hard, and then he smiled. "It was right after you hurt your foot. I remember because I brought you flowers from my garden, and then I went fishing." He frowned. "I figured somebody threw it out, so it was okay if I took it."

I thought my cheeks would crack from the effort it took to keep smiling. "I think you're right, Jimmy. Somebody definitely threw it out. Lucky you to have found it." I put my hand on his arm. "I'm not feeling too good right now. I think it must have been something I ate that doesn't agree with the baby." My smile began to falter. "Can we talk about the garden later?"

His face showed his concern, and even in my distracted state I realized how easy he was to read, as if his face were a road map to his emotions. And how different that was from Matthew.

"Sure," he said, stuffing the plans back into the briefcase. "Just call me when you're ready."

I nodded, then ran inside to the bathroom, emptying my stomach until there was nothing left. Then I curled into the fetal position on the floor, my cheek against the cool wood, and began to shake.

CHAPTER TWENTY-SIX

Pamela

I watched as Dr. Enlow emptied a small measure of powder into a glass of wine before handing it to me. I stirred it vigorously with a spoon, then lifted it to Geoffrey's dry and cracked lips. His skin was pale, his cheeks gaunt, but his blue eyes remained the same, and my heart leaped as they met mine.

He turned his head away, and I almost spilled some of the precious liquid down his chin. "Geoffrey, you need to take this. Please. It will make you better."

His eyes softened. "I heard the doctor telling you that there is barely enough for a full course of medicine for one person, much less two. Dividing what is available between Robbie and me will not cure either of us. Give it all to Robbie. I am much stronger than he is."

I shut my eyes, as if that would make his lie disappear. I was being punished by God for the sin of choosing Geoffrey over my sister. And now I was being forced to choose between Geoffrey and our son.

I shook my head and opened my eyes again. "Dr. Enlow has more medicine at the headquarters on Cumberland. He is working on obtaining it, and it will be here soon. Please, Geoffrey. Please take it."

He shook his head, the effort nearly exhausting him. "I am already feeling better. I will take the medicine if I need it when Dr. Enlow procures more. Give it to Robbie."

I did not doubt the doctor's promise that more medicine was forthcoming. If I could get both Robbie and Geoffrey started on the medication now, that would at least sustain them until the rest of the medicine arrived. "Please," I whispered urgently in his ear, as if I'd ever been able to change his mind.

He reached for my hand and squeezed it. "Forever," he whispered back to me. "Remember?"

I nodded, unable to trust my words to respond.

"Then do not fear my leaving you. It will all work out."

Slowly, I stood, knowing I could not dissuade him. "You are looking better. I will give this to Robbie now, then give you a dose when Dr. Enlow returns with more." I smiled, as if I believed that two lies could make a truth.

I led Dr. Enlow out into the hallway and closed the bedroom door. My hands were shaking so badly that he had to take the wineglass out of my hand.

"It is a blessing that you are not ill, too, Mistress Frazier. I normally see entire families afflicted."

"I thought so, too, last summer when they were both so ill. We had been to a wedding in Savannah and returned home late, so that all the biting bugs were swarming around us. They do not like me and I sustained no bites, but Geoffrey and Robbie were covered in red welts. It was shortly after that they both became ill." I met his troubled eyes. "At the time I did call it a blessing. Now I find that I am truly cursed. I would die with either one of them rather than survive alone."

His voice was stern. "Do not speak of dying. I will not allow you to go into your son's room with that word on your lips. Think of the love you have for your husband and son, and let that be your strength."

I thought of my mother and how she had always grieved for things that had not yet happened, and for a life she had thought to have. Her grief had blinded her to the parts of her life that were good, so that in the end, none of it mattered enough to bind her to this earth.

I nodded, then took the wineglass from the doctor with a surprisingly steady hand before walking into Robbie's bedroom.

After leaving both patients in Jemma's care, I escorted the doctor from the house. Georgina had gone, but I could see smoke from the kitchen house, where I assumed Mary had gone and was in the process of preparing food. I could not remember the last time I had eaten, and I felt a grudging appreciation for my sister's gift.

The doctor took my hand and kissed it. "You have much courage, Mistress Frazier. Have faith and we will see your family whole again."

"Thank you, Doctor. And my Christian name is Pamela. I am beholden to you for all of your help."

He gave me a sad grin. "No, Pamela. I am beholden to you for your help with the verse to send to William. I will return now to my tent and write down what you and I created so far, then post it to my wife, Catherine, in England, as I do not know when I will have time to finish it. I hope it makes it home before I do."

My heart was too heavy for me to return his smile. "Then I wish it Godspeed." I watched as he mounted my horse.

"Thank you for the use of your horse. You have saved my feet the long walk back to camp."

"You are more than welcome. When do you think you will have the medicine, Dr. Enlow?"

"As soon as I can possibly get it—you have my word. And you may call me Thomas." He settled his hat on his head. "I will be back before nightfall to return your horse." With a wave of farewell, he dug in his heels, then trotted away down the drive.

As I turned toward the kitchen house, a familiar figure stepped out from behind the shelter of the oak tree, startling me.

I held my hand over my heart. "Nathaniel. You frightened me. Why did you not make your presence known?"

His gaze was focused on the road and the back of the retreating Thomas. "I was not sure you would want to be interrupted."

I frowned at him, wondering what Georgina must have told him of my visitor. "Did your wife tell you that he is a British doctor who agreed to come see Geoffrey and Robbie?"

"She did, yes." His gaze scanned my face, taking in the dark circles under my eyes, and my hair that had not been brushed since morning. "You have been suffering greatly along with your husband and child, Pamela. You must rest."

"I cannot. But I do appreciate Georgina bringing me Mary. I have great need of her."

Nathaniel continued to study me carefully. "I've come to see your husband. Geoffrey asked Georgina that I come."

I wrapped my cloak more tightly around my neck, although I knew the sudden stab of cold had nothing to do with the scuttling clouds or the harsh wind that had begun to stir the dead leaves at my feet.

"Why would he need to see you?" My voice cracked on the last word.

Nathaniel regarded me with compassion. "We are no better than prisoners here, Pamela, and Geoffrey is ill. He will want to ensure that his affairs are in order."

"There is no need . . ." I began, but my throat closed and I could say no more.

"I've already instructed Georgina to hide her jewelry and other small valuables, and I would advise you to do the same. I will spread the word that there is fever here, and that might protect you from looters. But I would rest better knowing that you had taken precautions. Do you have a hiding place?"

I nodded. "We have a loose stone in the chimney in the upstairs portion of the kitchen house with a small space behind it. But I have no valuables. Nothing that anybody would want to steal."

"No jewelry?"

I shook my head. "Father gave Mother's jewelry to Georgina. I did not want it, but she had always loved bright and shiny things."

"What of your wedding ring?"

My right hand clasped my left hand, feeling the ridge of the wide band of gold through the worn red leather. "It has not left my finger since the day Geoffrey placed it there."

Nathaniel cupped my hands in his own. "Even more reason to keep it safe. Better off your finger and in a safe place than taken from you and worn by the wife of a British sailor."

I closed my eyes and nodded, understanding his reasoning. "Thank you, Nathaniel. You are right, as always, and I will take care of it now. The secret space in the chimney is a secure place. Please tell Georgina that she is welcome to make use of it."

He squeezed my hands. "I will tell her. And I will come speak with you before I leave, to see if there is anything else you need." His strong brow furrowed. "Georgina led me to understand that the doctor was staying here with you."

Before I could find the words to answer him, he was shaking his head and holding up his hand. "No, Pamela. You need not answer. I fear Georgina's imagination has taken flight once more. I will not trouble you for a response." He held my gloved hand to his lips and kissed it just as Thomas Enlow had done. "You know I hold you in the highest regard."

I watched him enter the house, his words doing nothing to soothe my soul. I glanced up at Robbie's bedroom window, feeling the pull to return to him and to Geoffrey. But first I needed to hide what valuables I had before returning to my husband and child.

I began walking toward the kitchen house, then paused as I remembered the two small oil miniatures in a silver double frame that had been delivered only the month before, when the traveling artist had returned to St. Simons. I had been saving them for Geoffrey's birthday in March. They would not be valuable to anyone but us, but I shuddered at the thought of the rough hands of a sailor touching the delicate silver frame. Or worse, tearing out the small oil portraits to use the silver for something else.

Quickly, I retrieved the miniatures from where I'd hidden them in my sewing basket, then retreated to the kitchen house. A fire blazed from the fireplace, broth simmering in a pot hanging over it. I greeted Mary, who was in the process of kneading dough.

After assuring her that Geoffrey and Robbie both loved buttermilk biscuits, I climbed the stairs to the upper room that had been Leda's bedroom. Crossing the room, I knelt by the fireplace, then slid off my gloves. I warily eyed a mouse hole in the baseboard, hoping I would not have company, before working the large stone back and forth in my hands to loosen it. There were no windows up here and I did not have a lamp, but I needed no light for my task. Eventually the stone gave way, and I pulled it out to reveal a dark hole behind it.

I took out the framed miniatures and kissed the top of the cold frames before sliding them into the small space behind the stone. Because of the cold, my wedding ring slid easily off of my hand. I traced my little finger against the inside, feeling the slight indentation of the engraved word there. *Forever.* I swallowed back the sob in my throat before placing the ring inside next to the miniatures and inserting the stone back into place.

Then I stood and brushed off my skirts, feeling that my actions were irrevocable, that I had somehow set into motion a series of events I could not alter, like pushing a stone from the top of a hill and feeling helpless to stop its momentum.

Gathering my cloak around me, I descended the stairs and returned to the house and to Robbie and Geoffrey, even more determined to make them well and to quell the sickening feeling of inevitability that seemed to follow me like a shadow.

CHAPTER TWENTY-SEVEN

Ava

St. Simons Island
July 2011

I blinked my eyes, wondering what the ringing sound was, and why I felt so cold in the middle of a St. Simons summer. I sat up and realized I was on the sofa in the parlor, where I must have moved from the bathroom. The ringing continued until my gaze focused on my cell phone that lay facedown under the table in front of me.

Still bleary headed, I answered it without looking. "Hello?"

"Hi, Ava, it's Tish. You sound groggy. Were you on call last night?"

I scratched my head, still feeling disoriented, seeing a stone fireplace instead of the yellow-and-blue toile of the sofa. "No. What's going on?" Even in my confused state, I remembered that Tish needed to be coerced into giving out information.

"I heard back from Dr. Hirsch at the archaeological institute."

I stood, hoping the motion would help orient me so that I would stop expecting to see gray winter skies outside instead of clear blue. "Dr. Hirsch?" I asked, as much to prompt her as to remind myself.

"Yes—remember? We found lyrics written by a Royal Marine but submitted by a Catherine Enlow. You recognized the lyrics, and Adrienne apparently knew them, too. An associate of Dr. Hirsch's accessed the archives in London to find the list of names of the marines here on St. Simons during the winter of 1815. Guess what he found?"

I knew. I wasn't sure how, but I knew. "That there was a Royal Marine with the last name Enlow."

"There were actually two, but only one was a surgeon. Guess what his first name was?"

"Thomas." I hadn't meant to say it out loud, but I couldn't stop it from tumbling from my numb lips.

She sounded surprised, like a child who'd been told there was no Easter bunny. "How did you know?"

"Lucky guess," I said. "There aren't that many names that begin with a 'T.'"

"No, I suppose not. And you're absolutely right. So now that we have a name, Dr. Hirsch has asked his associate to do a little more research to determine what happened to Dr. Enlow. He might even be able to tell us if there are any descendants."

"That's great," I said, wanting to tell her that Thomas had auburn hair and a son named William at home in Northumberland with his wife. But I couldn't. My head began to spin again, so I began to pace. My gaze settled on the music box on top of the curio cabinet, Mimi's words when she'd given it to me swirling through my thoughts: *Some endings are really beginnings. If you don't remember anything I've ever tried to teach you, remember that.*

"Are you sure you're all right?" Tish's voice sounded worried over the phone.

"Yeah, I'm fine. I just woke up, so I'm a little out of it." I turned at the sound of tires on gravel, thinking it must be my mother's car, until I remembered that she and Mimi had taken a senior citizen's bus tour of Savannah for the day.

"Tish, I've got to go. Matthew's home early."

She gave a wistful sigh. "Oh, I remember what it was like to be a newlywed. You won't have much time alone once that baby gets here, so you're smart to be doing it now."

I didn't correct her by telling her that I had no idea why he was home in the middle of the day, or why Adrienne's briefcase had turned up on the banks of Dunbar Creek four years after her death. "Call me when you hear more."

"Will do. And don't forget the next meeting of the historical society is Thursday. I'll pick you up at six thirty."

"Great. I'll see you then."

I hung up my phone and waited for Matthew to come inside. When nothing happened, I went to the front door and threw it open. He stood behind his car and was unfastening rope that attached a small aluminum boat on top. The boat was flat bottomed, with a square front instead of a "V" shape, wider than a canoe but about the same length. Even upside down I could read the word painted in bright red letters on the side: *Ava.*

His expression was like the one he wore after asking me to marry him, as if he were pleased with the world and expected everyone else to be, too. I couldn't reconcile this Matthew with the same person who might be capable of lying to me, who could look me in the face and tell me that he didn't know what had happened to Adrienne's briefcase.

"Surprise!" he said, his arms open wide as he approached me. He wore his dress pants and button-down shirt, but his tie and jacket were off and his sleeves were rolled up to the elbows.

All the things I'd prepared to say to him, the accusations, the questions, the doubts, vanished as I allowed myself to be enfolded in his embrace, his scent drawing me toward him like a butterfly to pollen. I hated this part of me, the part that erased all reason when I was with Matthew, the part that made me forget that I was separate from him.

"What is this?" I asked, stepping away so my thoughts could clear.

"It's a johnboat. I've needed one since mine sank in a storm last year. I thought that since you think you're ready to test the water, this would be a better choice than a sailboat. Sort of like learning to walk before running." He shoved his hands into the front pockets of his pants. "But I'm not going to force you into doing anything you don't want to do. It'll just be there when you're ready."

I looked at the small boat, imagining I could feel the steady rocking of water underneath my feet, see bright stars sprinkled across a night sky above me, and suddenly felt shrouded in a strong sensation of being *home*. It was a memory of an event I didn't remember experiencing, only that I knew that I had.

Although I was the one who had suggested I was ready to sail, I opened my mouth with an automatic response to explain that I didn't like water, much less boats, that I needed to ask him about Adrienne's briefcase, but instead all that came out was, "I can't swim."

He gave me a reassuring smile, then opened the door to the backseat of his car. "Don't worry. I got life jackets." He pulled out two adult-size fluorescent orange life vests and dropped them on the ground, then reached into the backseat again and pulled out a tiny replica of the two larger vests. "For the baby when he or she is older, and with his or her mother's full consent, of course."

I stared at the tiny vest, a voice in the back of my head reminding me that I had been the one to ask to be taken out on the water, and that he'd done this for me. I focused on the bright red letters of my name emblazoned on the side of the boat and thought again of the briefcase and all it implied, remembering something Matthew had said to me shortly after we'd moved to St. Simons. *I don't want any secrets between us.* I wanted to speak to him now, to give him a chance to defend himself. But I wasn't ready to face what would come next if he couldn't.

"They're not red," I said through stiff lips, trying for levity.

"No, but I did look. Spent almost an entire day between patients calling all over the country for red life jackets in adult and child sizes, and they're really hard to find. I hope these will work anyway."

"They're fine. They're great," I said, trying to reconcile what had transpired that morning with how I felt right now. I blinked, close to tears. "It will be all right, won't it?" I stepped closer and buried my face in his chest so he couldn't see my eyes.

Misunderstanding me, he said, "I'll be with you. We'll take it really slowly, and if at any point you're not feeling comfortable, we'll come right back."

I didn't want to tell him that my reservations weren't about the water at all. I nodded into his shirt, then pulled back. "Before I reconsider, let's go now; let's change our clothes and put the boat in the water."

I quickly slid out of his embrace; then we ran upstairs to change. I left my clothes on the floor so I wouldn't have time for second thoughts. We walked downstairs together, holding hands but not speaking, the old wooden floorboards whispering beneath our feet.

I helped Matthew carry the *Ava* to the dock, then watched as he put her in the water. He kept asking for assurances that I felt all right, that I wasn't fearful. I wasn't, and I told him so, unable to explain how I felt almost numb in the way one feels when going through familiar motions. Yet I'd never been on a boat before, had never wanted to be this close to the water.

He helped me put on my life vest, then secured his own, and then with one last assurance that I was all right, he helped me onto the boat and settled me on one of the two seats before untying us from the dock.

I watched a swarm of gnats dance around the dock post, undulating with the water's movement, cohesive in their uncertainty. Matthew picked up the oars he'd stored on the johnboat. "Are you ready?"

I nodded. "Yes. Definitely." I tilted my face into the warm breeze as he pushed off from the dock. I kept my hands resting on my knees, feeling no need to clutch the sides of the boat or to flail at the air like a dying butterfly. The world moved beneath me like a hand rocking a cradle, and I imagined that if I closed my eyes I'd feel the night wind on my face and hear the loud, harsh squawk of the yellow-crowned night heron as my boat propelled me toward *him*. I opened my eyes, blinking in the harsh light of a summer afternoon, trying to see the face of the man who'd been waiting for me.

"What are you thinking?"

I faced my husband, my thoughts jangling together like two colliding trains. "I'm thinking about how natural this feels. As if I've been doing it all my life."

Where I'd been expecting to see relief in his eyes, I saw hesitation, a flash of uncertainty, a sense that he'd had this conversation before. But not with me.

He glanced away, focusing on moving the oars through the water, pushing the boat away from the dock and the house. "I thought we'd just stay in this area here, where you can still recognize where you are until you're more comfortable."

I shook my head. "No. I want to go as far as the Frederica River, maybe farther. I want to . . ." I paused, no longer remembering what it was I wanted, only that I felt the need to reach the end of my journey, wherever that was, where somebody would be waiting for my return.

I looked at Matthew in astonishment, wanting to share with him what I'd just discovered, but I swallowed back the words when I saw the reservation in his eyes, as if he were ready to turn around now and head back to the dock.

"Let's get as far as the river," I said instead. "Then we can see how we feel and decide what to do then."

His chin set in a hard line. "The johnboat is made for calmer waters, so we won't be able to go much farther than the river. The flat front isn't designed for cutting through waves, so we have to steer clear of other watercraft. It can get a bit busy this time of year."

I nodded, not really listening, as I was too preoccupied with the onslaught of conflicting sensations. The fear had returned, but it had retreated behind all the other emotions, as if waiting its turn. I wasn't sure whether it was because I was on the creek and not the Atlantic, that my shoreline was filled with cordgrass and fiddler crabs instead of dunes and screeching gulls. But my anticipation eclipsed all other sensations, even the fear, and when my gaze drifted to Matthew's broad shoulders and the strong, capable hands grasping the oars, I knew his presence was helping to keep the fear at bay.

I was aware of the slap of oars against water as Matthew navigated our way through the fingers of the creek, aware, too, of the heat of the day and the cloudless sky. We spotted an osprey nest tucked inside the cradle of the branches of a dead tree, and a tall egret standing elegantly still, but I was aware mostly of a serenity that had settled on me like a shawl, as if my whole life had been leading to this moment.

We passed three people fishing from small boats like ours but with motors on the back, and every once in a while we could hear the moan and whir of engines in the distance, the sound like persistent mosquitoes. The marsh became sparser as we neared the river, the water wider, yet I still wasn't ready to go back, was still unsure of my destination.

I was about to tell Matthew that I wanted to row, to see whether it felt the way I imagined it would, the way my hands seemed to remember it, when the sound of something scraping against the side of the boat made me whip around to see what it was.

A gnarled and twisted limb from a long-dead tree floated past us in the current, spinning in circles as if the years trapped inside it were struggling to escape. Tangled in the twiggy fingers of a branch was a lady's scarf, wide white stripes against a sea of red. I thought of the woman who owned it, and how it had found its way into the water, and whether she missed it still. And I wondered about all the lost things in the water, and how most of them would be carried out to sea and never seen again.

I looked up to find Matthew watching me as if he'd heard my thoughts, as if we'd been in conversation and I'd spoken out loud. "Jimmy Scott found Adrienne's briefcase in the creek."

He stopped rowing for a moment, the air suddenly still around us. "He didn't tell me."

"He didn't know it was hers, because all the papers had been ruined by the water. But I saw her initials on the lock."

His expression gave nothing away. "How did he find it?"

The whirring of an engine droned in the distance, but neither of us looked away.

"He was fishing. It must have gotten stuck on something in the creek; otherwise it would be somewhere out in the Atlantic by now."

The droning became louder, but our gazes were locked in a dance to which neither one of us knew the steps. I waited for him to tell me that he knew nothing about the briefcase or how it had ended up in the creek. The water rocked beneath us as I held my breath and waited.

"Yes," he said, leaning forward slightly, his eyes widening. "It should have."

I'm not sure what I meant to say as I reached for an oar, wanting only to begin rowing back home, as if I could escape from a truth I couldn't face. Before my fingertips brushed wood, we both became aware that the droning was no longer in the distance, but saturated the air as a slim white boat erupted from the bend behind us, its trajectory in a direct line of collision with our boat.

I half stood in reflex, forgetting all the safety rules Matthew had drilled into me before he'd allowed me to step foot inside the boat. With a powerful tug on the oars, Matthew barely managed to push our boat out of the way, avoiding collision but turning us parallel to the choppy wake left behind by the other boat.

"Ava! Don't stand. . . ."

His words were lost as a large wave hit us broadside, and the last thing I remembered before my body hit the warm water was Matthew's hand reaching toward me.

I tasted briny water as the world went silent around me, a liquid world I vaguely remembered from the beginning of a journey. What was only seconds felt suddenly like a lifetime, a moment in time spent immersed in the peacefulness of knowing everything and nothing at the same time, of understanding how the water could carry us in any direction regardless of how hard we fought against the current.

Hands tugged on my life jacket, lifting me up, yet all I could think about was Jimmy saying something about flowers needing to figure out how to bloom wherever they were planted. I looked up into the faces of strangers, searching for Matthew, feeling angry and confused, yet seeing with brilliant clarity all that lay behind me and all that was in front of me, and how I was simply in the middle of my journey working to understand what to plant in my garden, and what to weed out.

I was lifted up and then over the side of the white boat and laid gently on a bench seat. Through stinging eyes I saw Matthew bending over me, hearing his words again: *They think I killed her.* I turned my head away as I was handed towels and asked whether I needed a doctor.

I insisted I was fine and allowed them to help me back into the john-boat, touching Matthew's hand briefly as he helped me into the boat, then letting go quickly. I felt the water move beneath me again as the boat turned toward home, trying to make sense of all I'd seen and why Matthew had not seemed surprised that Adrienne's briefcase had been found in the creek.

CHAPTER TWENTY-EIGHT

Pamela

ST. SIMONS ISLAND, GEORGIA
FEBRUARY 1815

A cold rain pricked my skin, the wind blowing it nearly sideways. I barely noticed as the numbness grew from my insides like a cancer. I was nothing more than a hollow shell left on the beach, waiting for the next wave to sweep me into the ocean.

Robbie was getting stronger with each dose of the nearly depleted medication, but despite Geoffrey's assurances that he was getting better, too, I knew from the dullness in his eyes that he was fading from me, his ghost already inhabiting his shadow. He had been unable to hold down any food for two days, weakening his already fragile state, and although the fever and chills had stopped, I knew that it was only a matter of days before they began their round again.

I urged the horse forward, my aged mare hardly noticing. My hands were frozen, the wind and rain easily cutting through the worn leather of my red gloves, but I kept my gaze firmly on the road in front of me. Each day for over a week I had not waited to hear from Thomas, but had sought news from him in his camp. I knew he had responsibilities, but I was too impatient to wait for him to come to me. And waiting for the sound of his horse had been like a knife slowly cutting into flesh, the disappointment of his absence like the severing of a limb.

I had become a familiar sight in the camp, yet I saw virtually no one, as most of the soldiers encamped there had retreated into their tents to escape the inclement weather. I had the hood of my cape pulled far over my face, trusting my horse to find the way. I tied my horse behind the big house, then trudged through the mud toward the medical tent, where a large oil-cloth had been stretched on poles over the space in front of the opening to protect it from the rain. I drew up abruptly in front of the closed flaps at the sound of a familiar female voice.

"I have the money to pay you, Thomas. My husband is a very wealthy man."

Thomas spoke in low tones, his words unintelligible.

"It is a very small thing I ask. I know you can help me if you wish to."

I recognized the animosity in my sister's voice, the very sound making me want to take a step backward, Georgina's unforgiving nature having made a permanent mark on me.

Thomas's voice was louder, as if he'd stepped closer to the tent's opening. "It is not a question of money, ma'am. It is simply that I am not allowed to leave St. Simons without risking getting shot as a deserter. I assure you that I am doing everything that I can to obtain the medicines I left behind on Cumberland."

Georgina's voice came back as a hiss rather than the deceptive cajoling tone she usually used to get her way. "Do not think I am without influence. I can make things very uncomfortable for you here. I am hoping that the next time we meet you will have a more satisfactory answer."

The tent flap opened suddenly and I fell back, finding myself staring into the astonished faces of both my sister and Thomas Enlow. He looked apologetic, while Georgina looked only smug.

"I hope you have not come to ask for the doctor's help, sister, as he is quite unwilling to do anything for us."

I put a hand on her arm. "Have you come for Geoffrey and Robbie?"

Her eyebrows rose as if she were considering my question. "Yes," she said slowly. "They are so ill, and Dr. Enlow is our only hope." A spasm shook her and she raised a handkerchief up to her mouth as she turned away to cough.

I frowned at her back. "Are you ill?"

She nodded, dabbing at her mouth with her handkerchief, her eyes on Dr. Enlow. "You know how the wet and cold always seem to settle in my chest. As soon as it warms up, I am sure I will be fine."

She turned to the doctor with a smile. "Remember what I have told you."

"It would be difficult to forget, ma'am." He made a short bow, but I saw his sardonic smile.

"I must go." A thin smile stretched Georgina's lips. "Geoffrey has asked that I visit more often. I hope you are not neglecting him."

I knew there was no use in defending or explaining myself. She had always had the ability to turn and twist one's words so that they fit into her side of any argument. She would claim that she had won, when in actuality her opponent had either simply given up or refused to participate.

"You are welcome to visit as often as you like, Georgina. Robbie especially enjoys your company, as you help him forget that he is ill. He keeps asking when you will bring him another caterpillar. His last one changed into a butterfly in the fall and she flew away."

Her clear eyes widened, as if they were seeing more than me and the rain and the muddy encampment. "They do that, don't they? They go to sleep as caterpillars and then awaken as butterflies. It is fascinating, is it not?" Her eyes met mine. "Tell Robbie I will bring him the first caterpillar that I find in the spring."

She coughed again, her handkerchief covering her mouth as she waved to me, then stepped out from under the cover of the oilcloth and into the rain. She turned back once more, her eyes bright, as if she were hiding a secret. "I would return home to your husband, Pamela. Each day you ride here, he watches you leave and then watches you return. He is sick but not blind. Do take care." She dashed away before I could respond, but I continued to stare after her for a long moment until the heat in my cheeks faded.

Despite Thomas's invitation to join him in his tent, I stayed outside under the makeshift porch in full view of passersby, huddled in my cloak. "Any news?" I asked, knowing from his expression that there was not.

"I've been given no leave as yet. I promise I will get word to you as soon as I do. Trust me to understand the depth of your need."

I nodded, looking down at the muddy hem of my skirt and boots so that he could not see the tears in my eyes. "I know you do." I reached under my cloak for my reticule, then drew out two pieces of paper. "My son and I created two more stanzas for you. He is getting restless staying in his bed all day, so I asked for his help. I thought he was very clever."

A weary smile lit the doctor's lips. "He is a very clever boy—very much like my William. Thank you—thank you both." His eyes were soft. "I am sorry I have nothing to give to you in return." He hesitated. "But maybe some advice for now?"

I looked at him warily. "What sort of advice?"

He pursed his lips, measuring his words. "Trust your heart, and your own eyes and ears. You cannot be misled by them."

I tilted my head as I regarded the doctor, not entirely sure what he meant. "I shall try, Thomas."

"Good. Now go home and sit in front of a fire to thaw out before you return to nursing. You are no good to either patient if you are not well."

"I cannot rest, Thomas. It is better for me to bathe foreheads and change bed linens to keep my mind occupied. I am afraid of where my thoughts might travel if they are not otherwise engaged."

He took my hands as his eyes warmed. "I know what it is to love deeply, and I understand your pain."

"Do you?" I asked. "Do you know what it is like to share a breath as if it came from one body? To die a little with each moment spent apart? I did not think that such a love was a common thing."

"It is not, Pamela. Therefore you and I are two very lucky souls."

I smiled and pulled my hands out of his grasp. "I hope you are right."

I took my leave of him and rode back to my tabby house, oblivious of the icy rain as I thought of caterpillars and butterflies, and of a love that was meant to last forever.

When I stopped in front of my house, I looked up at our bedroom window and saw Geoffrey staring down at me. I lifted my hand to wave, but the only response I received was the curtains falling back into place, and I was left staring at the empty window as if he'd never been there at all.

Gloria

St. Simons Island, Georgia
July 2011

I stood on the back stoop with a glass of iced tea and looked at Ava's garden, wondering why there were stakes in the ground marking off a path, but no other work had been done. I stepped closer, feeling Ava's absence the way a person feels the sun fade on a winter's day. As a baby she'd clung to me, following me from room to room as if she, too, could find no warmth without me. That's when my aversion to the phone began; I always feared when the sun might leave me forever.

Thoughtfully, I studied her practical garden, full of herbs she didn't know how to use in her kitchen. But I could see where flowers should be, right up to the kitchen house, where visitors to the backyard would be greeted with a fragrant and colorful surprise. I wondered whether she'd thought of that, of at least placing her beloved passionflowers where she might enjoy them.

The first flower name Ava ever said as a young child was "passionflower." It was so much harder to say than "rose" or "daisy," but nothing Ava did surprised me. The passionflowers attracted the Gulf Fritillaries like brilliant stars falling from the sky, as if she'd known all along that's what the flowers were for. For Ava, the rest of my garden was simply a place to dig in the dirt, to grow things with the sun on her back. But her passionflowers were her personal claim to magic.

Her love of the passionflower caught me by as much surprise as did her fear of water. Mimi said it was because Ava was an old soul, and told me that I could see it in all the shadows of Ava's brown eyes. But all I could ever see in her eyes was my own reflection, and that scared me most of all. Why would a little girl gaze out into the world with all the questions and uncertainties of a middle-aged woman?

A sound came from the direction of the path that led to the creek, a place I had not yet visited because of the sheer number of mosquitoes I knew were lying in wait for me. I looked up to see Ava and Matthew, both soaking wet, walking toward me. I knew immediately that something was wrong by the simple fact that they weren't touching each other. They were like a magnet and metal, and to see Ava walking a good ten feet in front of Matthew alarmed me; seeing her pale face and numb expression simply scared me.

I placed my glass on the ground and rushed toward them. "Is everything all right?"

Matthew started to speak. "Ava fell in the water. She and the baby are fine, but Ava's still pretty upset."

The air around me seemed to lose its oxygen as I watched them walk toward me, almost as if they were moving in slow motion. I thought of all the years I'd spent on the periphery of Ava's life, never understanding her fear of water or her doggedness on a soccer field. I'd been the ambulance carrier on a battlefield, nursing the physical wounds without considering how they got there. Now, looking at Ava's lost expression, I knew how very wrong I'd been, regardless of my reasons, just as I knew that a seed planted in the most fertile soil would never bloom without sunlight.

I turned to Matthew. "What was she doing so near the water? Didn't you know that she's terrified of it?" From the corner of my eye I watched Mimi leave the potting shed, where she'd been tidying up, and felt relief sweep through me. I was on uncertain ground, but Mimi had always navigated Ava's emotional life with the precision of a surgeon.

"Of course I knew. She . . ." Matthew stopped, as if realizing that nothing he could say would excuse his actions to an unsympathetic audience.

I waited for Ava to notice Mimi's approach, but she didn't even turn her head. "Mama."

As if I'd been doing it all of my life, I held out my arms and Ava fell into them, and she was my baby again and I was there for her, and for a brief moment I thought that I was being given a chance to start all over, as if do-overs were possible.

Matthew stopped behind us. "Ava, please . . ."

She trembled in my arms, holding her breath as she had when she was a little girl, preferring to pass out than to allow others to see her cry. She didn't step away as she faced Matthew.

"I need you to go. Now. To the apartment in Savannah for a few days. I need to sort things out in my head, and I can't do that when you're near me. Please?"

"No, Ava. We need to talk this out face-to-face. And we can't do that if I'm in Savannah."

"I can't." She drew in a shuddering breath. "I can't. Not now." She shook her head. "I need to sort things out. Alone."

He reached up a hand to touch Ava's hair but dropped it. "I'm sorry. I shouldn't have let you out on the water—it was too soon."

Ava shook her head again. "You know why I'm upset. And if you don't, then we have nothing to talk about right now."

It looked like he was about to argue, but I already knew it was pointless once Ava had made up her mind, and he must have known it, too. He set his jaw and nodded. "All right, but just for a few days. We need to work this out."

He walked up the steps and pulled open the door. Ava stepped away from me and stood on the bottom step. "Matthew."

When he turned around I had to look away, the pain in his eyes so much like what I'd seen in the eyes of mourners at funerals.

"You didn't deny it," she said, her voice soft but full of hope.

He didn't say anything for a long moment and Ava seemed to shrink, as if his silence diminished her. Finally, he said, "I didn't hurt her."

"Then tell me how her briefcase ended up in the water."

I could tell she was close to tears, but she was very adept at holding them in. She'd had a lifetime of experience.

Matthew's grip on the door handle tightened. "It's not that easy, Ava. Nothing ever is."

She squared her shoulders, her hands resting on the soft swell of her baby. "Love is."

He looked as if he'd been struck. "We'll talk about this later." He opened the door.

Ava took another step toward him and spoke, her voice raw. "It's like she's trying to pull us apart. Don't you see? Adrienne saw what I've been seeing, didn't she? What else did she see, Matthew, when you put her under hypnosis that you don't want me to know? What else did she discover that would make you toss all of her notes into the creek?"

His face hardened, and for a moment he no longer resembled the Matthew I'd come to know. I thought he would argue with her, but instead all he said was, "I love you, Ava. That should be enough." Then he turned and went through the door, shutting it softly behind him.

She stared at the closed door for a long time. Eventually, she turned to me, her face fragile like a flower after a heavy downpour. "What should I do, Mama?"

I think that might have been the first time she'd ever asked me that question, and it took me a moment to think, to find an answer that Mimi would have given. "Is this about Adrienne?" She'd told me very little about Matthew's first wife; Tish had been more than willing to fill in the rest.

Ava nodded.

"Do you love him?"

"Yes."

I took a deep breath, searching for words I'd long thought but never had reason to speak out loud. "Sometimes you have to make a huge leap of faith between love and trust, even when there doesn't seem to be a bridge between them. Do you think he had anything to do with Adrienne's death?"

She didn't hesitate before answering. "No. But he's hiding something, and he won't talk about it."

"Well, then you will fight to make this all work out. You're a fighter, Ava, in more ways than you will ever know."

She looked closely into my gray eyes, my mother's eyes, and I wondered whether she was seeing a truth too many. And in her eyes I searched for any blame for a lifetime of looking back to avoid seeing what was right in front of her.

"So what do I do?" she asked again, her eyes still searching mine, something I'd never seen before. I realized how very lost she was and how unprepared I was to help her find her way. It was as if Matthew had taken a part of her when he left, leaving behind an Ava I hardly recognized.

I glanced back to see whether Mimi was there to tell us the answer, but she was staring at the unfinished garden. I followed her gaze to the turned soil and stakes, to the one place where I'd always known all the answers, and remembered another garden from long ago. Remembered, too, another mother telling me that her children were her garden of souls.

I pushed a strand of wavy blond hair off of Ava's forehead, tucking it behind her ear. "I'm not going to tell you to find the truth at all costs. You have to figure out that part on your own. What you need to decide is whether or not you're strong enough to face whatever truth you find."

"Do you think I'm strong enough?"

Ava squinted up at me, looking so much like the strong-willed toddler I remembered that I almost laughed. The image quickly faded, and, perhaps for the first time, I saw her as she really was—a grown woman about to become a mother herself, and I realized I knew the answer to her question, that I'd always known it. That all those years of trying to protect her, I'd only been trying to protect myself.

"Yes," I said, swallowing hard. *But am I?* "But you have to believe it yourself."

Mimi came to stand next to me as Ava took a deep, shuddering breath. I waited for Mimi to explain to both Ava and me what should happen next, but she remained silent, as if she were retiring from her position as the person who knew all the answers, and had appointed me as her heir.

I took a step toward Ava, leading everyone into the house, feeling more confident now that my practical side could begin with the physical acts of setting things right. "Go take a shower and change. You'll be able to think more clearly then."

Ava nodded and moved slowly through the kitchen and up the stairs, her feet heavy. Mimi gave me a withering glance, as if I'd just failed in the first task of my new position.

"I'll make more sweet tea," I said, moving toward the refrigerator.

"And then what?"

I thought for a moment, staring into the refrigerator, welcoming the cold air on my face, trying to push all my practical thoughts aside. "I guess we'll go hang all three portraits of the pink dress in the nursery."

I turned to look at my mother as she sat heavily in a kitchen chair and looked back at me with the same expression of hope that Ava had given me. "Finally," was all she said.

CHAPTER TWENTY-NINE

Ava

St. Simons Island
August 2011

The waves rolled quietly over the rocks, their foamy edges reaching between each stone, leaving nothing untouched. I sat on a bench in the shadow of the lighthouse, watching joggers and casual walkers on the boardwalk in front of me. At the edge of the pier, a young boy and an old man perched with fishing rods, while another man wearing dark socks and sandals stood nearby shouting into his cell phone.

On the beach sunbathers baked in the heat of the morning. We were in high summer now, where even the mornings gave no cool-air respite. Mimi called them the dog days of summer, when even dogs didn't venture past the shade made by cars and trees. Two young girls, wearing matching bathing suits, sat under a broad yellow-striped beach umbrella and constructed a sand castle with pink plastic pails. Their mother lounged nearby under a wide-brimmed sun hat, reading a ladies' magazine, while an elderly man walked a large black dog close to the rocks. It was past nine thirty—when all dogs were supposed to be off the beach—but the man had probably been walking a dog on this beach long before there were leash laws.

Behind the beach lay the St. Simons Sound, the round curve of Jekyll Island in the distance. And beyond that the great Atlantic Ocean, rising and falling in its ancient rhythm. Two black skimmers flew over the water, arcing and diving in their perpetual survival dance, and I waited for the fear to come, for the aching in my chest to begin. But all I could feel was anticipation, as if I'd been walking down a long hall with a blindfold on for all of my life and I was about to have it lifted from my eyes. I even imagined a presence beside me, holding me close the way a person does before saying good-bye.

I was checking my watch for the third time when I heard my name being called. John McMahon took a seat next to me and slid off his sunglasses, treating me to his aqua eyes and warm smile.

"I'm glad you called," he said. "I didn't think you would after the last time I saw you."

"I know. I didn't think I would either, but things change. Thanks for coming."

"Don't worry about it." He handed me an envelope. "Sorry. I can't seem to help myself. Everywhere I go now, I'm looking for cameras. It's amazing how many are discarded with undeveloped pictures inside them."

I had to laugh as I took the envelope. "No need to apologize. I haven't had the chance to go garage-sale hunting in a while. Anything good?" I held up the envelope.

He shrugged. "See for yourself."

There were only three photographs, all taken of the same people but in different poses. It showed three women of three generations. They all had the same elfin chins and wide almond-shaped eyes that marked them as being related. They stood in front of a Christmas tree surrounded by brightly wrapped presents, and each wore identical matching knit Christmas vests. From the expressions on their faces, I could guess that the vests were some kind of an inside joke.

It was the youngest woman, in her late twenties or early thirties, who caught my attention. Her vest was unbuttoned from the breastbone down, her red turtleneck covering her pregnant belly as it protruded over her pants. In each of the three photographs she held up a sonogram picture, as if the photographs had four subjects instead of just three.

"It's not sisters," John said, "but I thought you'd like them anyway. It's a shame we don't know who it belongs to, because these are fun pictures I'd imagine they'd want to keep."

I nodded as I slipped the photographs back into the envelope. "I agree. But thanks—they're perfect."

He waited to speak until I'd carefully tucked the envelope into my purse so I could keep them awhile before discarding them with the rest.

"So what did you want to talk about?"

A gray-haired couple with matching caps of tight curls strolled by holding hands, and I stared wistfully after them. "I wanted to talk to you about Adrienne."

He waited for me to continue.

"Did your sister ever talk to you about undergoing hypnosis therapy?"

He looked surprised. "Yes, actually. She did. At least twice—that's all she told me about. She was a smoker—had smoked since high school, I think. I'd been trying to get her to quit for years, and so had Matthew, but she wasn't interested. And then one day, like, all of a sudden she decided it was time to quit, and she wanted it done yesterday. She wasn't interested in any medication or low-nicotine cigarettes. Nothing that would take any time. She wanted to go cold turkey, and she told me she'd read about using hypnosis. That it was one of the quickest ways."

"Why was it so important that she do it right away?"

Half of his mouth turned up. "I'm not sure—she never said. But that was Adrienne. Sort of impulsive. All it took was a mention about midwifing from Matthew to get her to want to become a midwife. I figured she was just being Adrienne."

"And Matthew did the hypnosis."

"Yeah. He did. I think it worked, too, because I didn't see her smoking after that. Not that I had the chance to see much of her."

"What do you mean?"

He looked out over the sound, and I imagined he was picturing his lost sister out on a sailboat, the wind tugging at her hair. "It was about four or five months before she died." He blew out a short laugh. "If I'd known, I would have told her to just enjoy her cigarettes."

"Did she say anything to you? About the hypnosis itself?"

"Not really. But . . ." He stopped.

I put my hand on his arm and his eyes met mine. "But what, John?"

"She seemed . . . changed. At the time I thought it was because of nicotine withdrawal. But there seemed to be more. She was definitely different."

"That was when she gave you her wedding ring, wasn't it? When she told you it didn't belong to her."

"Yeah. Exactly. Ava, what's this all about?"

I sat back against the bench, grateful for the hard wooden slats to keep me grounded. "I'm not sure." I considered my next words for a moment. "I found Adrienne's briefcase."

His head jerked toward me.

"Actually, Jimmy Scott found it. In Dunbar Creek."

"And . . . ?"

I shook my head. "Everything inside was ruined, so he threw it out."

"How did it get there?"

I studied my hand with the gold wedding ring, afraid of this question as much as I was afraid of the answer. "I don't know."

"Have you asked Matthew?"

"He didn't deny it, and unless there's proof I'm not going to jump to conclusions, and I don't think you should, either. He told me he didn't hurt Adrienne, and I believe him."

John's eyes narrowed. "What about her daily planner?"

"Jimmy said that he only found papers."

He took my hands in his. "Don't be blind. He won't deny tossing away the briefcase because then he can always say he didn't lie to you. I have no idea what might have been in there that he would have wanted to destroy, but there's nobody else who could have had it in their possession other than Matthew."

I wished now that I hadn't told him about the briefcase, that I could call back the words the way the ocean's tides call back the waves. But I thought of my mother's words, of how she thought I was strong, and knew I had moved beyond the place where I could avoid looking back to see what pursued me.

"I hardly know what to think anymore. But I do know that I love my husband, and whatever the truth is won't change that."

He shook his head, his gaze focused on our clasped hands as he slowly disengaged his fingers from mine. "So what do you need me to do?"

"Nothing—for now. But I don't want you to tell your parents yet about the briefcase until I know more. I'd like you to do that for me. For Matthew. For the friendship you once shared."

He looked out over the water, his eyes reflecting the sky. "I'll do it. For you."

I leaned over and surprised him by kissing his cheek. "Thank you. You're a good friend."

Glancing at his watch, he stood, his hands in his pockets. "There's something I haven't told you."

I stood, too, listening to the shrieks of the two little girls as they chased the waves.

"Matthew came to me once, that last summer. He said he thought Adrienne was having an affair. With a doctor in her practice. A mutual friend spotted them at a restaurant once, and in a park, having pretty intense conversations."

Whatever I'd been expecting him to say, it hadn't been that. "Did you ask Adrienne?"

"Yeah. She just laughed. And then said that if either she or Matthew could be accused of being in love with somebody else, it wouldn't be her."

It was hard to get my jaw to move. "Why are you telling me this now?"

"Because it all has to do with motive. And why Matthew wouldn't want anybody to see her notes."

I turned my head toward the shore and watched the endless roll of the waves, recognizing something familiar and comforting in their repetition. A distant memory tugged at the corner of my consciousness, but all I could hear was Mimi's voice. *Some endings are really beginnings.*

"You're wrong about Matthew, you know."

John's aqua eyes searched mine for a long moment. "I hope so, Ava. For your sake."

He said good-bye, then set his lips in a grim line as he walked away. I began walking in the opposite direction, toward the lighthouse and downtown shops, aware of the constant pull and suck of the ocean behind me, a reminder of how things changed while still remaining the same.

Bells tinkled over the door of Eternal Carnation as I entered the flower shop, the mixed fragrance of moist greens and scented blooms like a balm to my soul.

Arrangements sat in vases in various displays around the front of the store. The window was draped with blue and green streamers, with accents of yellow and orange mums and sunflowers shouting from clay containers in a nod to summer. It was eclectic, yet warm and tasteful, just as I would have expected in Tish's store.

"Hello?" I called, just as Beth emerged from the back. She'd been helping her mother in the shop for a few hours each week during the summer.

"Wow, you must be a mind reader! My mom was just getting ready to call you. Apparently the British are very meticulous in their record keeping."

When she didn't continue, I almost rolled my eyes, recognizing the resemblance to her mother, who also liked to withhold important information until the words were dragged from her.

"Really?" I said calmly. "What did she find out?"

Tish appeared from the back of the store, her green apron with ETER-NAL CARNATION printed in bold white letters nearly obscured by clinging baby's-breath buds. She carried a ubiquitous yellow notepad and waved a paper in her other hand. "Dr. Hirsch's assistant just faxed this over."

I stared at her expectantly until she slid the paper across the glass counter, where various stuffed animals, mugs, ceramic vases, and balloons on sticks were displayed. I had to squint to read the very tiny handwritten script on the faxed sheet, as a flourish seemed to ornament the end of each letter, making it almost impossible to read.

"What is this?"

Tish and Beth looked at each other, their cheeks puffed out in identical expressions of pent-up excitement.

"Please. Could you just tell me instead of playing fifty guesses?"

With a sigh of disappointment, Beth came over to my side of the counter. "I'm used to reading old script, so it's not too hard for me. These are the records of officers in the Royal Marines commissioned after 1793. They give full details of service, and some even include the name and profession of the officer's father. Cool, huh? Except for the fact that even if they were married, a wife rarely gets mentioned."

"Interesting," I agreed, as I watched her finger slide down the short entries, trying to make out a name I recognized.

Her finger paused on a name and she tapped it with her fingernail. "Here's your Thomas."

I squinted at the fancy script, deciphering the entire name of Thomas Edward Enlow. It didn't include a notation about a wife or child, but it did mention that his father's name was John Patrick Enlow and that he was a sea merchant. The last part of the entry was written in a separate script, even harder to read than the first part. "What does this say here?"

Beth moved the sheet of paper so she could read it better, then raised her gaze to meet mine. " 'Presumed lost at sea. March 1815.' "

A breath of cold air shot down my spine. "*Presumed* lost at sea? Wouldn't they know for sure?"

Beth shrugged. "The British were excellent record keepers, but their retreat from United States waters was pretty hasty. Both the Battle of New Orleans and the occupation here on Cumberland Island and on St. Simons happened about a month after the signing of the Treaty of Ghent, which ended hostilities between the nations and basically told the British to leave.

They sure could have used a couple of smartphones and texting and saved themselves a lot of trouble, huh?"

She laughed at her own joke, but I couldn't shake the numbing coldness that seemed to have settled at the back of my spine, and barely managed a smile.

"So who knows? It's all conjecture at this point," she continued. "Because it says 'presumed,' could mean that he's our 'T.E.' who was buried with a bullet to the skull. Maybe it was assumed he was on another ship— they brought several warships to St. Simons—and when they eventually discovered he was missing they just assumed he'd gone overboard."

"But wouldn't they have done a roll call before they left?" Tish asked.

Beth nodded. "Probably. But then they would have all piled into smaller boats with all of their supplies to get to the bigger ships. Lots of confusion involved, I'm sure. So if something happened to our Thomas Enlow, it might have gone without notice."

"But who would have wanted to shoot him?" Tish asked. "He's the guy in Ava's book who helped out with a malaria outbreak." Her eyes widened. "Hey—isn't the wife of Matthew's ancestor supposed to have committed adultery with one of the men stationed here? Maybe there was a love triangle going on. That could certainly explain a bullet to the head."

"No."

Both women looked at me in stunned silence, and I realized I'd shouted the word.

"Sorry," I said. "I just . . . I don't think that was the case. I have a strong feeling about it; that's all." I studied the paper so I wouldn't have to look at their matching concerned expressions. "So he never made it back to Northumberland?"

"Northumberland?" Tish asked. "How did you know he was from Northumberland?" She frowned down at her yellow notepad. "I know Dr. Hirsch's assistant told me that's where Thomas Enlow was from, but I don't remember telling you."

The bells rang over the door as another customer entered the shop, and Beth went to assist him.

"So what happens next?" I asked.

"They'll probably search for an ancestor and then be able to do some sort of DNA test—it's kind of difficult with bones that are so old, but Dr. Hirsch is hopeful, because the skull still had some hair on it."

Was it auburn? I wanted to ask, but didn't, because I already knew.

Eager to turn the conversation to something else, I asked, "Do you by any chance have a computerized list of the graves we inventoried in Christ Church cemetery?"

"Sure do. I just finished typing them up last week for the next historical society meeting."

"Do you have access to the file here, by any chance?"

She shook her head. "Nope, sorry. But I could e-mail it to you when I get home—although that probably won't be until after nine o'clock to-night. I have another wedding consultation."

I drummed my fingers on the counter. "How well do you know the graves in the cemetery?"

"Try me. I'm always amazed by what useless bits of information get stored in my brain."

"Smith. Georgina and Nathaniel."

She frowned, deep creases forming between her brows. "There are Smiths all over that cemetery—there was more than one branch, and then they married into just about every other family on the island. I can't say for sure that I've ever heard of Georgina, but that doesn't mean her grave isn't there. But I know for sure Nathaniel Smith isn't on that list."

"Why is that?"

She surprised me by answering right away. "Because he died up north somewhere—Boston, I think. Didn't that lady at the library tell you that?"

I thought back to our trip to the archives, and my conversation with the research librarian. I'd been so intent on my search for Thomas Enlow that I'd completely forgotten. "Yes, I guess she did—but I don't think she said his first name, and the name 'Smith' didn't jump out at me."

"I just know it was Nathaniel, because I went with Beth and her class to a field trip to the Savannah History Museum and saw the exhibit."

Tish's mention of the museum sparked a memory. "She gave me something—a brochure about the exhibit."

"Do you still have it?"

"I'm sure I do—I wouldn't have thrown it away." I thought hard, trying to retrace my movements, but coming up with nothing. "I have no idea what I did with it."

"Don't worry; I'm sure it will turn up. Things always do. But why the interest in Nathaniel and Georgina Smith?"

"I think that Pamela and Georgina were sisters."

Tish crossed her arms. "Pamela the midwife—the one I read about in the archived letters?"

I nodded. "She was Geoffrey Frazier's wife. The one who supposedly ran off with the British marine when they left the island in 1815. But I don't believe it." Before she could ask me why, I said, "The research librarian said something else about Nathaniel, too. Do you remember what it was?"

I was pretty sure I remembered, but I wanted to make sure.

"Yes. She said that at some point he sold his plantation on St. Simons and moved up north with his son and a freed slave."

"That's what I remember, too," I said. *But Nathaniel had no children, because Georgina couldn't have any.*

"What?" she asked, her eyes wide. "You look like you're about to say something else."

"Yeah. I was just wondering whether his wife moved up north with him, since they don't mention her."

"Good question. I'll send over the list from the cemetery as soon as I get home, and that might at least give you one answer."

I picked up my purse from the counter and put it over my shoulder. "I might not need the list. I've got a few hours before I'm on call, so I'm going to stop by the cemetery and see what I can find."

I waved good-bye to Beth as Tish walked me to the door. "Is everything all right? With you and Matthew? I called him earlier about an order for houseplants for his office, and he sounded so down that I had to ask, and he told me he'd been in Savannah for a week. I'm sorry if I'm intruding, but I just wanted you to know that I'm available if you want to talk."

I'd managed to occupy my thoughts with Nathaniel and Georgina so that I hadn't had time to dwell on Matthew or my inability to confront him. I managed a smile. "We're going through a little rough spot, but it'll be fine. I don't know how, but it will be."

She smiled, then hugged me. "Good. I've never known two people who belonged together as much as the two of you." She held open the door. "Call me and let me know if you find anything."

"I will—thanks."

The door jangled shut behind me and I stood still for a moment on the sidewalk, confused for a moment as I stared at the lighthouse that was the same but different, and the surrounding shops and restaurants that shouldn't have been there at all. Then I abruptly turned and headed for my bicycle, eager to get to Christ Church and find Georgina one way or another.

CHAPTER THIRTY

Pamela

St. Simons Island, Georgia
March 1, 1815

The smell of the sickroom, of sweat and fever and ashes from the fireplace that had not been taken outside in nearly two weeks, permeated the house like a constant reminder that we lived within ever-shifting possibilities and waning hope. Geoffrey had banned me from the room for the last three days, allowing in only Jemma, Georgina, and Robbie, who was now well enough to leave his own sickroom. Georgina had assured me that it was because of Geoffrey's feverish state that his thoughts and actions had become unreasonable, and that it would be best if I would comply so that he would not be overly agitated and sicken further.

I did not argue, having little energy left for anything except physical movement. But during the hours in which he slept I did not leave his side, and kept my hand on his chest to feel the reassuring beat. My heart ached, but my goal was to make him well, and with that accomplished we would take care to mend the frayed edges of our lives. He would then understand that my daily trips to Dr. Enlow were for him, and no other reason.

I looked up from where I sat in the parlor, repairing a hole in the knee in a pair of Robbie's breeches, listening to the sound of a horse's hooves pounding up the drive. I stood to peer out the window, nearly sick with anticipation, hoping against hope to see Thomas. For nearly a week the freezing temperature accompanied by rain mixed with snow had made it impossible for me to reach Thomas. My excitement plummeted as I recognized Nathaniel on his black gelding, its sides slick with sweat, plumes of steam rising from the large nostrils.

I stood as Nathaniel entered the house, the door swinging hard against the wall as he threw it open. He spotted me as I rushed toward him, my mending still clutched in my hand, his greatcoat bringing with it the smell of burning leaves and winter air.

"They're leaving. All of them. They're leaving today." He held up a copy of the *National Intelligencer*. "John Couper found this at Cannon's Point, left behind by the British. It's more than a week old, but it says that a treaty with the British was signed in Ghent on December twenty-fourth, and ratified in Congress on February sixteenth. That was two weeks ago! Which means their confiscation of our property was unwarranted, as the war has been over for more than two months."

I looked up to see Jemma at the top of the stairs, having heard the commotion from the sickroom. She looked down at me with questioning eyes, but I could not reassure her. All I could think of was Dr. Enlow and the medicine he had promised. And now he was leaving, and all of my hope would be gone.

"No. They cannot be leaving. I must go find Dr. Enlow and see when he plans to return."

Nathaniel regarded me with compassion. "They have already struck down the tents at Cannon's Point, and they've begun rowing supplies and soldiers down the Hampton River and to the ships anchored out in the sound. For several days now, they have been stealing wagonloads of our people and belongings. It is unconscionable."

Jemma came down the stairs to stand next to me, as if she knew that Nathaniel's news would be the final blow to my weakened state. I glanced down at the mending in my hand and saw that the wool was tear-splotched, the thread hopelessly tangled. I allowed it to slide from my hand. "No," I said. "That cannot be true."

"It is. I heard it from John Couper himself when he brought the newspaper to me. I wanted to head out to the encampment immediately to find the doctor, to see what could be done about procuring the medicine for Geoffrey, but Georgina insisted she go herself, since she already has an acquaintance with him and would know where to find him. I agreed, seeing as how it would expedite matters, and insisted she take our man, Aaron, for protection. I am afraid we do not have much time."

He took his watch from his waistcoat. "Wait here and continue as you were. I told Georgina to return here directly to let you know what she has learned. In the meantime I need to alert our neighbors so they will have time to petition to have their people returned before the ships sail."

I shook my head. "No, I cannot wait. Sitting here will kill me. If I head for Cannon's Point, I will surely pass Georgina on the road. I will take Jemma with me so that I will not be alone. Mary will be here to care for Geoffrey and Robbie, and to explain the circumstances to Georgina if we should miss each other."

He frowned down at Jemma, who would pose no threat to anyone who meant me harm, but I could tell that he knew I would not be dissuaded. "So be it. But I insist you take my pistol for protection."

He drew out a small flintlock pistol from his waistband and handed it to me. "You know how to use it?"

I nodded. With no son, my father had taught me how to be an adequate hunter, and proficient with firearms. Gingerly, I took the pistol and tucked it into the deep pocket of my skirt.

"It is primed and loaded, but you have only the one shot, so aim well."

He waited for me to nod my understanding before continuing. "Return here as soon as you have news so that I may be reassured that you are safe. With Geoffrey ill, your welfare is my responsibility."

"Yes, Nathaniel. I will." Without waiting to say good-bye, I rushed upstairs to find Mary and give instruction, then say good-bye to Robbie.

"You are the man of the house," I said, kissing his forehead as he sat on the floor with the wooden soldiers Geoffrey had carved for him. "Until your father is better," I added.

"Yes, Mama."

"I love you, Robbie." I surprised him by hugging him tightly, something he seemed to welcome less and less as he grew older.

"Good-bye," I said, trying not to see the worry in his blue eyes, memorizing them at the same time, as if our parting might be permanent. Then I turned and left and headed toward the sickroom.

The man lying on the bed was merely a shadow of my beloved Geoffrey, a skeleton being held together by skin stretched too tightly over bone. His eyes were glassy and unfocused, as if he were already seeing into another world. I sat on the edge of the bed, wondering whether he was even aware of my presence.

I rubbed the heels of my hands into my eyes, averting my face.

"Why are you crying, Pamela?"

I blinked to hide my tears, hope rising at the sound of his voice. He was lucid, meaning another bout with the fever was passing. I watched as he tried to lift a hand, but it fell limply by his side.

"Because I have missed you," I said, swallowing back tears.

"But I have missed you. When I awaken, it is never your face I seem to see."

"I was told that you did not want me in here."

"If I did, it was the fever speaking. Forgive me."

I placed my head against his chest, listening for the reassuring beat. "No, darling. There is no forgiveness necessary." I sat up and took his hand, and I watched as his gaze drifted to my fourth finger.

"Where is your wedding ring?"

His suspicious tone was foreign to me, almost as if the words had been spoken by a stranger. "Nathaniel told me to hide my valuables from the British. Their raiding parties were stripping the plantations of everything—not just silver and jewelry but cotton and slaves, too." I had yet to tell him of Zeus's desertion. I held up my hand. "My ring was the only thing of value that I could think of." I tried to speak lightly, but his expression showed grave concern.

"You once told me that it would never leave your finger. That it would show your fidelity."

I recalled Georgina's words of warning regarding my neglecting my husband, and his presence in the window after I'd returned from seeing Thomas, and I could not help but wonder what sorts of poison Georgina had included with her nursing.

Trying to keep my tone light, I said, "Then I will fetch it and put it back on my finger, if that will give you ease. But first I have an important errand to run. I am leaving you alone here with Mary and Robbie, and they will take good care of you until I return."

He struggled to sit up. "Where are you going?"

"The British are leaving. I need to determine when the medicine will get here."

Bright spots of pink appeared on his sunken cheeks. "You will go to this Dr. Enlow again, then?"

I paused, thinking I should lie, but knowing I could not. "Yes. He is the only one who can help us."

"Please do not. I have need of you here. More so than any medicine."

I felt like a doe I had once seen caught in brambles, struggling to free herself, yet the more she struggled, the more entangled she became. My father had shot her to end her suffering, yet I had not had the heart to eat venison for a good while afterward.

"Geoffrey, I need to go. When I have the medicine and you are well again, you can scold me as much as you like, and remind me of my vows to honor and obey. But not now."

He struggled to pull himself up to sit, and I had to grasp my hands together so I would not help him. "You mean to leave me. Do not go, Pamela. Do not leave!"

I was weeping openly now, despite knowing his irrationality had much to do with his state of malnourishment and prolonged fevers. But the truth did nothing to ease the tightness in my chest as I bent to kiss his forehead. "I will be back. I promise."

With surprising strength, he gripped my elbows. "I will find you. Wherever you go, I will find you."

"I am not leaving you, Geoffrey. I am trying to save you, as I would rather die than to live one day without you. Forever, remember?"

I kissed him again, then pulled away easily, his strength gone. "Be well, darling." My last glimpse was of him struggling to sit up, his head falling against the pillows as I ran from the room. I flew down the stairs, fastening my cloak as I ran outside, the pistol in my pocket bouncing against my leg.

Jemma had already harnessed the mare to the wagon and was waiting for me by the time I left the house, still shaking from the encounter. I took the reins from her and headed for Cannon's Point.

There were few roads on St. Simons, yet I did not pass anyone on our race to Cannon's Point. I assumed it was because the most direct route for the British evacuation would be by boat down the Hampton River. I did not notice the cold, or the draped alleys of oak, hickory, and gum trees that normally comforted me the way a familiar blanket on a cold night would. Now they only blocked the light, distracting me from my singular goal of saving Geoffrey's life.

As we neared the bend in the road that led to the old fort at Frederica, I heard the sound of a horse's hooves. I slowed the wagon, wondering whether I should seek shelter in case they were British soldiers looking to scavenge what they hadn't already taken. Jemma strained in her seat to see ahead, then touched my arm in alarm. I began to look for a place to turn off the road when the horse and rider pulled into sight.

The rider pulled her horse up tightly, making it rear so that her cloak fell back from her face, revealing yellow-blond hair.

"Pamela," Georgina shouted when she had regained control of her mount. "Thank goodness. I was afraid that I would have to ride all the way to Dunbar Creek."

I handed Jemma the reins, then clambered down from the wagon, uncaring of how high I had to lift my skirts. I grabbed the horse's bridle and looked up at Georgina. "What news do you have? Did you see Thomas?"

She began to speak, but her words were lost in a coughing spasm. She held a handkerchief to her mouth, and when she removed it I saw the telltale drops of blood, scarlet against the white linen.

"You are ill! Why have you not told me?"

I studied my sister for the first time in a long while and noticed how her hair lacked its usual luster, and how sunken her cheeks were. I had been so preoccupied with my husband and son that I had not noticed.

As if I had not spoken, she said, "You must hurry, Pamela! Thomas is already at the beach, prepared to be rowed out to one of the ships. He said he could take you with him to Cumberland and see that you are returned here. But they cannot wait. It might already be too late!"

She quickly slid from her horse. "Here, take my mount. I'll take Jemma with me, but first we will head home. Thomas told me we might need bribe money, and I have Mama's jewelry. I will take a faster mount and meet you if I can near Mr. Gould's light—that is where the British warships are waiting, and where Thomas said he would wait for you. But do not wait for me. I will find a way to get the jewels to Cumberland if you are not at the beach when I get there."

"But where is Aaron? It is not safe for you to ride alone."

Her face showed scorn. "He left with the British as soon as we reached Cannon's Point. We will see how he fares in the icy-cold winters of Canada. That is where I heard they will be taken. But do not worry for me, sister. I have come this far unscathed, after all."

I embraced her tightly. I knew how much our mother's jewelry meant to her, and how hard it must have been for her to offer it to me. I felt the heavy weight of the pistol in my skirt, reminding me of its presence, and I pulled it out.

"Take this," I said, offering it to her. "I have nothing of value that can be stolen. But if anyone tries to take the jewelry from you, you will need protection."

With only a brief hesitation, she took it, nodding her thanks. I had taught her how to fire a pistol when we were younger, and while she was not an excellent shot, a weapon might pose enough of a deterrent to a would-be thief. She could at least hit the broad chest of a man if he got close enough to her.

"I will find a way to get the jewelry back to you," I promised as I lifted my skirts again and mounted the horse without assistance.

"I know you will," she said, an odd light in her eyes. "Remember, do not wait for me. It is low tide now. If they have already left the beach, you may still be able to reach them. If you need courage, remember that you are doing this for Geoffrey. That will give you the strength you need to do what has to be done."

When she handed me the reins, I squeezed her hand. "Thank you, Georgina. I will not forget your kindness."

Her face stilled. "I do not do this for kindness. You are my sister."

Swallowing heavily, I nodded. "Geoffrey is at home, too weak to leave his bed. Please let him know that I am doing this for us, and that I will return to him as quickly as possible." I then turned toward Jemma. "Do whatever Mistress Smith asks of you. She will ensure that you make it back home. She will send word to Master Geoffrey." I choked back a sob. "Godspeed to us all."

With serious eyes, Georgina said, "Do not stop for anyone; do you understand? If there are deserters on the island, they will be desperate men in want of a horse. Or worse."

I nodded in understanding before turning the horse around, then dug in my heels, the wind freezing my tears as I tore down the shell-covered road, feeling nothing except for the fear that seemed to pursue me, its hooves pounding nearer and nearer as I headed toward the sound and whatever fate awaited me there.

CHAPTER THIRTY-ONE

Ava

St. Simons Island, Georgia
August 2011

My leg muscles burned after the long bike ride to Christ Church, and I wished I'd thought to bring a clean and dry shirt along with the large bottle of water I'd tossed in my purse. I took a long drink before crossing the road and entering the gates to the churchyard.

Although I had since become familiar with the meandering paths of the cemetery, I still could not push away the lingering feeling that there were too many gravestones that didn't belong here, that there should have been more empty space.

I found the Frazier plot easily, relieved to see no sign of tourists or anybody else in the shady space. The scent of tuberose lifted to my nostrils from the large vase in front of Adrienne's grave, letting me know that Jimmy had been there recently.

I squatted in front of Adrienne's headstone and read the inscription again. MOTHER OF UNBORN CHILDREN. My hand drifted to my swollen belly, feeling a quickening deep within my womb. It was too early to feel my baby's movements, but I sensed it inside of me, swimming in its watery world.

With trepidation I approached the final row of tombstones, of Geoffrey and his two sons. The confusion and grief I'd first experienced were still there, like an old bruise unexpectedly touched. But there was something else this time: a feeling of expectation. Just as I had felt earlier sitting on the bench at the beach and watching the waves tease the shore.

I stared down at the cold stone, wondering why I couldn't get past a niggling thought that I was missing something important. I waited a few moments longer, imagining I knew what Geoffrey looked like and wishing I could find a portrait of him to see whether he had blue eyes. Because then at least I'd know . . . what? That he was the man I saw in my dreams? That he was real and that I somehow *knew* him?

Eventually I turned around and began walking toward the front of the enclosure, examining the other graves sandwiched between generations. I stood and walked toward the back of the plot, seeing the graves of Matthew's parents, who had died while he was in college, two of his grandparents, and intermittent gray slabs of ancestors who'd come in the generations between Geoffrey Frazier and Matthew.

I hadn't expected to find Georgina here, but I allowed my gaze to glance at each name as I walked by, which was probably why the name didn't register with me at first, and I had to retrace my steps after I'd already passed it.

ROBERT WILLIAM FRAZIER
b. December 13, 1806, d. May 9, 1879.
The thing that hath been, it is that which shall be;
and that which is done is that which shall be done;
and there is no new thing under the sun.

Robbie! I almost shouted aloud. It had to be him. His year of birth followed the births and deaths of the two boys buried with Geoffrey, and he would have been eight and a half years old when his parents died. I knelt in front of the gravestone, my vision blurry as the dates and letters danced in front of my eyes. He had survived and lived to be an old man. And, judging by the nearby graves, he'd had a wife and children of his own. I sat back on my heels, doing an estimated calculation, figuring that Robbie was most likely Matthew's great-great-great-great-grandfather.

My fingers brushed over the engraved name, a name so familiar to me, but for no reason that rational thought could produce. Yet I could see his blue eyes and dark curls, knew what his small hand felt like pressed into mine. I knew his scent, and that he liked to be read to before he fell asleep but not sung to.

I pressed my hand against my mouth. Was this what it felt like to lose one's mind? Or were things that Matthew said were illogical somehow possible in a universe we were still struggling to understand? Mimi's ancestors claimed that the life of a man is a circle from childhood to childhood. I didn't know the answer. But maybe I didn't need to.

I stood, a feeling of contentment stealing over me. Robbie had lived out his days on his beloved island, near the ocean and marshes that were like the blood that ran through his veins. He had married and raised his children in the house where my unborn child would live. It was a circle, a continuation of a family connected like the estuaries and creeks that surrounded us, a watery womb to nourish us.

Realizing I still had much of the cemetery to go through, I stepped away from Robbie's grave, then paused, remembering something the curator had said, something Tish had reminded me of. Something about Nathanial Smith. *He ended up selling everything, then moving up north with his son and a freed slave.*

I turned back to Robbie's grave. If both of his parents had died in 1815, then who had raised him? Could he be the son that Nathaniel brought up north and raised? If there was an exhibit of artifacts from his estate at the Savannah History Museum, it was certainly possible that I could find out.

I returned to my stroll through the cemetery, my thoughts as twisty and wandering as the paths, my hope that by finding Georgina, all the other puzzle pieces would finally fall into place. My dreams had stopped, my flashbacks leading me only as far as my childhood in Antioch. But I needed to know more, needed to know what had happened to Georgina and Pamela. And Thomas. Because somehow all of this was connected to me. To Adrienne. I couldn't explain it, but I knew that whatever driving force was pulling me apart from Matthew had its roots in something that had happened before I was even born.

I found several clusters of Smith graves, and even that of a girl named Georgina. But her last name had been Hamilton, and she had died at the age of seven. I had covered nearly the entire cemetery when I found myself near the four graves of Jimmy's family.

Like Adrienne's grave, they were well tended, the faces of the stones wiped clean of dust and dirt, and fresh yellow gladioli placed at the base of each grave. A faint smile touched my lips as I recalled Jimmy telling me about his sisters, and I thought, too, of his burned hands, and how he had tried to save his family from a burning house.

A bright pop of yellow at the rear of the plot caught my attention. It was Jimmy's gardening gloves, and I knew he'd be missing them. Stepping carefully around the graves, I bent to retrieve them, noticing as I straightened something I hadn't seen before.

A small trellis had been erected slightly behind Mary Anne's grave, between her headstone and Scooter's, a blooming passionflower vine now creeping up the base. A brilliant orange Gulf Fritillary perched on one of the blooms, its wings moving slowly in the heat. The vine had not been there the last time I was at the cemetery, when I saw Jimmy and he told me about Scooter and Skeeter, and how his mother had loved her garden.

I walked back to the front of the stones, an eerie sense of déjà vu tiptoeing across my brain. I remembered standing here with Jimmy and taking photographs for Tish. I'd had them developed but hadn't yet given them to her. There had been something off about the pictures I'd taken of Jimmy's family, something that had given me the same feeling I was getting now: the feeling of somebody walking over my grave.

I stared at the stones again, and read the single inscription on Mary Anne's grave: FROM THE WITHERED TREE, A FLOWER BLOOMS. It was a beautiful epitaph, but I wondered where it had come from. Jimmy had been only fifteen when his parents died, and he'd had no other family, which was why he went to live with the McMahons. But even if the McMahons had been generous enough to pay for the burial and headstones, I couldn't imagine a stranger would have written that epitaph.

The butterfly left the vine and fluttered in the air until it found purchase on the smooth stone of Mary Anne's marker. My gaze traveled down to the inscription, to the death date that was the same on all four headstones, and the skin over my skull tightened. June 30, 1980.

I recalled the phone conversation I'd had with my mother after I'd met Jimmy, when I'd asked her whether she'd remembered the family, or the tragedy. *We'd already moved, so I don't remember too much. It was a hectic time for us, with your granddaddy getting sick so sudden-like, and your daddy having to move up to take over the business. And your brothers begged to stay to watch the Fourth of July fireworks on the pier, which meant we ended up sleeping on mattresses, because the movers had already come. It's no wonder I don't remember much of anything else happening that summer.*

But my father had worked for the coroner's office before he became a funeral director. If there had been a major fire with four deaths, he would have known about it. Most likely he would have been involved in the recovery of the remains. Which meant my mother would have known about it in every excruciating detail. *And your brothers begged to stay to watch the Fourth of July fireworks on the pier.*

I focused again on the death date: June 30, 1980. Five whole days before the Fourth of July. The butterfly continued to move its wings up and down in a hypnotic rhythm, but it was as if I were no longer seeing it, but instead was watching a movie of me participating in my own life.

I took a step backward, smelling ashes, like a harbinger of a storm, as gooseflesh rippled across my back. I could see the tall flames and hear crying and shouting and little pops and hisses as the world around me caught fire and exploded. I saw coats hanging above me and I knew I was in a closet, just as I knew that I had run there to hide. I reached out into the dark space beside me and found it inexplicably empty. And I realized then that

that was why I could hear crying outside of the closet where I hid. Because we were not together. Because I was all alone.

I dropped Jimmy's gardening gloves onto the dusty ground and I stared at them, surprised that I was still in the cemetery instead of inside the waking nightmare. Spots began to dance in front of my eyes, and I lowered myself to a sitting position, afraid I would faint. I wrapped my arms around my legs and placed my forehead against my raised knees, hoping to make it all go away.

But the smell of smoke and ashes was even stronger now, the sense of fear and danger erasing my defenses like a flame slowly burning paper. I sat holding my knees, but I was in the closet again, and I was coughing and trying to shout, but I couldn't. I didn't want to, because the crying outside the door had stopped. I was so tired, I leaned my head against the wall, and my eyes started closing even though I didn't want them to.

And then the door opened and familiar arms were reaching for me, and then I was being lifted and carried outside, the scent of flowers heavy in the night air. I was tucked under a large and leafy plant that smelled of summer, and watched the sky turn red. The warm arms left me and I was alone in my soft bed of dirt and flowers, the scent reminding me of my mother.

I sat on the ground in the cemetery, stunned and breathing heavily. I wasn't sure what I'd just experienced. They were clearly memories of something long-buried and forgotten, something traumatic and life-changing. The only thing I was sure of was that they weren't memories from somebody else's life. They were memories from my own.

The sound of nearby voices quickly brought me back to the present, and I scrambled to my feet as a small group of people with cameras around their necks sauntered past. Still disoriented, I stayed where I was, my gaze focused on the passionflower vine, wondering why it was there. I had no recollection of telling Jimmy that it was my favorite flower, or that I loved them because they attracted butterflies.

Who was that girl hiding in a closet? And whose hands were those that lifted her to safety? Just like the images of Pamela and Georgina, the people and events were *real*: a movie played on the canvas of my subconscious. When I was under hypnosis, Matthew had brought me to a door marked SECRETS, and told me to open it, and I had. And then I'd stepped through it. I remembered, too, the unseen presence that had been there with me, pushing me forward, and I wondered whether she belonged in the room of secrets, too. It was as if I'd been suddenly thrown into a world of stunning brightness that illuminated everything, including things I didn't want to see.

I needed to go back to that place, to that secret room, so I could try to retrace my steps and close the door behind me. I did not want to see into the dark corners, where things like fire and grief waited to be touched with light.

With shaking hands, I reached for my phone and hit Matthew's speed dial. Despite everything, his was the sole voice I wanted to hear. And he was the only one who could take me back to the place where all of this had begun. The call rolled over to voice mail, and I hung up without leaving a message. The sound of his recorded voice had brought every emotion to the surface, and I didn't trust my voice. He'd see that I'd called and call me back, and I felt some comfort, as if I'd just made the first step of a long journey.

I waited a few minutes, until I was sure I was steady enough to make it across the street; then I got on my bike and pedaled home as quickly as I could, eager to erase the past and all the secrets that weren't meant to be shared.

❦

My mother's car wasn't in the driveway when I returned home, and I felt only relief. I still wasn't ready to speak to anybody about what I'd seen and felt, and wasn't even sure whether I ever would be. I started chewing on my fingernails, a nervous habit I'd temporarily lost while in nursing school, when I'd finally realized that there were bigger worries out there in the world and that I could do something about them that was more productive than chewing my nails to the quick.

My hand fell to my abdomen as I thought about stress and its effect on unborn children. I stopped inside the front hall of the old house, listening to the antique grandfather clock that never told the right time, and realized that what I was feeling wasn't stress. It was the pervasive sense of anticipation, like waiting for a jack-in-the-box to spring.

I attempted to block those thoughts, remembering instead the period of time before I'd hurt my ankle and opened Pandora's box. The ghosts of the old house pressed against me as I moved to the stairway, touching again the old newel post, recalling how I'd known how it would feel under my palm before I'd even touched it. I looked behind me at Adrienne's painting of the house hanging between the windows in the front parlor, not understanding why it had looked so wrong to me until I'd seen Adrienne's sketch that showed the house the way I remembered it, as if it existed in my memory. Like she'd seen the house before, too.

It was as if the spirits of those who'd lived in this house before were chiding me for closing my eyes, for leaving them in unknown graves, their stories buried with them, the truth hidden between the covers of history books and in the memories of people long since dead.

I climbed the stairs to the master bedroom, and was nearly overwhelmed by the smell of ashes. But the hearth was bare, as no wood had touched this fireplace since Matthew had done the renovations and replaced the wood-burning fireplace with a gas log. It looked wrong to me, and would be restored to the way it had been if I had anything to say about it.

I turned on the shower and stripped out of my sweaty clothes and stepped under the stream of water. Closing my eyes, I let the water run through my hair and along my skin, giving me a few moments of mental serenity that I desperately lacked. After a few deep and cleansing breaths, I reached for the soap, my gold wedding band catching the light. I froze. The steam rose in clouds around me, the water growing warmer as it sluiced down my body, but all I could feel was a cold winter's day and a warning to hide my valuables in a secret place.

"Go away," I said out loud, as if Nathaniel's voice had been real, as if Pamela's trek out to the kitchen house to hide her wedding ring had been real. *But what if they were?* I tried to push away the unwelcome thoughts and focus on relaxing under the stream of water. But my body refused to cooperate, the feeling of sick anticipation returning, as if I couldn't stop myself from winding the jack-in-the-box. *But what if they were?* There was only one way to know for sure.

I dropped the soap and shut off the water, barely pausing long enough to dry off with a towel and throw on fresh clothes and grab my phone before rushing out of the house to the potting shed. The door banged against the wall, stirring up dust motes along with the ghosts, and I didn't pause to close it before making my way up the narrow stairs. My pregnancy and fear for my safety were the only things that kept me from taking the steps two at a time.

Gingerly, I made my way across the darkened room with the slanted ceilings, the only light that from the stairway, then knelt in front of the fireplace. My hands knew where to go, knew which stone would not be secured by mortar to its neighboring stones. In the dim light it would have been hard to tell without testing each stone, but I didn't need to see.

I worked the stone back and forth a few times until it came loose in my hands, revealing a black hole. *How did I know this was here?* I stared at the hole like a Gypsy staring into a crystal ball, except instead of seeing the future, I was about to glimpse a part of the past.

Still, I hesitated. I was deathly afraid of spiders, most likely because I'd grown up with brothers who enjoyed putting them on me. Leaning closer to the opening, I blew hard, hoping to scatter any webs and their occupants. Then, before I could think any more, I thrust my hand inside, my fingers immediately coming into contact with what felt like a small book with a soft cover, and carefully pulled it out.

I blinked at it in the dimness, as if that would somehow enable me to see in the dark. I'd expected to find the two oil miniatures Pamela had placed in the hiding place along with her ring. *But her ring had already been found.* Matthew's mother had worn it, and so had Adrienne, and I had held it in my hand. Whoever had pulled out the ring must have discovered the miniatures, too. But I had to know for sure.

Clutching the book in one hand, I reached in with my other and spread my fingers wide, moving them back and forth. I wished for my mother and her large hands that would be sure to feel all the corners of the space and pluck out anything that might be hidden there. Disappointed, I pulled my hand back, my fingers having grabbed only air.

Holding my prize gently, I moved to the stairs and quickly descended, eager to examine what I'd found. When I'd reached the bottom step, I held up the book, my mouth opening in surprise. Although, I supposed, I shouldn't have been surprised at all.

I brushed loose dirt off of my potting table, then pulled up the tall stool and sat down. The book was made of soft leather, worn smooth from heavy use. I knew whose it was even before I saw the *AMF* imprinted in gold in the bottom right corner.

Adrienne had known about the hiding place. *But how?* If Matthew hadn't shown it to her, then how would she have known it was there? From looking at the fireplace, it had been impossible to tell that one of the stones was concealing a compartment behind it. *Unless Adrienne had learned about its existence the same way I had.*

I took a deep breath, then opened the cover to find a spiral-bound calendar insert. *Daily Planner, 2007.* The year Adrienne had died. The planner that had been missing ever since, and important enough to Adrienne for her to hide it. With a calmness I hadn't known I possessed, I began turning the pages.

It had clearly been used as a datebook, with appointments and reminders jotted in their time slots, along with memos to pick up dry cleaning, and her work schedule as well as Matthew's. But she'd also used it as a doodle pad, although her doodles were a lot more sophisticated than any others I'd seen.

There were half-drawn faces of people, sketches of shorebirds and insects, of the lighthouse and a close-up of an azalea. I could almost see Adrienne waiting in line at the grocery store or the bank and starting to draw in her datebook. It made sense to me that her parents would want it. But not why Adrienne would have hidden it.

I continued to flip through the pages, noticing how around the middle of March her sketches changed. These were all of children and babies, some full-bodied, others just of their faces. I recalled the faceless baby sketches in her studio, the ones Matthew had given away, the ones that made me think of the epitaph on her tombstone. *Mother of unborn children.*

As I glanced through her appointments, a name jumped out at me. Dr. Bill Walker. The first one had been on April thirteenth, and then another appointment the following week. His name appeared more and more frequently, with several of them with a restaurant name listed alongside the entry. I remembered John telling me that Matthew had thought Adrienne was having an affair with a doctor in their practice. That would be reason enough for Adrienne to want to keep her datebook hidden.

The entries tapered off around July, as if nothing were going on in her life. But there had been. She and Matthew had been preparing to sail in a regatta the following spring, and she'd taken the print of the house in to be framed, along with the three other prints to be stuck inside, hidden. She'd had two hypnotherapy sessions with Matthew, because she was trying to stop smoking. And she had met her brother for lunch at least once, to give him the wedding ring that she said didn't belong to her. She had died at the end of August, but according to her calendar, her life had ended sometime in July.

I flipped a few pages back and saw two more entries for Dr. Walker. I knew he was an ob-gyn and had consulted on several cases in my own practice, but that was all. I pulled out my cell phone and called my coworker Diane Wise, who'd stepped into the role of my mentor and had become a good friend in the short time I'd been with the practice. She'd also lived and worked in the medical field in Brunswick for more than twenty years, and knew pretty much everybody. She answered on the second ring.

"Hi, Diane, it's Ava. Do you have a minute for a quick question?"

"For you, always." Her chipper and no-nonsense voice was like a mental massage, kneading out all of the tension and confusion that had been bombarding me since my visit to the cemetery.

"What do you know about Dr. Bill Walker? I know he's an ob-gyn, but that's about it. Is he married?"

"Very. What an odd question, and now you've got me curious as to why you want to know."

"I'll tell you later—promise. Do you know whether he's happily married?"

"Yes, but I will tell you that his spouse is another man. Is that what this is about?"

I was too stunned to say anything for a moment. "No . . . no, not at all. I'm just . . . Well. Never mind. It doesn't matter." I bit my lip, trying to think of another question that might salvage the conversation and perhaps get me the information I needed. "Would you know whether he's in charge of human resources at his practice, or anything to do with personnel?"

Diane laughed. "Like he would have the time. I wouldn't think so— he's a specialist in high-risk pregnancies, especially the ones with genetic implications. Pregnant women from all over the world come to see him. I've sent him a few patients of my own, actually."

Mother of unborn children. The pages in front of me seemed to blur and refocus.

"Ava—you there?"

I cleared my throat. "Yes, thanks, Diane. You've been a big help." I ended the call, feeling as if I were playing with one of those puzzles where you had to pull out all the pegs so that only one remained. Except I was still left with more pegs than holes.

My phone buzzed and I saw it was Matthew, calling me back. I waited for it to stop before picking it up and clicking on the messages icon to start my text. *I'm not ready to talk right now. I'll call u later.* I clicked the send button and stared at my screen for a moment before picking up the phone again and texting, *P.S. I love you.*

I waited a moment until he texted back. *I love you, too. Please let me come home.*

I stared down at Adrienne's datebook, and the two entries in the same week of June for appointments with Dr. Walker, and added another peg to my already overcrowded game board. *Not yet,* I texted back.

"Ava?"

I looked up to see my mother peering through the door. "I saw your wet towel on the bedroom floor, so I knew you couldn't be too far."

I stood, holding the datebook against my leg so it wasn't noticeable. I wasn't ready yet to share what I'd found. "I didn't hear your car pull up or I would have come in. Did you need something?"

"Just you." Her smile was hesitant. "We finished the nursery and we're ready."

There was something in her voice, something that made me pause and study the face I thought I'd memorized by now. But the expression she wore was new to me, her eyes showing a hesitation I'd seen before. Gloria Whalen had always been a woman who made up her mind and stuck with it, and never thought twice about her decisions. She'd once told me that making a decision—regardless of whether it was right or wrong—was always better than not making any at all.

She surprised me by holding out her hand, and I surprised myself by taking it. I don't think I'd held hands with my mother since I was very little. As she led me from the potting shed toward the house, I noticed a small white trellis lying on the ground, as if somebody had placed it there in preparation for planting it to grow a vine.

My mother let go of my hand to open the back door, and I stopped, my gaze still on the prone trellis, trying to remember where I'd seen one recently. *The cemetery.* It had been placed between two graves, and I recalled wondering how it had gotten there, and whether I'd told Jimmy that it was my favorite flower because it attracted butterflies.

I took a step toward it, away from my mother, who was waiting by the back door, but it was as if I were transported again to that dark closet, and I could hear the crying and the shouting, feel the sense of being alone, could smell the heavy scent of ashes.

"Ava? Are you coming?"

I nodded, still feeling as if I were in a trance, and followed her into the house and up the stairs. I was vaguely aware of my mother pushing open the nursery room door and me stepping inside a fairy tale of a child's dream, created with love by two women who loved unseen the baby growing inside me.

The smell of ashes was still strong, my internal fight to ignore it making me light-headed as I stood inside the soft green of the room. Light white curtains with tiny hand-stitched passionflowers fluttered on the windows, while a ceramic carousel of plump, sleepy circus animals danced on a mobile over the white-painted crib. The rocking horse from the attic, freshly painted in pastel colors, was stashed in the corner by the window, exactly as I remembered it. *But how?*

I spun around the room several times, trying to take it all in, and knowing that no thanks could ever be adequate.

"Do you like it?" Mimi asked.

Speechless, I nodded, noticing the hand-stenciled egrets and herons that soared around the perimeter of the room beneath the cornices as if watching over their own young. And a painted passionflower vine that grew up the wall in the corner of the room, bright orange butterflies hovering over the purple blooms. "It's beautiful," I said, still turning slowly, before stopping in front of the crib, noticing for the first time the three framed portraits lined up on the wall above it, with space on the end for a fourth.

The room stilled as I leaned forward to examine them, wondering whether the intake of breath from behind me had been my imagination. Everything about each subject was the same: the pink dress, the black patent-leather Mary Janes, the lace-edged ankle socks. Even the small pink bow barrettes in our hair were almost identical. But that was where the similarities ended.

"I didn't know your hair was brown, Mimi," I said, my voice sounding very small. "I've only ever known you as a blonde."

In the portraits, Mimi and my mother both had dark, almost black hair, and eyes the color of storm clouds. My hair was blond, almost white, and my eyes a deep and dark brown. My entire family, my mother and father, my brothers, even most of my nieces and nephews, shared the same coloring, except for me. Maybe because I'd been the only girl and was supposed to look different from them, I'd never thought to question it.

My gaze drifted back to the painted vine on the wall, and I thought of the vine and trellis and the cemetery, suddenly certain that I had never told

Jimmy about my favorite flower, and yet still I wondered why it was there and who had planted it.

I looked back at the three portraits and gripped the crib railing, finally seeing, *really* seeing what I was sure they had wanted me to see. I had never seen the portraits all together before, and after looking at them now, I finally understood why.

I stood motionless for a long time, my body shaking uncontrollably as I pictured Jimmy with a nose that zigzagged down his face, and how he spoke to his sister's graves as if he expected them to come back. And I thought of my own inexplicable bone breaks, sustained when I was very young. Mostly I thought of all the years my mother had kept me separate from her, naming me her daughter in every place except her heart.

What you need to decide is whether or not you're strong enough to face whatever truth you find. My mother's words reverberated in my head as I wrestled with my answer to a question I had never thought to ask.

I turned to face them, leaning against the crib for support. Of all the questions I wanted to ask, only one came to my lips. "Why?"

CHAPTER THIRTY-TWO

Gloria

St. Simons Island, Georgia
August 2011

When Ava was a little girl, her favorite question was, "Why?" Why was the sky blue? Why did moths throw themselves against a light until they died? Why were there no more dinosaurs? She'd lose interest while I was halfway through my explanation, as if it were more interesting to know only the possibilities instead of actual answers. Over the years, I'd come to understand her reasoning, as I'd learned that there are some answers you'd rather not hear. I'd come to St. Simons prepared with answers, yet when the question came, I still wasn't ready. I'd worked so hard for so many years not to hold on too tightly for fear of losing my daughter. Yet looking at her face as she examined those pictures made me realize that I was going to lose her anyway.

She turned away from the crib and her eyes traveled from me to Mimi and back, as if she were hoping somebody else was in the room to jump out and tell her it was all some bad mistake. Her eyes seemed dead when she said that one word that held over thirty years of secrets and all the love a heart could hold: "Why?"

I exchanged a glance with Mimi before stepping forward, while Mimi settled herself into the glider chair. "There's no easy answer to that, Ava." I held my chin up so I could go on pretending that I was strong. "You needed a mother. And I wanted a daughter." It sounded so simple, and, in its way, I suppose that was really all it ever was.

"So you took me? And pretended that I was yours?"

"You *are* mine. I have never doubted that for one minute."

She was shaking her head even as I spoke, unwilling to listen. "How? How did it happen?"

Her second-favorite word. I almost smiled.

I sank down onto the ottoman in front of Mimi's chair, keeping my back ramrod straight and my hands clasped. I had the fleeting thought that I should slouch once in a while, that maybe if I leaned into the wind, it would be easier to face a storm. That maybe I could face the ringing of a phone that might be the dreaded call letting me know that somebody knew what I'd done. But none of that mattered anymore.

I took a deep breath. "I only saw you once before . . . before the night of the fire. You and your sister were in the backseat of Mary Anne's car in the carpool line at school, and you had casts on both legs. Mary Anne said you had fallen, but I didn't believe her, because I'd heard stories about her husband, and had seen Mary Anne with black eyes more than once. She tried to tell everybody she was clumsy, but I remembered the one time I'd come over to see her garden and I'd met Floyd, so I knew better. She must have set your casts herself, because he wouldn't have allowed her to take you to an emergency room. Too many people to ask questions."

I looked up at Ava, wondering whether she needed me to stop, but from the set of her stubborn jaw I could tell I wasn't going to get away so easily. "I did try to reach out to her a few times after that, but she shut me out. Insisted she was fine and could take care of herself and her children. She slammed the door in my face and I went away."

I watched Ava as she took it all in, every emotion showing. It was why she was such a terrible liar. She'd learned early on to act first and ask forgiveness later, so she never had to deny a misdeed. Mimi was headstrong, too, and Ava always said that was where she got it from. I wondered whether she was thinking about that now.

"So what happened—the night of the fire?"

I spread my hands on my skirt, recalling a summer evening when the sky was more stars and moon than night. "Henry and I were planning on building a bigger house on that spot of land that used to be the Smith Plantation. Mimi insisted that we needed to know what it looked like at sunset before we made an offer."

I began rocking back and forth on the ottoman, as if I were consoling one of my babies. "Right after nightfall we were heading back to the car, when we heard what sounded like an explosion, and then a baby screaming and a boy shouting for help. So of course we went to investigate—the Scotts lived through the woods a bit." I swallowed, remembering, tasting smoke. "The house was already on fire when we got there, and we didn't see anybody except Floyd Scott, who was laughing and staggering around like he was drunk, and a shovel was at his feet. That's when we saw what he was laughing at."

I closed my eyes, trying to block out the scene I'd carried around in my head for so long. "I heard Jimmy shouting and a baby screaming from inside the house. And I saw the woman on the ground." I didn't tell Ava about the blood or the damage a shovel could do wielded by a large man against a delicate woman.

"It was Mary Anne, and we could tell she was dead." I didn't elaborate. There are some things that should never be remembered.

The sun sank lower in the sky, shooting rays of gold through the slats of the shutters into the nursery. The light brushed my face, but I shrank from it, still reliving the night that my greatest wish had been granted, but at a cost I was never sure any of us could really afford to pay.

"We heard Jimmy shouting inside for his father to come help. The entire upper story of the house was on fire by then, with flames shooting out from all the upstairs windows." I paused. "I think I might have seen you first, in the garden. You were wearing a white nightgown and I saw that, standing out in the darkness, tucked beneath the passionflower vines like an uprooted camellia."

Ava was breathing hard to keep from crying, and I knew she'd learned that from me.

"I started walking toward you, afraid that you were hurt, but Floyd saw me and turned, and soon saw you, too." I began speaking quickly, to make this story end. "He picked up the shovel and began walking toward you, and he was closer than I was. I couldn't run very fast—I had tripped in the woods and fallen on something and had cut open my knee, and Henry was running toward the house to get Jimmy outside and didn't see what Floyd was doing.

"And then Jimmy was there and he saw his father moving toward you. I could tell he was burned badly. The fire was making it almost as bright as daylight, and I saw that there was no skin left on his hands. But when he saw where Floyd was headed, it was like he wasn't hurt at all. He picked up one of those large rocks Mary Anne used to edge her beds as if it didn't weigh anything. Floyd was lifting the shovel over you, getting ready to bring it down when Jimmy hit him. Hard." *Hard enough that the big man crumpled like a marionette with suddenly severed strings.*

Our eyes met in mutual horror, the silence of the house interrupted only by the chime of the antique clock downstairs.

"Henry told me to get in the car and wait for him. I didn't think to question. That's how things like that are—you're living your normal life one minute, and the next something extraordinary happens that you're not prepared for. So I didn't think. I just picked you up, and you put your little arms around my neck and laid your head on my chest. And I was lost." I struggled for a moment to put air back into my lungs so I could speak. "I loved you from that moment as if I'd always known you. As if you'd always been mine."

I swallowed hard, trying not to cry, as if the two of us were having a contest.

"I took you to the car and waited. I heard things exploding and glass shattering as the house burned. It's a pretty isolated spot, which is probably why nobody had called the fire department yet. I held you until Henry got back to the car. All he said was that he'd taken care of everything, and that Jimmy would be fine. And then he started the car and we left, and I was afraid to say anything. To ask any questions that might mean letting you out of my arms."

"What did he do?" Ava asked, her voice cracking as if she'd been inhaling smoke and burned air. As if she were remembering, too.

I quickly glanced at Mimi for reassurance and then continued. "Everything was crazy, and nobody was thinking clearly. Jimmy begged Henry not to tell anybody what he had done. He was convinced that he would be sent to one of those juvenile delinquency places. And no matter what Henry told him, how he was just trying to protect you and there were witnesses, Jimmy wouldn't believe him."

I lifted my chin, as if that one movement would explain what could be explained only by the scent of a baby's hair, and the feeling of soft, small hands on a mother's cheek. I thought for a moment, trying to pinpoint the exact instant when everything had changed. "I don't think it occurred to Henry that we would take you until Jimmy took off, running into the woods. Before he ran, he told Henry to take care of you. Maybe that's what started this whole thing. I don't know. But Henry knew Jimmy wouldn't get far—he was too badly injured. Because he was a volunteer fireman, he carried a two-way radio in his trunk, and when he called in the emergency after he got back to the car, he made sure they knew to look for Jimmy, that he would need an ambulance.

"Henry then moved the bodies into the burning house so it looked like Floyd killed himself along with his family, so nobody would be pointing fingers. Henry wasn't going to call the fire trucks until everything was pretty much ashes, where it would be hard to determine forensically what exactly had happened. As it was, since both Mary Anne and Floyd were found by the door, it looked like they'd been trying to escape but were overcome by smoke."

Ava was looking at me like I imagined a drowning person would look up through the water toward the sun. I wanted to stop, but knew she wouldn't allow it.

I continued. "When we got home, Mimi—who was visiting us at the time—had already put the younger boys to bed, and the older boys were in the basement watching a movie. We kept waiting for the phone to ring, to let us know that they were coming to pick up the baby, thinking that Jimmy must have told them. But when it didn't, we began to make plans." I tried to smile. "By then, we'd both fallen in love with you. You were so happy to be with us, as if that nightmare had never happened. And you helped us forget, too."

"And my sister?"

"They found some remains. Henry wrote in his report that it was the remains of two toddlers, and he had enough seniority to convince others to agree."

Her beautiful eyes were wide, and I could almost read every word she was thinking, trying to determine the one last piece of information that would place all the guilt on me.

"But why? Why would Daddy risk everything?"

I was silent for a moment as I studied my fingernails, clipped short, without polish, searching for the words I needed to make her comprehend the incomprehensible. "Because he loved me. I had just had another miscarriage, and the doctors told me I shouldn't try anymore. I was an emotional wreck. That's why your father thought we should build a house for us and the boys—to get my mind off the daughter I couldn't have but couldn't stop wanting."

She was pressing her lips together so hard they'd turned white. "So you packed up everything and moved to Antioch, where nobody knew that I wasn't really yours and wouldn't think to question. Where the funeral business would come in handy when in need of a new identity for a stolen baby. How convenient for you all." She paused a moment to take a deep, shuddering breath. "But what about Jimmy? Didn't he miss me?"

"I didn't go to the funeral, not wanting to leave you, and afraid of Jimmy demanding that I give you back. But at the funeral, Jimmy recognized Henry, and Henry was sure that would be the end of it, that we'd have to surrender you and face the consequences. But Jimmy had a secret to hide. All Jimmy wanted was for Henry to promise that he would make sure that you were raised by a loving family. Henry said that he could come live with us, but Jimmy didn't want to leave St. Simons and his mother and sister, and we couldn't stay. Jimmy was already living with the McMahons and was happy there." I shrugged. "Maybe by giving you to us he was making sure his secret was safe." I regarded her silently for a moment. "He just made Henry promise him one thing."

Ava's eyes were hostile. "What?"

"That you be taught how to garden like your mother. I'd only ever been a reluctant gardener, planting the requisite gardenias in pots by the front door, or attempting vines on the mailbox. But I learned, with you at my side, because that's what Jimmy wanted. Because I knew that Mary Anne would have taught you if she'd been here to see you grow."

She looked at Mimi as if for confirmation and must have seen it in her grandmother's face. Turning to me, she said, "My whole life has been a lie. All my life I haven't known my real name, and you never thought I might want to know?"

I shook my head. "No, it wasn't like that at all. You were our daughter and sister and granddaughter. None of that was a lie. And we did plan to tell you; we did. But as you grew older, there never seemed to be a right time. You were a happy child. How could we tell you and ruin your happiness?"

Mimi leaned forward in the chair, and I could tell by the way she was shaking that she wouldn't have been able to stand. "Oh, Ava, your life has not been a lie. You have a family who has loved you without question since the moment you appeared in our lives. *That* is not a lie, regardless of what name we called you. I fought your mama and daddy for years, trying to get them to tell you what had happened, and I'm so glad they never listened. Because that would have been the second-biggest tragedy of your life." She closed her eyes for a moment, the lids translucent. "You will leave this room confused and angry, and we won't blame you. But even then, you will still be loved with all of our hearts. And we can't be sorry for that."

A spot of blood appeared on Ava's lip where she'd bitten it too hard. She turned to me again. "I don't know what's harder to take—the fact that you've lied to me every time you said my name, or that none of this was really about me. I was just a convenient baby girl to fill a void for you. Somebody to wear the pink dress and have her picture taken so you'd have another picture up on the wall."

I didn't know it was possible to hurt so much without having been physically touched. "No, Ava. You're so wrong. I love you because you are who you are. Because you're tenacious, and you always step first and look second, and because you're honest, and kind, and smart. And because you love so completely. You just step in headfirst and give it all you have. I think that's why your brothers accepted your sudden appearance in our lives—because you were so giving in your love." I hiccuped, realizing that I was finally crying. "I love you because you're my daughter, regardless of who gave birth to you. And I always will."

She was shaking her head as I spoke, as if the mere action could negate everything I said. "You are not my mother. My mother is dead, and no matter what you call yourself or tell me, that will never change. My whole life has been a complete lie. Because of you. And I don't ever want to see you again. Any of you."

She headed for the door, but not before I could see her own tears. She stopped, her back to us. "So which one am I? Christina or Jennifer?"

I hadn't thought of those names in so long that it took me a moment to remember. "You're Tina. Christina Mary."

Ava's chin fell to her chest. "Scooter. Jimmy called me Scooter. Because I couldn't walk and just scooted around on my bottom. I guess that's the only memory I'll ever have of my real family."

She lifted her hand to the doorknob, but I stopped her. "I named you Ava because it means 'life.' Not because you were starting a new life, but because you'd given me back mine."

Ava hesitated only a moment before opening the door. "Don't bother to say good-bye. Just go." She walked out into the hall, then shut the door quietly behind her, as if she were afraid of dislodging any more ghosts.

CHAPTER THIRTY-THREE

Ava

St. Simons Island, Georgia
August 2011

I normally slept lightly on the nights I was on call, so when I woke up the following morning at eight o'clock, I jolted out of bed. My mind must have simply shut down, unable to process everything that had been thrown at me in such a short time. I checked my phone to make sure I hadn't missed any calls, grateful that none of my patients had gone into labor. I'm sure my experience and professionalism would have taken over if I'd been required to deliver a baby, but my mind would have been in a different place, a night filled with violence and roads taken, a place where I couldn't stop thinking that I had been somehow left behind.

I showered and dressed, and when I picked up my phone I saw that Tish had called three times while I'd been in the bathroom, but hadn't left a voice mail. I put the phone in my pocket without calling her back, not ready to speak to anybody yet. There was too much in my mind to sort through, and I needed to do it by myself. And there was only one place where I knew I could: the place where it had all begun.

The air hung heavy with moisture, the moss on the trees limp with their own weight. I took my car, wanting the comfort of air-conditioning as well as not trusting that I'd have the energy to last if I rode my bike the long distance and back.

When I passed the spot for the turnoff to the Smith Plantation, I noticed there were more cars and activity there than I'd seen before, and I wondered whether the new imaging equipment Tish had told me about had finally arrived.

I slowed down and took the first right onto a shell-and-sand road, following it for a short distance before I saw the ruins of the old house with the magnificent garden beside it, looking like an old woman wearing a flamboyant dress.

The blooms drooped in the heat, and I imagined the smell of ashes still heavy in the air. But birds chirped in the trees, and two squirrels bounded into the encroaching woods like a reminder that life was resilient and somehow remained and coexisted with devastation.

I walked slowly through the meandering beds of brilliant blooms and bright foliage until I found the trellises with the passionflower vines against the charred bricks of the old chimney. I hadn't seen them the first time because I hadn't been looking for them. My gaze traveled to the ground, where the vines erupted from the soil, and imagined an almost two-year-old child cowering under their sparse shelter.

"Hi, Miss Ava. You here to talk about your garden?"

I turned around quickly, my heart thudding. "Jimmy! I didn't see your truck."

He motioned with his chin. "I parked it on the other side of the house. You can't see it from here."

He wasn't wearing his gloves, and I remembered the pair I'd found in the cemetery. "I found your gloves, but I left them in the basket on my bike. I'll bring them to you later, if you like."

He took off his UGA hat and swiped his forehead with his sleeve like I'd seen him do so many times before. But this time I was noticing his blond hair, darkened with sweat, and his slender, capable hands. Like mine. I wondered whether we'd inherited them from our mother.

"Or I could come get them when I come to work in your garden." He smiled, and I knew he was thinking of the flowers he was determined to plant there. He wasn't one to easily take no for an answer, either, and I wondered who'd win this battle.

I stepped closer to him. "Do you know who I am, Jimmy?"

He tilted his head and nodded shyly.

"How long have you known?"

He scrunched up his face as he thought. "I think it was when you hurt your leg real bad, but you didn't cry. You didn't do that when you were little, either. Even when Daddy hurt you and your legs got broke, you didn't cry. I figured there couldn't be two people like that." He smiled brightly. "And you look like me."

I wanted to laugh out loud. "Then you're a lot smarter than I am." I stepped closer and took his scarred hands in mine. They were cooler to the touch than I expected, as if the scars should somehow carry the heat of the fire three decades later. "Thank you," I said, staring into a pair of eyes as brown as my own. "You saved my life."

He shrugged, but he was smiling, too. "Nah. I just took you out of the house. Your mama and daddy did the hard part."

"No, Jimmy. What they did was wrong."

He regarded me closely, and I remembered how I'd once thought that Jimmy was a lot smarter than people probably gave him credit for. I squirmed under his scrutiny, trying not to hear the truth of his words. "I was the one that ran. I was that scared I was going to jail, even though your daddy said that I wouldn't. But I knew jail was filled with men just like my daddy, and that's all I could think of."

He squinted into the sun. "See those dead flowers over there by the wood railing?" He jerked his head to an area separated from the woods. "I planted tuberose bulbs in the spring and only one of them grew. And that was because it was the only one in full sun. I don't think I did the wrong thing by planting the rest in partial shade, because if I hadn't done that, then I wouldn't have found the perfect spot for them."

I frowned up at him, wondering whether I'd been wrong about him, wondering whether he really understood what I was saying. "If my daddy had told the authorities what had happened, we could have been together. We could have grown up together."

He moved to a bed of leggy petunias and began pulling them out by their roots, adding them to a pile he'd already started. "I didn't know who Gloria was at first when she came to the cemetery to see the graves a few weeks ago. I didn't see her the night of the fire or at the funeral, so I didn't know she was your mama. But I recognized her from that time she came to see Mama's garden when I was in Joshua's class. I liked her. I liked the way she listened to Mama as if Mama had something important to say. It was funny, because she was saying that she'd never planted a garden before and needed help with her wisteria. And Mama told her to be patient and plant what she loved. That she couldn't make mistakes, because mistakes were just chances to learn. Like my tuberoses." He paused. "I knew she was your mama when she brought the passionflower vine for me to plant."

Jimmy focused again on the petunias, and I followed him as I swallowed my frustration. "You're not making any sense, Jimmy. What has any of this got to do with my parents stealing me and lying to me all these years? Don't you care? Aren't you mad?"

He didn't look up as he continued to yank up the flowers. "I'm mad that Mama and Skeeter aren't here. Sure, your parents lied to you, but maybe because they didn't want to hurt you with the truth, because it's a pretty big, awful thing. And maybe you just weren't ready to hear it until now. Even as a baby you didn't like it when the truth wasn't what you wanted. You'd break a toy and still expect it to work just because you wanted it to." He sat back on his heels and looked up at me. "Seems to me that you and me ended up blooming anyway."

I dropped down on my knees, needing an outlet for my anger, and began yanking petunias out of the ground. "I've only known that you're my brother for less than twenty-four hours, and we're already arguing."

He gave me a lopsided grin. "Feels good, huh?"

Despite all my conflicting emotions, I felt a laugh bubble to my lips. "Feels normal."

His expression became thoughtful. "Do you think your parents would get into trouble if everybody knows now?"

I wanted to say that I didn't care, but I knew that wasn't true. "I don't know."

"Then I don't think we should say anything to anybody who doesn't need to know. The bad guy is already dead. Can't kill him twice."

I stopped yanking out flowers, remembering something he'd said before. *Then you'll know what you want to take root, and what you want pulled out.* I didn't want to admit it, but I knew he was right. He'd suffered much more than I had, yet he understood what was important to hold on to, and what was okay to weed out. My family had kept an unimaginable secret from me. But they'd also given me a wonderful life, and more love than could last a single lifetime.

I stared at my brother for a long moment, then threw my arms around him in a tight hug, catching him off guard so that he staggered a bit on his knees before regaining his balance. "I think you might be the smartest person I ever met."

"Shh. Just don't tell anybody, okay?"

His body shook as he chuckled, his hands patting me on the back, the same hands that had carried me out of a burning house and into the arms of a family who would love and cherish me regardless of where I came from.

⌘

I half expected to see my mother's car in the driveway when I returned home. Despite what I'd said, neither Gloria nor Mimi had ever given up anything without a fight, and I figured they wouldn't have already headed back to Antioch without communicating with me again. Since Mimi hadn't already called, that meant that they were giving me time.

I was trying to decide whether I should call first or show up unannounced at their condo when I spotted Adrienne's datebook that I'd left on the kitchen counter the day before as my mother led me to see the nursery.

I picked it up, holding it lightly as I recalled my conversation with Diane Wise, and the appointments Adrienne had made with a specialist in high-risk pregnancies. Adrienne and Dr. Walker had worked in the same practice together, so there were several reasons why they would have met. But only one of those reasons kept returning to me, spinning its web like a spider preparing to lay its eggs.

I walked upstairs to the nursery, the datebook still in my hand. Mimi and Gloria had closed the door when they'd left the house, and I hadn't had the heart to look inside it this morning before I'd seen Jimmy. But my talk with him had changed things, had made me see things differently, like a blind person who'd been suddenly given the gift of sight. I suppose that, in a way, I had.

I stood in the doorway, smelling the fresh paint and seeing everything that I had seen the day before: the rocking horse, the crib, the three framed portraits. And the miniature murals on the walls of flowers and birds and butterflies. It was as if they'd known what my vision of the perfect nursery was, down to the mobile over the crib, and made it come to life with needle, thread, and paint. And love.

The stirrings of guilt that I'd been wrestling with since my conversation with Jimmy worked to overtake all my other whirling emotions. Mimi and Gloria had driven across the state for me because they knew I'd needed them. Not just to tell me the truth of what happened too many years ago to count, but to be there to let me know that I wasn't alone. And then they'd given my baby and me this beautiful nursery. *Seems to me that you and me ended up blooming anyway.* Maybe if I started now, I'd have enough time before I died to thank them.

My phone buzzed in my back pocket, and I saw it was Tish. I quickly took a deep breath to calm my voice before answering, belatedly remembering the three phone calls she'd made earlier that I hadn't returned.

"Hi, Tish."

"Where are you?" she asked, sounding breathless.

"At home. In the new nursery." My voice wobbled, and I hoped she hadn't noticed.

"I've been trying to get hold of you."

"Yeah, sorry about that. I saw you called, but you didn't leave any messages, so I figured it wasn't important. I've been . . . busy," I said.

"I bet you didn't find Georgina's grave in the cemetery, did you? I could have saved you the trouble, because I didn't find her name on the grave list, either."

She paused and I sat down in the glider, wondering how long it would be before I could get Tish off the phone and be alone with my thoughts. "So that means she moved up north with Nathaniel and it's just not mentioned. Or she's still here."

"Bingo."

When I didn't ask her to elaborate, she said, "So which do you want first—the good news or the bad news?"

I closed my eyes, having no energy to play our little game. "Tish, I'm not feeling very well, so if there's something you need to tell me, could you please just spit it out?"

I heard voices in the background before her voice came back on the phone, and I knew she hadn't heard me, so at least that was one less person I needed to apologize to. "I'm sorry—I'm at the site of the old Smith Plantation, where you found the grave of the British doctor. Right after you left my shop, I got a call from Dr. Hirsch. They've found something pretty big."

I was listening with only half an ear, still feeling consumed with my mother's story of how I came to be her daughter, and my conversation with Jimmy. And feeling desperately alone because I'd sent the one person I wanted to talk to right now to Savannah.

"Aren't you going to ask me what they found?" Tish's voice sounded impatient.

"Found where?" I asked, realizing too late that she'd probably already told me.

"Near the doctor's grave. They found more remains. And these appear to be those of a female."

My field of vision seemed to shrink to a tunnel as memories swirled around in flashes of colors and faces. I saw Georgina and Pamela on the road to Cannon's Point, and heard the word "Godspeed." And then I saw Pamela hand a pistol to Georgina.

"Ava? Are you still there?"

"Yes. Sorry. I was just thinking who it might be. I know it's early, but can they tell how she died?"

"You mean like a bullet hole or something like we found in the doctor? No such luck. And there's no makeshift grave marker either. Like she was just dumped into a hole and covered. But it doesn't look like she was shot. From the skull fragments, it appears it could have been some kind of puncture wound. They're not sure what could have made it, but they're pretty sure it wasn't a knife."

"You're right. That's pretty big news." The images of Georgina and Pamela returned, and I struggled to follow them to the next scene. But all was blank. "Look, can I call you back? I . . . need to go." Without waiting for her to answer, I hung up the phone, feeling light-headed. I tried to remember how much water I'd had so far, and wondered whether I might be dehydrated.

I stood to get water from the kitchen, and the datebook I'd placed in my lap fell on the floor, the back cover splayed open. Inside the leather flap used to hold the yearly inserts in place was a familiar black-and-gray film, with small letters and numbers in white in the top right corner.

I began seeing spots in front of my eyes before I realized I was holding my breath. Slowly, I let air into my lungs, then leaned over and picked up the book from the floor, then very carefully slid the sonogram out of its spot. I studied the image of the sixteen-week fetus with the eye of a clinician, seeing its rounded head and soft nose, the curled hands and retracted legs. At sixteen weeks, the baby would have been covered in a protective down, and fat would have just been starting to form underneath the skin. The baby would have been able to hear external voices, and even experience dreams. Squinting at the small lettering on the sonogram, I read the date: *August 15, 1997.* Two weeks before Adrienne died.

I sat down again in the glider and rocked back and forth for a long time, experiencing the sense of being in an open elevator as it fell through the shaft, the floors flying by with impressions of color and faces, all of them turned to me with expressions of expectation.

I stopped rocking, hearing my mother asking me whether I was strong enough to hear the truth, and her telling me that I was. I returned the sonogram to the back of the datebook, then pulled out my cell phone. After hesitating for only a moment, I hit Matthew's speed dial.

I didn't know any of the answers I needed. But I knew that whatever they were, he and I were meant to discover them together.

CHAPTER THIRTY-FOUR

Ava

St. Simons Island, Georgia
August 2011

It was nearly sunset when I heard Matthew's car outside. I sat on the sofa in the dying light, preferring to stay in the shadow. The key turned in the lock and he stepped into the foyer.

The first thing I noticed was that he still looked the same, and that my heart and body still ached just by being near him again. The second thing I noticed was that he carried a bouquet of red roses in their trademark iridescent pink paper from Eternal Carnation. Tish would have had to meet him right at the curb with the flowers already wrapped for him to have made it to our house from Savannah in such a short period of time. That and he must have gone seventy-five the whole way.

He headed for the stairs, but I called him back. "Matthew."

Surprised, he turned to me, his smile fading when he noticed my expression, then disappearing completely when he saw the datebook and sonogram on the small table in front of me. Laying the flowers on the hall table, he walked toward me, his hands hanging loosely at his sides. I wanted to end this now, to go back to the moment when we'd first met and we'd seen only possibilities. But hiding from the truth didn't make it go away.

He read my face and didn't approach me, as if he knew his touch would be my undoing. And that would be the unforgivable. He sat in the chair opposite the sofa, and a dark wave of hair fell over his forehead. I wanted to reach over and push it away, but knew that I could not.

He brushed his finger over the datebook, then picked up the sonogram. I wished then that I'd turned on the lights so that I could read his eyes.

"Where did you find them?"

"Upstairs in the kitchen house, behind a loose rock in the fireplace. Adrienne must have hidden them there."

He looked down at the sonogram in his hand, the baby barely visible in the dim light, but its presence between us as large and looming as the ocean itself. "I didn't know about the hiding place."

"I know," I said quietly. "Or else you would have destroyed the datebook like the briefcase."

His eyes were guarded as they sought mine. "Do you think I killed Adrienne?"

I was glad he hadn't tried to lie to me again. "All the evidence is circumstantial, but it all seems to point to you, doesn't it? Why was she in the car that night, and where was she going? I don't think she was having an affair—there's nothing to really indicate that—although John says that you thought she was, which of course gives you motive.

"And then there's the way you cleared out the potting shed of everything that had belonged to Adrienne, and you found her briefcase in the attic before I could, and then you threw it into the creek after you went digging for it in the old root cellar. And every time I asked you about these things, you always had a good and ready excuse that I accepted. Because I trusted you. Because I loved you."

I indicated the datebook and the sonogram. "The pregnancy must have been on the autopsy report, but I think you already knew about it."

When he looked at me, I was relieved to see Matthew's eyes: eyes I'd seen warm and tender and sparking with laughter. He didn't say anything.

I continued. "It's why she wanted to stop smoking, because she was pregnant. Which is why she asked you to try hypnosis that first time. But things didn't go as planned. She saw something, didn't she? Just like I did. She saw something that changed her."

He placed the sonogram carefully on the table and sat back in his chair, his palms spread on his knees. "What do you want me to say? That I killed her because she was pregnant? Is that what you really believe?"

"I want you to tell me the truth. Because there's only one thing right now that I know is true, and that is that I love you. I think I always have, even before I met you."

His eyes flickered in understanding, but he didn't interrupt.

"I know you didn't hurt Adrienne. I believe you're trying to protect her, and are willingly accepting all accusations, because that's who you are. I believe you when you tell me you had nothing to do with her death, although everything I've discovered, all of your lies and misdirections, tell me that you did. That's my leap of faith, Matthew. I love you and believe you. And because of that, I want you to take a leap of faith, too."

He took a deep breath, his chest rising and falling slowly. "I only meant to protect you, Ava, and I'm sorry if I've hurt you. But the truth is very hard to hear."

I tensed but didn't avert my eyes, remembering my mother's words. *What you need to decide is whether or not you're strong enough to face whatever truth you find.* "I'm strong enough to hear it now."

He leaned forward with his elbows on his spread knees, his hands clasped between them. Everything was silent except for the old house, sighing with its subtle creaks as it settled in to listen.

"She didn't tell me she was pregnant. I'd told her that we should wait, and she'd told me she was on the pill, so she didn't think I'd be happy. But I wasn't suspicious when she asked for help to stop smoking. She'd talked about it before, so it didn't occur to me that there was a reason she'd chosen then to quit."

"And you said yes."

"Yeah. I said yes. I figured the worst that could happen would be that it was a waste of time for both of us, and the best would be that she'd quit smoking. I was inexperienced, and I didn't take it seriously enough to understand that the process is different depending on the goals of hypnosis. My only mission was to access her subconscious mind." He scrubbed his hands over his face. "And I did." He stood abruptly. "Mind if I get a drink?"

I nodded, wishing desperately that I could have one, too. I didn't say anything as I watched him move to the small table under the side window and pour two fingers of Scotch in a glass. He studied the world outside through the blinds as he took a sip and then another before speaking again.

"It reminded me a lot of that when I put you under that first time, when I told you to close the door and you stepped through it instead. Maybe because you're both so strong-willed." He shrugged and took another sip. "The script I used was a basic one for smoke cessation—although it was very similar to the one I used with you. We spent time relaxing, and then I moved her down a flight of stairs to a walled garden with a key that represented the place she wanted to be as a nonsmoker. Her task was supposed to be to focus on weeding the garden of the stresses in her life, the triggers that caused her to smoke." He stopped.

"And what happened?" I prompted.

He looked at me, his face half in shadow in the growing darkness. "She found another door, with another key, and she went through it."

I went very still, afraid he'd stop talking.

Matthew continued. "She went back to her childhood, to before the McMahons adopted her. And she saw her biological mother." He returned to sit in the chair across from me, and I reached up to turn on the lamp beside me, casting us both in its yellow glow but keeping his eyes hidden in darkness.

"Her mother was confined to bed, unable to speak, and a nurse tended to her—there was no sign of her father. But what Adrienne focused on were the soap operas playing on the television on the dresser across from the beds, and how the nurse would wait to feed her patient until her show was over."

He sloshed the liquid around in his glass and stared into the pale amber.

"She didn't tell me any of this until much later, after I'd found the sonogram. And then I knew why she hadn't told me.

"What she saw prompted her to search for her biological parents, something she'd never even considered before. She found the adoption records, and discovered that both of her parents were deceased, about six months before she was adopted. Her father died in a motorcycle accident about a month before her mother." He paused.

"And her mother?"

"She killed herself." He glanced at me briefly. "Adrienne asked the McMahons what they knew about her birth mother, but all they knew was what was on the death certificate."

I sat up, listening to the persistent ticking of the clock, but neither one of us said anything as we waited for the old ghosts to gather around us.

"Without my knowledge, she hired a private investigator, who told her everything she wanted to know."

I thought of what Diane had told me about Dr. Walker, and my breath turned icy cold. "And everything she didn't."

His eyes were dark as they turned inward, and I felt an irrational stab of jealousy that I was excluded from his thoughts and memories.

Carefully, he placed his glass on the table and clasped his hands. "Her mother had Huntington's." He was silent for a moment, as if to allow the word and all its implications to sink in.

I knew about Huntington's from classes on genetic diseases I'd taken while studying to become a nurse-midwife. As if Adrienne's ghost were nearby, I felt her despair. In addition to being physically and mentally debilitating, Huntington's disease was always terminal. If a parent carried the gene, his or her offspring had a fifty percent chance of inheriting it, and of those, one hundred percent would eventually begin showing symptoms and die.

"She underwent genetic testing to see if she had the gene. It was positive." He picked up his glass as if forgetting it was empty, then put it down, but not before I noticed that his hand was shaking. "Still, she didn't tell me while she waited until the pregnancy was far enough along and they could test the baby for the gene. It was positive, too."

I felt Matthew's grief as if it were my own, only imagining how he'd felt when he'd seen the faceless baby sketches in Adrienne's studio, mourning the child he'd never have a chance to hold. I wanted to curl up on the couch and erase all that I had learned, no longer wanting to know the truth. But his story wasn't finished, and I knew that to move forward, I needed to look behind me.

I clasped my hands together so I wouldn't reach out and touch him. "When did she tell you?"

"She didn't. I found the sonogram by accident. I was looking for the bottle of aspirin she always kept in her purse, and there it was. When I showed it to her, she told me everything. She shouldn't have carried that burden alone for so long. And the whole time she'd been suffering alone, I'd noticed how she'd changed, but I was so ignorant. I even thought she was having an affair."

His gaze moved to my hands, which had found their way to my belly, cupping the soft life that grew there. I didn't say anything, and waited for him to continue.

"I told her that we would handle it together. That I would take care of her and the baby, that she didn't need to be afraid of anything, that I would stay with her no matter what."

I didn't want to ask the next question, content in my dark corner to believe only in possibilities instead of the truth. But the secrets were like silk scarves pulled from a magician's hat, one connected to another, the beginning and end indiscernible, and the truth hidden somewhere in between.

"How did Adrienne die?"

Matthew stared down into his Scotch as if he were watching the events played back, and when he first started speaking, I thought he hadn't heard my question.

"You would think that with my training and experience, I would know the signs. But maybe when it's somebody close to you, you're blind to them. The light had gone from her eyes, but that was understandable under the circumstances. That's why I suggested we participate in the regatta, to show her that she had so much more life to live. Most Huntington's patients don't begin to exhibit symptoms until well into middle age.

"And it did seem to lift her spirits, enough so that she was almost back to normal. It wasn't until . . . after that I understood why."

I sat up, a cool brush of air touching my neck. I remembered seeing Adrienne's datebook, where I could find no more appointments after July, as if her life had ended then, and how I knew that wasn't the case, because she'd taken the print to be framed, and had lunch with her brother.

My eyes widened as our gazes met in mutual understanding. "She killed herself, didn't she?"

He nodded, the movement slow and labored, as if it hurt. "I'd been so happy to see that she was acting like herself again that it didn't occur to me that she was happy because she had a plan. Everything she did leading up to her death was tidying up loose ends—a typical sign to look for in suicide risks. And I missed it all because I didn't want to see."

I moved to him then, took the glass from his hand and curled up in the chair with him, my arms holding him tightly. "I'm sorry," I said, knowing my words were inadequate, but knowing, too, that he would understand. I laid my head on his shoulder and waited for him to speak.

"She didn't leave a note. But I knew when I got the phone call from the highway patrol why her car had run off the road. The only part that I didn't understand was why she chose to drown."

Cold air like a breath moved across my skin again, and I began to shiver.

"The one thing I think I understand is that she was so far from home because it took her that long to work up the nerve. Despite being a midwife, Adrienne was pretty squeamish. She never really got used to the smell of blood."

I recalled Tish telling me how Matthew encouraged Adrienne to be a midwife, and how she was good and competent at her chosen profession, but that it was never her passion. The shivering grew worse, and Matthew pulled me closer.

I pressed my face into his neck, melding myself to him. "And you let

John and his parents believe the worst of you so they wouldn't know what she'd done."

He pushed me away, then cupped my head in his hands. "And you never doubted me. Despite everything you knew, you never doubted me."

I shook my head, then placed his hand on my heart. "Because I *know* you. It's as if we share the same heart."

He brought his lips to mine in a gentle kiss. I pulled back, searching his eyes, hearing his words. *She told me once that sometimes when I looked at her it was like I was seeing a ghost instead.* "That's not the whole story, is it? She went under hypnosis again, and she saw something else, didn't she? That's how she knew where the hiding place was in the old kitchen house, even though you didn't."

I could feel him pulling away, but I held firm, my hands clasped behind his neck. "It's your turn, Matthew. For your leap of faith. I want you to put me under hypnosis again. I can't explain it yet, but I have a feeling that Adrienne and I were somehow connected . . . before. That everything that has happened was meant to happen."

He began to shake his head, but I took his jaw in my hand. "I never doubted you, Matthew. Please don't doubt me now."

His eyes became dark and serious. He pushed back my hair and kissed me again. "All right." His resistance softened beneath my fingers. "When do you want to try again?"

I slid from his lap and reached for his hands. "How about now?"

CHAPTER THIRTY-FIVE

Pamela

St. Simons Island, Georgia
March 1815

The light of the day began to dim as I headed back down Frederica Road toward the St. Simons Sound, glad for the faster horse. Remembering Georgina's words to stop for nothing or nobody, I did not slow at the sound of horse's hooves as I flew down the road on my race toward the beach, where the sand hugged the water by the St. Simons light. Judging from the sound, I was far enough ahead to avoid pursuit, but I dared not look behind me.

When I reached the thick sand of the dunes, I pulled the horse up short, knowing I had a better chance of getting to the water's edge on my own without stumbling, and I did not want to risk his breaking a leg. I slapped him on his rump, hoping he would find his way back home, then began running toward the water, my whirling thoughts distracting me from the cold.

I found myself wishing that I had brought my birthing instruments, in case I reached Thomas before Georgina arrived with our mother's jewelry, just in case I needed them either to barter my services or the instruments themselves. But I had left them in their leather case in the wagon, and trusted Jemma to keep them safe.

As I climbed to the top of the dunes, I looked around me, hoping to spot Thomas. Nothing on this barren beach resembled the beach of our summer-afternoon picnic, when Geoffrey and Robbie had slept beside me, and the sun had warmed my face as I dwelled in my contentment. This desolate place and murky ocean were foreign to me, as if I had already left my beloved home behind, and for the first time I began to feel the cold.

I looked out toward the horizon, where a giant warship lay at anchor and a smaller boat with about eight men had begun to row from the shore out to it. I began running, stumbling once in the hard, cold sand, shouting for them to stop. But the wind blew my words behind me, depositing them in the tall grasses of the dunes.

"Thomas!" I shouted again, waving to the boat, the ocean taking it and all of my hopes farther out of my reach.

A man in the boat turned, and I ran to the end of the beach, the water soaking my skirts, but I barely noticed. I strained to see Thomas's face, but even with the dim light and the distance between us, I could see that the man turned to face me was not Thomas, but a familiar face nonetheless. It was the young man who'd first given me directions to Thomas's tent, and whom I had seen frequently on my visits to the doctor.

"Liam!" I waved frantically, my boots now in the surf, numbing my feet. I turned behind me, expecting to see whoever had been pursuing me so ardently appear on the dunes, ready to drag me away from the shore. "Where is Thomas?"

It took two tries before he could understand me over the sound of the waves. "I haven't seen him—must already be on the ship. Us here are the last to leave."

I nearly stumbled into the waves, my legs unable to bear me up any longer. "Liam—come back for me! I must get on that ship!" But again my words were lost to the winter wind.

I heard a shout from behind the dunes, and I turned quickly to see my pursuer, fearing already that I had lost. But whoever it was remained out of view, giving me precious seconds to still escape. Panic filled me as I recalled Georgina's words of warning about the desperation of deserters.

I jerked my head back toward the sea, where Liam and the others on the boat had begun rowing again. I was a good swimmer from long summers as a girl growing up on the island. I tried to measure how far the ever-widening distance was between the boat and me, remembering Georgina's words. *If you need courage, remember that you are doing this for Geoffrey. That will give you the strength you need to do what has to be done.*

Liam was still looking at me, saying something that I could not hear. "Wait for me. I am coming!" I shouted. Without thinking further, I removed my cloak and let it slip to the sand before diving forward into the icy surf.

The cold sliced me like a razor, stealing my breath. But I pressed on, my desperation moving me forward into deeper water more effectively than my frozen arms. I opened my mouth to shout to Liam, but he had turned his head, the oars continuing to move. A large wave washed over my head, filling my mouth with salty water and dying hope. *They do not see me,* my mind screamed. I pressed forward toward the boat, the current fighting me with every stroke. I tried to kick my feet, but instead found myself sinking downward, my heavy and wet skirts tangled around my legs.

I managed to bob my head above the waves, clinging to the hope that Liam might see me and start rowing back, but all I could see was his boat getting smaller as it neared the great warship where Thomas waited.

I heard my name—coming from the shore, not the boat. Blood pounded in my ears, and all warmth left my body as I struggled to keep my head above the water. I was so tired, my arms wooden. I heard my name again, closer, and my heart recognized the voice before my ears did. *Geoffrey.*

A wave pushed me up, high enough that I could see him standing near the shore, holding a lantern that swung in the wind like a fleeting star, looking past me to the disappearing boat. But Liam was too far to hear, too far to see me.

"Geoffrey!" I shouted, but my voice fell like brittle ice back into the water. I saw him turn his head, as if sensing that I was near.

"Pamela—come back! Please come back."

Another wave pushed me up again and I saw him stumble to his knees, the lantern falling from his hand and extinguishing itself in the sand. "I will find you, Pamela! Wherever you go, I will find you!"

I wanted to call out to him that I would never leave him, but I had already begun to slip beneath the surface, my body having given up long before my spirit. The moon crept from the clouds, a beacon of light through the murky gloom of the quiet beneath the water's surface. I reached upward, as if the moon could pull me out of the hateful winter ocean, as if it could place me back on the summer beach with my husband and son once again. But the moon drifted farther and farther away, the cold, faceless orb fading above me until I was no more.

Ava

St. Simons Island, Georgia
August 2011

I awoke, blinking into the darkened room lit only by the bulb of a single lamp. My face was wet from tears, a sense of loss squeezing my chest. Matthew helped me sit up, then joined me on the sofa, his eyes searching mine. "So Pamela died, and Geoffrey swore that he would find her, wherever she was." He smiled softly, but his eyes were troubled. "And that has something to do with my leap of faith."

"Part of it," I said. I touched his cheek with my palm, knowing this wouldn't be easy for him, but, like pulling a splinter from a finger, it was necessary for us all to heal. "You remember how I said that I thought that Adrienne and I were connected somehow?"

He nodded, the wariness not leaving his eyes.

"I need you to tell me about the second time you hypnotized her. I need to know what she saw."

"I don't understand any of this," he said, his voice very quiet.

I realized how hard it was, as a scientist, as a psychologist who dealt with reality every day, to admit that there was something beyond his realm of knowledge. I took his hands in mine to let him know that he wasn't alone in this. "I don't either. Maybe we just need to open our minds to the possibility that the universe is bigger than we know, that there are things that can't be taught, things that can't be understood anywhere except in our hearts."

He looked down at our clasped hands for a moment, then slowly let go before settling himself back against the sofa.

"All right," he said, taking a deep breath. "The second time Adrienne went under was after I'd found out about the pregnancy. She said that she wanted to see her mother again, before her mother got sick. She didn't want the only picture she had of her biological mother to be the one of her so ill. And I thought it was a good idea."

I reached for his empty glass and stood, his story almost unbearable to hear. I could only imagine what it had been like to live it. I poured a generous amount of Scotch into the glass and returned, placing it in Matthew's fingers.

"Go on," I said.

"So I did. And we were back in the garden that we'd found the first time." He paused. "But she found another door and went through it."

He jerked to a stand, the Scotch sloshing over the edge of his glass and onto the floor, but neither one of us moved to wipe it up. With angry steps, he walked back to the window, although the world outside was now black, the colors of the day swallowed by the night.

"What did she see?" I asked, but I already knew.

"Georgina."

The word echoed in the empty room, flitting like a ghost around the furniture, coming to rest in the space separating Matthew and me.

He took a sip from his glass before continuing. "I listened as she told this remarkable story—because that's all I thought it was—about a woman who'd lived here two hundred years ago. What I found so remarkable was that Adrienne told the story as if *she* were the main character. And when I brought her out of the session, I let her think that I believed that she was the reincarnation of Georgina Smith."

He returned to the chair opposite me, as if he, too, found it easier to think when we weren't so near each other. "It was after that that she became obsessed with my family history, gathering all that data in her briefcase, visiting the archives in Savannah. And I humored her, just happy to see that she'd found something to distract herself from her diagnosis, something to occupy her mind and give her satisfaction that her job never seemed to be able to deliver."

I attempted a smile. "So it must have been something of a shock when I went under hypnosis to find out why I couldn't remember breaking my legs as a child, and instead started talking about Pamela and Georgina."

His eyes met mine, but he wasn't smiling. "Yeah, you could say that."

Hesitantly, as if my mouth knew I didn't really want to know, I asked, "Did she tell you how Georgina died?"

Studying me carefully, he said, "Yes. She did." He leaned forward again, his elbows resting on his knees. "She told me how Georgina sent her sister off with the British, to punish Pamela for taking the one thing Georgina wanted but could never have. She must have believed that she could make Geoffrey believe that his wife had deserted him, so that even if Pamela returned, he wouldn't want her back."

I closed my eyes. *Geoffrey.* "But she was sick, with tuberculosis, I think. She must have known she was dying. That she would have no chance to be with Geoffrey even with Pamela gone."

"I can't believe I'm talking about all of this as if it's real. But it *can't* be. It doesn't make sense."

"I'm not asking you to believe it, Matthew. Just listen and open your mind. A leap of faith, remember?"

He nodded, and then continued with Adrienne's story. "Until the end, Georgina thought the British doctor would have medicine for her. But she also believed that he was too concerned with Pamela, and putting Pamela's needs before Georgina's. It enraged her, believing as she did that she had always placed second in everyone's affections except her mother's. And her mother had died while Pamela was attending to her, adding more fuel to Georgina's growing sense of displacement."

I recalled my conversation with Tish about the second grave found near Thomas's, and how they were sure the remains were those of a woman. "Did Georgina die that day, too?"

"According to Adrienne, yes." He sighed heavily, as if finally letting go of the years of secrets, unraveling them like yarn. "I didn't want to tell you any of this, thinking it was all a figment of Adrienne's imagination. Even when you started talking about Pamela and Thomas Enlow, and your reaction to the sketch of the house as Adrienne had seen it through Georgina's eyes. I didn't want Adrienne's story to become a self-fulfilling prophecy."

"And now?"

"I'm still not sure."

Neither one of us spoke for a few moments. Finally, I said, "What happened to Georgina?"

"She'd told Thomas to meet her at the Smith Plantation, that Pamela was there waiting for him, and that it was a matter of some urgency. After Georgina ensured that Pamela was headed toward the coast, she returned home to find Thomas waiting there. When he discovered that Pamela was not there, he would not be persuaded by Georgina to wait any longer, and he threatened to leave."

Matthew paused again, his face closed to me as he remembered. "Georgina hadn't really thought out her plan, because she would have known that she couldn't keep the doctor waiting when the rest of the British were evacuating and he was expected to go with them. Or even that Geoffrey would find the strength to leave his bed and go searching for Pamela. Maybe her illness was interrupting her thought processes, or maybe her anger at her sister had festered so long that she wasn't thinking clearly. Whatever the reason, she found herself in a desperate situation."

"And with a weapon," I said, imagining the weight of the pistol in my own pocket, and the cold feel of the metal as Pamela had given it to Georgina.

"Yes," Matthew said. "Adrienne wasn't clear on the next events, but if you believe that she was relating the last moments of Georgina Smith's life, that would be expected."

We regarded each other silently, his words like sharp bullets.

He continued. "I want to believe that what happened next was an accident, but if we believe Adrienne's story so far, we are left to wonder how Georgina was prepared to explain Thomas's presence on St. Simons after the evacuation and Pamela's disappearance, unless Georgina had some plan to send him to Cumberland Island on his own. Regardless, Georgina meant only to hold the doctor at gunpoint until she knew it was too late for him to reach Pamela. Adrienne said only that Georgina was pointing the pistol at the doctor, but that a shout came from behind her, and then she experienced a blinding pain to her head before she heard the report of the gun. And then she remembered nothing else."

It was my turn to stare at him in confusion. I thought back to my own flashbacks of Pamela, of the last day during her desperate rush to the ocean. *And how she hadn't set out for home alone.* "Jemma," I whispered. "Georgina had Jemma with her."

We looked at each other in mutual realization. "It had to have been Jemma. She must have thought that Georgina meant to shoot the doctor, and tried to stop her." I closed my eyes for a moment, thinking hard. "Tish said they found another body today, near the doctor's grave at the Smith Plantation. They're pretty sure it's that of a female. There was a small puncture wound in the back of the skull. They don't think it was a knife, but they're not sure what it could have been."

I sat back on the sofa, feeling exhausted, as if I'd just relived the events of that long-ago day. "Poor Georgina. And poor Jemma." I thought for a moment, listening again to the silence of the old house that wasn't anything like quiet, more like a murmuring from behind the wall of years that separated us. "Nathaniel must have buried them and given them markers. Georgina might have had one, too, or maybe he kept hers unmarked so that nobody would draw their own conclusions. There's no marker for her at Christ Church, and there's no mention of her traveling with Nathaniel when he moved to Boston."

"If this all happened the way we're thinking it did, then I'd bet that there's a letter from Nathaniel in the archives somewhere to a friend or relative that mentions Nathaniel sending Georgina ahead of him sometime in March of 1815. He would have needed to perpetuate a rumor he would have spread among his neighbors on St. Simons to explain Georgina's absence. He might even have said she needed a change of scenery to escape from the stigma of her sister's treason and adultery, since it was believed that Pamela had fled with the British."

I nodded, almost hearing the click of the pegs being removed from the playing board one by one, then set aside. "And Jemma must have been the freed slave who accompanied him and Robbie to Boston. Since she was mute, she either figured out a way to tell him what happened, or he witnessed it. Either way, Dr. Enlow and Georgina were dead, and Pamela had disappeared. Geoffrey must have died shortly afterward. Only Nathaniel was left to pick up all the pieces."

Matthew rubbed his face, and I wondered whether I looked as exhausted as he did. He surprised me by smiling. "But Robbie came back, didn't he?"

"Yes. His grave is in the cemetery, along with his wife and children and most of the family members between him and you. Like it was meant to be all along."

He stood, and I stood, too, allowing myself to be enfolded in his arms. "Do you believe it, then?" he asked. "Do you believe that you and Adrienne lived before as Pamela and Georgina?"

"I don't know. How can we? I don't think we'll ever know for sure until we die. But there's some comfort in believing that we return to earth to get a second chance. What if that's what we're here for—to learn lessons or right wrongs from previous lives? Like the ultimate do-over." I frowned, feeling my brain trying to wrap itself around all the thoughts and ideas running through it. "What if Pamela's fateful sin was to accept things as they were, to never question what she was told? Maybe that's why I'm here, to learn from her mistakes and try again."

Matthew kissed the top of my head. "Then I'd have to believe that

Adrienne's sickness was her punishment, and that she was never meant to have children or to live to be an old woman. And I don't want to do that. Adrienne was a good person, and I loved her. I want to believe that she was born with a clean slate, that she determined her own fate."

I accepted his words, understanding his need to believe what he did, and knowing, too, that the truth lay somewhere in between. I nuzzled his neck, imagining I could smell the lingering scent of pipe smoke. I didn't want to talk any more, but there was still one more thing I needed to tell him. Pulling back, I looked into his eyes. "Adrienne didn't lose her wedding ring. She gave it to John before she died."

His face registered surprise.

"She told him that it didn't belong to her." A thickness formed in my throat as I finally understood what she'd really meant, and it had nothing to do with it having once belonged to Matthew's mother and other ancestors. It belonged to someone Adrienne had never met, a woman Matthew was somehow destined to meet and with whom he would fall in love. It belonged to *me*.

He rested his forehead against mine. "Does John still have it?"

I nodded. "He showed it to me. It has the word *Forever* engraved inside of it." My brows puckered as I considered something else. "Pamela told Nathaniel where the hiding place was, and he must have recovered the ring and oil miniatures before he left, then given them to Robbie when he returned to St. Simons. I wonder what happened to the portraits of Geoffrey and Pamela."

We didn't speak for a long time as we held each other, and I thought of a love that was meant to last forever, and of a husband promising his wife he would find her wherever she was.

There was a short rap on the door, and we pulled apart so Matthew could answer it. I smelled the scent of talcum powder and Aqua Net before I heard the voices of my mother and Mimi.

They crowded into the entranceway, apologizing for intruding, their faces devoid of any remorse. They stood together, instead of one in front of the other, vying for position, as I usually saw them.

Gloria spoke first. "We know you told us you didn't want to see us again, but we needed to see you. To ask for your forgiveness one more time."

Mimi stuck her thumb out at Gloria. "She won't leave, and you know I can't drive, so we're stuck here."

All three heads turned to me expectantly.

I couldn't move, feeling as if I'd been standing on an escalator that had suddenly stopped. I could feel a forward momentum, but all I could do was hold on tightly to keep from falling.

"Matthew . . ." I began, realizing I hadn't told him anything about the grave in the cemetery that was supposed to be mine, and of the night that I had become Ava Whalen. Or how it seemed that I was always meant to return to St. Simons and the briny water of the marshes and the ocean that pulled at me still.

"Matthew," I said again, falling back onto the sofa, no longer trusting my legs to keep me standing. "I recently discovered that I'm Jimmy Scott's sister, Christina. I was supposed to have died in the fire, but Jimmy took me out of the house so that I lived." I bit my lip and met my mother's eyes. I stared at her for a long moment as I wondered how anger and love could inhabit the same corner of one's heart. "And Mama and Daddy saved my life."

My husband knew to step back, understanding that he'd hear the rest of the story eventually, but knowing, too, that the story wasn't yet over.

I looked into my mother's gray eyes, so different from mine, yet holding within them all the years of loving me without condition, of waiting for the dreaded phone call to tell her that I was no longer hers. And of not knowing that none of it really mattered. I'd been hers and she'd been mine since the first moment I'd put my arms around her neck and rested my head against her heart.

"I'm so sorry, Ava—"

I didn't let her finish. "Please don't. I'm still a little confused and in shock, and even a little angry, but I had a conversation with Jimmy, and he helped put everything in perspective." I tasted salt on my lips, the same salt that ran through the tidal creeks and estuaries like a tethering ribbon from one life to the next, and I smiled. "I should be the one asking for forgiveness."

My throat closed, and all I could do was run to my mother and hug her fiercely, my tears melding with hers. Her arms came around me, her hands patting my back as she held me tightly, as if we'd always been this comfortable with each other, as if we both remembered how.

"I am sorry, Ava. I'm sorry for always keeping you at arm's length. I was too afraid that I would lose you, and knew how painful it would be if I allowed you to get too close. I should have known that it was impossible. But everything I've done, I've done because I love you. Nothing will ever change that."

I held her closer, finally comprehending how hard it would be to let go, and seeing that she had known that all along. Some are called to be gardeners of souls, and she'd tended hers with a blind dedication that accepted the floods and famine along with the sunshine. I couldn't put into words yet how glad I was that she was my mother, that she had taught me how to be a good and passionate gardener. All I could do was hug her tighter and say, "I love you, too."

I turned to Mimi and hugged her. "You don't have to dye your hair blond anymore," I said, smiling through my tears.

She ran her fingers through the blond strands, still thick and shiny like mine. "Well, maybe just a little longer—at least to get me through all the photos I'm sure we'll be taking at the family reunion."

I pulled back, confused. "What family reunion?"

Mimi and my mother exchanged a glance. "Your father and brothers and their families are all coming to St. Simons for Labor Day weekend. They all want to meet Jimmy. We've already found condos for all of them and paid their deposits."

I stared at them in astonishment before realizing that I shouldn't have been surprised at all. It was one of a million reasons I loved them so much.

Matthew came up beside me and put his arm around my shoulder. "Well, I'm glad we don't have to wait until Christmas. It'll be wonderful having everybody together."

I smiled up at him and saw some of the weariness leave his eyes as he smiled back at me. "Yes," I said, rubbing the small swell of my belly. "It will be."

EPILOGUE

Ava

The smells of barbecue wafted through the backyard as my brother Stephen took control of the grill in the new outdoor kitchen. To Jimmy's great delight, I'd agreed to his plans for the garden, and late-summer blooms sprang from the ground in riotous displays between the new brick paths. It was partially a nod to the gardeners in my life, Gloria and Mary Anne, and partly for Adrienne, too, who'd left her garden in my care. I'd tend it well, along with the other flowers in my life, always remembering what Jimmy had taught me. *Know what you want to take root, and what you want pulled out.*

Tish and Beth were there with their respective spouses, and Adrienne's parents were there, too, along with John. Matthew and I had agreed that John should know the truth, but we'd left it up to him as to whether or not to tell his parents. We didn't know what he'd told them, but they had accepted our invitation and greeted me warmly, and I knew the healing had begun.

I felt Matthew beside me before I turned and saw him. He gave me the smile I remembered seeing from across the room the first time I'd seen him, the moment I'd felt as if I'd loved him my entire life. "Let's go to the dock. I need a break from having to share you. Are you okay with that?"

I nodded. Although I hadn't attempted to get in a boat since my initial excursion on the creek with Matthew, the water no longer had power over me. I didn't think I'd ever be comfortable swimming in the ocean, but the mystery of the unknown had been erased, the question of why finally answered.

The moon was full and the stars bright, making it easy to find the path and make our way onto the dock that had been strung with twinkling lights and paper lanterns for the party. Tree frogs chirped as we passed, a night bird flitting over us, startled out of its perch. The night was warm and wet, like a cocoon, as if expecting a sea change from what we'd been and understood.

We sat on one of the dock's benches and looked up at the sky, painted with stars that had shone for thousands of years in their same constellations. Generations before us had guided their ships and wished upon these same stars, and I found myself wondering whether Pamela and Geoffrey had ever sat in this same spot and looked up at the sky that never changed while the earth revolved beneath it.

"Dr. Hirsch called today," I said. "He wanted to let me know that they're shipping Dr. Enlow's remains to England to be interred next to his wife. He's also releasing Georgina's remains so that she can be buried in the Frazier plot at Christ Church. Next to Pamela's new marker." *Beloved wife and mother.* I had thought to add a verse to Pamela's stone, but then I realized that the epitaph I'd chosen said everything Pamela would have wanted the world to know.

I'd been to the cemetery often after my discovery of the identity of my biological parents and my twin sister. It had brought me comfort to lay to rest the enduring presence by my side that had given me reassurance since birth. I hadn't felt the need to collect other people's photographs, or felt Jennifer near me since the night I'd learned about the fire, as if we both knew it was time to say good-bye.

Matthew kissed my temple, and I leaned into him. "I'm glad to know Thomas is finally going home," he said. Then he lifted my left hand, and I felt something cool slide over my knuckle above my gold wedding band. It fit perfectly.

I raised my hand to see better in the twinkling light and saw a familiar gold ring. My eyes met Matthew's.

"John gave it back to me. Said it wasn't his to keep."

Carefully, I slid Pamela's ring off my finger, then held it up to the light. The band felt heavy in my hand, like a bridge of years that carried with it the hope and love of those who'd gone before. Matthew took the ring from me and slid it on my finger again, and I imagined I could feel the word *"Forever"* pressed against my skin. I lifted my hand to the light, feeling like the ring had always been there, and that I'd just been reunited with an old friend. "Thank you," I said, seeing the light in his eyes that rivaled that of the stars.

"It belongs to you," he said softly. "I think it always has." His kiss was long and deep, ending only at the sound of a wave of laughter coming from the party, reminding us that we needed to return.

"I almost forgot," he said, sliding something out from his back pocket. "When I was vacuuming the inside of your car today, I found this." He handed me a bifold glossy brochure that had been folded in half to fit in a pocket. "I haven't had a chance to look at it yet, but I thought you might still want it."

I blinked at it for a moment, then recognized the brochure for the Nathaniel Smith exhibit at the Savannah History Museum.

He continued. "It must have fallen between the seats. I was thinking that if it seemed interesting, we could take a big group down to Savannah tomorrow to do some sightseeing and maybe stop off at the museum."

I took it from him, then held it under one of the paper lanterns to see better. I tapped the cover with my finger. "This portrait of Nathaniel must have been painted when he was an old man. I think that's why he didn't seem familiar to me when I first saw this." I opened up the brochure and started skimming through the text and photos.

I paused at the first photo, a picture of a midwife's kit. The instruments lay in their respective places on top of the leather wrap they would be rolled in. But there was one empty spot, indicating a missing tool. *A perforator.* I wasn't sure how I knew, but I could see the two-handled instrument with the sharp point at the end used to either break the water sac or to assist in the removal of a dead fetus in the days before cesarean sections. *How did I know this?* The skin tightened on my scalp as I saw Pamela on the beach, wishing she had her kit with her but feeling reassured because it was in Jemma's care.

I jerked my head toward Matthew. "The skull that was found that we believe was Georgina's—Tish said it had a small puncture wound, right?"

"Yes. Why?"

I looked down at the midwife's tools, the glaring omission telling me more than any archaeological dig. I would never know for sure, but I felt sure that Jemma had tried to save Thomas's life, and in doing so had taken Georgina's.

"I'm not sure," I said, still wary of how wide Matthew's leap of faith had been. "Just thinking about something." I smoothed my hand across the photo. "Did I tell you that Beth did research on Nathaniel Smith in Boston? The freed slave he brought up with him, Jemma, became a well-known and much sought-after midwife in the city."

"Maybe they'll have more about that in the museum."

"I hope so," I said, smiling to myself as I continued to skim through the brochure. I was halfway down the second page when I saw it.

"Look," I said, pointing to the photograph of two miniature oil portraits in a silver double frame. The woman had dark hair and eyes, with a deep widow's peak and a soft smile. I knew that face, just as much as I knew my own. Just as I'd known when I'd seen Adrienne's sketch of the same woman. *Pamela.*

I read the caption out loud. " 'Geoffrey and Pamela Frazier, St. Simons Island, circa 1812. From the Nathaniel Smith collection, donated to the State of Georgia by the descendants of Mr. Smith's ward, Robert Frazier, 1923.' "

I lifted the brochure higher, wanting to see the portrait of Geoffrey, and the air seemed to shatter around me. *It's you,* I thought. I studied the eyes and saw that they were a brilliant blue, just like I remembered. I turned my face toward Matthew, seeing now the resemblance. Except for the color of the eyes, it could have been the same man.

Wherever you go, I will find you. I touched Matthew's face as he studied my own, my heart singing in recognition. "You found me," I said, wrapping my arms around his neck. "You found me," I said again.

"Yes," he whispered in my ear, and I wondered whether he'd understood, and knowing, too, that it didn't matter. We had found each other.

I allowed myself to melt into him, aware of the falling night and the water around us like a womb, and the sky above watching silently the journey of souls below. Matthew took my hand in his, his fingers touching the ring like a talisman, then led me back toward the ancient house, the house with memories like an ocean's waves with no beginnings and no endings, its sighs reminding me of how impossible it is sometimes to distinguish between the two.

Photo by Lee Siebert

Karen White is the *New York Times* bestselling author of fourteen previous books. She grew up in London but now lives with her husband and two children near Atlanta, Georgia.

CONNECT ONLINE

www.karen-white.com

Sea Change

KAREN WHITE

This Conversation Guide is intended to enrich the
individual reading experience, as well as encourage us
to explore these topics together—because books,
and life, are meant for sharing.

QUESTIONS FOR DISCUSSION

1. Have you read any of the author's previous works before? If so, did you enjoy the more supernatural elements blended into White's story?

2. The spray of the sea, the rich, musky air of a root cellar, the persistent kudzu vines. White conjures up a strong, vibrant sense of place for the reader for life on St. Simons Island. Did you feel like you were transported there (and even into the past) while reading the story? What other descriptions sang out to you?

3. How do the multiple voices in the book come together to tell one story? Do you think the story would be as layered or successful without one of the voices, like Pamela's?

4. Do you think Ava does the right thing by attempting to dig up the truth behind Adrienne's final days? Could you have lived with so many secrets or rooms closed off to you? Did you think Matthew was guilty of her murder?

5. Do you think objects, like Pamela's wedding ring, can carry powerful energies that connect us to the past? If so, how? Are there beloved items in your own collection that might have a similar kind of special energy? What are they?

6. Why do you think Matthew allows Adrienne's family to think the worst of him after her death? Do you think he goes too far—especially as his actions become more secretive and troubling to Ava—in trying to protect her legacy?

7. Describe the relationship between Pamela and Georgina. Do you think all relationships between sisters are as emotionally complex—or perhaps complex in other ways? How so?

8. Do you think it was ethical for Matthew to hypnotize both his wives, even if the intentions were to be helpful or to unlock their connections to their ancestors? What are the dangers of opening up these psychological doors that have remained closed for so long? What were the results for the two women?

9. Ava is a lifelong collector of undeveloped photograph film (from yard sales and other places). What do you think is behind her attraction to those images, once printed, that feature sisters?

10. Do you think it's true that "being a mother is like being a gardener of souls"? How is that true for the women in the book? How might it be true in your own life if you yourself are a parent? Do you see this as your role, and how do you nurture your little "seedlings"?

11. Were you shocked by the revelation of Ava's biological parents? Do you think it was best for Gloria and Mimi to keep her in the dark for so long? What are Jimmy's feelings?

12. Do you believe in the possibility of reincarnation? Why or why not? Do you think Geoffrey and Pamela are finally together?